Perdita

by Arwen Spicer

Arwen Spicer is a science fiction writer and writing instructor.
She holds a doctorate in English literature
from the University of Oregon.
She is the author of *The Hour before Morning*.

I wish to particularly to express my undying gratitude to the memory of Nye Joell Hardy for her support across the years and to thank Erin Wilcox for her copyediting and proofreading. My thanks, too, to Aaron Williams, this book's longtime supporter and spaceship designer, and to Eric Eisenhart for digitizing the map to the original edition way back when. And special thanks to Glenn Peters for unflagging support, lots of technical help, and a fantastic cover design.

To the good folks at the Novel Project, who critiqued this book, and to my parents. Without all of you, this project would never have been possible.

PROLOGUE

The years since humanity abandoned Mother are lost in the black of space. We know only that our ancestors left her, the world we evolved on, to settle a planet they engineered and gave the name of Daughter. Now, you may ask why I'm beginning a history of jae technology with such an ancient story. I'm doing so because the origins of jae and the origins of humanity are one and the same. Long before a technology exists, it exists in the mind of a dreamer. Healing existed before vaccines and killing before there were guns. No technology is anything but what the actions of its makers make it.

Thousands of years ago, the depletion and pollution of Daughter triggered a collapse in its biosphere. Our ancestors fled into space. Over the millennia, they made new homes and new discoveries. They discovered that by translating particles into another dimension, a spaceship could travel between any two real-space points almost instantaneously. This technology, called jae, might have made our age-old superlight travel by rippling obsolete, but only one empire ever implemented it. That empire is as dead as Daughter.

The History of Tachyon-Quark Technology, Commonly Called Jae by Sylan del-Disal West-of-Now, Division of Physics at Melnar and Nevan West-of-Now, Division of History at Melnar

2028 After the End

PART ONE
THE KIRI SHIP

CHAPTER 1

Everything about her husband aggravated Sylan these days.

All Nevan had done was fall into the copilot's seat and ask, "Where's the planet?" and it made her want to slap him.

"It's supposed to be there." She pointed to a blank grid square on the readout. "At 45 million kilometers."

"Did you double-check the coordinates?" he asked.

"No—would you believe it? That never crossed my mind." He rubbed his beard.

"The coordinates check," she said, "but, then, since the War's End there's been no record of Berdida. So our coordinates are two thousand years old. Who knows if they're accurate?"

Nevan nodded.

Sylan's hair was in her way: a red haze over the console. She twisted it into a knot behind her head, but it immediately slipped free. Her mother's message had told them to meet her on Berdida. But in the three months since, she hadn't answered any of their comms. Even for Sylan's eccentric mother, that meant something was wrong. She was stranded or dead. The planet itself wasn't there.

"It would be awfully silly if we were dealing with a scanner malfunction.," said Nevan.

Sylan's look was acid. "Do you think I haven't scoured this ship's systems?"

"I'd expected you did," said Nevan. "I'm just running down the possibilities." He took her hand. "So let's assume it's the right place. What's your theory?"

"The planet could have been destroyed, assuming an agency to remove the debris."

"Destroyed without anyone registering the explosion? And how? Who?"

"I'm just running down the possibilities." Sylan disentangled her hand.

"Right. But if it were destroyed, then your mother would have tol—"

4

"Yes. Assuming the coordinates are correct, the only other explanation I can think of is that it's shielded."

"I like that one," said Nevan. "It would mean she got through and is waiting for us."

"She still would have sent a message to prepare us for the shielding."

"But if communications are shielded—"

"She'd have gone back into orbit to send it."

Nevan shrugged. "And this is all guessing. But if Berdida does have information about the War's End, well, that would make it important enough to shield."

"To protect. At the cost of killing my mother?"

≈•≈

Nevan was a nervous space traveler and well aware that his wife found it irritating. But after three months in a cramped ship, with his mother-in-law lost and the destination itself missing, panic became hard to resist. Especially so for a Kiri: Kiris didn't belong in space. Leddies like Sylan thought of spaceflights as a morning's outing. Short flights, anyway, where nothing went wrong.

There has to be a logical explanation.

Nevan reviewed the vid Sylan's mother had sent three months ago. She'd been excavating on Toldurn. There, in the ruins, she'd discovered something—she would not say what—that had pointed her to Berdida. Berdida, she was sure, would unravel that riddle of the millennia, the fate of the Sama Empire.

Sylan and Nevan specialized in the War years, she in its technology, he in its history.

"Bring your *Jae History*," Sylan's mother had told them.

For twenty years, the *Jae History* had been the cornerstone of their studies. It was common knowledge that the Samas' use of jae in space travel had resulted in the Quark-Shift Plague that claimed billions of lives during the Kiri–Sama War. That was easy to explain: jae shifted particles into another dimension, but partial shifting resulted in unstable particles that tore apart molecular bonds, causing massive cellular damage. It was inevitable, therefore, that the first reaction after the War's End had been to blame jae. Yet post-War quark-shift contamination, far from having skyrocketed, was lower than the War-era baseline. No one had ever explained why.

Nevan massaged his brow, wanting nothing but a breeze from the meadows of his home on Onáda.

"I tell you," he said, "I need to make planet-fall."

Sylan said, "There it is."

It hovered in space like a tarnished coin, as if its sun hardly found it worth the effort to light.

"So it is shielded," said Nevan. Conventional shielding obscured an object from a distance but could not conceal it completely close up.

The scanner flashed the planet's position now, spilling out contradictory gravitational and electromagnetic analyses. Soon the moons came into view, two gray spots, circling a larger gray smudge.

"The moons have shields, too," said Sylan, "or booster stations to channel the planetary shield."

Behind them, a curtain swished, and feet padded over the mossy floor. Jasen rested a hand on the back of Nevan's seat. *He's getting so tall*, Nevan thought as his son towered behind him. *Why did we bring our children here? Why not leave them home safe?*

"Is that it, *Mila*?" Jasen asked Sylan. Though the family usually spoke Nevan's native Keshnul, the children had always called Sylan "mother" in her own language.

"Yes, that's it. Put on your shoes—you too, Nevan. With luck we'll be landing before the next sleep cycle."

Nevan rose. "Quietly, Jas. There's no need to wake Miri yet."

When they returned, Nevan gave up his seat to his son.

"Shielded?" Jasen looked at the brightening moons.

"That's right," said Sylan. "The shield scatters electromagnetic waves as they leave the outer atmosphere, so we can't perceive them easily. But as we get closer, the jumbled patterns haven't had as much time to disburse, so we can see better."

"I know what a shield does," said Jasen.

"I was talking to your father."

"So why is it shielded?" Jasen swiveled in his seat to stare at Nevan. His telepathic blocks were partially in place in the normal Kiri way, but Nevan had grown used to the feel of the question: what had happened to his grandmother. Over the months it had become an accusation, as if Nevan and Sylan had failed her.

"That's what we're going to find out." Nevan sat in one of the backseats.

Near orbit, the gray cast fell away, and white-blue Berdida shone marble bright. Now, it had a living look. The Samas had engineered Berdida to be capable of maintaining a livable, Daughter-type biosphere without human management. A rare and beautiful thing in the Sama Empire.

"It's the right place," said Sylan. "Look, you can see the two continents."

Each no more than fifteen hundred kilometers wide, the planet's only continents lay like two yellow eyes in the ocean's face, soon to be obscured by falling night.

Sylan said, "I can't read electrical signals through the shielding."

"Can you try sending out a general hail?" asked Nevan.

"I have," said Sylan. "No answer yet."

"She's dead," said Jasen.

Sylan's face was hard. "We'll have to move in closer to get a signal through."

≈•≈

As Jasen watched the planet swell in the viewscreen, his heart began to pound. If his grandmother had died there, or was trapped there, what was to stop them being next?

"I still can't get any clear electrical readings," said Sylan.

As she spoke, the ship lurched, throwing them against their harnesses.

"What was that?" gasped Jasen.

Sylan, busy at the controls, only shook her head.

"Jasen?" His little sister's voice came from behind the sleeping curtain. "*Mila?* Dad?" In his mind, Jasen could feel her fear shoot up.

"It's all right, Miri," Nevan called. "We've just hit a little turbulence."

"I'm coming—" began Miri.

"No, sweet, stay in your sleeping harness," called Sylan. "Nevan, go sit with her."

Nevan cleared his own harness and started for the curtain as the ship lurched again. He fell against the mossy wall, then continued into the children's cubicle.

"Is it the shield?" Jasen held tight to the copilot's console as the ship began to rattle.

Sylan made an affirmative noise. "It's feeding scrambled signals to the relays between the helm and the engines. I didn't think it would affect us so far away." She scrunched over in her harness and opened an access port.

"What can you do?"

"Take everything offline but manual control and try to countermand any skewed signals that still get through." She worked at the switches.

"Will that work?"

"It should, but we won't have full inertial damping, so hold on."

Jasen looked at the viewscreen; they were careening over an expanse of cloud and ocean. He found himself listening for the muffled reassurances his father was giving Miri as Berdida spun toward them. It was like zooming in on a satellite picture, the clouds steadily more like clouds, the water more like water. They were going to crash—and they'd swept right over the continents. There was nothing but water.

"*Mila*, we're going to hit the ocean."

Sylan glanced up. The ship pitched, and they rocked into a cloud bank. She swore and turned back to her work.

"See if you can get a fix on our position," she told him. "I want to know how far we need to go to get back to a continent."

For a moment, Jasen stared. Then the ship dove down sharply, Miri cried out, and the ocean pulled out of the clouds. In a flurry, he ran through the navigation readouts.

"I think . . . I think . . . It doesn't make sense. The computer's scrambled."

The ship pitched up, though whether that was due to the shielding or his mother, Jasen was not sure. They whisked over the ocean, the rattling subsiding.

"Are we out of it?" asked Jasen.

"We're under the shield," said Sylan, loud enough for Nevan and Miri to hear. To Jasen, she added, "We've suffered some damage to our helm controls, though."

"You can bring us down, though, can't you?"

"I'm your mother, aren't I?"

She steered the ship toward the looming horizon of the eastern continent, out of the sun, into the night. They decelerated rapidly—without inertial damping, it was a thickheaded feeling. Relief surged through Jasen all the same. *We're slowing down. Thank God.*

They swooped past the ocean over a flat land. A mountain range reared up; they knocked and jolted as Sylan pulled them over it. In the middle of the mountains was a vast lake, glassy gray. Then, they dropped down once more, and the land skimmed by them faster and faster, though the tugging of Jasen's harness told him that they were still slowing down.

Trees rushed by in a blurred mass. His mother wasn't even looking as she fought with the controls.

"You'll overshoot the land," Jasen blurted.

She started and cursed again, gunned the reverse thrusters. The ship rocked back, head over heels. In the night sky, stars whirled past the viewscreen—Miri screamed. Sky for land and land for sky. Then down, zagging past the treetops.

"We're coming in," Sylan shouted. And they roared through branches into darkness.

CHAPTER 2

Ethan sped downhill, jumped a dew-soaked path, and dove into a thicket growing dense around a tree. Tearing through the brush, he slammed his back against the trunk and held still until his blood stopped drumming and he could hear the forest.

The tramping of his pursuers receded; the rustlings of the dusk grew bolder. As night veiled the sky, rivers of fog descended into gullies. He began to shiver. An hour later, the world gray and black, he got up on numb legs and peered into the shadows. Seeing no sign of his pursuers, he picked his way down the hill, feet lost in fog.

As he crossed into the lamplight of the paved expanse that marked the observatory, Torna came to his side. She was in her eighties, middle-aged, but looked older after months of army life in this forest.

Ethan knew that he, too, looked too old for his thirty-nine years, his hair already whitening. The army could do that. But it also meant a chance to protect Perditan civilization.

"We were worried for you, Warchief," said Torna.

He nodded. "The rebels are encamped by Sorel Falls. They'll be gone by the time we can send a team out, but they may leave behind some evidence to lead us to their network. I'll organize a search and radio my report to Lashen." He lifted his eyes to hers for the first time. "Did anything happen while I was gone, Lieutenant?"

"Everything's well, sir. Get some sleep."

"You can give me your daily report tomorrow morning." He plodded past her, past makeshift wooden buildings and night guards. He scarcely saw the grand white tower of the telescope that was the observatory, the eye to the beyond.

≈•≈

"Hurry. They'll be on us soon." Sherayna's voice was just loud enough for the fifteen remaining Borderal soldiers, including Leric, to hear.

Yes, it was the right tone of voice, Leric thought—confident, careful, but her footsteps were weary. He watched her hair escaping from its knot at her neck, dark in the blue night fog, though he knew that it was gold. He watched her pause to retie it, then go back to stuffing her bedroll into her pack, her expression cold.

He saw Illia was studying Sherayna too, observing all that Leric saw and probably more. Illia, dark in the daylight, was a shadow in the moon. But he could see her shoulders droop, and that was a bad sign for her.

"We did what we could," Illia ventured to Sherayna.

Sherayna glared at her foster sister. "The fourth time." It seemed she whispered to keep from shouting. "The fourth time that man has found a base of ours. We came to Iltan to close down the observatory, and instead we run and run."

"An old story, Commander," said one of the northerners, walking past.

"That doesn't mean that I accept it." Sherayna cinched her pack shut and crossed the camp to review the escape plan with the next-to-last walking group.

"It's the nature of a guerilla war," called Illia. "We've always known what to expect."

Leric came over and slipped an arm around her waist. "You're trying to douse a volcano with a bucket." *I should get my ladies home.*

His thought was shattered by thunder. Out of nowhere came a roar, then a screech. Everyone plunged into the undergrowth. A shrieking yellow swept past them, trailing a wind that made the leaves jump. The branches were still billowing when the pitch lowered fast and a single boom shook the ground.

≈•≈

Silence. Cautiously, the Borderals emerged from the brush and spoke in hushed voices.

"A jumper," said Illia. "It crashed."

"The jumper routes don't run over this part of Iltan," said Sherayna.

"Navigational error?"

"Or it's not an airship at all, but some weapon the City's deploying against us."

"Gods, I hope it's a weapon," said Leric. "I'd like to think their aim's that bad."

"A weapon we're meant to bring ourselves to," said Sherayna.

"Weapon or not," said Illia, "We have to find out what it is. Ignorance is not power."

"Yes." Sherayna cut her off. "I'll go. With Tyora, Enom, and Illia."

"And me," said Leric.

Sherayna hesitated. He knew what she was thinking—she still didn't trust him, after all these years, to be serious and do the job—always accusing him of talking too much.

"I did break the Iltan–Mesa code last year," he reminded her. It might well have been the wrong thing to say, because she didn't trust his interest in ciphering either.

But she answered, "Yes, all right. Leric instead of Enom. The rest of you head fast for the new site." Resolutely, she stepped out from the shadows, and the moon Olay shimmering through the mist outlined her in silver.

≈•≈

Ethan had scarcely closed his eyes when he was shaken awake by the trembling floor and a memory of sound. Voices shouted; footfalls thumped. He switched on his lamp, head still swimming. Groping for his boots, he flung open his door to the freezing night fog, saw a footman running toward him.

"Warchief," she called out.

"Well?"

"A ship's crashed, sir, about three measures northeast."

Ethan plucked his jacket off the floor. "I wasn't informed of any ships crossing Iltan airspace tonight."

"Neither was I, sir."

Ethan pushed past her out into the night. "Identification?"

"Unknown, sir. Lieutenant Torna is trying the radio in field control."

"I'll join her, then. Return to post, Footman."

≈•≈

Ethan blinked in the fluorescent light of the control center, his steps echoing through the makeshift building. He sat beside Torna.

"No response." The lieutenant pulled off her earphones. "They could be badly damaged."

He ran an eye over the flight logs. "The nearest flight scheduled is over Mesa. Two hundred measures is more than a little off course."

"This may sound insane, but could it be a rebel ship?"

"The way they feel about air and space tech? Much more likely rebel sabotage."

"They did restrict guns for a while, and gave it up when they found that arrows are seldom a match for bullets. When it comes to it, their denial of high tech is pragmatic." When Ethan made no response, she added, "Either way, the ship's crashed a good measure nearer their camp than ours."

"Yes." Ethan rose. "And whether the Borderals planned it or not, they'll be there."

≈•≈

Sherayna motioned her companions down into the ferns and flattened herself beside them, breathing in the damp soil. In the blue light of Olay, now bright overhead, the ship lay in a wreckage of decapitated trees, a lopsided oval with a flat projection slanting upwards. A few flames were failing in the dewy undergrowth. She could smell wood smoke on the fog, and other, strange things, tangy—unnatural.

"Look at the poor trees," whispered Tyora. "City things!"

Sherayna hushed her with a gesture. "Do any of you know that type of ship?"

"It's a fish," said Leric.

"Leric, for our love for the gods—"

"Commander, look, there's a mouth, an eye—that shadow looks like a gill. That wing thing is painted with veins like a fin. You can even make out scales."

"He's right," whispered Illia.

Sherayna nodded. "I'll investigate. The three of you fan out. Leric, you'll assist me if I find anything." She was glad now she'd let him come. On a ship like that, there might be machines they'd need his help to deal with.

She crept through the branches, scarcely snapping a twig as the ship loomed before her. It was some 115 meters long; close up, the painted scales were obvious. But the gill was not paint. It was a door, partly open. And dangling out of the door was a hand. Sherayna stepped over the last ravaged branches. Her handgun ready, she stooped and watched for movement.

Nothing.

She pulled at the heavy door. A shape slumped to the ground in a crackle of leaves. Even as Sherayna drew her gun, she knew there was no need; no one feigning unconsciousness fell like that, hard against the head. She knelt by the body: a woman in a long gown with a bruise across half of her forehead.

She whistled a cricket call for assistance.

Leric came to her side. "How is she?" He touched the bruised forehead lightly.

"Not bad, I think. I want you to carry her to our new camp."

"Any files for me to crack?"

Sherayna glanced through the black entrance. "I think the machinery's dead. Wait, and I'll check."

She pulled the door back, letting in a flood of moonlight, and climbed inside. The room gave off an earthy smell, like a forest, but not like the one outside. There was no sign of active power, no instruments Sherayna recognized, though her knowledge of airships was scanty.

Slumped over a panel was another body: a young man. Sherayna checked him over, releasing his safety straps in the process. She'd gotten him slung over her shoulders when an owl call sounded: the City approaching.

"From the west," supplied Leric as Sherayna leapt down from the door.

Leric carrying the woman, they staggered back the way they'd come. A shot rang out to the west, just as they reached the cover of the ferns. They split apart and followed separate paths to the new camp.

≈•≈

A human shape rustled out of the brush. One of Ethan's footmen fired, and everything went still, even the crickets.

"Shall I see if I got him, Warchief?" said the footman.

"No," said Ethan. "Just keep watch." A moment before, through the trees, he'd seen the ship rise out of the fog like a whale from the ocean. One glimpse of its dome had told him it wasn't any licensed ship. Experimental perhaps. His mind went to his father, and his pulse quickened with the old dreams of space.

He wanted to race through the trees. If he knew the rebels, their band had already retreated. Even so, how odd this impulse to throw caution to the wind!

He led his team onward with wary steps.

At last, they stood before it. "Lieutenant, do you know what this is?"

"I'm not an air-transport specialist, sir."

"It's a Kiri ship. Look at the painting. The forward sensors are made into a mouth."

"And that hatch is open. Someone's come out, or gone in."

"Yes," said Ethan, "I'll look." *Oh, to see this in the daylight!* He switched on the icy beam of his hand lamp.

The layout of the controls meant nothing to him, but the vegetation on the walls was quintessentially Kiri, so too the carvings on the chairs, the designs on the curtains. Behind one of the curtains lay an empty sleeping room; behind the other, two bodies were strapped to beds: a man and a child perhaps nine or ten, both unconscious but breathing. The man was bearded and had dark-brown hair, a common Kiri trait, rare on Perdita. The girl had hair a little lighter.

No ship from space had come to Perdita in six hundred years. The ship that had crashed then held a crew of the genetically engineered beings called sverra, like humans but stronger and longer living. Only three had survived. They had brought the news of the end of the War, the Samas' defeat. And long ago, they had vanished into legend.

He wondered what legends were in the making now?

CHAPTER 3

The boy awoke first, just after they reached camp. He was fifteen or sixteen, Sherayna guessed, brown-haired and dark-eyed, wearing an odd knee-length shirt and tight pants. The woman had small, firm features, and hair blood red in the firelight. Illia seated the boy by the fire in the great tent, the woman on a bedroll beside him. When Illia offered him water, he bathed the woman's head. Sherayna posted four guards behind the prisoners. She and Illia sat in front of the prisoners placing all four on equal standing, suitable for talking, not intimidation. For though the strangers were City, they were civilians—at least the boy—and so not to be treated like army prisoners.

But the boy did not speak or seem to understand their questions. Yet his eyes were keen, and he could hear, for he moved to noises behind him. Perhaps he'd suffered an injury that had damaged the language centers of his brain.

After a silence, Illia voiced the question: "Could they possibly be offworlders?"

"The City, out to trick us," said Sherayna. And yet these people dressed so strangely, were colored so exotically. . . .

Leric entered the tent and knelt beside her. "Tyora's not back. I want to look for her, Sherayna."

Sherayna nodded. "Be careful."

After a time, the woman groaned and opened her eyes. The boy spoke to her in some strange language, not Tapanayn, while he helped her prop herself on her pillow.

"Can you understand me?" Sherayna asked the woman.

The woman and the boy exchanged glances.

"A triflingly," the woman enunciated with great deliberation.

"Who are you?"

"Who are I?"

"Yes, who are you?" Sherayna nodded.

"Sylan," said the woman, then pointed to the boy. "Jasen." Then she grew thoughtful and muttered words to herself. "Of, now . . ." She paused, fell into a quick conversation with Jasen. "West," she said. "West-of-Now."

Sherayna turned to Illia. "Does this mean anything to you?"

Illia shook her head. "But I recognize the language."

"And?"

"It's Kiri. I heard the words for 'yes' and 'no.' I read that once in an old story."

"You think they truly are offworlders, then?"

Sylan was waving a hand to get their attention. She pushed herself into a sitting position. "Seek?"

The woman's speech was not simply unskilled; it was old, not so much Tapanayn as Old Dabunè, the Sama tongue from which theirs descended.

Sherayna tried to answer her. "We found you."

"From the skiff?"

"The ship. Yes."

"Seek daughter my—my daughter—and . . ."

Jasen said, "Father."

Sylan pointed at Jasen. "Her—"

"His!" the boy corrected.

"His father . . . and sister . . . from the . . . ship."

Illia leaned close to Sherayna. "Did you search the whole ship?"

"Of course not. The City came."

"Then the daughter and her father will be gone." Illia's tone was not indifferent but hardened by many such sunderings.

"Gone—whence?" Jasen glared at Sherayna.

She met his eyes. "We will search for them."

He started to retort, but Sylan put a hand on his arm. "Ydan del-Disal?"

Sherayna could only shake her head.

"We don't understand," said Illia.

Sylan closed her eyes in concentration. "My mother, Ydan del-Disal, she did voyage hither prior to that we did voyage."

"In a spaceship?" asked Illia.

Both Sylan and Jasen nodded.

"We have never heard of her," said Sherayna.

The mother and son exchanged a few words that rose quickly to the pitch of an argument.

Sylan barked a command that silenced Jasen, and turned to Sherayna again. "Convey you me hence—for our ship."

"Us," put in Jasen. "Us two." He pointed to himself and his mother.

"No," said Sherayna. "Neither of you. There is danger there." She pointed out of the tent. "We will search. We know how."

"By rapidness," urged Sylan.

"One is searching already. More will search soon. Now, you should rest." She stood. "May you help the gods."

With that goodnight, she gestured for Illia to follow her.

"We'll never find them." Illia hugged herself against the chill. "The City will already have them. And they'll use them to learn their tech secrets."

≈•≈

When Nevan was ten, his father had took on a seeing trip into the north of the continent of Shálien, where the firs and the sedúma trees hid their heads in mists and barred the ground from daylight so that grass seldom grew. In the camp, the fire had warmed them at the same time the fog soaked their clothing.

"Dad, I need another blanket," he said and opened his eyes onto a low mattress.

His head hammered, and only slowly could he make sense of what he was seeing: a tiled floor, a stony wall, and Miri on her back on a mattress almost touching his. At the sight of her, he sat up with a jolt, pain stabbing his neck.

"Lemur-kin, are you all right?" He felt for a pulse in her neck.

Even as he found the pulse, a man's voice answered him. The words were familiar but made no sense. The man repeated them, and Nevan realized that he was speaking some simplified sort of Dabunè. He was saying, *"The child isn't badly hurt. She will be well."*

And Sylan and Jasen? Nevan searched with eyes and mind, but they were not nearby.

He turned toward the voice, twisting so that a pang leapt from his neck to his head. A heater box glowed red. Near the box, an electric lamp on a neck of snaking metal cast a white-yellow light. Next to the lamp, the man who had spoken sat cross-legged on the floor.

He was old—that was Nevan's first thought—but that couldn't be right: he hadn't passed the prime of life. His eyes gave the illusion of age, his short hair pale as an autumn field. His clothes were dark blue, a shirt and pants, three gold bars at one shoulder. He was clean shaven like Sylan's father. The thought snapped Nevan back to his wife and son.

He started to speak in his native Keshnul, corrected himself to Dabunè, blessing the history studies that had forced him to learn the dead language: "Where are the others?"

"We found only you and the child. The four seats in your navigating room were empty."

Nevan shook his head. "They would not have left us."

"It's almost certain they were taken by the rebels before we could reach you."

Nevan's heart fell into his stomach. "Who are the rebels?"

"They are ones who go to the far edge, who look down on technology."

"Oh." Nevan felt like a criminal caught in a spotlight: a Kiri on a Sama world.

When the Kiris and the Samas had fought long ago, ownership of the Seven Planets had been the vehicle for a battle of ideals. The Samas had thought to improve human life through improvements in technology. The Kiris had deemed reliance on high technology enslaving. On Berdida, it seemed the battle was still being fought. And he, a Kiri, would be considered sympathetic to the rebels. They might well guess he was Kiri by his dark hair, his red face. And his wife was a physicist. She ought to be here, not with the people who shunned technological advancement. Nevan took his daughter's limp hand in his own.

"When will she wake?" he asked.

"I don't know. But our healer has found nothing wrong with her, at the side of a few bruises and knocks." After a moment, he added, "Your great ship crashed."

"Yes."

"Can it be made whole?"

"I know not." Nevan stroked his daughter's hair.

"I will take you back to look tomorrow."

"Tomorrow you must help me in the finding of my wife and son from the rebels."

"We always search for the rebels. Often we find them. We will do what we can."

Nevan sensed a pulling back in the man: a sympathy, a sorrow—a self-doubt. He was far from certain he would find Sylan and Jasen. Somewhere, Nevan noted that the man could not read minds. He had the facility, like everyone, but his mind was closed imperfectly, in the way of instinct rather than a practiced block.

This isn't surprising, Nevan's thought. *In the days of the Sama Empire, the Samas rejected training in mind reading, holding that only an untrained mind was open to the gods. These people are descendants of that empire. Therefore . . .*

At the same time, his heartbeat hollered: *Sylan* and *Jasen.* "I require you to find them."

"We will do what we can. At the same time, we require that you supply us with information concerning your great ship." The man paused. "You are the first offworlders we have seen on Perdita in six centuries."

"Six centuries? You have seen ships not in six centuries?"

"No."

Just how cut off would they be on this Berdida, or *Perdita,* as the man pronounced it? And Sylan's mother—what of her? "We came here to seek a ship. You do not know it?"

"No. Why were you looking for it here?"

The truth was potent: the War's End. Nevan chose a lie instead. "My wife's mother, her final message came by near this part of space."

The man stared with an intensity that Nevan did not like. He would not volunteer anything more.

Seeming to see his unease, the man drew back. "My name is Ethan from Mesa. I am the official-having-rank in the Iltan forest."

Forest: *shalo.* Not a Dabunè word but from Keshnul, the Kiri tongue.

"My name is Nevan, Nevan West-of-Now. This is Miri." She stirred at her name, and Nevan again stroked her hair, flooded with relief to see her moving.

"West-of-Now?" Ethan frowned. "Make plain the under-meaning of that title."

Nevan considered refusing, but no, he could make use of this. "My wife—she is a physicist—is from planet Vorshtamor in Leddra. She is Leddie, not Kiri." *Not a technology hater, not one of your enemies.* "*Vorshtamor* is 'west harbor' in Vunizh, but *mora* is 'now' in my tongue, and so we made our name West-of-Now: our children are both Kiri *and* Leddie."

Ethan eyed him with dissatisfaction. "I will leave you to rest. A footman is outside to see to your needs. May you help the gods." He walked out.

CHAPTER 4

Ethan's footmen found nothing of value at the Sorel Falls camp. He ordered them to scout for the new campsite.

The night was old by that time, and Torna had gone to bed. But Ethan had no hope of sleep and needed to talk to someone. He rapped on her door four times before she called for him to come in.

He opened the door to a rush of warm air. Torna, a dark shape in the second moon, Tori's, fading glow, rubbed a hand across her eyes and drew herself onto her elbow, pulling her blankets around her.

He sat by her mattress and switched on her lamp.

"Lieutenant . . ." Sitting by her knees like a pensive adolescent, he had lowered his standing from commander to friend; he should address her as a friend. "Torna, this ship changes everything. Think about it. Why do we have an observatory in Iltan?"

She yawned. "Because in summer, the atmospheric conditions are good for stargazing."

"Partly. But mostly because the rebels have a fetish about Iltan. They crusaded for decades to end logging in the forest. So we reasoned that they'd hesitate to launch a major assault here. They'd have to bomb us, and that would mean damaging the trees."

"Ethan, it's late. What's your point?"

"The point is that our reasoning was ridiculous. They won't bomb it—but they don't need to. They make life so difficult that we have no hope of doing science here; astronomers won't come here just to be shot at. So we sit here defending an idle building."

"Will all that be in your next report to the warmaster?"

"I never wanted to do this. All I've wanted was to reach the realm of the gods. How much closer we would be to the rest of creation if only we could reach space. Torna, you were a seer. . . ."

"I was once."

"Can you see how this will end?"

"Not without the ceremonies. You know that."

"To think what we might accomplish here." His voice was quiet; he kept it so whenever he was excited. "We have access to an interstellar vessel. If we can examine it, we can learn what we've done wrong all these years. We could rejuvenate the Space Project—so fast the rebels won't have time to stop us, not again. The rebels don't matter anymore. The ship is the thing that matters."

"And finding the Kiri's family?"

"Yes. That matters. The woman, Nevan says, is a Leddie and a physicist. If that's true, she probably knows more about spaceflight than he does. My scouts have orders to search for her and the boy. But protecting the ship from rebel vandalism must be our priority."

Torna sat up and shivered in the night air. "If you want the Kiri Nevan's help, you will have to be mindful of his fears for his family. If you want to help the gods, you should be mindful anyway."

He looked down, embarrassed. "Yes, that's so."

≈•≈

It was dawn when Jasen awoke in the great tent. His mother was asleep beside him, the bruise on her forehead darkening and swelling. *Normal*, he told himself. He looked at her profile, caught between dying fire and the premorning glow that flowed in a column through the smoke hole.

She'd brought their ship down safe.

He looked around the tent. The guards from the night before were gone. In their place sat a man dressed, like all his people, in a shirt and pants mottled in brown, green, and purple-blue. He smiled and came to sit by Jasen, handing him a water flask and hard, grainy bread.

"My name is Leric. I had the honor of bringing your mother back to our camp last night."

Jasen could feel his rusty Dabunè coming back. He was pleased that he understood Leric.

"Why?" he asked, drinking some of the water. "Why do you bringing us back to your camp?" He was painfully aware of how poorly he spoke.

Leric's smile faded. "At first, we thought you were City people. We wanted you as prisoners. But we soon saw you were offworlders, and so it is our duty to put a roof over you from the City." Jasen started to speak, but Leric laid a hand on his arm. "I know you must be worried to a great dance of excitement for your father and sister. But we have people looking for them now."

The milky dawn lit Leric's face. He was younger than Jasen's parents, with pale skin and gray-blue eyes, his dark-blond hair short, like all the men's here. Like all the men, too, he was clean shaven, unnatural to Jasen, who had been raised as a Kiri.

"We want not to fight with you or City," said Jasen. "We want us four to go back at our ship and to find my mother-of-my-mother."

"I know. I wish it were possible. But the City will not let your ship go. If you return to it, they will only capture you, too—"

"And then, so?"

"They will not let you go. They will keep you—only to question you, to learn about your ship. Not to hurt you. But they will use you."

Jasen felt a sudden cynical sympathy for this man doing his utmost to make Jasen fear this City, yet to comfort him simultaneously. He smiled.

Leric laughed at once. "I am glad to amuse you. I was beginning to worry I'd have to trip on my feet and land square in the mud to get a smile."

Jasen was not sure he'd heard this correctly. "This do you often?"

"Only to break Sherayna out of one of her moods—so, yes, constantly."

As he was speaking, one of the women from last night came in. Not the fair-haired commander, Sherayna, but the one with dark-brown skin and black hair in two braids. Illia.

She sat beside them, her face drawn. "We've found Tyora. She's dead."

Leric made a small, distressed sound and took her in his arms. "She'll be a good pilgrim to the gods."

Tyora. Jasen had heard them speak of her, one of the people who had gone to find their ship.

"You," he began, losing his Dabunè in a panic, "you anger to us . . . that the lady to die our ship to find?"

"No, no," said Illia. "You're not to blame. Only the City can be blamed."

What sort of planet have we fallen onto? "What does City do very wrong?"

"The City—they don't care anything about the planet," said Illia. "They'll do anything to get into space. They believe tech can solve everything. They refuse to see how high tech hurts things instead."

"They refuse to hear us," Leric put in. "They made it against the law for us Borderals to speak against them."

"Border . . . ?"

"We call ourselves 'Borderals' because they've pushed to the borders, not geographically but by silencing us."

Illia broke in. "They use pesticides on our crops that poison the plants and animals and get into our water. They've dammed and logged and overfarmed so much that whole ecosystems have collapsed. Erosion has been an animal raging—that is, very bad. Whole species have gone extinct. They use fission in their space program and other chemicals pollute the land."

Leric laid a hand on her back, but he did not look much calmer.

Jasen swallowed. "I am not pro-that." Indeed, if what they said was true, it went very much against his Kiri upbringing. But how did these people propose to change these policies? It seemed they lived like bandits running from the law. Maybe that was their only option.

"We are none of us for it," said Leric. "So you see, you have found friends in us."

CHAPTER 5

Nevan felt Miri awaken in the night with pains in her head, neck, and back. Nevan kept his mind open to her, for as distressed as she was to see his fear, she'd be more distressed to be locked out. He tried to assure her and himself that Sylan and Jasen were alive and well and that they would soon be reunited. She'd cried, complained, asked questions he could not answer, cried again, and finally fallen into silence in the interminable dark before morning.

A foggy whiteness had filled their room's single window when Miri, awaking from a fitful nap, asked if Perditans used chamber pots or toilets. Nevan told her he'd have to ask the footman on guard outside.

Miri said, "Please hurry."

When he stepped out the door, he nearly plunged to his death. Their room perched on a ledge overlooking a precipitous drop down a curving white wall to a cement expanse dotted with buildings like boxes. Far out beyond the buildings, fog wreathed a sea of bluish trees. He recovered his wits against a flimsy railing.

Then he looked out again at the landscape. It was like home—not that it looked exactly like any place he'd lived. But it was forest, after months in space. *Trees, trees*, his mind repeated. *Trees*—his own name came from the word: *Nevi, nevi.*

At length, he became aware of their footman staring at him. He related Miri's question to her, not without difficulty, as his vocabulary was lacking.

The footman led them to a room called the "washroom." Waiting for Miri outside the door, Nevan eyed the stern young woman. She had black hair and a pale face, almost unheard of among the Samas, common among the Kiris. *How did she come to look so Kiri?* Miri, meantime, was gone quite a while, trying to discover how to work the alien toilets, he supposed.

Nevan felt good. It seemed so unapt with his wife and son missing that as soon as he realized it, he was miserable. But even then, a sense of relief continued. It came from the forest and the planetary sunlight. That realization eased his conscience a little, for what could be more natural than to rejoice in the living land?

The footman took him and Miri down an elevator and outside. The building they'd been lodged in was a broad, stony cylinder, ending in a dome out of which a dark projection pointed at the sky.

"What is that, Dad?" Miri held tight to his hand.

"It looks like a telescope," said Nevan. He asked the footman, who concurred after some linguistic confusion.

The footman led them to the boxish buildings, Miri clinging to Nevan when the blue-clothed Perditans stared at them. They were deposited in a room much like the one they'd slept in. In it were a heater, a lamp, a mattress, and an object that appeared to be a combination of a chest and desk, set low to the ground and padlocked. The footman asked them to wait and left.

In a few minutes, a gray-haired woman brought breakfast grains and dried fruit and reconstituted juice as vile as space food. She introduced herself as Lieutenant Torna and sat on the floor with them while they ate.

"We have people in the forest now searching for your family," she told them.

Nevan translated that for Miri and felt her mood lighten.

"Today, the warchief will take you back to your ship so you can cast a glance on the damage and collect your belongings."

Nevan nodded. "Lieutenant, are we your prisoners, or are you holding us for our safety?" He did not expect an honest answer but hoped to glean something of her motives.

"For now, Nevan, both. But we will not hold you long."

Nevan was startled by her seeming candor. "Do you speak as authority, with sure knowledge?"

She smiled at Miri. "I do not know the plans of my superiors, and yet I believe what I say to be true."

Miri smiled back uncertainly.

≈•≈

By midmorning, the fog had burned away and an azure sky blazed through skinny branches. The sun lifted Nevan's spirits as the warchief Ethan's party marched Nevan and Miri to their ship. Nevan found himself watching Miri more than anything.

He could see her noticing things he didn't, her eyes pulling this direction and that.

At the ship, he told her to pack what belongings she could easily carry. Then, he surveyed the damage.

"Flying ferrets," he whispered as he knelt by the open helm port. Then to Ethan, "My wife has taken mostly all the directional . . . things off-line. Let me see. . . ."

He had reconnected several relays when one discharged with a pop and a shower of sparks.

"Ferrets!" cried Nevan, shaking a singed hand.

Miri ran from her cubicle to his side. Ethan, who had wandered off, bolted from the other cubicle. Nevan told Miri he wasn't hurt and asked her to pack up some of his things, too.

To Ethan he said, "There's more damage here than I know how to fix." He clambered into the helm seat. "I'm not sure what my wife did, even, and especially not what broke in the first place."

Ethan flopped down in the seat next to his, caressed the panels with his fingers but said nothing.

"You think I'm saying that in order that you'll search more for my wife and son."

"The thought had occurred to me."

"Still, it is true. Sylan understands spaceships. I study history."

Miri stuck her head out of her parents' cubicle. "Dad, should I pack things for *Mila* and Jasen?"

"Oh, maybe a few, in case we find them before they get back here."

"Should I pack your *Jae History*?"

"No, Miri. I don't think there'll be much chance to work on it for a while." It wasn't safe on the ship, of course. If they left it there, no doubt the Perditans would find it sooner or later. On the other hand, the baggage they took with them would surely be searched. Leaving the *History* here might at least buy Nevan time to find the right person to reveal it to. Nevan glanced sidelong at Ethan to see if the word "jae," a Sama word, had affected him.

But Ethan pursued their conversation as if there'd been no interruption: "Nevan, you are a Kiri with a Kiri ship. How could you understand it less than Sylan?"

"Easily. On my world, Onáda, spaceships are not known for many people. I did not study them. Sylan came to study on Onáda, and she did study them."

Ethan rose. "Can you access any of your logs?"

"No, I cannot bring power online," Nevan said, though he probably could have.

Ethan fixed him with a measuring stare. Then he nodded and ordered his footmen to redouble the search for Sylan.

CHAPTER 6

Sylan and Jasen sat silent on a fallen tree trunk. Nobody openly guarded them, though there was always at least one camouflaged watcher in sight. The sun climbed the sky. Sylan's head ached when she moved, but at least, passing through the shield's disruption field shouldn't have hurt them. All such shields were programmed not to damage organic life.

As Sylan waited on the fungusy log, she was reminded of the day she'd waited twenty hours for her first child, this young man staring into space beside her, to be born. She was gazing at him when Illia hurried toward them.

She started out speaking impossibly fast but slowed down at desperate signs from Sylan. Something about how they had to leave. Another Borderal arrived and placed a pile of clothes before them.

In the ill-fitting pants and shirts, they looked very much like Borderals. As men and women swiftly packed up the camp, Leric appeared and told Sylan and Jasen to follow Illia. They set off at a sharp clip into the trackless forest, Leric bringing up the rear.

Never had Sylan been so lost; purplish tree trunks and purplish dirt, ferns, bushes, low herbs, falling needles, rotting snags, roots jumbled in swirling succession. At least the air had a leafy freshness—one of the things Sylan liked about Onáda. But she was out of condition and breathing hard. The blood pounding in her head made her bruised face throb.

She had fallen into a state of mindless misery when Leric shoved her down into a ditch obscured by a toppled tree and gestured for her to stay there. She huddled beside Jasen, while Illia and Leric disappeared into the forest. At first, listen as she might, she could hear nothing but her own breathing and her son's. When they were quieter, she caught the sad fluting of a bird, tiny rustlings of animals or breezes—or people?

A long time passed. Sylan's leg fell asleep. She shifted it.

Jasen whispered, "What will we do if they don't come back?"

"Look for food and water."

Jasen gave a voiceless laugh. "Here, where we know the ecology so well."

"There must be common Daughter-world plants."

A distant explosion trembled through the ground. A cry. Another explosion—and another. Three more. A shout.

Sylan realized she'd stopped breathing and resumed. She searched for Jasen's hand and squeezed it.

The sun found a chink in the canopy and warmed them for a few minutes before passing. A thousand times, Sylan played over what she'd say if the City found them: *We're strangers on this planet. We didn't choose to go with them.* Silently, she rehearsed dozens of conversations in stilted Dabunè.

But what if the City shot first and questioned later? What would become—or had become—of Miri and Nevan? And how far from them would she and Jasen have to trek?

The shadows lengthened. And what if no one came? That would be worst of all, trapped in an alien forest with no provisions and no idea how to get back to their ship. In the icy damp, Sylan and Jasen sat up in their ditch and put their arms around each other for warmth. She didn't try to touch Jasen's mind; her own was so frightened she would be of no comfort.

"How long do we wait?" Jasen whispered, his voice loud in the stillness.

"Until morning. Where would we go at night, anyway?"

The sun set, taking with it the last illusion of warmth. Thirst gnawed at Sylan. She wondered how much water she could lick from the dew.

The footsteps came on them so fast she scarcely had time to panic. Then Illia dropped down beside them and swung a sack off her shoulder. For a moment, Sylan thought she would faint, so great was her relief. Illia pulled out a water flask and dried food, making some apology for not leaving the sack with them.

Sylan handed the flask to Jasen. "Miri and Nevan?"

"No word."

Leric joined them as the fog was rolling in. After he'd eaten, they plodded on. Now, in the cold, Sylan was not so easily winded, and once they had walked a ways, her head did not ache badly. Imperceptibly, the blackness turned gray and the chirping of crickets surrendered to the fluting of birds.

The sun had not yet risen when they came to a cave covered over with ferns. Inside was a flattened floor of dry sand and some piles of stones. Buried under these was a chest with food, blankets, and plain gray clothes. At Illia's instruction, they changed into the clothes, abandoning their forest camouflage. After they'd eaten, they slept again.

≈•≈

The next day, the four of them reached a grim coastline looming over a stale, colorless sea. Sylan's legs felt near to buckling as they scraped down the cliffs to a pebbled beach. Boats sprinkled the water.

"We walk public?" whispered Sylan to Illia in surprise.

"The Veshna fishers won't hurt us. They stay out of our way, though most will never actually be with us."

By afternoon, she and Jasen were belowdecks in a motorboat humming through the waves. Sylan was exhausted and sore, and Jasen sprawled on his sitting cushion, his face miserable.

"Do you have any idea where they're taking us?" he asked.

Sylan had been watching the course of the sun through the window: from west into east, according to the rotation she had observed from space. "South, I think."

"Dare I ask how we're going to find Dad and Miri now?"

"The best thing to do is learn all we can about the planet. For all we know, they have a comprehensive communications system for tracking down lost people."

The truth was they were at the mercy of the Borderals. They both knew it.

CHAPTER 7

Ethan had Nevan and his daughter escorted back to the observatory while he himself stayed with the ship. The first thing he did when the Kiris had gone was pocket the book-sized computer pad he suspected might be the jae something the girl had asked if she should take. It was just text, probably. Anything literally jae powered would surely have been far too massive to remove.

It was lucky he'd managed to catch that exchange. As a boy, he had studied the Kiri language, Keshnul. He hadn't understood, then, why he'd had to bother, but his father had insisted it was important to understanding the history of Perdita. Now he wished he had studied more diligently.

He made a final perusal of the ship. It had a Kiri artistry: decorative rafters accentuated the mossy walls. The Kiri use of mosses to oxygenate spaceships was unique as far as Ethan knew—though who could say, after all these centuries. Perhaps all the Nations used mosses now. Such mosses, he'd been taught, were engineered not only to produce oxygen in vast quantities but also to be incapable of reproduction outside of laboratory conditions. He suspected that, among the Kiris, the introduction of foreign organisms into an ecosystem was a grave offense.

He pressed his fingers into the browning moss, then strolled back behind the bedrooms through the tight-packed storeroom to a large, dim hold that housed the main engineering access panels and the gleaming silver pods in which travelers slept in the course of long space voyages. How long had it taken them to come here? He conjured up old lessons in astrohistory: from the Kiri Empire to the Afebat Galaxy . . . two intergalactic tide portals to cross? And how many light-years besides? He ran his hand across the sleek metal of one of the pods. If only his father were alive to see this!

His reverie was shattered by a commotion outside. He hopped down from the outer hatch to see two footmen striding toward him, holding a rebel, her face blue-brown with dirt.

"Where did this one come from?" he demanded.

"She was hiding under the tail of the ship, Warchief."

"That suggests unacceptable laxity, Footman. Tighten your watch."

Ethan ordered the woman bound and taken into custody. He saw the area searched and ordered the guard round the ship redoubled, leaving only a skeleton force on duty at the observatory.

≈•≈

Ordinarily, the capture of a rebel prisoner was welcome, but under these circumstances, Ethan found her an inconvenience. The ship was the vital thing. He had no desire to see his attention diverted.

He radioed Lashen's office and asked to speak with the warmaster. The warmaster, predictably, was not available. Yet less than an hour later, he radioed Ethan back.

"What's the latest with your offworlders?" Lashen's voice was jovial.

"The man and his daughter are secure, the woman and son still unaccounted for, presumed taken by the rebels." He ran down the facts fast, eager to get to his point. "Sir, I wish to request immediate backup for safeguarding the ship. The significance of this find cannot be overestimated."

"Reinforcements. I see." Lashen's laughing condescension rankled Ethan. But after years of serving together, Ethan knew the warmaster's dedication. So he kept his peace till Lashen said, "That's the only reason you requested a direct call?"

"It's the most vital, sir. In addition, we've taken a rebel prisoner. I request authorization to transfer her to Mesa at once. We don't have the resources here."

Silence a moment. "I'm afraid you'll have to keep her, Ethan."

"May I ask why, sir?"

"Surely, you see that a rebel's your best lead for finding a woman and a boy who have been stolen by rebels. And the woman's a physicist, no? She's our best link to understanding that ship. I'm surprised at you, asking permission to give away such a source of information."

"I doubt she'll talk, sir."

"Well, that's your business: get her to."

≈•≈

That afternoon in a holding cell, he saw to her interrogation. Her wrists were secured to the wall where she sat: movement deprivation. He didn't intend it that way—only to keep her from attacking or escaping. But she wouldn't understand that. She stared at the floor while he placed the requisite questions, lies, insinuations. It dawned on him halfway through his performance that he had seen her when he had spied on rebel camps: her slanting blue eyes, her sun-yellow hair. She wore a necklace. He remembered seeing it glint in the sun, an unusual risk for a rebel. When he had finished the standard speech and learned nothing, he switched to the minimal, but original, strategy he'd mapped out after speaking to the warmaster.

"Sherayna." She looked up at the sound of her name. "The arrival of this ship is not a City thing or a Borderal thing." Her eyes narrowed at his use of her people's name for themselves. "Parliament has made no ruling regarding it. It is not the subject of any particular law, yet. The Borderal perspective of the issue could be heard—"

She snorted.

He leaned back against the wall, lessening the gap between their social standings. "I have a proposition. I know you have the Leddie woman and the boy. If you return them, I'll ensure amnesty to a Borderal committee—two people in exchange for two people—who can speak to Parliament in Senarna and make their case for the fate of this ship. You could go yourself."

She spoke for the first time. "You don't have that kind of authority, Warchief."

"I have the warmaster's ear. That's more authority than you'll see again."

She leered like a wildcat and looked at the floor.

Ethan continued. "You're thinking that if Parliament didn't listen to the Borderals before the Progressive Tech Statute, it isn't likely to listen now, when you've turned from politicians to open outlaws. But remember the offworlders. They alone have the knowledge to use the ship. To use it, we must have their cooperation. And the man is Kiri, the ship is Kiri. He will most likely side with you."

"Then why would you give us such power?"

"Because I don't believe he will side entirely with you or that the woman will. But a compromise, for both of us, is better than nothing, no?"

She made no reply.

"Think about it." Crossing to the door, he knocked for the guard.

She was right, of course. He had nothing like the power to offer amnesty to rebels. Only the king had the right to do that, and he was a devoted pro-tech. He was lying; she clearly knew it. His goal was to get her to doubt that knowledge, but the odds of that were slim.

And yet, was it really such a lie? *Make a lie near the truth.* It was an ancient adage. Would he give her amnesty if he could? The freedom to speak her views openly? "We do not fear to hear ideas," his father had said. "It is they who fear to hear ideas."

≈•≈

Two guards came to feed Sherayna. One held a gun on her, while the other spooned dry cereal into her mouth and then held a glass of water to her lips. When they had gone, she stared at the wood panels of the room—purple wood, torn out of Iltan itself—and looked for an escape.

She could not break the shackles on her wrists or twist her hands free of them. When they'd first left her here, she'd tried until her wrists were raw. But leaving her alone at all marked a breach of procedure. Usually, when the City took prisoners, they left one guard in the cell and one outside the door. It seemed she had only the one guard outside. The warchief was diverting his personnel to the ship.

The City must not keep the ship. Yet she was relieved that the diversion of City troops meant greater hope for her own rescue. She must escape before the City could transfer her to their own ground for interrogation.

Interrogation. The word hardly applied to her interview with the warchief. What sort of game was he playing: amnesty in exchange for the offworlders! A bargain well above his standing.

They needed Sylan to run the ship, he'd said. They'd never make sense of the ship without its owners' aid. *Gods, if only that were true!* No, with their doggedness, they would figure the ship out on their own—given time. But they wouldn't get the time, and the warchief knew that. Was that what he meant by needing the offworlders: to learn to use the ship before the Borderals could stop them? Was there any chance that those words might be half true? Might he indeed have the warmaster's ear and the warmaster the king's?

No, the idea's folly. You look at a man with some intelligence in his eye, and you want to believe him. That's a child's belief.

So her thoughts rolled as the day cooled into night.

She jerked up at the sound of a thud against her door. There was scrabbling and a click of the lock, and Enom dove into the room, his friend Callin behind him, dragging the body of her City guard.

"He won't be out long," Callin whispered.

Enom darted to Sherayna's side, inspecting the chains at her wrists.

"Close the door," Sherayna hissed.

Callin obeyed, then gagged the guard and tied him up.

"We won't have much time before they notice the guard's gone." Sherayna held up her wrists. "Can you cut the chain?"

Enom inspected them. "Iron. We could have cut a plasti-chain." He rifled through the travel pouch at his waist.

"We'll have to pull it out of the wall," she said. "I can't pull hard facing backward, even if I grip the chain, but if you two pull with me. No, one of you pull with me, the other work on the wood itself. You have an awl, a knife, anything?"

Enom already had a stout knife in his hand and was chipping at the wood around the thick iron staples that secured the left chain, while Callin and Sherayna pulled on it.

The chains scarcely budged. "Damnation," said Enom. "These walls look as flimsy as paper. They should . . ." He trailed off, re-angling his knife to get under the chain.

They pulled till Sherayna's arm and back were burning. Little by little, the staples slipped, until, with a final wrench, the left chain came free, knocking Callin and Sherayna onto their sides so hard Sherayna's still-chained right arm tore out of its socket in a burst of pain. She suppressed a cry, clenching her teeth while Callin realigned her shoulder.

While Callin worked, Enom crossed to the unconscious guard and delivered a calculated blow to his head to make sure he'd be out a bit longer. It was difficult, Sherayna knew, to strike a helpless being. She saw the tightness in his face as he knocked the man's head against the floor. But it was that or kill him.

Then they were back to work at the right chain.

They were so intent on their task that they only heard the door when it was already half open. Sherayna flattened herself on the ground. Callin lunged at the footman, knocking her to the floor as her gun went off. Then, Enom was on her, his knife in her ribs. Whether the woman was dead or alive, the shot would bring more guards in moments. Sherayna braced her foot against the wall and tore the chain from the battered wood, falling hard onto her back.

Gathering the chains so she could run, she leapt to her feet. Voices were heading toward them; a shot rang past as they sped out of the door and around the corner, running for the trees.

≈•≈

Ethan dreamed he was a child at a picnic with his parents, by the shores of a shadowed lake. He wasn't looking at his father, yet he could see his father laughing. His mother was perched high on a rock. At her throat gleamed her gold pendant, the ideogram for *destusee* (we overcome): the motto of the Samas. She dove into the lake.

A gunshot had roused him, but the rebels were gone before he reached the scene. He must have helped the gods because they lived out his wishes and fulfilled them. The prisoner was off his hands.

In his report to Lashen, he stood by his decision to shift the balance of his footmen from the observatory to the ship: "The loss of the rebel Sherayna is insignificant next to the protection of the Kiri ship." He relayed the message and received concurrence from the warmaster.

≈•≈

But they failed to find the Leddie Sylan and the boy. In point of fact, all the rebels vanished.

Building an observatory in Iltan was always folly. Those people move through the forest like owls. Better to hide an observatory in the middle of

Senarna, in decent pro-tech land. Better not to hide at all. We are the right; we are the law. Why should we hide from terrorists?

The loss of the offworlders was a grave blow. The woman's expertise with the ship would have proven invaluable. And Ethan's frayed temper was not mended by Nevan's constant, thick-accented demands that the search be expanded, as if the number of footmen in Iltan were infinite. And then, as if in final proof of the heartlessness of Wolsena, the orders came.

The king called Ethan to the capital. He was to escort the two offworlders to a royal audience at the towers of Ayer Senarna. He was being torn away from the ship and required to present himself before King Rarion himself—and worse, before that creature the king called his wife.

CHAPTER 8

Nevan's Journal
Perdita: 26 Mid-Spring, 15.05.2033 After the End

When I asked Ethan for writing materials, he gave me
paper and a pen instead of something to type on. That made
me glad, for it reminded me of home. Yet this planet reminds
me too much of home. The people, for instance: most are fair-
haired like Samas, some dark-skinned like Ránlans, which isn't
surprising, since numerous Ránlans immigrated to the Sama
Empire over the centuries. But many show Kiri ancestry, pale
or bronze skin and dark hair.

And then there is the language, a descendant of Dabunè
but rich with words from the Kiri language, Keshnul,
particularly for landforms: *forest, ocean, mountain.* The shifts in
sound values (Berdida to Perdita, and so on) also suggest
Keshnul. I am writing this journal in Sylan's Vunizh tongue,
because I begin to think that my own language might be better
understood here than I had first imagined.

Today we set out for Senarna, the capital city. When Ethan
told me we were leaving, I almost refused. But then something
came to me, an impression through the untrained block of his
mind. *He winced.* I saw that he didn't want to go any more than
I did. We are both prisoners. And perhaps the power of the
capital can help us find Sylan and Jasen. At any rate, that's what
I told Miri. She argued at first, then grew quiet. Every day, I
revile myself for bringing my children into this. They should be
safe on Onáda with my parents.

We took a hydrogen-powered ground car from the
observatory south to Mesa, about 180 kilometers, or 200
"measures," as they call them. A footman drove, and Ethan sat
in the front with him. After about 70 kilometers, the forest
thinned into a patchwork of deciduous and coniferous trees
interspersed with fields: like my birthplace on Onáda, only
flatter.

Mesa is a city in the sparse woodlands just outside the
floodplain of the North Oja River. I say "city" as if I were
using our Keshnul word, *onar,* when what I should say in
Vunizh is "town," for it is not large or dense. The buildings are

low boxes, painted bright, with yellow roofs that look as if they are hoping to pass for thatch. Many have flower gardens. In their way, they are pretty. The only truly ugly thing is the broad roads made to allow for heavy traffic.

It took us four hours to reach Mesa by car. Once there, we boarded a light airship called a jumper. (The channel between this continent of Veshna and the west continent of Keeri-Semlona is named the Jump.) On the ship, I could finally sit next to Ethan and ask him questions.

"You said that six centuries ago, a spaceship crashed on Perdita. Were the people on it Kiri?"

"No. Why?"

I explained my observations of the Kiri influence on Perdita.

He said, "During the War, Perdita was a prison planet. By the War's End, about one-eighth of the population consisted of Kiri prisoners. There were no permanent superlight ships stationed here. With no ships, when the empire stopped communicating with us, we were planet bound. After some years, a decision was made to release the Kiris. For centuries, the two peoples struggled to live together. At times, there was carnage. But about a thousand years ago, a peace accord was ratified." He barely smiled. "At times, an accord more on paper than in fact—but it did call for the recognition of Perditans as a single people, neither Sama nor Kiri but belonging to our own nation. That idea at least has held."

This made sense to me. Though it might no longer be identified with National ancestry, the ideological chasm that stretched between Sama and Kiri had yet to be bridged.

I asked him who, if not Kiris, had come here six centuries ago in that ship. Sverra: three survivors. The word "sverra," *swerra* among the Perditans, was applied notoriously loosely by the Samas, often referring to any nonhuman, but humanoid, engineered species. More properly, it refers to the species we call the *Tralorváti* in Keshnul: the "strong humanoids."

"A very strong, heavy-bodied people?" I asked, and he assented. "A very long-lived people?" Again an assent. "What became of them on Perdita?"

"We don't know. The woman, the adult, was revered as a seer for a time. Then, she and her two children fell from our view."

"Do you think they're still alive, Dad?" Miri asked from my side.

"They can live for fifteen hundred years or more," I told her. "It's certainly possible."

42

CHAPTER 9

Micor could hear his son Olloan on the stairs.

"Here it is." Olloan's tall form emerged from the basement of the Northwestern Regional Oja Library, holding up some papers. A light-brown dye disguised his face and hands, almost as pale as his father's. They would never look quite human, but they passed because no one expected to see anything else. Micor took the pages, peering at them in the light of the filing computer's monitor.

"Sobai's floods," he said, "it is the schematic for the isolation field. And I'd hoped we'd found all the copies long ago."

"Did you find anything else?" Olloan nodded at the computer.

"Not on this list. And I'll have this one erased in a minute." He turned back to the computer.

Ten minutes later, they had left the library, the door secured behind them by one of their Borderal operatives. The operative didn't know what they'd found, of course. But she trusted Micor. He knew it was enough for her that he and Olloan had removed a dangerous tech plan.

The next morning, as dawn floated through stone windows cleft in the mountainside, Olloan knelt by Micor's bedroom hearth and set a match to the laminated document. Oily smoke slithered up the chimney to disease the air, a small price to pay for the eradication of another threat.

Pensive, Olloan watched the flames.

"What is it?" asked Micor.

Without looking up, Olloan said, "Does it ever strike you, Micor, that we are like the people who drive off the locusts?" *The fools who drive away locusts, rather, should go where the locusts are not.* It was a proverb so ancient that Micor wasn't sure where it came from—maybe all the way from Daughter.

"Yes," said Micor. "Unfortunately, we carry our locusts with us."

Olloan stirred the ashes. "I wonder if we'll see the day when Perdita ceases to make tech its locust. The day it has something to watch, beyond."

A knock at the door. "Micor?"

"Enter."

The man stuck in his head. "Sherayna has driven from Iltan to see you."

≈•≈

Sherayna honored Micor as their supreme leader, insofar as they had one. He didn't organize all Borderal activities—that kind of centralization would have been deadly to their guerrilla war. But when a major action needed coordination, or when one's path was not clear, he was the guide.

As soon as Sherayna arrived, she was shown to a room where he sat by a fire with Olloan. She had known the two of them all her life, yet every time she saw them, part of her was surprised. Olloan was just a little fairer than normal, his eyes a little brighter. He looked the same age as Sherayna, though she was thirty-two and he over four hundred.

Micor was whiter than his son, with sea-gray eyes. When he smiled at Sherayna, the lines stood out around his eyes and mouth. If he had been a full sverra, there would have been no lines—not at just over six hundred years old. But his father had been human.

"It's good to see you, Sherayna." Olloan gestured to a cushion. "We got your message yesterday."

Sherayna sat down hastily. She had been standing far longer than was proper, leaving her superiors sitting below her. "And you, Olloan, Micor."

The room was crammed with faded wooden furniture—bed, desk, shelves—and sitting cushions, less worn than the rest. The windows gazed out over cedar-dotted slopes.

"You have two of the offworlders?" Micor asked.

"Illia and Leric are taking them to Meena."

"And their ship?"

"The City is guarding it. We weren't able to mount an effective assault against it."

"And you would authorize the ship's destruction if you could?" Olloan asked.

Sherayna's eyes leapt to him. "You wouldn't, Olloan?"

"The ship is not merely a Perditan matter. It's the property, or at least in the trust, of the offworlders."

Sherayna hesitated. "I don't wish to create difficulties for our guests. But surely the protection of Perdita comes first. With that ship's tech, they could turn Perdita into one great cement spaceport. We can't allow expansionism to undermine the fragile ecological balance of the two continents. Think of the Lost Lands."

"Yes, I remember the Lost Lands—living within a hundred measures of them is still considered a health hazard. And no, I wouldn't like to see what you describe."

"Well then?"

Olloan studied her. "Sherayna, I am a commander, not the coordinator." He glanced at his father.

Sherayna, too, looked at Micor. "Coordinator?"

"What happened to your wrists?"

"The City had me chained up overnight."

Micor nodded. "Yet you told them nothing about the offworlders."

"Or course not."

"I expect no less from you, Sherayna. You are a rock among our people. And you must not let them take the offworlders, especially the physicist, Sylan. This takes precedence over the ship, over everything."

CHAPTER 10

Nevan's Journal
Perdita: 27 Mid-Spring, 16.05.2033 After the End

We stopped overnight at the airfield outside Senarna. The land was ocean cold. Both continents lie in the northern hemisphere, and Senarna is the northernmost continental city, poised on the Gulf of Crimson. *Senarna* itself means "crimson tamed." When I asked Ethan why, he said it had once been bathed in blood but became the first seat of the unified planet. It has been the capital for eight hundred years.

Just after dawn, we took a car into the city. Miri was so enthralled that for a few moments I could feel her mind relax and forget her fears for our family.

It is a true metropolis, this city: buildings precipitating out of the ground like crystals. The streets are gray but the buildings white, or meant to be—some are stained and faded. The preference is for tapering towers and glass-paneled ceilings. Solar heating is useful in sunny, chilly Senarna. I expect storms are mild, nothing that would be likely to shatter all that glass. (Or is it a synthetic?)

They love water as well. Little streams skip down algae-blue canals to be pumped into fountains sculpted like sea animals. Like Mesa, Senarna has an admiration for flowers—to the exclusion of the other plants. Trees are few, and most of those heavy with huge blossoms. The almost mathematical interspersing of blooms with greenery suggests that the gardens are planted with an eye for seasons. By the time the buds of this spring have withered, no doubt the buds of summer will be gleaming on sister plants.

The city is pleasing to the senses. When the sun is right, it is radiant, the glass casting white light on the buildings. And onto this persistent whiteness, the flowers shine life. The chatter of running water almost blots out the engines of cars. And the air has a scent of ocean and nectar.

There are more people than I am comfortable seeing. They dress in pants and shirts, like the soldiers, though in a variety of colors; or else, they wear loose robes. They drive in cars of varying size or walk so determinedly down the roadsides that I wonder what is so urgent. Yet I know this is the way of cities. I have seen it in Leddra.

The castle of Ayer Senarna is like the rest of Senarna's architecture but bigger, down to the sprawling gardens that separate it from the city. The servants who escorted us into one of its towers were dressed in white, as if extensions of their castle. Inside, the halls were also white but draped in carpets of intense colors like flowers seen through half-closed eyes. These halls were warmed, by heaters I presume, since no fire was evident.

They took Miri and me to a room with a mattress, sitting cushions, and lamps. There, they laid out new clothes for us, suits of green and brown. I found it difficult to lay aside my own clothes. Like leaving the Iltan forest, it was a step in the wrong direction.

Ethan met us in an anteroom. He was wearing a wine-colored suit with three gold bars, his sign of rank, placed diagonally over the right ribs. They reminded me of cat scratches. Emblazoned in gold on the suit's left shoulder was the old Sama emblem, representing a nearly horizontal circle encircling a vertical one: the universe of the gods crossing the universe of humanity. He wore it easily—yet ill at ease—as if he had often come to court but never made its ways his own.

He gave us some rules of conduct, surprisingly few for a Sama court. "You will have no trouble with King Rarion so long as you are respectful. The king is a simple, common-sense-expressing man." He paused. "Watch Queen Laynia, though. She's a Wolsena's promise."

Wolsena's promise. I could not guess what he meant by that. Our goddess, Volsénlla, is not personalized in that way.

"I did not know Wolsena made promises," I said.

"Why no. Wolsena's an equivocator."

≈•≈

When the three of us entered the royal hall, I held Miri's hand and she smiled at me to comfort me, as if I had become her child. The hall was long, carpeted, lit by fluorescent lamps—the first windowless room I had seen in Senarna. It was also the first I had seen to have chairs: two, hewn from marble, at the end of the hall. In them, the rulers of Perdita lounged. Underneath robes like the midnight sky, King Rarion was an uninspiring man, gaunt and graying. In a loose gown the shade of pine, the equivocal queen looked younger.

We bowed our heads and sat before them, Miri and I on either side of Ethan. Rarion greeted us by our names, and we affirmed our hope that he and his wife would help the gods and feel their love. So saying, we were permitted to gaze on them.

She dragged me to her eyes. *I am seeing my wife's eyes,* I told myself, for they were green. Yet that was not it. Sylan's eyes are like emeralds, Laynia's slices of jade. Her hair, falling loose to her shoulders, is red-gold. Her face is ivory. She did not look alive but like an illusion. In the instant she retreated within herself, I knew that her mind had touched mine. The contact broken, I became conscious of the king, rattling away like any competent, untalented orator.

Rarion asked me many of the questions Ethan had. I was about to ask the king if he would lower the shield, but a warning iced my brain; the queen's eyes blazed. I told the king I did not know why we'd lost control of our ship.

Finally the king said, "We wish to help you, Nevan. We are searching for your family. We will help you to fix your ship and see you on your way, provided you grant us access to your technical information."

I wanted to say, *And if I refuse?*

But Ethan had said, ask no questions. "I thank you for your generous offer, my King."

I saw the queen smile.

≈•≈

When the audience was over, Miri and I were treated to dinner, which, from its variety—and artistically piled vegetable slices—I suspect was one of Senarna's best. It was too salty for our taste, a risk inherent in farming the ocean.

Near sunset, a servant announced that we might walk in the Glass Garden, a greenhouse in the top of the low tower at the center of Ayer Senarna. There, great blooms gave off an insistent perfume. One could get lost of the jungle of vines, were it not for the mumbling reference point of the central fountain. Miri and I liked this garden. The plantings had a random look, almost like the living land.

While Miri played in the greenery, I looked through the glass walls past the towers and courtyards, over the city glinting red in the sunset, out to shadowed cliffs and a russet ribbon of ocean. I did not hear the doors open. But suddenly the queen was in my mind, calling me to the fountain.

When I reached her, Miri was already there. Laynia, sitting on the fountain's edge, looked as she had in the long hall, but now her gaze was far away, her fingers stirring the waters.

"Miri," she said, "you may listen here if you wish, but I have much to speak of with your father, and I fear you will be waiting a long time before I'm ready to speak with you. Perhaps it would be best if you amused yourself in my garden."

Miri had not caught every word but understood enough. I saw that she did not want to go, yet I found myself urging her to do as the queen suggested. She gave me a glance that was not quite reproachful, a distancing glance that tore at me. But then she was gone, and my thoughts were of Laynia.

"It is important, Nevan, that you tell no one about the shield."

"I had assumed it was common knowledge, my Queen." I was standing in front of her and remembered suddenly that this made my "standing," as they call it, superior to hers. Quickly I sat on the damp stone floor.

She made no response to my action. "Of course, you assumed so. But, in fact, knowledge of its existence is severely restricted. In Ayer Senarna, only I know of it."

Ask no questions, I thought. Did that apply to this audience? "Why is knowledge restricted, my Queen?"

"A long story, Nevan. Tomorrow, I will take you and your child where we can talk of it." She leaned forward, elbows on knees; I wondered if that changed her standing. "Now we must talk of other things. Do you worship Volsénlla?"

This was the last question I had expected, and it brought Ethan's words back to me: *Wolsena's promise.* "Yes, I worship her," I said truthfully.

"You believe then she is the creator?"

"I do not know if she exists, my Queen. But I worship her universe through worshipping her."

She leaned in close and whispered to me, "So do I. Do you know what she is on Perdita?"

I shook my head.

"She is hated, Nevan. 'Wolsena the Non-intervening,' and 'Heartless Wolsena,' and 'Earless Wolsena.' A few of us remember how the Kiris knew her: the Lady of Nature."

I do not know quite what she meant. The Lady of *Midia*, is what she said. I had heard this word used for "nature," as we say: *tórvalla*. Yet, she spoke "Volsénlla" in the Kiri tongue, and I wondered if she didn't mean *mirlla*, as we mean it, which is to say: "the process of nature, the physical laws, the actions of the dimensions, the survival of the fittest." And if that was what she meant, then Kiri ways are still living here, albeit relegated to an enclave.

"I wish to take you and Miri to our place of worship," she said. "We speak with our minds there, as you do. We have more power on Perdita than is known, the power that comes of being able to feel minds."

"Most Perditans' minds are naturally veiled, surely?"

"Indeed, but the strong readers can still gain impressions. Those are useful."

"And easily misinterpreted."

"That's why we train."

They train to manipulate minds as well. The proof is that, then, I was not thinking it.

"If you stay here," she said, "you will be my husband's pawn. Your ship may be mended, but you will not escape, for the shield will not go down but by our words—I do not threaten." She laid a hand on the sleeve of my shirt. "I say only what is true. We have much to discuss that can only be said on Zerin. It's not far. If there's news of your wife and son, we will hear it almost as fast as in Senarna."

"Where will Ethan go after he leaves court?"

"Oh, probably back to your ship. That one always has an eye on the stars." There was dismissal, if not derision, in her voice, and inside I drew away.

But I said, "I will go with you, if Miri agrees."

She called Miri over and asked her if she would like to see a place where people were like her people, with the same religion and the same mind knowledge.

"Will be my mother and brother there?"

"No, I'm afraid they are not there," said Laynia, "but if there is news, you will hear it there, fast as anywhere on Perdita."

Miri looked at me and saw that I wanted to go. "I'll go where my father goes." There is no gift so undeserved as a child's loyalty.

CHAPTER 11

As an officer of upper rank, Ethan was required at the court banquet. This one reminded him of all the others: the room too hot, the music too loud, the people too gaudy, the food excellent but impossible to enjoy in the midst of the general unpleasantness. He wore his uniform unadorned and brooded close to the walls.

I'm a simple soldier, his attitude shouted. *I am with you, but I am not one of you.*

But one god at least was treading water, for there was Lashen, in a red and gold robe, dancing with some woman. When the dance was over, Ethan pushed through the throng to the warmaster's side and followed him out into the corridor.

"Gods, but they do delight in chest-rattling music these days." Lashen rubbed at his graying mustache and motioned Ethan down the hall.

"Warmaster," said Ethan, leaning on the wall, "have you had a chance to examine that computer book I delivered?"

The warmaster crossed his heavy arms. "My encryption team reports two facts. First, there's no password: the files are simply openable. My instinct is that's a bad thing. I wouldn't be surprised if all we find is some half-rate children's story. Second, the alphabet is standard and the language is Vunizh, an obscure language and probably much changed from our most recent records, but translatable."

Ethan nodded. "I'm well pleased, sir. I mentioned that the document may be jae related?"

"You did, my friend, and I told you vain hopes gain nothing. But we'll translate it. Even a children's tale from the space-faring worlds could be of use to us." He peered at Ethan. "Iltan hasn't been good to you, my boy. Get back in the sun."

"I hope to return to Iltan, sir, as long as the ship is there."

≈•≈

Lashen went back to the banquet, which obligated Ethan to follow. The music at least was softer now, making conversation possible. He wished all at once that it weren't, for here came the queen bearing down on his wall.

"Ethan, you are a treasure to us as always!" She took his hand. "What a find you have brought us in this ship and these people!"

"I thank you, my Queen." Ethan pressed his back against the wall. "I look forward to returning the people to their ship so that they may assist us with repairs."

She looked suspiciously as if she was about to kiss his cheek. "Of course, you do. Unfortunately, the powers declare that Nevan and Miri, who are not mechanical experts, will aid us far more by staying in Senarna and sharing their knowledge with the academicians."

"I see. I shall be returning alone then, my Queen?"

"Unless you wish to remain as a technical advisor in Senarna. I have been authorized to offer you such a post."

If only she would let go of his hand. "I am at the king's disposal, my Queen. I prefer, however, to return to the Kiri ship in Iltan."

"Then, you shall. And all the more reason, surely, to enjoy yourself while you're here—on which note, I must mention that you are as always welcome in my bed."

Every time it was the same. She could not legally compel him to be her lover, but his refusal revealed that he did not find her palatable. It was tantamount to admitting that he questioned the king's choice of consort, thus, the king himself. And here in the middle of a crowded hall, how many of those blank faces were eavesdropping?

"I must respectfully decline."

Laynia reclined against the wall next to him. "Dear me, how monotonous."

≈•≈

Ethan knocked on Nevan's door and did not receive a reply. But after a silence, Nevan opened the door, and it seemed a weight lifted from his face when he saw Ethan. He welcomed him into the chamber, poorly lit by the dimmest of its lamps, then closed the door to the adjoining room where his daughter slept.

When they'd sat down like equals on cushions, Ethan said, "I doubt we'll have another chance to converse for some time."

"It seems not likely. Miri and I will be leaving Senarna in the morning."

"Indeed?" So where was she planning to hide them?

Nevan spoke as if abashed. "The queen will show us an island."

"Zerin?"

"Yes. How did you know that?"

"It's the queen's homeland. She was raised there by the Jethor, who study mind reading."

"Ah, that's why she could reach my mind."

So Nevan had felt her. "Do you read minds as well?"

A nod.

"Have you mind-read me?"

Nevan met his eyes. "No, not hardly. People who haven't learned to mind-read have closed minds naturally. If I tried, I couldn't sense more than a few emotions."

"She can."

"Yes. She's very strong. She controls—" He broke off and rubbed his hands over his face. "She held me tonight. I closed her from my mind. I felt my walls holding. She held my mind even still."

"She has such power over many."

"Over ones so recently parted from a wife they'd live and die for like a termite for her queen?"

Ethan had no comfort to offer. He found the termite image odd, and it surprised him that Nevan had bothered to learn the word in Tapanayn.

Nevan gazed at the floor. "My wife has been in my thoughts today. Not just in fear for her and my son, but in memory like the dead. I was born in the city of Kórfyntan on Onáda. You would not call it a city. It is . . . not a place where a human meets many humans. I wanted to learn human history, so I went away to crowded Melnar, where the great university on Onáda is. Sylan was there to study our technological history. Because many thousand years ago, when the ancestors left Daughter, the Kiris were a great technological power, and the records are there still. From the day I met her in our jae history class, my eyes would search for her everywhere, and no one ever could turn my eyes from her . . . till this day."

I have nothing to say to this. What can he want me to say? "The queen is a seducer born and bred. Stay vigilant."

"I will hold a watch in the tower of myself, yes."

"I came here to offer you my postal address, though I'd counsel you not to employ it lightly. Always assume she, and others, will see what you write."

"Do you not have audio or video communicators?"

It seemed an odd question to Ethan. "Yes, we have radios for official communiqués, military coordination, that sort of thing—not for private talk."

Nevan nodded as if satisfied.

"Why?" Ethan pressed. "Do you use such things for personal communication?"

"We Kiris don't, of course. But most other peoples do." He whisked his journal and pen from the bed and opened the book to the last page. "Will you write your address here?"

Ethan jotted down his Senarna listing, which forwarded his private letters. His ears were hot; he felt like the butt of someone's private joke. Most peoples routinely used higher tech to stay in touch! *And we, we are like the Kiris. I am like the Kiris. Think how efficient communication would be if we could all just radio each other—and it never even occurred to me.*

Ethan was burning to get out of the room. "Now, I will leave you." He started to rise, but Nevan stopped him, touching his knee with his fingers.

"Wait, please. There is something on my ship, a computer like a small . . . uh . . . square-with-four-long-sides box. On it is a writing about jae. I ask you to find it and take hold of it."

Ethan's heart constricted. "I thank you for your confidence."

"Before you thank me, listen. I am much worried for this writing. I know your people want to travel in space, and jae is a fast way of travel. But jae caused the plague that killed much Sama-world life. There is nothing in it to help Perdita. It will kill Perdita."

Ethan kept his expression still. *He is thinking like a Kiri. Kiris make an art of overestimating risks.*

"I understand you, Nevan. Do not fear for us. Help the gods."

Nevan gave him a sidelong look. "You help the gods also."

≈•≈

Ethan's conscience was sizzling as he closed the door. *I have done nothing wrong. I took custody of an important document from a ship under Perditan jurisdiction. I gave it into the hands of the proper authorities.*

Still his conscience stung. Absorbed in thought, he was startled by footsteps clapping down a side hall. He glanced over to see Lashen meet Laynia in a fierce embrace and suppressed revulsion for Lashen. It wasn't his fault that Laynia made the warmaster play second choice to a warchief. Lashen could only accept her—and look foolish as a replacement lover—or refuse her and look more foolish for seeming to nurse his hurt pride.

In his room, Ethan sat on the mattress and thought about the art of writing: placing one's thoughts on record. It was power and vulnerability both. He thought of Nevan scribbling for hours in his notebook. Nevan was a historian; perhaps he wrote to find the truth behind human existence, perhaps because he did not know how not to. Ethan's father had written as well. He had once been a major commentator in the pamphlets.

Ethan had always been silent.

Perhaps too silent—even with myself.

He found some stationery and wrote many pages recounting the past several days. At the end, he wrote:

> *A word is a lance between our universe and the gods', so I have heard. I have also heard that a word is the truest bridge between minds, truer than the mind reading. It follows that a word is also a bridge within a mind. There is much to be bridged, much sundering to be undone. So I have determined to follow your example, Nevan, and set down my thoughts in these pages. I set them down for you, so that you may understand our civilization.*

CHAPTER 12

They were going to Meena, so Illia told Sylan. And where was Meena? It was south by sea to the Gulf of Grass and northeast up the South Oja River. And what was Meena?

Meena was home.

On the boat, they dyed Sylan's hair brown with walnut juice. Red hair and pale skin made a rare combination on Perdita, the first thing the City would search for. They adapted Jasen too, trimming his hair and shaving his beard, which made him sour.

"But you must understand," said Sylan during these ministrations, "we want the City to find us. We want to be by Miri and Nevan."

"I know you do," Leric said as he drenched Sylan's hair. "But we must unite you by finding them, not by letting the City find you. You have knowledge they would treasure too much."

≈•≈

After four days, they came to the Gulf of Grass, a stretch of calm ocean rounding sandy cliffs—no grass at all. But when they churned up the mouth of the South Oja River, the land vindicated the gulf's name. On either bank, grasses waved high and supple, a second sea of airy swords.

They would not have to hide belowdecks again, for the border guards of Meena were allies of the Borderals.

Jasen stared at Illia. "All with you?"

"Almost everyone in Meena is with us," she said. "But we're always cautious. Within the town precincts, you must be very careful of what you say and do. We can vouch for our border guards, but we cannot vouch for everyone. We'll hide you as much as we can while you're new, but you must learn how to act Perditan as soon as possible."

"We'll be here forever," said Jasen in Vunizh, which they had taken to using over Keshnul for privacy.

Sylan shook her head. "If all else fails, my father will come looking for us when he realizes we've disappeared."

"What if his ship crashes into the shield?"

"That's why we've got to get the shield down."

≈•≈

Leric and Illia led Sylan and Jasen on foot down a dirt road. They followed it through a prairie dotted with yellow, purple, and red spring blossoms. Birds startled before their steps.

"We'll go straight to our house," said Illia. "It isn't in town but out by the claw-wheat fields. When we leave, we say we're going to market the wheat or check on the production of our competitors in Semlona. But in fact, my parents do most of that work."

"And you fight," said Jasen.

Leric laughed. "Not if there's the remotest chance of doing anything else. Mostly we spy and sabotage. In fact, with the loss of very few lives, we've managed to halt progress in the Space Program for twenty years."

Sylan disliked the pride in his voice.

At a fork, they turned down a narrower path along a wooden fence. Inside the fence, a span of soil lay fallow, and beyond that nodded high, homogeneous waves of green wheat, mounted with bulbous grains.

"That is not *claw*-wheat? Where are claws?" asked Sylan, nodding to it.

"You wait until the autumn," said Leric.

"It is all one wheat," said Jasen. "Where is the ecosystem?"

"Increasingly compromised," said Illia. "Perdita has farmed this way a long time, even though the pests have increased with the pesticides, and irrigation has eroded the hillsides, and the wheat encroaches on wild species decade by decade. We'll keep fewer monocultures someday."

Sylan asked, "Why not now?"

"The Grains Consortium makes guidelines for how we manage our fields. If we ended our contract and turned to small-yield farming, we'd go out of business and fall under suspicion for being 'rebel sympathizers.'"

Sylan was trying to determine if this argument was reasonable, when she grew conscious of a swishing through the windless fields: some animal rushing toward them, in and out of the pale stalks. They all noticed it at the same time and stopped dead, staring.

"What is it?" hissed Sylan.

A second elapsed, and the tension evaporated. Leric said to Illia, "It's Kara." He sidled up to the fence as the thing came hurtling forward. "Now then, magpie," he called out, "up you come and fly for true!"

In a heartbeat, a little girl sped out of the field, over the fence beams, and did seem to fly—right into Leric's waiting arms.

"Papa!" she cried, then "Mama!" swinging herself into Illia's embrace.

Why didn't they mention they had a child? thought Sylan with a surge of pique for which she felt instantly guilty. The child was not more than six: a tawny brown with long black curls. There was nothing about her like Miri.

Wise parents leave their children safe at home.

Jasen's arm stole her around her waist. Unable to look at him, she opened her mind a crack instead—but found his sealed.

Illia and Leric introduced the girl, Karmeena.

"As like the town?" asked Jasen.

"Why, yes: Karmeena of Meena." Leric heaved her up onto his shoulders.

Illia said the name meant "nurturing sanctuary."

Nice, but too flowery, thought Sylan. *My children are "Honor" and "The Daughter of Mirlla." If only I could shape their lives as easily as their names!*

≈•≈

The house was a wooden rectangle, a focal point drawing together tilled field, wild grass, and an ill-maintained paved road. Before the porch, a flower garden nestled in the shade of a lonely walnut tree. Karmeena ran inside and hauled out a tall, dark man, still youngish—perhaps not more than sixty.

Illia and Leric embraced him, the man looking nervously at Sylan and Jasen all the while.

"Papa, you're never going to believe this," said Illia. "These people, they're offworlders. They crashed in Iltan, and we've rescued them. Where's Mama?"

Illia's father tore his eyes from Sylan. "I . . . she's mending the irrigation line."

"Sylan and her son, Jasen." Leric introduced them. "This is Illia's father, Shoshec."

Karmeena tugged Jasen off to play. The rest went inside, Leric telling of their crash in words too fast for Sylan to follow. Inside, a long hallway was lined with ten or twelve doors. At the far end, they entered a room Leric called "the center room." Its walls, covered in warm-hued rugs, suggested autumn leaves. The room was rustic, not un-Kiri with its organic fabrics and carved wood furniture. But unlike a Kiri home, this house had electricity: lamps mounted on dark walls.

Before dinner, Illia's mother returned: Rajaneen, a round brown woman, who, after her initial shock, embraced Sylan and Jasen as if they were long-lost children.

"Don't worry. We'll keep you safe here," she promised.

≈•≈

Nights in Meena were a crystalline, clear cold, punctuated by the blueness shed on the fields by the moons: Olay, "Beloved Light," and Tori, "Steadfast Follower." Watching the swaying grasses, Sylan half-believed she was tossing again on a sea, drifting ever farther from familiar land. A footfall sounded behind her.

"We call them the 'Eyes of Perdita.'" Leric nodded at the moons. "There's a story about them."

"Oh yes?"

"Since we never see the sunlight from the same angle on both, they never come full or new in phase with one another. Thus, the eyes are never both wide open or both completely shut. They say the Eyes of Perdita see things as Perdita does. Perdita sees nothing wholly clearly and is wholly blind to nothing."

The frost stung Sylan's eyes. On impulse, she said, "You are married with Illia?"

"On Perdita there is only one marriage: between the king and queen. It's symbolic of an alliance of powers." He chuckled. "Perhaps because one person's two eyes are never both wide open, but we dream that two of four eyes may be."

This last bit was difficult for Sylan to follow. She said nothing.

After a moment, Leric said, "When you said you and Nevan were married, we thought at first you must be very powerful rulers."

Sylan laughed. "To your sadness, we are common people only."

"No, indeed, we're glad. We are not friends with our rulers."

Another step came up behind her; a warm hand was laid on her shoulder.

"Come in by the fire," said Rajaneen. "It's bad enough to freeze yourself to death, but to suck all the heat out the door!"

Sylan let Rajaneen lead her back into their amber-lit center room. Illia and her father lounged on cushions by the fire. Karmeena sat on the carpet, building castles out of wood while Jasen assisted her, lying on his stomach, a tender sadness in his round face, exceedingly like his father. Sylan would see to it that they were together soon.

CHAPTER 13

Nevan's Journal
Perdita: 28 Mid-Spring, 17.05.2033 After the End

I suspected last night that Ethan had absconded with our *Jae History*. Today, Laynia confirmed it.

But let me not get ahead of myself. This morning, Laynia took Miri and me out of the city by ground car. Like a common citizen, she wore a shirt and pants and drove the car herself. The influence she exerted on me yesterday had dulled—but since she kept her mind closed, I cannot credit myself with surmounting it.

She drove us to a harbor on the Crimson Gulf. There *is* something crimson about it, not in color, but in spirit: a vividness in white buildings, sparser than in the city, dipping waterward on lazy hills, in stout grasses and stunted pines, in breakers like wild children of the pearl-blue veil beyond.

We caught a boat called the "Refomin ferry," which hauls travelers from Senarna to the island of Refomin, thirty kilometers to the north.

"I thought we were going to Zerin," I said.

"Refomin is the southern brother island of Zerin," said Laynia. "The only ship to Zerin is the Sennac ferry from Refomin. Zerin is a private place. There are no airfields either."

The small island of Refomin has the look of the Senarna coast but with fewer buildings and a corresponding rise in the predominance of pines.

As we drove north across the island, Laynia said, "We have your files, Nevan."

I started.

"Your jae files. Ethan found them and turned them over to Warmaster Lashen."

"Isn't that bad, Dad?" asked Miri.

"Yes, Miri, it is," I answered, but at her silence added, "we'll work it out." I touched her mind lightly, saw she wasn't really worried. She's too young to understand just what jae means.

62

As for me, my initial reaction was anger—at him and myself. As I say, I had suspected something. The cast of his face had been guilty last night.

"The files are dangerous," I said.

"I know the risks," she said. "I don't need your counsel to convince me to fight jae. But my influence over our government is not as great as you imagine. My husband is king by descent. The power is his, not mine. It's tradition for the monarch to marry a person of Zerin, so our mind-reading skill can help in policy matters. But my role is advisory. And my personal hold over Rarion has been taxed in bringing you to Zerin."

I had a vision of myself as the vector for the particle-shift infection of an entire biosphere. But, understand, such responsibility is more than a human can comprehend. It did not affect me much.

"Ethan took my files without my permission, you know."

"Of course." She was silent a moment. "He's not a bad man, Nevan. But he is an idealist and self-involved. His judgment is unsound."

I decided to bait her: "I do not think he likes you."

"He hates me."

"Why?"

She laughed. "Because when he was nineteen, still grieving after two years for the death of his papa—his only relative—he was a rising star in the Space Project. Like you, Nevan, I made the mistake of thinking him a potential ally. I tried to enlist him to Zerin's cause, to convince him that now is not the time for Perdita to explore space. That, of course, was antithetical to his fantasies. He didn't try to denounce me. He knew I was too high for him to depose. But he considers me a traitor, even after twenty years."

≈•≈

On the other side of the Sennac Water I found a different world. The landscape itself is much the same, but buildings give way to forest so pure it is almost Kiri. Electrical machinery is forbidden on the island. Instead, we set forth in a cart pulled by two striped animals called *shezmar*: heavyset antelope with sloping necks. They resemble nothing so much as the child of a donkey and giraffe.

The cart ride excited Miri. In fact, it was so difficult to hold her still that we finally let her ride one of the shezmar. Miri is a fine horsewoman, and despite the low sloping of the shezma's back, she was soon at ease and casting glances around the woodland.

Past the waterside village of Nac, the woods grow denser. The squat, knobby pines of Senarna give way to a tall and erect species, its long needles almost black—the "Zerin pine." I am told that the snows have only just cleared, leaving the turf packed and spongy.

Though Miri looked rosy enough in her excitement, my fingers and toes were soon numb, despite my coat. The air breathed an oceanic cold, heavy with wet salt, even when we felt no wind. The coldness here is deeper than Senarna's, all the more so when the trees block out the sun.

Our destination was Wolsenond: "Wolsena's Home," an inflammatory name in a world that despises her. Laynia told us that outside Zerin, we must call the town *Vojin*: "The Little Place by the Voj," which is a river of sorts. It is fifty kilometers from Nac to the Voj, and it was nightfall before we came there. The cold got the better of Miri at sunset, and she relinquished the shezma to bundle herself in the cart by me.

If a river were a bird, the Voj would be a stubby nesting grouse. It feeds off the Water Plain, a series of alluvial fans that freeze in the winter and run with streams pouring down off the hills in summer. The Voj, strictly speaking, is a canal built to drain the Water Plain and spare Wolsenond annual flooding. I have refrained from observing to Laynia that any sensible people would not build a town on a runoff plain. And to see such a town, named with defiant pride for the honor of our goddess of *mirlla*, I find offensive.

Across the bridge that spans the Voj is Wolsenond itself, two rings of wooden buildings surrounding a large, round hall they call "the keep." The settlement crouches on the rocky slope of the drained portion of the Water Plain. South and west of it lies the beach, east the hills, north the forest and the swamp.

Laynia deposited Miri and me in a bedroom lit by oil lamps. Their flickering light calls me back to my childhood.

But it makes writing difficult. And Miri is fast asleep, so I will end for tonight.

CHAPTER 14

On their third night in Meena, Sylan and Jasen made their escape. In their guest room they dressed by the blue light of the moons, quieter than the rodent nibbling in the walls. Sylan reviewed their plan in her head: they would get away, turn themselves in to some City person who could take them to Nevan and Miri, even if that meant into a prison cell. And if they were recaptured by Borderals, Sylan doubted they'd be much worse off than they were now. For however much she resented being shuffled around by these people, she did not fear them.

Sylan opened the door a crack. The house had twelve rooms, the large center room paradoxically at the far end of the hallway. The front door was by the kitchen at the other end. They hadn't dared to sneak food out of the kitchen during the day. It would be their first stop now. They crept into the hallway.

All at once, a figure loomed out of the shadows, tall and gaunt: Shoshec. Sylan had feared they were being watched. But the sudden confirmation tore her nerves.

Her anger flared. "You let go of us! We are people, not your things!"

Shoshec held up his hands placatingly. "Please. There is much of the mutations of this universe you don't understand."

"I understand much," she snapped, just as Illia and Leric, in their nightclothes, darted into the hall.

"It's late," said Shoshec. "We should discuss this tomorrow."

Now Rajaneen had appeared and Karmeena, who went to her grandmother's side at once, grabbing her hand and whining sleepy questions.

"Not tomorrow," said Sylan. "You imprison us."

"Listen," said Illia, "we've told you, if you let yourselves fall into the hands of the City, you'll merely be taken prisoner."

Rajaneen knelt by Karmeena, offering reassurances. Sylan hesitated, not wanting to upset the child. But now Rajaneen was leading her back to her own room.

"We are prisoners now," said Sylan, "but with the City we are prisoners beside our family."

"You don't know that," said Illia. "And the City won't just hold you, they'll demand information from you."

"Maybe I will give information. Maybe that is not bad for me."

"Simple. We go," said Jasen, "or you kill us."

Sylan gaped at him.

Leric shook his head. "You're here for your own well-being, so that we can protect you."

Jasen took a deep breath and stepped toward Leric. Sylan kept close behind him. Everyone else stood frozen, surrounding them. Then, as Jasen moved to step past Leric, Leric seized him and twisted him back into the circle. With instinctive fury, Sylan hurled herself at Leric, wrenching his arms away from her son. Someone pulled her back, pinning her arms behind her. She struggled alongside Jasen, till, with a cool efficiency, the Borderals pushed them facedown to the ground.

Illia's voice came from just above Sylan; it must be Illia's knee in her back. "Now, we will let you up because you are intelligent enough to see you can't run, no?"

"Yes," replied Sylan.

The weight lifted off her back.

"You have politics." Sylan stood up beside Jasen. "But no politics says you can keep prisoners illegally."

"This is war," said Illia. "We must think of the higher good of the planet."

"And you must understand," put in Leric, "if the City catches you coming out of Meena, they'll guess we held you here. They'll come for us. So you see, we can't let them find you: for our friends and family, for our child."

"Then take us another place," said Sylan. "And let us find the City there."

Illia shook her head. "We can't let them have your knowledge."

"So you keep us forever?" Jasen demanded.

The Borderals glanced at each other. At last Illia said, "We are only speaking of the present. For the future, we have to confer with our people."

Shoshec cleared his throat. "Let me make tea. It breeds companionship."

≈•≈

Sylan considered the electric lights an insult to the night: a desperate wakefulness. She and Jasen sat around the kitchen table with Illia, Leric, and Shoshec in silence, drinking Shoshec's spiced tea.

"Surely you understand," said Illia finally. "The higher good is to save Perdita from the irresponsible tech policies of the City."

"Then why should we not tell what we know?" said Sylan. "We can teach the safe tech."

"It isn't the knowledge, it's the way it's used," said Leric. "Fire is a simple and useful thing, but misapplied it can wreak a kingly savage destruction."

"But I think you trust the City to use fire," said Sylan. "Or do you fight that too?"

Leric smiled weakly. "You call out the cards exactly, Sylan. Do I trust the City with the knowledge of fire? Not particularly. But it would be silly to try to fight fire. There's no way to eliminate the knowledge of how to use it. But spaceships, energy plants, complex chemical poisons—that kind of knowledge we can eliminate, or at least keep from being implemented. And those are the projects that do lasting damage. Those are the great powers."

"There are big problems with your thoughts," said Sylan. It was vital that she make them see. Their lives might well depend on it. "You know not of the Two Laws here."

"What laws are these?" asked Shoshec, eyes narrowing.

"The Law of Reversibility and the Law of the Irreversibility of Knowledge." Sylan had learned how to name them in Dabunè years ago. "The Law of Reversibility means no technology be made unless the knowing to unmake it."

Leric gave her a baffled smile. "Again, please?"

Sylan thought. "You do not make a poison unless you know a cure. You do not control the weather unless you know the way to make it again natural weather."

"That's not possible," said Leric. "I can't see how anyone could ever know all the consequences of implementing a new tech without seeing it in action. One might build a road, imagining that the road could be torn out and returned to the wild, without realizing that the road may pack the soil down so much that the old plants would simply not return. There must always be an element of trial and error."

"Yes," Sylan agreed, "the law is never quite done. It's a goal not reached but attempted."

"It's a good idea," said Illia, "but the City would never apply it. And the other law?"

"The Irreversibility of Knowledge means no knowledge can truly be lost, once it is known. You attempt to forget how to make nuclear bombs, but you never know when someone will find the knowledge again."

Illia answered briskly, "But even if that were true, it doesn't mean we should all be manufacturing bombs. We have to let go of the tech that's harmful."

"But can we? Even the Kiris keep the old knowledge in their tech centers, like weapons for defense if an attack comes."

"Then the Kiris are wrong," said Illia. "There are some things that we should strive to forget."

"But at the same time," said Leric, "to overcome the City, it's sometimes necessary to employ their methods. Yes, I know, Lia, but it's the truth. We've tried low-tech ways, and the City has vanquished us."

Sylan frowned at him, surprised and somewhat relieved to see some pro-tech sentiment among them.

"But we're careful," Shoshec put in. "We use only those machines we need to use."

Illia scoffed. "Oh, be fair, Papa. You can't say we've never gone too far."

Shoshec opened his mouth to speak, but Leric interrupted him. "We needed those computers, Lia."

She leaned over the table at him. "Why?"

"To break the Iltan–Mesa code."

"We didn't need to know that code."

"We found out about those shipments of optics to the observatory."

"We'd have found that out by conventional spying, Leric."

"Then be so good as to explain why we didn't."

"You got in first," said Illia stiffly.

"I got in only sixty hours before the shipment left Mesa. Honestly, Lia, sometimes I think you *would* choose suicide sooner than use one City advantage."

"Papa?" Karmeena was frowning in the doorway. "Why are you yelling?"

Leric stared at his daughter and managed a smile, holding out his arms to her.

"I'm sorry, Kara," he said when he'd pulled her into his lap. "We were just talking about the City. I shouldn't have taken it so seriously."

"I hate the City," Karmeena said.

CHAPTER 15

Nevan's Journal
Perdita: 29 Mid-Spring, 18.05.2033 After the End

Today Laynia gave us our first real look at Wolsenond. It is
no larger than a Kiri town. The buildings are functional,
constructed to provide shelter from the Zerin cold. Almost
every wall and floor is carpeted. Beds and chairs are thick with
down. While the houses seldom have more than two rooms,
public kitchens and dining halls provide gathering places.
Agriculture is scanty on Zerin. And though a portion of their
food is harvested from the sea, most is shipped across the
water from Semlona.

The settlement houses about sixty people: women, men,
and children. They are powerful and highly trained mind
readers, except for a handful of children who did not inherit
their parents' gift, and some adults designated as
"companions" to novice children. Novices are potentially
strong mind readers recruited from all over the two continents.
In their daily lives, the Zerins keep their minds open to strong
emotional impressions and closed to specific thoughts, much
as we do on Onáda.

They call themselves the *Jethor*, "the priests," after the Kiri
teacher class, the *jetháti*, and all adults are vowed into the
worship of Wolsena. When engaged in some official activity,
they dress in loose gray robes. The rest of the time, they dress
like their mainland relations. They are taught to translate
Keshnul but, as far as I can tell, do not speak it.

Late in the morning, Laynia took Miri and me into the
center building, the keep, to meet with Olwer, the High Jetho
("*Im Jetho*," they call him, *Im* signifying "the preeminent one").

The keep is large enough to hold thrice over every
inhabitant of Wolsenond, yet it has nothing in it: a plain
wooden floor and walls, with high slits of windows, designed
to admit light and no other sight. An elderly man sat in the
center of the floor, perhaps 150 years old, of average build,
wearing ritual gray, like Laynia. She sat down before him,
motioning for Miri and me to do the same.

Olwer greeted us amiably. "I must learn from you," he said, "and tell you of us in return. May I ask you a question?"

I nodded.

"No living Perditan has met a Kiri till now, Nevan. You are one of our ancestral peoples, ancestral to the religion of Zerin, in particular. Will you tell us, then, about the religious practices of your people?"

I answered in the way I've learned (though in words less polished in Tapanayn than those I set down here): "We hold to the Two Assertions: that 'nature is everything' and that 'everything is a part of nature.' We hold that *mirlla*, the way of nature, sustains the universe. We hold that the use of technology to dampen the immediacy of human contact with the living land typically results in a negative impact on ecosystems and human society. We therefore reject the use of machines that require extensive infrastructure to build or maintain."

"Yet you came here in a Kiri-designed spaceship."

It was a familiar query. "The great exception to our limits on technology has always been space travel. The reasons are twofold: first, in space, the systems are much simpler, so disruption by human activity is much less likely. Second, to live in the living land, we need only simple tools, but to travel through space, we require spaceships. To relinquish them would be to relinquish the Convention of Kiri Worlds."

"But," said Olwer, "Sama spaceships once destroyed numerous ecosystems simply by landing and launching."

"That's why Kiri ships have never been jae powered. For superlight travel, we ripple: use small space distortions as ships have done for thousands of years. It's slower, but it works."

Olwer nodded. "Nevan, we are of similar mind. And because of that, I feel I can share our plans with you. You may not agree with all of them. We do not ask you to. But it is vital to the health of Perdita that you not compromise our efforts." When I made no reply, he continued. "You Kiris, I believe, hold that Volsénlla created the universe but does not interfere in creation?"

"Well, Volsénlla is an idea, and if any part of her is based in a real consciousness, it is certainly nothing like the humanoid woman in the paintings. Personally, I find the depiction of her as human a little offensive."

Olwer laughed. I was not sure why.

"But, yes," I went on, "the idea is that Volsénlla need not, will not, should not, and perhaps cannot violate *mirlla*, the laws of nature."

"And why should she never supersede her natural laws?"

This is a question I have never understood. The answer to me is obvious.

"There is no need."

I could feel Miri fidget. She did not like Olwer's question.

Olwer went on. "Isn't there much suffering and mass destruction—of ecosystems and whole planets?"

"Yes."

"Should she not then avert these things?"

"No. *Mirlla* works. Why should she tamper with it? If people cannot live at peace with its laws, then they will always be unhappy, requiring some power from above to rescue them from their own stupidity, or from natural dangers that *must* claim someone's life—for without death, there is no life. Why then should some lives be more sacred than others? Why should the creator have to choose which of her beings will die at any given moment? Surely that is the highest injustice."

"The highest justice, some would say. Nevan, I agree with you that Volsénlla cannot be like a human—it defies logic— yet, unlike you, I find it highly beneficial to regard her as such. Humans need to believe that the universe is motivated by human love, a personal love. The truth of this has been proven on Perdita. There was a time, soon after the War, when the Kiris gained philosophical supremacy and destroyed most of our technical records, devolving our tech to a pre-Daughter level.

"But even at the height of Kiri power, the Samas reviled the Kiri goddess, Wolsena, as a soulless fabrication—because she did not love as humans love. They rejected her and Kiri philosophy with her. And so Kiri rule collapsed and a dangerous infatuation with tech development came to threaten the balance of life on Perdita.

"It is our goal to regain hegemony. To do so, we require a religion that can promise human love and personal help. We can't use Wolsena. Her name is anathema. But there is another goddess, one who works just as well to teach the people to tread lightly on their planet. We call her Leva."

"I've never heard of a Leva," I said.

"Ah, but you've heard of a Léyvia."

Miri said, "But Léyvia isn't a goddess. She was the Kiri queen during the War."

"Precisely, Miri," said Olwer. "In the Shonac tradition, the spirits of the dead are thought to travel to the realm of the gods for a time, before returning to new mortal bodies. But sometimes a mighty spirit moves permanently into the hierarchy of gods. Thus our Leva. She died heroically in the War, we are told. Now she lives to defend Perdita. Year by year, we are spreading her word."

"And this word," I said, "this word teaches that Perditans should live like Kiris?"

"You partly have it, Nevan. Our Leva is not a Kiri goddess. She does not teach that tech development—or ecological management—is wrong. But she does teach that it should be conducted slowly, careful not to set unintended consequences in motion."

In a word, she'll teach the Law of Reversibility—common sense at last.

"But Leva isn't real," protested Miri. "You're making it up."

"Quite so. *Mirlla*, passing through the beneficent hands of the nature healer, Leva."

"If you care about *mirlla*," said Miri hotly, "why do you build your town on a flood plain? Why do you always fight the river to keep it from being washed away?"

"She's right," I said, unable to suppress a smile.

Olwer smiled too. "Your people teach that *mirlla* cannot be overcome. Our people demonstrate it yearly. Reshoring the canal reminds us of what a tenuous grip we have on this world."

I had not thought of it that way. No Kiri town would act in such a way. These people are very like us and yet trouble the waters of our minds with new currents.

CHAPTER 16

The night of Sylan and Jasen's eighth day in Meena, Sylan was thinking again of the shield. Presumably, the Borderals kept it active as a means to avoid contact with space. So much for their pretense of disdain for high tech. A disdain for space travel only, perhaps? And since the City apparently had a strong desire to go into space, it was logical to assume that the Borderals' shield generator was hidden—and a major asset in combating the City. Therefore, it was doubtful they would lower it just to allow the West-of-Nows to depart. On the other hand, if lowering the shield meant getting rid of a piece of tech as unwelcome as their ship, then perhaps they would agree.

She was on the point of going to bed when a sudden resolve galvanized her: she would broach the subject of the shield. She threw on a robe, telling Jasen to stay put, and stepped out to find Illia on a cushion in the hall, clothed in the heavy, warm tunic Perditans slept in.

"I do not run," she said as Illia's head snapped up. "I came out because I need help to be able to move on from this place—with no harm done."

"I am so glad," said Illia, rising. "I was beginning to worry about you. You want Leric?"

Of the Borderals Sylan had met, Leric seemed the nearest to a tech expert. "Yes," she said, puzzled by Illia's enthusiasm.

"Just a moment." Illia vanished into her room.

Sylan had waited rather longer than a moment when Leric emerged and closed the door behind him. Standing close, he looked down at her gently. Certain that she was missing some signal, Sylan stared at him in the blue glow of the moons.

Looking perplexed, Leric said, "Are you ready to go to bed with me now?"

"What?"

"You're ready for my help in saying your good-byes, no?"

"What?"

They frowned at each other. "I thought you had come to tell me you were ready to mourn the loss of your lover—I mean, your husband."

"I don't understand," said Sylan.

"Your people don't do that? Mourn the loss of a lover by making love to him through another's body?"

"No, we do not."

Leric leaned back against the wall. "I'm sorry. What is it you wanted?"

"I came to talk about the shield."

"What shield?"

"The shield around the planet." Sylan waved her hand at the ceiling. "The big shield that made us crash." He stared. "The shield . . . the shield that . . . keeps away the planet light from space."

Still frowning, Leric took Sylan by the arm and ushered her back into his bedroom. The three of them sat on the low square bed, while Sylan repeated her explanation to Illia, elaborating on the crash of her ship. Both Illia and Leric denied all knowledge of such a device.

Then Illia started. "Leric! Remember the *Outbound*?"

"I was eight, Lia, naturally I remember it."

"What is it?" asked Sylan.

Illia said, "Twenty-two years ago, the Space Project developed a ship, the *Outbound*, that was designed to exit the atmosphere and make an orbit of Perdita. It exploded only a few minutes after launch. Of course, the Borderals were blamed for sabotaging it. But we did no such thing. Oh, we had plans for blowing it up on the ground. But we wouldn't ever have blown it up during launch because Jessec from Mesa was on board."

"And who was he?"

"The director of the Space Project. He favored rampant tech expansion, but he was an upstanding man too. He was the last tech progressive to insist that the Borderals be listened to in Parliament. He said that only by open debate would his side be proven right. He was wrong about that, he'd have been proven wrong. But everyone respected him, the City and the Borderals."

Leric said, "For years, we've suspected that the City itself had the *Outbound* destroyed in order to lay Jessec's death on us. It certainly seemed no coincidence that barely a month after the tragedy, Parliament passed the Progressive Technology

Statute that made it criminal to advocate a halt to tech development." He looked at Illia. "Perhaps this time we were as wrong to blame the City as the City to blame us."

Illia glanced from Leric to Sylan. "You think the shield could have caused this explosion?"

"In a first-trial, simple-orbit impulse spaceship? Yes, easy. You think the City also does not know about the shield?"

"Perhaps they do," said Leric. "If it was a plot to kill Jessec, as we thought. Except that a successful orbit with Jessec in command would have been much better pro-tech propaganda than just defaming us. Funny, I've never heard anyone point that out. It's obvious."

Sylan felt the tears brim in her eyes. "But if no one knows about the shield, how will I ever find it?"

Illia embraced her. For a minute, the only sound was Sylan snuffling like a child.

Then Leric said, "Micor might know. It could be his ship was brought down the same way."

Sylan glanced up. "Who is this?"

"He's a great leader in our cause. A sverra—you've heard of them?"

"Yes, yes," said Sylan. "You must bring me to see him."

"I'll talk to him. I'm scheduled to meet with him soon."

Sylan shook her head. "No. You bring me."

"It's not wise for you to leave here yet," said Leric. "You don't know the language well enough."

"You bring me," Sylan repeated, "or you must lock me up and always watch me. And I keep you from doing your other jobs." It was an awkward threat, in both form and content. They could easily keep her locked up. And what about Jasen? Most certainly, he'd follow her lead: he'd been spoiling for action. Still, should she make ultimatums without his even being there?

"There's no need to be hasty," Illia said. "We'll see what we can do, if you will be a little patient."

Sylan nodded. She could be patient for the shield. But just how much more patient could she bear to be without any word of her lost family?

CHAPTER 17

When Ethan finally got back to the Iltan Observatory, he encountered more irritations. Lashen had authorized the transfer of fifty additional footmen to Iltan. Ethan did not object to the increase: a more solid defensive force was welcome. But in a matter this sensitive, he wanted to screen the troops' records personally. Moreover, the footmen were natives of Veshna, and Veshna was the continent with stronger rebel sympathies.

So Ethan sat down to familiarize himself with the service records of these new people, only to find that most records had not yet been transferred from their prior posts. He put in a request for immediate transfer of the records and filed a complaint against Lashen's peremptory reshuffling of undocumented personnel. With nothing more to be done, he headed for the ship.

Walking through the forest in the company of two footmen, it was as if a fog he'd been living in evaporated. True spring was dawning: the leaf litter crunched underneath his feet, firmer and drier than when he'd left. The purple-tree larks were bolder too, their low whistling as common now as it had been rare a month before. The breezes carried a woody scent.

He could be happy here. The transfer of the footmen was a passing annoyance. It would be dealt with, and the summer months would fly as he investigated the secrets of this discovery the gods had flung down. He quickened his step; he could not count the years since his spirit had floated so light.

In a fraction of a second, the world ground to a halt. There was a flash—too close. His vision faltered. There was a sound so loud it was more pain than sound. He ran. Light spots beat before his eyes, but as long as he could steer himself, he went forward—without seeming to move—nightmare-like. He knew precisely what had happened and why and how—but his thoughts would not articulate it. Years went by. He fell once, had no recollection of hitting the ground or rising.

Like a tidal wave, the wreck loomed before him. His first thought was, *It's not as bad as I thought.* The hull was intact, even its painted scales in place. But like some weird aquatic dragon,

it belched black smoke from its upturned mouth-hatch: a
lopsided fish, flat, dead.

Someone with his eyes was appraising the damage, noting
that the fires were few and already sputtering on the moist turf.
Someone was giving orders in his voice for injuries to be
assessed.

He pressed his palms against the hot hull. His eyes teared
in the oily smoke; his lungs tore. He was trying to get inside to
evaluate the damage, while some being in control of his body
balked at walking into the broiling blackness. Now someone
else was pulling him back, and he let himself be pulled. Now
the dark, twisted rectangle of the hatch was getting smaller.

Now, he sat in his room at the observatory. He sat on the
floor, not much aware of anything, except a rawness in his
throat that made him cough. A knock sounded, and Torna
came in without waiting for permission. She was covered in
soot and sweat. She sat down opposite him. It occurred to him
that he ought to be outside giving orders.

"Have I been relieved of command?" His voice was a
croak, not his own voice at all.

"No. I've given out that you're on private radio to Senarna
and I'm acting under you."

"Do we know who . . . ?"

"We have six likely suspects. But to be safe, I've ordered
five of our footmen—our *real* footmen—to escort the fifty
transfers into custody in Mesa."

"Five to fifty?"

"Well, no doubt the majority of those fifty are loyal. I've
told them that we don't suspect any particular individual,
which is overstating the case a little. Most took it reasonably
well. Eight are logging protests. I'm sorry, Ethan, the protests
will turn up against you, unless you want to officially hand
command to me."

"I'll take responsibility for the protests."

She gazed at him. "Have you seen your face?"

He must have shaken his head, because she picked up the
scratched square of mirror from his desk and handed it to him.
His face, dirty as hers, was blistered and swollen. So were the
palms of his hands, throbbing as he held the mirror.

He looked up at her, surprised. "I wasn't that close to the blast."

"No, you got too close afterward. I had to hold you back. You should get cleaned up—and be checked for vision and hearing loss."

He set down the mirror. "What are the casualties?"

"Two dead, one critical, three with hearing and vision loss, probably temporary, seven minor injuries, excluding yourself, since you haven't been examined yet."

It flickered at his mind to ask about the ship. But he could not think of that yet.

≈•≈

When he had been pronounced medically fit and had washed his face and hands, he gave some rote encouragement to the footmen and ordered them to begin salvage efforts. That minimal duty done, he sent a brief report to Lashen and retired to his room. He felt as heavy as the inside of the planet, melting under its own weight, oozing and thickening, until finally, at bottom, it solidified again under pressure greater still. He fell asleep.

He dreamed. He was back on the plains west of Cudonond. He was watching the silvery bullet-shaped glint of his father's ship climbing the sky. Then, soundless, an orange blast, like a funeral firecracker, blazing where the ship had gleamed. Then the noise, like a gun going off in his ear.

He opened his eyes to the darkness and the tired embrace of his bed. *It was only a dream.* Then, it came to him that it was not a dream at all. His father was dead, the *Outbound* was gone, and all his aspirations gone with it—and the new ship, the new hope, that was gone too.

Tears came into his eyes.

CHAPTER 18

Jasen could hear Shoshec sneezing in the kitchen. Illia's whole family had a cold, most likely from exposure to Sylan and Jasen. It made Jasen feel like he'd tracked mud in the house. The West-of-Nows had taken their immunity boosters before leaving Onáda and showed no signs of illness.

They were sitting down to dinner when a voice from the open front door called out, "It's Rayna."

All of Illia's family bolted to the doorway, Jasen and Sylan behind them.

Sherayna looked dusty and serious. "Mama, Papa, would you take Karmeena out for a while?"

Efficient as soldiers, Karmeena and her grandparents walked into the sunlit fields.

Sherayna faced Jasen and Sylan. "There is no easy way to say this. Yesterday, your ship was destroyed."

The floorboards bent away, like a dream the moment one realizes it's actually a nightmare.

"Completely?" he heard his mother ask.

"Irreparably. Three bombs were set inside."

"By whom?" she demanded.

"By us." Sherayna's face remained immobile.

Jasen wanted to strike her. "You planned this from the beginning, didn't you? You pretend to protect us, while you take us from our family and our hope to leave this sick planet that thinks the War is going still." He looked from Sherayna to Leric to Illia. They stared out of lifeless eyes. "So now you kill us, too?"

"Of course not." Illia's voice was a machine's. Then she coughed, a human sound.

"We're not murderers," said Sherayna.

"But that is exactly what you are," replied Sylan.

Sherayna rubbed at her forehead tiredly. "It was not our intention to cause you grief. But there are greater issues to consider. The War is still going on for us. I don't think you understand that. Perdita has no tech policy—none. Oh, the City has a few little rules about safety precautions and waste disposal, no overarching ethic. It places *no* limits on population expansion. It has outlawed *no* system of energy generation, except in weaponry. And this sick planet, you would see it go out into space? To import offworld organisms, diseases that could wreak havoc on our ecosystems? I am sorry, but your ship made a terrific threat and your access to it a small reward."

"And who are you," burst out Jasen, "to choose what Perdita does, what we do? You're as crazy as any human ever!"

He turned and walked straight through the house, out the back door, toward the trails through the fields. In the corner of his eye, he could see Shoshec and Rajaneen with Kara, dark shapes among green stalks. He started down a trail that would take him away from them—but, of course, they would be watching. His mother came to his side and marched with him down the footpath.

Abruptly, he stopped. "I won't stay with them," he said in Vunizh.

"Where will you go?"

"I'll turn myself in to the City."

Sylan sighed. "They are probably right about one thing, anyway. If the City finds out you were hidden here, you could bring them down on all the Borderals in Meena."

"Good!"

"Is it? The Borderals have done wrong, but does that make the City right? Or even if they're right about Perditan tech, they execute convicted Borderals, you've heard so on the radio. Do you want that blood on your hands, Jas?"

Jasen was still boiling. "I won't tell them I came from Meena."

"Do you think their intelligence is really so poor that they won't be able to figure it out?"

"Well, what do you suggest we do? Sit here while they wreck our lives?"

Sylan turned back in the direction of the house. Jasen turned, too. No one else was in sight. "We don't want to be anyone's prisoners, Borderals or City. That means Illia was right: we need to learn to pass for Perditans. Until we learn the language and the customs well enough to impersonate residents of one of the backward islands, we need to stay where they'll hide us."

"Stay trapped here!"

"There's more. I've been chipping away at Illia and Leric. Soon I'll convince them to bring me to this Micor, and he just might have the answers we're looking for. And Rajaneen herself has been talking about how we ought to have access to their library records. We might learn a lot just by research."

"Spoken like a researcher," said Jasen sourly.

"All right, what else can we do?"

"I don't know. There must be something. I don't know."

As they walked back, Jasen could hear the wheat swishing, their captors following. When they got to the house, everyone was hovering by the back steps but Leric. He emerged from the wheat a few seconds behind them, not bothering to hide anymore. Karmeena stared up at Jasen with wide eyes—her nose running, thanks to some exotic pathogen he'd given her.

"I'll stay," he said.

≈•≈

Sherayna could see the hatred in Jasen's face and scarcely less in Sylan's. She was too tired to face that now. Best she leave.

"Mama, there are so many things to be done, and I can't afford to catch your cold," she protested when Rajaneen insisted she stay.

But as Sherayna was walking out the door, she heard her name. She waited for Illia to join her on the porch. Illia held a garland made of walnut leaves with which she tickled Sherayna on the head.

Sherayna smiled. Long ago, she'd papered the walls of her room with sketches of walnut branches woven into weird designs. She took the garland.

"Well, put it on," said Illia through a stuffed nose.

Sherayna plopped it on her head.

Illia hugged her. "I don't think you'll be back soon."

"It'll take time." Sherayna nodded to the house. "I don't want them to hate me, you know."

"Maybe time is what they need."

≈•≈

Nevan's Journal
Perdita: 11 Late-Spring, 30.05.2033 After the End

It was late afternoon yesterday when Laynia told me the rebels had blown apart our ship. Miri was playing with the Zerin children. I took her aside, steeled to recite a litany of hopeful half-truths: if we got the shield down, we could call for help; her grandfather, Sylan's father, would find us. Before I could begin, she recited this litany to me, her hazel eyes big with fear and trust.

"And besides, Dad, we can't go before we find Jasen and Mila anyway."

Strange. Those simple words made me see how deep we've sunk. Our ship gone, our family parted. And I, here, in the stronghold of the queen and the Im Jetho, what have I done to find my wife and son?

When Miri was asleep, I went to Olwer's lodging and banged on the door till he let me in. I demanded to know what was being done to find Sylan and Jasen. Smiling cordially, he told me that I'd have to ask Laynia.

I went to her and repeated my demands.

She coughed. (She's just recovering from some sort of virus, caught from Miri and me most likely.) Then, she sat me down and took my hands. "The army is looking for your family. I also have contacts of my own. They already have some idea of where your family is."

"And that is?"

She was silent, then seemed to make a decision. "In Veshna. In the south. Alive and well. Nevan, the wheels move slowly, and to push for their rescue right now would be to put them in harm's way."

"How so?"

"Sooner than see your family taken by the pro-techs, the rebels would kill them." I must have blanched, for she pressed a warm hand against my cheek. "I'm sorry, but you came here for the truth."

Her thoughts were veiled, and I felt her exert no mind power on me. "Give me a reason to believe you," I said.

"I told you the truth about your *Jae History*." (I have no iron proof of that, either.)

"When can we see them?"

"I can't say. But you can tell Miri that they're safe in the south."

≈•≈

Approaching my own door, I could feel Miri awake and frightened.

I peered into the dark room. "Miri?"

"Dad!" She hurtled out of the shadows and flung herself into my arms. "I thought they'd taken you away."

I held her close. She was tiny in her rumpled nightshirt. "No one could tear me away from you, lemur-kin. I just went out to talk to the Jethor—I left a note on your bed, but it seems you didn't see it."

"It's dark," she snuffled.

"I know. I should have woken you up to tell you I'd be out. I'm sorry."

She relaxed her grip on me. We sat on the corner of her bed, and I stirred the embers of our fire. "I have some good news, Miri. Not the best, but it's good."

She rubbed her eyes. "What is it?"

"Laynia's had word that *Mila* and Jasen are safe. They're down south on the continent of Veshna, where we crashed."

Miri bounced up. "Can we go see them, Dad?"

"I wish we could. But we have to let them be for a while."

"Dad! Why?"

How to say this? "Because there are some people who might hurt them, and if we went to see them, we might lead these people to them."

Miri stiffened. "What people? We've got to stop them!"

"They work for the king, I think. And Laynia's going to stop them. She's the queen, so she has the power."

"Are they going to be all right?" Miri asked in a small voice.

"Everything will be fine, you'll see."

She snuggled close to me. "I hate this, Dad. I wish we could go home."

(later)

Ethan sent me a letter. It came, as far as I can tell, unopened, so perhaps communication is freer than he suggested. It was brief:

> *Mark how these rebels betray you and choose your course wisely, Nevan. Do not believe for a moment that these maniacs are your kind. If you are not an insane man, then do not let them use you. If, as a Kiri, you cannot join us, then stay out of our affairs.*

The Tapanayn word for "rebel" is old Dabunè for "the ones who make change"—on Perdita, the ones who hate change, who hate new knowledge. And my wife and my child, their heads full of new ideas, are among them.

CHAPTER 19

The ship did it, Sylan realized. It was shame at the pain they'd caused Sylan and Jasen that convinced Illia to take Sylan to Micor. Shame and prudence: they could no longer expect Sylan's cooperation without cooperating in return.

They traveled by ground car—an elegant machine, ergonomic and solar powered, with a hydrogen cell to be used when there was no sun. It was the only piece of truly well-designed equipment she'd seen on Perdita, a product of centuries of necessity, no doubt. She and Illia drove northeast to Oja through an agricultural countryside and into a mountainous forest.

That night, in a roadside hotel, Sylan dreamed of driving. She was looking out the window from the highway into the pale Oja River. All at once, the water was turquoise and vast, spreading out like an ocean. And she was not on Perdita but home on Vorshtamor, a child, hopping the islands in the backseat of the skimmer, the wind whipping her hair. In front sat Father, and next to him, Dienzhok, her parents' husband, whooping with delight. Father dove the skimmer down so low across the waves that the spray showered Sylan and Miri, who was with them.

But as she looked at Miri's face, she saw they were standing in the grass by the house: tough, yellow coastal grass. It was day, but the sky was black, punctuated by too many stars. Suddenly Mother's voice boomed, "Come to me on Perdita."

Sylan reached for Miri, but her daughter was gone.

With a start, she awoke, gazing up through the window at unfamiliar stars.

≈•≈

The next day, they angled north, high into the mountains, till the trees surrendered to raw rock. Illia stopped the car and explained apologetically that Sylan would have to go blindfolded the rest of the way.

"This land has been Micor's home a long time, and no one but the most trusted Borderals can know just where to find him."

They drove on for perhaps half an hour, then walked up what felt like a dirt path. Abruptly, their steps began to echo and the air grew warm and earthy. A door clicked, and Illia removed Sylan's blindfold. The stone room was bare except for a bed, a wood chest, and some cushions. A fire burned in the grate; a window looked out onto a blue sky and mountains of faded violet.

Illia looked uncomfortable. "I have to go. I'm told there'll be a . . . guard outside your room. If you need anything, just ask."

To combat anxiety, Sylan rifled through the wood chest and found old Sama books of the doings of the gods. They failed to distract her.

After an hour, a knock sounded at her door, and a man entered who could only be Micor: albino white with dark, round eyes. He took a cushion next to her so their standing was equal.

"Are the gods loving, Sylan?"

"I don't know." She'd heard the ritual hello at the hotel but still wasn't sure how to answer.

He smiled a little. "I'm Micor. Illia tells me you wished to speak to me."

Sylan felt her strength flow back. She was her mother's daughter now on the quest for answers. "I need to know what you know about the shield."

"Illia spoke to me of this. It was the first time I'd heard of it."

Sylan laughed, not surprised he had started by lying. And his mind was fully blocked, not like the others'. He'd been trained.

"You hide the truth. But I will find it."

He did surprise her then: he addressed her in her own language, old-fashioned and accented, but plain and fluent Vunizh. "You prefer to speak the Leddie language?"

"Thank you. It's gratifying to hear. But in Tapanayn or in Vunizh, I still need to know about the shield. I know you know something: you must after six hundred years here."

He gave a shrug. "Name me an unobservant fool, but I can tell you of no shield. Since such a device would elucidate why my ship and yours crashed, I'm inclined to credit that it exists. But I never knew wherefore my family's ship crashed, being naught but a child at the time."

"And when you grew up, no one spoke to you of it?"

"My mother, the sole adult survivor, seldom spoke of the crash—remembrances of her family's death pained her—and she herself had not flown the ship."

"How convenient for your story."

"I cannot change the only truth I have to tell."

"Bravo. Very equivocally stated."

He laughed. "Not by intention. I am speaking your language as best as I can. I have naught but my son with whom to practice."

"Then you and I have something in common. I have no one but my son to practice with either. I was ripped from my daughter and husband by *your* people."

After a moment, he said, "Sylan. I do know many things. Permit me to open my mind to you. Not fully, for we all must have our secrets. But permit me to share my intentions with you. Mayhap, you can judge if my words be sincere."

"Intentions can by mimicked. You could be lying to yourself—or just very good at playacting."

"Yes. But it's the best I can offer. Look."

Grudgingly, Sylan reached out toward his mind. It did feel part open, like an honest face, like those grave eyes on hers.

"I know your family is safe," he said. "I know where they are. I will make sure you encounter them again, yet it may take some years."

She wasn't sure she'd heard him right, except she knew she had. "Some *years*! I will not wait 'some years' to see my daughter again. I will not let the years roll by while she grows up without me. I will not sit on this backward planet for years while my family in Leddra thinks I'm dead."

"Would that I could see you reunited at once. But we must preserve the security of our work. I wish you no harm, Sylan. But before I let you jeopardize us, I would see you dead. Yes, and your son, if it came to him or us."

The threat to Jasen made her want to strike him, but it frightened her enough to make her refrain.

"Moreover," he said, "your daughter and husband are safer without your seeking for them. They are with friends of ours.

But the king will not allow them to be moved, and if we try, he would imprison them where we cannot reach them."

Sylan scoured his mind down as deep as he would let her. He felt sincere, like his voice, like his eyes. But she couldn't be sure. It was all surface work, and even deep readings were unreliable.

She thought for a moment. "If you truly know of my family, tell me something you know about them. Then maybe I can judge if you know anything or not."

"I have not seen them myself. But I hear that your daughter likes to talk of philosophy, though she's but a child—and she likes to dance. And your husband occupies his days by studying books."

As far as it went, that was Nevan and Miri. It sent a pang through her to think of them not far away, living lives not so unlike theirs at Melnar, not long ago.

≈•≈

Micor always marveled at the way the mountains caught the afternoon sun in Late-Spring. He sat on his perennial rock, letting the heat suck every vestige of stoniness out of his bones. Since the offworlders had come, he'd often caught himself remembering the terror of his own ship falling, that rickety, War-era ship from Shi Durn. He was just six years old, and all at once his human father was dead, Taman's parents too. He and his mother and Taman, only five herself, all with broken bones, all sverra or part-sverra, were surrounded by a throng of humans.

But they'd lived, and years later his mother had found the papers. She'd guessed their significance and stolen them for safekeeping. And when the Kiri and Sama sides had started fighting again and his mother was killed, he and Taman fled with the papers into the wilderness of Oja and later shared the secret with Olloan, their son. And ever since Taman had sickened and died in the Lost Lands, Micor and Olloan had carried many worlds' weight in their arms, alone.

He heard a heavier-than-human step on the rocks leading down to him and looked around. His son emerged from the trees and sat by him.

"How was your journey to Raratin, Olloan?"

"The Raratins don't like the loss of the ship. They say it turns the City harder against us. They say it was cruel to the offworlders, and that we should have helped them get back to their ship and leave Perdita."

"As if it were that easy."

Olloan squinted out at the mountaintops under the setting sun.

"My informants say you got back from Raratin ten days ago. Why didn't you come to see me?" Micor said.

"I needed time to think."

Micor waited.

Olloan glanced at his father. "You helped Sherayna plan the destruction of the ship?"

"As you know."

"It *was* cruel. We could have helped them leave. If we could smuggle two bombs on board the ship, we could have smuggled the offworlders on—after the City made repairs."

"But they still couldn't have left with the shield in place."

"You could have gotten the shield down. You could have negotiated it."

"Maybe. But we aren't ready for the shield to come down, not till the Perditan people are wiser." He paused, decided to say it aloud: "Not till we can figure what to do about the papers."

A silence fell. The sun sank to eye level, blotting from sight all but the rocks by their feet.

At length, Micor said, "Did they ask you about the shield?"

"Oh, yes. And they asked you, of course."

"Yes. They brought Sylan to me. She's diamond-hard, Olloan. She may find the shield, given time."

"Yet you said you knew nothing about it."

"Yes."

"I don't like lying," said Olloan. "Illia came to me six days ago, asking if I knew about a planetary shield. I told her no. She went to bed with me. I held her in my arms and told her lies with a trustworthy face."

The sun was passing below them redly, into the familiar cleft between Mount Bluestone and Mount Dwarf.

"They deserve to know," said Olloan. "Not all Perdita. But our Borderals, some of them, the ones who'd understand. They die to guard their planet. They deserve to be made guardians, of the shield and of the Sama papers."

"You just said it was wrong of me to destroy the ship. Perhaps even I am not wise enough to be trusted with what I know. Sadly, you can't erase my knowledge of those papers. But should we extend that kind of power to those whom you just accused of acting cruelly?"

Olloan smiled tightly. "Just a few. But no, you don't have to say it. News travels. No, you're right. But, Micor, I do think you've acted wrongly. And you and I *are* guardians. And if I think you're wrong and you think I'm wrong to think so, at least one guardian is making mistakes."

"I'll review my motives."

Olloan nodded and rose to go.

"Olloan? This hasn't opened a breach between us?"

Olloan sat by his father's side once more. "No, no. Of course not. How could there be a breach between thee and me?"

"Since your mother died, you're my only friend."

"I know it," said Olloan. "Don't be afraid. There's only one thing I love more than I love you. And that is rightness of spirit, which you love as much as I do."

PART TWO
THE WEST-OF-NOWS SUNDERED

CHAPTER 20

Nevan's Journal
Perdita: 21 Late-Spring, 5.06.2033 After the End

I am back in Zerin. Miri is asleep beside me, finally. They came for me in the night, soldiers in black. That is, their uniforms are blue but looked black in the lamplight. Five days ago. Only five days.

A voice said, "You are ordered to Senarna to answer questions for the king."

And Laynia was there. She said, "He is here under my protection by orders of the king."

Miri was calling me, pulling at me. Someone showed Laynia a paper.

"I'll go with you, Nevan," she said. "It will be all right."

"Dad, where are they taking you?" said Miri, gripping my sleeve.

Everyone tried to comfort her. I did, Laynia did, even the soldiers did in their fashion. We said things like, "It will be all right. Your father's just going away for a while." We said things like this to a little girl on a foreign planet with her mother and brother already gone. She screamed that she had to come with me. I wanted her on Zerin, safe—safer. It seems safer. Except it's not safe at all, is it? And overriding every practical concern was that deep guilt every parent has felt: that I was failing her. She needed me, and I was failing. They said she couldn't go, just me. She screamed. They tore me away from her. She screamed and screamed. I could hear her as they marched me to the cart and down the road. I could hear her after the lights of Wolsenond flicked out behind the trees. It took everything in me not to kick at them and run back to her. Yet a piece of me was relieved they had made the decision for me. I did not have to choose to take or leave her.

They locked me in a room, a windowless gray cell with a cot and toilet. A local jail? I don't know. People came. The king himself came much of the time. Not Laynia.

They asked me questions about jae, technical questions, things I couldn't answer—happy chance that I couldn't answer because if I'd known, I might have told them. They didn't torture me, not in the gross sense of the word. But they made me afraid. I'd never experienced anything like this, not as a scholar on Onáda. To be robbed of my freedom, even the limited freedom to walk around Wolsenond, and sit in a little room with the lights always shining and no measure of time. No water except at intervals on their whim. I contemplated drinking from the toilet.

The same questions over and over. They accused me of lying: I was an author of the *Jae History*, I must know all about it. They accused me of anti-tech sympathies and made it very clear that this was punishable by extended imprisonment, in other words, by throwing all I am away into that little room. I told them Sylan knew. I all but told them to go find my wife and do this to her. I am not a liar. I don't know how to lie, even to protect her.

If I said anything useful, it was once when I managed to spill out something about jae contamination in an awkward paraphrase of the *Jae History*: "In the central Sama planets where the plague was the worst, whole populations wasted away. Teeth would fall out, organs would melt from within, victims would cough blood, defecate blood, people would drown in their own lungs. The less sick dragged on through their lives in constant abdominal pain, nauseated, head in splitting pain. No cure, no treatment except replacement of organs and tissues, but even the replacements were soon contaminated. It wrecked humans, other animals, even plants. Forests became garbage piles."

I think somebody hit me. I don't remember being told to stop, but I was stopped.

My head pounded all the time. I don't know if it was something they gave me or just strain and dehydration.

They said they needed jae. It would break the stalemate with the anti-techs. It would get them off Perdita. It would reunite them with their sister worlds. I told them—truthfully—that our *Jae History* doesn't have precise enough specs to build a jae reactor. It tells a lot, too much, but it's not a blueprint. They refuse to understand. I don't think I mentioned the shield. They might think a jae ship could bypass such a shield by jumping out of real space from the atmosphere. It can't, of course. The emissions from the reactor spin-up would devastate a biosphere. Even the Samas at their craziest didn't launch jae ships in atmosphere.

It went on. I am certain I didn't do anything to convince them to release me. Eventually, Laynia was there, dressed in a gold robe like a queen, but her face crinkled like dry paper. "We're going back to Zerin," she said and pulled me up. I was embarrassed to smell so terrible. On the way, she told me, "I've convinced them that you don't know the technical specs. Still, they'll use your book to further their own research, and they'll be redoubling their search for Sylan."

So that is that. They are going to try to make a jae ship and coerce Sylan into helping them. My performance in front of their interrogators did nothing but save my own skin, for now. I was out of words. I was a lump of cargo all the way to Zerin.

Miri cried. She has scarcely stopped crying.

≈•≈

27 Late-Spring, 11.06.2033:

I woke up this morning to Laynia rapping at my door. She looked nothing like the queen I first met. Her hair was uncombed and tied back sloppily. Dark circles ringed her eyes. "I'm called back to Senarna."

I grabbed my coat and stepped with her out into the crisp morning air, closing the door to let Miri sleep. "Will they interrogate you?"

"No. Maybe. Mostly, I will—I have to—I have contacts back there. I need to make sure they're still on my side, I can make them see reason." Her words were jumbled in a way I'd never heard. She rubbed her temples and then looked at me. "I'll protect you to the best of my ability. And we will not let them have Sylan or jae." She moved to go, then stopped. "We were going to show you the shield," she said, "as a gesture of goodwill, but now, the less you know the better."

I told her I agree. Though I need to see the shield if I'm ever going to lower it and free us, I still meant it. I don't want to know anything. I don't want to be taken from Miri again.

(later)

Asked to see Olwer because he's the leader on Zerin. I don't know what I expected. He came to my room, which annoyed me. I realized I wanted to see his room, his bed, his books, his hairbrush, wanted to scour off his plain gray exterior. Instead, he gave me empty words: sorry they took you, sorry we couldn't do anything, Laynia is conferring with the king. Empty eyes, empty face, gray robe, gray hair like a figure far off in the mist, but his stiffness told me he was afraid, and that made me afraid too, and perversely happy.

While I was talking with Olwer, Miri got in a fight. After he left, I went out to meet her in the play yard and found her on the road in tears.

I sat next to her. "What's the matter?"

"This is a stupid island," she said in Vunizh. "I hate it. Stupid Tapanayn! Stupid Leva! Stupid humans who don't understand any of the simplest things!" She wiped her nose.

A little way past her, a young Jetho, Elri, one of her tutors, was hugging a tree.

"Elri . . . ?" I said.

"I'm sorry, Nevan. I was spinning her on the rope swing, and we were laughing. And I said, 'I'll wager this is the sort of thing you do at home with your family.' And she started to yell at me. She said we were nothing like her family."

"I said *you*, you stupid human," Miri shouted. "You are nothing like my family!"

Elri opened her mouth and looked from Miri to me.

"Miri," I said, "Elri didn't mean any harm."

"Like I believe that!"

I sat down beside her on the wet rock and took her in my arms. "I'm sorry, Elri," I said.

"It's all right," she said, clearly embarrassed, and left quickly.

Miri and I sat up late reciting poems our Kiri *jethâti* taught. We also invented our own tales, something we've done since she was very small. We made up stories tonight of King Átymar and of Fallingwind, our great theologian, in the days of the Convention of Kiri Worlds, when our planets were first united. It was comforting to remember our past—to remember that our worlds endure, and will endure, despite the antics of Perdita.

CHAPTER 21

Sylan decided to bide her time. On the one hand, Micor's threats had pushed her toward a kind of submission. On the other, his knowledge of Miri and Nevan gave her hope: if they were safe, then her actions need not be so urgent. And she could learn from the library books Rajaneen brought on the history of tech on Perdita.

Books in place of action. I'm as bad as Nevan, Sylan thought, but she studied the texts nonetheless.

Jasen didn't like her reasoning, but he claimed to understand it and agreed to bide with her.

≈•≈

Two months of work. Sylan wrote her observations in her journal: two thousand years of bickering, a world achieving neither progress nor stability. She wrote about it sedately, but inside she was fuming at the sheer scope of the waste.

Leric kept a small desktop computer, and one day when everyone was out of the house, she had at it. It was a fossil, keeping records on the wheat business and running a few stultified projections on climate and economic trends, never incorporating more than ten variables. She cleared a little memory by consolidating partially redundant files.

She also determined that this was the machine Leric used to break that Iltan–Mesa code that Illia would rather he'd left alone. He'd erased the files, of course, but not very well: she recovered almost the whole document. She had to admit, there was something pretty about that antique decoding program, something fundamental to all computer design as respiration to living organisms. It was like watching pi. She was paging through his code when a footfall made her jump.

"How did you find it?" Leric gasped, falling to his knees to lean over her shoulder.

"You didn't destroy the files. You only marked them all right to write over."

"But I checked. They were nowhere on the machine."

"Only the name was nowhere." She glanced up to find his face blanched. "I'll show you how to do it better."

He shook his head. "Illia would tell me to leave it."

"I call that superstition, Leric: like that Perditans don't use portable communicators."

He stared at her. "But then people could talk at you anywhere, anytime."

"That is the point."

"That sounds horrible."

She rolled her eyes. "Many cultures place limits. They say, 'Don't call me then,' or they just turn off the communicator. Only Perdita abandons communication for that reason, makes people write paper letters."

"And the Kiris?"

She laughed. "Yes. And the Kiris too."

"They're right. It's good to meet people face to face. To leave the machines." He stared at his computer.

"Do you want to leave it?"

He drew up a cushion. "No. Show me how to use it better."

CHAPTER 22

Jasen had done his best to hate the Borderals. But perhaps because of Karmeena, he couldn't stay angry at Illia and Leric. Sherayna seldom came home and as the months passed, even his rancor toward her faded. While his mother ensconced herself in library records, he followed the radio news. Little was said about the Borderals, the rebels. And though reports of the search for Jasen and Sylan sometimes surfaced, none mentioned his father or Miri.

"It's like they've never existed," Jasen said once to Shoshec.

"The City already has them," Shoshec answered. "Why would it compromise its security by publicizing the fact? Do we brag about having you here?"

"Do you have any right to brag?"

He dreamed of striking off on his own. But as long as he stayed, at least he and Sylan had each other, and they were learning things about Perdita here, things he could use to pass for Perditan and travel freely.

≈•≈

Near the end of Late-Summer, Illia pronounced Sylan and Jasen sufficiently Perditan to venture out into town, provided they speak as little as possible. They went to the prayer meeting, a minor ceremony held every six days.

Jasen's first impression was that the town was not un-Kiri: households scattered at broad intervals in the fields, with public buildings clumped into a tight, central mass. On the heels of this observation came a recollection of Vorshtamor, his mother's world, whose few habitable islands were thick with fields yellow like Meena's. Like Vorshtamor, Meena punctuated its grasslands with a sprawling transport center. It lay beyond twenty or so dusty buildings, which, fringing a broad north–south highway, made up the heart of the town. There the highway bloomed out into a huge, dark square of pavement on which ten wheat-transporting vehicles clung like chitons in a tide pool.

Set back from the main road was a silo. In front of the silo stood a crude statue—a man in white plaster, embracing a woman painted black and peeling to reveal the same plaster beneath. Hundreds of people gathered in a loose circle around this shabby pair.

Various inquisitive Meenans asked Illia's family about their guests. Leric introduced Sylan and Jasen as friends from the Remote Islands in the northeast. Jasen wondered how many of these people were Borderals and how many Borderals knew the truth. He thought he saw smirks behind their eyes and wished that their minds were not instinctively closed. At least his mother's mind was responsive: he held onto it as if he were still a child.

A few minutes, and the crowd satisfied its curiosity. Jasen found himself more or less ignored, at the back of the convention. Relieved, he asked Leric, "So who are the statues?"

Leric glanced at him as if surprised by his ignorance. "It's the Nama-Sor. Nama and Soruc. Sister and brother, dark and light, vacuum and matter, space and the stars."

Jasen thought a question to his mother, a feat of concentration, but their only secure way of speaking here: *I thought Naima and Soruc were brothers in the Shonac.*

It took her several seconds to formulate a clear answer: *Maybe the Kiri Perditans got confused because Naima sounded like a woman's name to them.*

People began singing a low incantation. They linked arms and rocked, or danced close, weaving in slow circles.

When blind and broken Fennoc fell,
Then sputtered stars their final breath
As candles gasping in a well,
That once made light, make mist in death.

When human hearts the blackness quell
With bold devotion, ware and wise,
As fire to melt the ice of hell,
Then whole and hale will Fennoc rise.

Jasen recognized the name of the old Sama king of gods, but he had never heard this story. The song ended and the crowd grew still. A man stepped in front of the statue.

Wizened and bent, he must have been nearly two hundred. Like the rest, he dressed casually, a straw sun hat shadowing his face. Jasen felt a surge of mind power, though he could not identify its source.

Someone from the crowd said to the old man, "Has Daros the Timekeeper spoken to Fennoc, Im Seer?"

"He has," the old man piped.

"Has Fennoc the Mover spoken to you, Im Seer?"

"He has."

"What do the gods tell us, Im Seer?"

"They know this: Meena will cease to be Meena."

Jasen cast a glance around the assembled Meenans.

They merely closed their eyes and said, "We help you and we love you, gods, for halting to speak to us." Then they all fell to one knee and rose, and the old man hobbled back behind the statue.

The man who had spoken to the seer stepped out in front. "We've been blessed today: a clear message from the gods! Must be because it's only ten more days to Monedor." This provoked a ripple of laughter. Then the man stepped back and the opening song was sung again. When it was done, people began to disperse.

But the man came forward again and raised a hand. "One more moment, my friends." The crowd quieted. "We have with us a guest today."

Jasen felt his throat close up. Were he and his mother to be put on public display?

But the man swept his arm out toward a woman robed in gray. "This Jetho has come all the way from the island of Zerin to speak to us." He stepped back as the woman took his place.

She smiled over the crowd. "I am glad to see you. As you know, we on Zerin are mind readers, and though we have nothing of the gift of the seers," she nodded to Meena's ancient seer behind her, "yet sometimes the gods can reach our minds. And recently, we've been blessed with a message from the goddess Leva."

She paused. The crowd listened politely.

"You've heard the name," she went on. "She's not a high god—yet she's watched us long and feared for us, seeing the strife between pro-techs and anti-techs. She mourned for the

Lost Lands and for the *Outbound* and reached out to teach us to live more wisely. Through Zerin, she has sent us a prayer in her honor."

In a low voice, she began to sing:

Dear Leva, when we make machines
To bring to dawn a brighter day
Let us not only make machines
But make them in a better way.

"She wants us to remember this prayer so that we may better love each other through the gods. This is the Shonac, the Golden Way." She smiled again—*too much*, thought Jasen. "I would be pleased to speak to any of you who wish to learn more of Leva." With a little bow, she withdrew into the crowd.

Jasen wondered at this Leva prayer. It sounded almost like something the Borderals might say. At any rate, it didn't sound like the City, not as the Borderals described them. He sent his perplexity out to Sylan's mind. She replied with a little mental shrug. Then, Sylan, Illia, and Rajaneen were absorbed into a knot of chatting women. Shoshec went off somewhere, holding Karmeena by the hand.

Jasen turned to Leric. "That Leva thing, it's not different much from the ideas of the Bor—"

"Not here in the crowd." With a light touch on Jasen's shoulder, Leric guided him to the silo, where food and drinks were being served. Jasen bought a wheat cake from a short girl with curly flaxen hair and piercing blue eyes.

"You're the one from the Remote Isles?" she asked as she handed him his change.

"That's right."

"Do they worship Mon over there?"

"Of course." People were pressing in around him to reach the counter. The girl grinned; he moved on quickly.

Leric, who had been behind him, joined him after a few moments. They sat down to eat in the shady grass by the far side of the silo, well away from the crowds.

"You're in there," said Leric.

"What?"

"For Monedor." Leric was grinning.

"I don't even know what Monedor is."

"It's the night of Mon, the love goddess. It's a very ancient holiday, very important. You truly haven't heard of it?"

"No."

"Well. At any rate, Worshena was inviting you to catch her."

"To what?"

"To go to bed with her."

Jasen flushed. "Me? Was that a code? I mean, I didn't make the response."

"There's no code. But it was obvious, no? And you did make a response. You said of course you worshipped Mon."

"Oh, gods," Jasen rubbed his hands over his face. "So she expects me to meet her on Monedor now?"

"Probably. You don't have to, of course. She doesn't know you, she can hardly be very hurt if you don't arrive." He studied the waterfruit he was eating. "I don't know why you wouldn't though. She knows who you are—really. Her family's worked with us for three generations, so it wouldn't matter if you didn't act just like a native."

"But I . . ." Jasen began. "I don't, I mean—what I mean is . . . I'm not on contraceptives . . . I mean . . . since leaving Onáda."

A tight smile spread over Leric's face; then he doubled over laughing.

"What?" cried Jasen. "What? What do you find so funny?"

"I'm sorry." Leric wiped his eyes. "Truly, Kiri men use contraceptives?"

"Naturally. Why not?"

"Well, I'd think it would be a little more appropriate for the women."

"Women do too, of course."

"But why both sexes?"

Jasen scoffed. "You'd let someone else make your choice for having children?"

Leric considered this. "I suppose there's a logic to that. On Perdita, though, we don't have male contraceptives. But we do have a strategy for letting men be part of childbearing decisions. We talk about it."

It sounded haphazard to Jasen.

"So? Worshena?"

"And what makes what I do your worry? That you're my host?"

"No, that I'm a meddler, with my eye on every doorway."

"Yes, you are." Jasen's face was still hot. "You want to help me, Leric? Tell me about that Leva thing. It seems a good idea your people would like: not to make tech foolishly."

Leric, suddenly sober, shook his head. "It's a City ploy."

Jasen was surprised at the tingle of fear that ran through him. "You think the City knows about Meena?"

"No. They've been preaching Leva all over Veshna for years. It's all of Veshna they don't trust, you see. Leva's a ploy to make it seem like they care about caution, to make us look alarmist. Then, they can justify anything they do by saying they still revere the teachings of Leva."

"And you don't believe this is the word of your gods?"

"I believe that Zerin is loyal to the king. They may pretend they can see like the seers, but they see for the City."

"Do you believe in the gods at all?"

"Of course. I just resent the City's cynical appropriation of their names."

Jasen thought about this. He knew so little of the Shonac that he wasn't even sure what the word "god" meant to Perditans.

He said, "Tell me the gods—the real gods."

Leric crunched his waterfruit for a moment. "You don't worship the same gods at all? You don't know about the gods?"

"I've heard a few names only."

"Ah. The gods, you see, are very powerful beings. They shape the whole universe, from our hearts to the courses of the stars. Sometimes they shape things purposefully, particularly Fennoc the Mover. But all of them also shape things just by the fact of their existence, like a rock jutting out of a stream makes eddies . . . well, maybe not quite like that. The seer once told me, a god is like a pregnant woman, who creates life and knows it, but without direct conscious control or full understanding of it. To further the analogy, the well-being of the gods is intimately connected to the well-being of all their creations.

"You see, the gods, most of the time, don't think very clearly. They live in a world of confusion: between our universe and their own plane, between linear time and timelessness, without any of the solid, physical truths that we use to root ourselves in our reality. And so they feel lost and alone. And that hurts us too, in our hearts and in the world. So from our peaceful, stable world, we uphold them with our prayers. We send them our love so that they'll reflect our love back in the universe. One day, at the end of the universe, we'll all be one."

That's the old Sama Shonac. Everything was one and will be one again. He remembered that from school, but the rest . . .

"Does that explain it?" Leric asked.

"Not truly." Jasen marveled that the Perditans could believe in such a convoluted, anthropocentric cosmology. "I mean, I suppose it's something that can't be explained."

Leric laughed. "Not by me, anyway. Maybe the seer could help you."

"What did the seer mean when he said, 'Meena will cease to be Meena'?"

"I don't know. We'll know in time. That's the way with prediction."

CHAPTER 23

Ethan spent the summer months in Kepot, tracking contacts to the rebels who had blasted the ship. The months were called summer, but the summer shunned the north port city. Day after day, fog thick as a seal's pelt reared out of the ocean and over the sea cliffs. Gray tides clashed against gray rocks. Gray on gray. All day, the foghorns moaned. The weeds wet one's shoes.

Inside, the rooms were no more than an escape from the air, artificially warm, well lit, like this record room of the local library, on these firm foam cushions at this false-wood desk.

Ethan had not once seen the stars in Kepot; he looked for them every night as he walked to his room.

But there were rewards. There she was, like the sun rising out of the waters, in a series of photographs from a consortium reception, a dozen days before the traitors who destroyed the ship had transferred from Kepot to Iltan. She was in the back of the crowd in a corner, but it was clearly Sherayna, little mouth frowning. Her presence in the photo was as good as proof that she had helped organize the ship's destruction.

Ethan signed for the picture and trudged with his bundle through the head-muddling fog of evening, the sea roaring over horns that groaned like wounded beasts. He arrived at his hotel room, toes numb and fingers red. He turned up the heat.

She was the key. She had been a leader in Iltan. He paced in the confines of his room, hands in coat pockets, waiting for the heater to dry the air. He would have to keep his operation small, so small it would not require the warmaster's oversight.

Ethan did not wish to think ill of Lashen. But Lashen had ordered the traitors to Iltan, and he had been in the arms of the queen in Senarna. And if Laynia had compromised him, he was in a prime position to undermine Ethan's attack. Ethan sat on the carpet, next to the heater radiating into his face. He felt his body unclench.

She must be sought subtly. He could search municipal records for information on Sherayna, but it was doubtful he'd find much. If she hadn't cleared her picture from citizen records, she'd almost certainly altered her appearance and name. Finding her real identity, family, home would be sheer luck. No, far better to bring her to them.

CHAPTER 24

Sylan went with the rest of them into town that afternoon for the festivities. She knew of Monedor: the word came unchanged out of Dabunè. It was a sex festival, like many others in the religions of the Nations. She'd taken part in some, but this one frightened her. Despite Rajaneen's encouragements, she hung back with the few who were old, infirm, or unwilling to take active part, leaving the others to the circle dance around the Nama-Sor statue. It made her miss Nevan and realize how little she'd thought of him in recent days—she didn't want to be unfaithful yet feared that she already was. She was nervous, too, for her son, who was still too young, for a Kiri, to have much experience with sex. She kept her mind closed and clapped in time to the dance, pretending to enjoy herself.

There had to be more to the festival than sex, for young children were in the dance as well. After the dance, there were songs, more dances, food and drink, no invocation to the goddess, Mon, that Sylan could catch. That was a change from the Sama days. As the dusty sun sank low, people wandered off in pairs. The children and elders now dominated the scene: there was Karmeena in a group of little girls with an older woman. Against her will, Sylan found herself looking for Jasen.

Instead, she caught sight of Leric, sitting on a railing kissing a young man. The wind blew dust eddies about the two of them, and they laughed and crossed out of sight behind a building. Of Illia, Rajaneen, Shoshec, she saw nothing.

Why did they bring me here? Piqued, she returned to the family's ground car. Its starting card was still inside, since theft was rare in Meena. Sylan liked motor vehicles, and the ground car was simple. She pulled out onto the road in the twilight and drove smoothly but for jerking the steering too hard. She imagined driving off to look for Nevan and Miri—and abandoning Jasen to the arms of some Perditan teenager. She turned the car toward the house.

≈•≈

She walked into the kitchen and stopped short. Sherayna looked up from the table with the wide stare of a child caught with her hand in the candy bowl. She'd been scribbling on a piece of paper: leaves and vines. Sylan hadn't seen her since she'd brought news of the ship.

"Why aren't you at Monedor?" Sherayna asked.

"Why aren't you? Your festival."

Sherayna sighed and set the kettle to boil.

Sylan watched her. "And why are you in Meena?"

Sherayna was fixing a dried soup mix, a mainstay of quick meals in Meena. "Monedor is my day of rest. It's a day when nothing happens, no one works, no one schemes, the City scarcely bothers to guard anything, and the Borderals can scarcely bring themselves to care. So I make it a point to come home."

"So you never keep Monedor?"

"I am keeping Monedor."

"It's a sex festival."

Sherayna looked up from the soup pot. "It's a love festival. And what is love if it isn't peace? Both exist so we can quiet the gods." She gave the soup a final stir and poured it into two cups, handing one to Sylan as she sat down—thereby lowering her standing below Sylan's, or perhaps indicating that standing was unimportant now. "And you? Why aren't you with the others?"

Sylan shrugged. "I have not the mood."

Sherayna laughed aloud—a sound Sylan had never heard, and it startled her so badly that she slopped her soup onto the table. "What is funny?"

"You aren't there because you don't want to be. It's the best answer in the world, yet people won't accept it. Never mind. I accept it."

Sylan stirred her soup. "Thank you."

CHAPTER 25

Nevan's Journal
Perdita: 20 Mid-Spring, 23.04.2034 After the End

I've been too tired to write. Now I must catch up. It's a year, by the Perditan calendar, since we first came to this planet. Since mathematics was always a nuisance for me, I've decided to make the adjustment between the calendars only once a year, a Perditan year coming out to 0.94 of a standard year, a net loss of 20.64 standard days—an orbit remarkably close to standard: one reason this planet was chosen for engineering.

What else must I force onto this bleached paper? I have looked through some shield documents. Olwer was reluctant to let me. I was reluctant to do so, afraid of what I might divulge if the king pulled me in again for questioning, but he hasn't. I've learned that the shield is powered by a fission generator, of all things. Perdita had fusion once, but the fusion plants were destroyed in an early tech war and the records expurgated. They have never rediscovered the technology.

I know roughly where the shield generator is. I won't write it here. But I've found nothing about how to power it down safely. It may be as simple as an off switch, or a complex sequence that must be input exactly to avoid a dangerous energy discharge or a slow dispersion of the field over decades.

Olwer also told me something. The shield, of course, has a monitoring system, overseen by guardians from Zerin. It has a record of the sverra ship crashing in Keerina in 1421, then nothing until the final month of 2032, when another ship fell into the trackless south ocean. The record shows that part of the ship's hull ripped off. Breached, the ship would have taken water fast. So even if the inertial dampers had remained online for the impact, any survivor would have drowned. Strange that I should be grateful to Olwer for telling me that Sylan's mother is dead, but it's better to know for certain.

Miri took the news hard, and fell into a moodiness that did not pass. It was the last half of Late-Winter, when Zerin is like a frosted pane of glass, windless and stony, when the laughter of children skating on the Water Plain vibrates through the island like ice crystals transmuted into sound. But Miri didn't play with the other children. Often, when she wasn't with a class, she would curl up in a corner of the library or put on her coat and boots and walk by the brink of the ocean. She kept her mind closed with adult skill.

But she ate well and slept soundly. Her face was round and her color bright, indeed scarlet from her walks in the white winter sun. She spoke reasonably, though she evaded questions touching on the change in her.

One day, she was sitting in my room by the fire. The east wind whipped down from the mountains, a sign, one of my Jetho friends told me, that spring was close.

"Dad, I've been thinking." Miri gazed into the coals: we speak in Keshnul now, a first tongue to us both. "The Jethor don't believe in *mirlla*. They think it's like Wolsena, not a truth but just a thing to control people's behavior, to get Perditans to be more sensible about technology. But that doesn't matter either, because *mirlla* does exist, and it will outlive all of us. To almost all of the universe, we don't matter at all."

It scared me how old she had grown. Longing to see the little child again, I said, "You're precious as amber to me." It's an image from an old tale.

Miri scoffed. "I'm not a baby, Dad."

"Of course you're not. But it's still true. We matter to each other."

"That's why I said, 'to *almost* all the universe.'"

"But if we matter to anything, then we do matter. Our actions matter, our thoughts and feelings." A very old piece of philosophy. Do I ever say anything that comes out of my own mind and not some twenty-times-recopied exegesis?

Miri said, "We only matter in a very insignificant way."

"Insignificant to whom?"

An expression of annoyance crossed her face. Finally, she said, "To me."

The next day, Miri was almost chipper, and as the sun climbed daily toward the equinox, she became like her old self, though more careful to shield her thoughts. Perhaps that's merely growing up. Jasen did the same thing. And cynicism, too, is often an adolescent phase. Perhaps Miri's just reached it early. She's had reason enough.

CHAPTER 26

It was Mid-Spring of the second year when the claw-wheat fields rolled languid under the high, rough-beating sun. For months, Sylan had watched Jasen move among the Meenans in ever-widening circles—learning skills, he said, that would soon enable him to pass for Perditan and walk through the continents looking for their family. He would be gone already if Sylan hadn't checked him. She was frightened of what Micor might do to Jasen if he left.

She'd come to know the local library like she knew her mother's face; the librarian recognized her by her footfalls. She'd found an old War-time supply report detailing the requisition of a refraction corrector: a type of wave-resequencing equipment used with large-scale electromagnetic shields. Planetary shields. It was written proof that a shield surrounded—or had once surrounded—Perdita. But she still had no information on where the generator was.

One evening, when the distant smudge of the Oja Mountains reached up to the reddening sun, Karmeena and Shoshec set out plates for supper. Rajaneen peppered her salad. Leric was in Mesa, doing something for the Borderals. Sylan sat with Illia and Jasen outside the back door, half-listening to the suppertime radio through the open kitchen window.

She was gazing at the spreading beige fields when the radio intruded:

"The rescue teams out of the western Tall Mountains report that the ship is of Leddie design. They have discovered the remains of two passengers killed on impact. Baggage-identification tags list their names as Dienzhok ik-Hrenok and Orkmaro ik-Udunan. We commend them with love to the gods. The ship itself has been declared unsalvageable. This is the second offworld ship to have been destroyed within the year in what is widely acknowledged as a rebel conspiracy."

Sylan and Jasen stared at each other with mounting horror.

Then Sylan turned away and gasped in Vunizh, "My God! My fathers."

≈•≈

Well after midnight, Sylan sank into bed and closed her eyes, but her mind refused to shut up.

My family tried to find me, and now they're dead, and I killed them. And Mother is dead too: she must have crashed. And Nevan and Miri may be dead for all I know, and Jasen and I trapped here, while somewhere up there, life leaves us behind.

These Borderals have kept us here in fear. If I hadn't listened to them, I'd have given myself up to the City and been taken to my family. I'd have told the City about the shield, and they'd have found it and taken it down because they'd want to—it's what they've been longing for. And the Meenans? Would they find the Meenans and kill them? Maybe.

And maybe I don't care.

≈•≈

Three nights after the death of her circle family, Sylan voiced her thoughts to Jasen as they sat late in her room. "We don't owe them anything, Jas. Oh, they've played at being kind, and in return, we've stayed hidden here to save their people from arrest, maybe execution. But now they've let our own innocents be killed."

Jasen met her gaze. "So what now?"

"Now we go to the City."

≈•≈

Their chance came abruptly, sixteen days after the crash: an uncommonly warm Late-Spring morning. Illia had gone off on Borderal business and would not be back until evening. Rajaneen and Shoshec took the car into town to drop Karmeena off at school and look into buying a new thresher. Gazing out the kitchen window absently, Sylan watched the car drive off. She was remembering a trip to Vorshtamor, and Miri, eight years old, dancing circles around Dienzhok.

"This is it, *Mila*." Jasen was suddenly by her side, dumping cereal into a disposable bag.

Reality clicked in. "Careful, Jasen. They might miss the food before they notice we're gone."

"I'm mostly taking things out of the big bins—nothing obvious."

"You have your money? Good. I'll pack the coats and blankets." She seized her research journal from the table. That too was going with her.

Ten minutes later, they were heading down the south trail along the fields at a jog. No reason to get off the main path yet. The family wouldn't be back for some time, and the sooner they struck off through the grass, the sooner they'd start leaving obvious traces. They took the south trail as far as it ran, passed a dead finch along the way. Sylan wondered what had killed it. When the trail forked, they went east.

Jasen said, "If we see a spot where the grass thins, we should break off and go cross-country, toward the coast." The land was rockier there, harder to track.

But the sun climbed high till the sweat poured down Sylan's forehead, and no good passage presented itself.

Sylan was out of breath. "Maybe we should just head off through the grass but go carefully. Otherwise, we'll never get off this trail."

Jasen seemed to ignore her for several paces. Then, he stopped. "All right."

After a time, they gave up any pretense of trying to hide their trail and went quickly, putting the wheat fields behind them, until all they could see was the wild plain and a few scraggly trees as they pressed southeast.

In the midafternoon, they paused near a couple of oaks. Sylan was trembling from muscle fatigue, and Jasen looked little better. They ate and drank in silence, waiting for their breathing to slow.

"We should go again," said Jasen, when they'd eaten.

"Not yet. We should wait at least half an hour to rest. It's no good if we collapse from exhaustion."

Jasen scoffed.

"Or me anyway. How far to the road, do you think?"

"It's been maybe a kilometer north of us for quite a while. But they'll be looking for us by now."

They went cross-country until sundown. Since night was falling and most people would be home, they decided to risk the road. For a quarter hour, they walked east, a night breeze chilling them through their coats. Sylan felt as she had trudging through Iltan, oblivious to everything around her, her eyes programmed only to register approaching headlights.

Jasen stopped short. Pulling up behind him, Sylan peered through the blue glow of Olay, which crouched just above the horizon of the western plain. Around them stood five—no, six—shadowed figures.

"You won't keep us," said Jasen.

"You're going to have to come with us," said a familiar voice, a man she'd met in Meena.

No one made a move.

All at once, feet pounded up the road in their direction. "Wait! Let me talk to them."

"We have nothing to say to you, Illia," said Jasen as she came to a halt beside them.

"Go back for the car," said Illia to someone. "We'll watch them."

A couple of figures bled off into the night, replaced within moments by another, the solid shape of Rajaneen.

"Is Shoshec going to be joining us too?" asked Jasen.

"He's home with Karmeena," said Illia. "She was very upset when she found out you'd gone."

Sylan heard Jasen swear under his breath. She said, "Karmeena deserves a better life. But also, so do we."

Illia began, "I understand you're upset—"

"Damnation to what you understand!" Jasen shouted. "You *killed* our family, you know that? You kept us from getting that shield down—it killed them!"

"And you think we enjoy this?" Rajaneen demanded. "We could have locked you up like convicts. Instead, we've treated you as friends. But if you think we'll let you put our own grandchildren at risk—"

"My heart bleeds," Jasen spat.

"Shut up!" Rajaneen said. A ground car pulled up beside them, and she pushed Sylan toward it. "You're coming back with us. I'm sorry. That's how it has to be."

≈•≈

For four days they were in prison, watched continually by at least one member of the family. Every day, Sylan watched Jasen try to mend things with Karmeena: offering to play or tell her stories. She turned away. She was seven years old, quick to be hurt and slow to forget it.

On the fifth day, two visitors came. One was Sherayna, dusty and worn. The other was Micor, his white skin dyed with brown juice so he looked like a passable Perditan. Sylan felt a surge of hope at his arrival, but she did her best to crush it. He might have power, but he'd showed no interest in using it to help her family. He took a quick drink of water, then asked them all to sit with him in the center room.

"I'm sorry for the deaths of your family," he said to Sylan and Jasen.

"I do not care," said Sylan. "I care for nothing now but going to my family."

Micor gave her tired look and faced the others. "Raja, Shoshec, Sherayna, Illia, I've known you all your lives, but there are things you don't know about me. You must keep what I'm about to say in the strictest confidence."

"Leric?" asked Illia.

"He is your family, and you may tell him when he returns, under the same conditions."

"We understand," said Rajaneen.

He turned back to Sylan and Jasen. "Your family is on the island of Zerin."

Sylan followed his gaze to the Meenans and was startled to see the looks of bewilderment.

"Jethor who are Borderals?" Illia gasped.

"Not precisely. Let us say that, in general, they're nearer to us than the City."

"So you'll take us to Zerin," said Sylan, "or we will escape, sooner or later."

"No, not Zerin. City agents on the island of Refomin are always watching Zerin. Even I would only go there in an emergency."

"Then the City knows that Zerin is against them," said Rajaneen.

"They don't trust the Jethor, Raja, because the Jethor read minds. But they do not suspect rebel sympathizers. And they must not learn it." He addressed Sylan. "We will arrange for you to meet your family in Senarna."

In response to the words, Sylan felt a swell of anger. There was no reason for it: she'd been given what she asked for. But it came so unexpectedly that her emotions had no time to adjust.

"Senarna?" said Rajaneen. "The center of City power?"

"It's our best compromise," said Micor. "You will meet in Senarna, and then Nevan and Miri will return to Zerin and you two will return here."

"No!" shouted Sylan, half glad to have a reason for her indignation. "That is not acceptable."

"The City has your *Jae History*," said Micor. "They have it. And they are bent on finding you."

The *Jae History*. She'd assumed it burned with the ship. *Dear God, we've put jae theory into the hands of techno-fast-trackers.*

"What is a jae?" asked Sherayna.

"I won't help them," Sylan cut her off, "even if they find me. The *History* itself has few technical specs."

"They will not give you a choice," said Micor. "Torture may be officially outlawed, but they can be very persuasive."

"What is this jae?" Sherayna repeated.

"It's a dangerous space-travel tech," said Micor, "but it isn't your concern, not yet. Olloan and I are doing what needs to be done."

"If we get the shield down and go away," said Jasen, "they won't be able to use us."

Micor leaned back and sighed. "You were right. I do know of the shield."

The silence hung heavy.

"How long have you known?" said Sherayna.

"Since my own family crashed on this world."

Sherayna laughed as if she did not know what else to do. "Did this shield bring down the *Outbound*?"

"Yes."

"And you never said? It could have exonerated us of sabotage charges, it could have blocked the Progressive Tech Statute, and you never said?"

"It is all that protects us. If I had told the City, they wouldn't have stopped till the shield was lowered, and our balance would be shattered. You thought your sabotage work was keeping Perdita planet bound. All it would take is one comm to the nearest inhabited planet, and our isolation would be broken."

"It should be," said Sylan. "Call for help to the other worlds. Call my people, the Leddie Confederation. They will help you explain to the City why not to use jae."

"They wouldn't listen!" said Micor sharply. "They are hungry to reach the gods. That's how they see it. They are hungry for tech power. We know them. And there's something else, Sylan. I know something of jae but not as much as you. We too may need your knowledge to stop a jae disaster. We can let you visit your family, but we cannot let you go."

CHAPTER 27

Senarna's green night lamps reminded Sylan of ghost stories from her childhood, but she saw little of the city. In a dank suite of two adjoining bedrooms, she and Jasen waited out the night with Micor.

At sunrise, an odd pattern of knocks sounded, a signal. Sylan strained outward with her mind and was sure she could sense them. Yet, what if that were only wishful thinking? Micor crossed the room. Sylan could feel him stretch out with his mind too. He swung the door open.

Miri flew past him and into her arms. A cry burst from Sylan as if the air had been forced from her lungs. Miri was so tall, so lean. Too big, too grown, too much time gone. Sylan cradled the familiar red cheeks in her hands.

Maybe she gasped, "Miri."

And heard Miri answer, "*Mila.*" Then, she ran to Jasen.

He released his hold on Nevan, catching Miri in his arms. And Nevan crossed the floor to Sylan in two quick steps. For a second, she could feel herself pull back. But then, they were in each other's arms and relief flooded her at the feel of his stocky, strong arms. He'd kept his hair cut the same. And he'd kept Miri safe. He kissed her. She looked into his beaming face, at the same old wrinkles around his eyes that he'd had when he was thirty.

"I can't believe it's you," he said in Keshnul. "Can it be I'd almost forgotten your face?"

"And I yours. I'd forgotten." She brushed his bearded cheek.

She looked at Jasen and Miri in tears, and felt a surge of love for Jasen, with whom she had endured so much. A silent understanding ran between them.

≈•≈

"Micor," said Sherayna when they'd retired to the adjoining room, "would it be all right—would it be safe enough—if Illia and I got some air?" There was something she hated about this reunion. Not that Sylan's family was together. Not that they were happy. But she felt trapped in an ants' nest: everything stung. She could hear them crying in the other room.

Micor exchanged a look with the tall, orange-haired woman who'd brought Nevan and Miri. "Yes, Sherayna. Go get breakfast."

She and Illia stopped at a stall for bread and fruit, but they didn't speak till they were in the open walkways, where they could easily watch for spies.

"That woman with Micor looks like someone," said Sherayna.

Illia nodded. "Like the queen, I think, like the pictures in the pamphlets anyway."

Sherayna's heart leapt. "You think she is? The queen, with us?"

Illia made no reply.

They walked on in silence. "Are you thinking what I am?" Sherayna asked at last.

"Not a Jetho, Rayna. What are you thinking?"

"About Micor . . ." She broke off and made a covert inspection of the walkway around them. Though she found no one following, she steered Illia down a side road anyway, to break from the pedestrians behind, just in case. "He lied, not only to Sylan but to you directly. Olloan lied too."

"He had his reasons." There was pleading in Illia's voice.

"Everyone has reasons. The question is . . ." She didn't want to say it. "The question is do we trust him?"

Nevan's Journal
Perdita: 27 Late-Spring, 25.05.2034 After the End

Impressions of our reunion: Sylan didn't look right. I think her brown-dyed hair disturbed me.

Jasen didn't either: so much older, even with his shaven face that ought to have made him look younger. I couldn't put my finger on it. He hadn't changed so much. His red-brown hair, his brown eyes—my eyes—were the same, his youthful face, his lanky form. He has been taller than me since he was fifteen—perhaps a little heavier now, but there was more to the change I saw.

I hugged him, surprised almost to feel his arms around me. His mind was open for me to see my own fierce love mirrored there. Then, I felt him think of Miri, like a physical pulling to the side.

And then, I with Sylan. I could feel her joying in me, and it surprised me a little; she had been distant in recent years. But now those years are wiped away. We existed without time.

But are they safe? Laynia said she had permission to take us to Senarna, but she had permission to keep me on Zerin too, and it didn't stop them from coming for me.

At some point we ate, and Miri taught Jasen dances from Zerin. I could hear her behind me, counting out steps: "One-and-two-and-three-four. Five. No, no, Jasen, three-four. *Five.*" Their feet jounced the floorboards. Behind the laughter and the clatter, Sylan and I took stock.

"Can we even be sure that the military has the *History*?" said Sylan. "Maybe Micor's people got it, and he's just using it to control us."

I shook my head. "The king's people have it. They took me in for questioning."

She gave me a dark look. "Are you all right?"

"I convinced them I didn't know anything, but they know you do." I realized only after I spoke that I hadn't answered the implicit question: had they hurt me. I decided not to answer it at once. I wanted to scare her. We should all be frightened.

"I need to get to that island," said Sylan. "I need to get that shield down and call for help."

"My love, we can't sneak you in. The whole Zerin coast is mountainous, impassable. There's no place for an airship, and every harbor is near the inhabited areas that are always under surveillance. It's not worth the risk."

She touched my face with her fingers. "That's such a very Kiri thing to say."

"They held me in a little room with almost no food or water—"

"*Mila.*" Miri's voice intruded. She sat down beside Sylan and looked into her face. "You can't let them take you. They only brought Dad back because he couldn't help them. If they took you, you'd never come back." Her voice caught, and Sylan held her close.

Jasen sat close to me. "Dad, what did they do to you?" I hated the fear in his mind, though I was glad he had the sense to be afraid.

I shook my head. "They just held me, questioned me." I shook my head again. It sounds so slight, and it is not. It is brutalizing.

Jasen took my hand. In that moment, he admired me, a strange reward for something I had no control over and was not particularly brave in facing.

Finally, Sylan pulled a stack of paper out of her knapsack. "Take these, then. It's all the information I've gathered about the shield. Maybe you can get it down."

"I'm no good at—"

"I know." She smiled slightly. "But even you can try."

She sat back and nodded. "After that, if we can't get to Zerin, maybe you and Miri can escape to us. At least we'd be together."

≈•≈

At sunset on the second day, it was time for us to leave, Miri and me before Sylan and Jasen. I have written enough of our tears, I think. I will only say that there were more, and bitter as they were, they could not begin to express the injury of our second parting.

124

CHAPTER 28

Nevan's Journal
Perdita: 15 Early-Summer, 08.06.2034 After the End

I asked to examine the shield control room. Olwer refused.
How can I shut down the shield if I can't reach it? I know
where the door is, but Olwer tells me it is guarded by Jethor
listening for a telepathic password from a mind they know the
feel of. Several of my Jethor friends independently confirmed
this. Moreover, part of me agrees with these anti-techs that the
Perditans must evolve an ethic of preservation before we open
up the planet to be transformed by rapid urbanization to
support offworld markets, or by invasive species designed to
increase crop yields.

Perhaps Miri will be a step in Perdita's evolution. She is
going to become a Jetho. I asked her why she wanted to
become part of a group she has often derided. She told me it
would give her leverage—not her exact words, but that was the
gist.

"As a Jetho, I'll have standing on Zerin," she said. "I could
even come and go from the island. I could visit *Mila* and Jasen.
I could maybe talk to the king about technology and things. *I*
could make things happen."

I did not miss the stress on the "I." I am proud of her will
to act.

For myself, I've begun that work with the crisis of the Lost
Lands. In the mid-seventeenth century After the End, the
Perditans were experimenting with a new chemical fuel source.
The fuel was low yield by space-faring standards. For the
Perditans, however, the energy yield would have been
appreciable, potentially replacing much of their fission power.

Unfortunately—inevitably?—a leak occurred,
contaminating the soil and groundwater of the entire peninsula
of Far West. Virtually all animal life and much of the plant life
of the region was eradicated—biodiversity there is still
minimal. Several hundred humans died before the area was

evacuated and redesignated as the Lost Lands: *Apatnar* in their language.

I have written to Ethan in the past about my studies. His replies have been few and terse. But he answered my mention of the Lost Lands with ferocious swiftness:

> *Again the Lost Lands! Let me enlighten you, Nevan, to a fact that the rebels conveniently forget. The disaster in the Lost Lands occurred because (and only because) the rebels assaulted the research facility with explosives that destabilized the containment tanks and led to a ground-level breach. If they had left us alone, it would never have happened. If they had left us alone, we would have fusion power and all of our energy crises would be moot. If you're looking for someone to blame for the ecological perils of Perdita, blame them.*

The records bear out his account of a rebel attack. Strange that I'd overlooked that detail.

I have a theory about Perdita: if the anti-tech forces triumphed, life on the planet would be stable and sustainable. If the pro-tech forces triumphed, the same might be true. Put them together, and it's only a matter of time before they form a synergy that will collapse the entire system. And yet, no better than all the rest, I felt obliged to rebut Ethan's letter:

> *I take your point about the Lost Lands: the rebels do deserve much of the blame. But Kiri philosophy would answer that it was the founders of the project who created the conditions that made the disaster possible. Your people laid the scorpion in Perdita's path, even if it was the rebels who made her step on it. The question is whether potential benefits outweigh potential risks. The answer is subjective, of course. But generally, a planet's ecological stability, in terms of its ability to adapt to environmental change, is proportional to its biodiversity. To take an oversimplified example: consider a disease that wipes out two species. If only those two species were present in an area, all life has*

just been destroyed. But if twenty species were present, eighteen still have a chance.

Now, every engineered planet is a contrivance. None has the layers of life history built to the level of complexity of a naturally evolved world. And Perdita, from what I have seen and read, has a simpler biospheric system than many engineered worlds. In terms of ecological adaptability, Perdita is an egg balanced on end at the edge of a cliff. Take care then what breezes you blow over her.

He answered me only with the words: "So much the more reason to reach for the stars."

CHAPTER 29

Sylan had talked with Jasen about being respectful of Perdita's polyamorous culture, but the knowledge didn't run deep enough to wipe the Kiri out of him. It had hurt him to see Worshena with other men. She hadn't understood his anger, and in Early-Autumn, they parted ways.

Shortly thereafter, he told Sylan he'd be traveling north, to be closer to Nevan and Miri, to share their air a while, he said. The journey needn't be too risky, he argued. He could pass for Perditan if he was careful, and Sylan, not he, was the one the City was bent on finding. After many nights of debate with Illia's family, they'd agreed to help him, perhaps because it was easier than resisting. With false identification papers, he'd gone to Refomin, taken a job at a fish market, studied Zerin. Perhaps he'd planned to stow away on the ferry to the island. Then his letters stopped.

≈•≈

Fifteen days with no word. Maybe he'd gotten distracted from writing, maybe letters had gotten lost. But maybe he was sick or captured or dead. With Illia and Leric away fighting, Sylan demanded that Rajaneen and Shoshec do something. Rajaneen said they'd alerted their contacts. It was all they could do.

Sylan thought hard about stealing the ground car. Risks be damned, she had to find her son. She sat in the center room, watching the sun sink over the shorn wheat like a lamp extinguished by the icy north wind. Maybe she could steal the car tonight. How far would she get before the City found her?

All at once, the door blew open, whipping the wind through the house. Karmeena was already rushing past into the hall.

"Papa!"

And in a moment, Leric was in the room—and staggering beside him, Jasen, one arm around Leric's neck. Sylan eased Jasen down onto a cushion.

Jasen coughed wetly. "I'm all right," he croaked. "I'll be all right." He coughed again.

Leric sat beside Jasen with Karmeena in his lap. "I found him in a hospital in Senarna. He has a touch of pneumonia. I told them I was a cousin and got him released to me—I've got his medication with me."

Sylan put her arms around Jasen and did not let go.

≈•≈

For two days, she scarcely left his side. On the afternoon of the third day, it occurred to her to thank Leric. She found him in the kitchen, with a cup of tea, fighting off a cold.

She sat across from him. "Thank you for bringing him back to me, Leric. Thank you for stopping your work to do it."

He smiled and sniffed. "It gave me an excuse to come home."

"I feared I would not see him again. Was it hard to find him?"

"No." Leric reached across the table and pressed her hand. "The hard part was getting Raja's message to me. All I did was search the local hospitals for his assumed name." He coughed.

"I hope you didn't get his sickness."

"I probably did, but pneumonia's just a nuisance. I expect Jasen got it badly because his immunity's different. You should be careful yourself."

Sylan groped for appropriate words. "Thank you."

He nodded, fingering his cup. "I'm sorry I wasn't here when your family's ship crashed. I was planning to come home, but with the Borderals being blamed for the crash, things got difficult for us in the field, and I was kept on. The next thing I know, I've been gone the better part of a year. And I never had a chance to say I was sorry about your family."

"I'm sorry you had to be gone so long from Karmeena."

After a moment, Leric said, "I'm home now. At least I'm able to go home."

"Sometimes I think the worst part of being trapped here is never seeing a familiar star. Sometimes I think nonlinear travel is a curse. It plays with our minds, makes us feel we're close when we're far, four hundred million linear light-years from the Diatonan Galaxy, where I was born."

"Where your family's ship came from. The two men on the ship. Shoshec told me one was your father. The other . . . ?"

"He was my circle father."

"I don't understand what that means."

"The circle parents are the people in the same circle marriage as someone's parents. When I was born, there were Ydan, my mother; Orkmaro, my father; and Dienzhok. On Vorshtamor, they had an island house, in the high grass, yellower than Meena's. It was long and low, the house. They had a flier that zipped among the islands. Going slow, you could ride with your head in the open. And inside the house, they had a big conference room with video and holographic links in their office."

"It sounds otherworldly. It sounds too good to be true."

PART THREE
MEENA

CHAPTER 30

Five years later

"Warchief?" Torna called over the Late-Winter winds as she thumped at his tent. "Warchief!"

"What? This isn't the time, Lieutenant."

"I wish to discuss the operation, sir."

There was a long pause, then, "Enter."

Like all the tents hastily erected nine measures west of the Oja City base, Ethan's was cramped and cold in the lamplight. He hunched over a writing board scribbling at his maps. He didn't look up when Torna sat opposite him.

"What?"

"I ought to be informed of your contingency plan, if we fail to locate the rebel commander."

"Go back to our spy network and start tracking her again."

"Is she worth that much effort?"

He looked up at her. "Are you suggesting I established the network to catch her alone? When we've brought in dozens of rebel leaders these past five years?"

"No, Warchief. I was simply wondering, if this campaign fails, will she still be worth more of our time?"

He looked back at his maps. "If she didn't mastermind the destruction of the ship, she knows who did. I'll wager she was in the middle of that Leddie ship's destruction, too. She's our best, our only, real contact."

Torna was struck by how the past five years had aged him, how his eyes glowed out of dark sockets. "Warchief, even eliminating the rebels for all time would be a worthless act if it robs the gods of our love."

"Eliminate the rebels, end the fighting. Less fighting, more love."

"I don't think so, sir. I don't think hate breeds love."

"Who said anything about hate?"

"Warchief, I have a prediction. Capturing this rebel will hurt you."

He gave her an icy look. "You can't make predictions without the ceremonies. I hope that you are cut by shame to misuse the name of seer so. And how dare you accuse me of hate? You are dismissed."

Torna stood up, stooping to keep from hitting her head. "It's a true prediction, Warchief."

≈•≈

That night Ethan dreamed of the dark lake. He was alone, its motionless surface stretching out before him to the horizon like a plain of shale. As he gazed, he saw a glow beneath it: a lamp sunk in a mire. Something was there, where his mother had plunged in.

The dream was gone as soon as he woke. Today was the day he had spent five years planning. With only twenty footmen under his command, he'd traced the patterns in rebel activity till he'd tracked down Sherayna. She had been in Oja City nineteen days. He'd set up camp under the pretext of hunting a band of rebels. In fact, the "rebels" were his own footmen. He'd moved in fast, forcing her to act before she could gather her own reinforcements. Yesterday, he'd arrested the false band. Tonight, Sherayna, who had been marking him since his arrival, would be there to free her supposed allies.

All day, through flurries of snow, his people shivered and played the parts of bumbling soldiers, pretending to get word of another rebel band, pretending to dispatch a patrol to search for the new interlopers.

Night fell. The camp seemed almost devoid of footmen. And there she was, crunching through the snowdrifts at the outskirts of the camp with two young men. He let them get close to the tent where the seven seeming rebels lay in wait.

She opened the tent, stepped inside with her companions. The prisoners she had set out to save opened fire on her two men. As they fell, she leapt back into the arms of the waiting footmen, who disarmed her, bound her, and handed her over to Torna.

"Gracefully accomplished, footmen," said Ethan, coming forward. "I congratulate you." They'd stay on full alert tonight and head back to the city at first light tomorrow.

Sherayna said, "My people—if they're not dead, you're required under the Laws of Humane Conflict to render medical aid."

Ethan nodded to a footman, who examined the bodies; they were dead. Sherayna turned away. Torna gave Ethan an insubordinate glance and marched Sherayna to the tent that had been set aside to hold her.

≈•≈

Sherayna watched the old lieutenant all night. Neither spoke. The tent's heater was a cheap box of metal, and Sherayna shivered despite her heavy coat as she lay on the ice-hard canvas floor, legs tied and arms bound behind her.

She wondered if the two dead boys had family. She'd hardly known them. They were native Oja iron miners, almost untried in scouting missions, the only companions she'd found in time to move in on the City before they left with their Borderal prisoners. And it had all been a trap. Just to catch her? Two lives lost for her? Why her? What was he going to do to her?

Sherayna had worked as a Borderal since the age of fifteen. It had been a long time since she'd been brutally afraid. In her mind, the possibility of death—or worse—had grown remote with the years. If it happened, it happened, she'd told herself. It had not. So she had come to assume that it would not, the way one assumed when one got in a car that it would not crash.

But he had looked at her with hatred. She shivered and tried to forget his eyes, only to dream about them.

Sometime in the night, the lieutenant turned the heater toward her and covered her with a blanket. She awoke almost warm, only to be seized by a footman who untied her feet and pushed her staggering into the snow. She saw the sky paling against the trees, and then she was bundled into the back of a transport, shut out from the light. Half-frozen, she jounced on the rough metal floor, feet and hands unable to find purchase.

Please gods, she thought as the floor cracked her knees, *please let him be done with me. Wherever you are sending me, please let his part be over.* She knew as she prayed that it wasn't possible. He had labored to find her, and he would be there.

In the afternoon, they stopped. The transport door swung open in a flood of white that dimmed fast to a gray sky. Two footmen dragged her through the transport yard into a long building, downstairs to a glaring washroom where they untied her hands, stripped and scrubbed her, and dressed her in a white prison coverall. Then down another hall to a cold little cell: a white room with an oily mattress, a toilet, and a sink with a drain but no tap. They locked the door and left her in deaf silence.

≈•≈

Time passed. She was bruised and consumed by thirst. She sat on the mattress and cried a little. She hadn't cried in—how long? Since word had come from Senarna that Leric's father had been executed: twenty years? She thought of not seeing her family again, and a wave of self-pity washed over her, so forceful that she sobbed.

Presently, she began to think like herself again. She would escape. She'd escaped before. Maybe not from a prison but from under armed guard. They wouldn't leave her here to starve. If they'd wanted her dead, they'd have killed her on the mountain. No, they wanted information, and that gave her leverage.

More time passed, and that conviction waned. Then, as if from nowhere, a step sounded by the door. The lock clicked; the door pulled back.

And there he was. The relief of seeing a human face vied with terror that the face was his. He came not alone but with a footman, which was comforting. Strange to be comforted by an icy-faced woman aiming a gun.

Sherayna managed a smile. "I think I'll take you up on your amnesty offer now, Warchief."

"Shut up." He seized her by the wrist and marched her to a larger room, white, empty. "Sit." He flung her at the floor. He turned to the footman. "You will wait outside the door."

Sherayna's heart jumped in her throat to see the footman leaving. She pulled herself up to a sitting position.

"You will tell me why you did it," he said.

Sherayna stared at the floor and said nothing.

"You will tell me."

"You just told me to shut up," she said to prove to herself she would not cower.

He came to within six feet of her. "I don't think you realize how deep in this mire you are. The waters have already closed over your head. The ripples are subsiding fast."

She swallowed.

"Why?" he said. "Just tell me why!" A sob cut him short; his tone was suddenly imploring.

She glanced up in surprise.

"Why what?" she asked helplessly.

"Why what?" he repeated. He sank to his haunches before her. "Why what!"

"Why did I become a Borderal?"

"The ship. Why did you destroy the ship?"

"I didn't," said Sherayna automatically. "I had nothing to do with the destruction of the Kiri ship. I was nowhere near Iltan. I was in Oja on the day it happened. I have alibis."

The warchief stood up. "Of course you weren't there! You had more than enough agents to do it for you. But you were behind it. Don't deny it. I know."

"Oh, you know. How?"

"I ask the questions, Sherayna."

"I have no answers."

He stepped back. "You will have no water either until you find some." He turned to the door.

"You'll get none if I die of thirst! And you cannot take actions that will lead to my death without due process. It is against the laws of humane conflict and the love for the gods."

He faced her coldly. "Do not speak to me about loving the gods—you who refuse to let us seek the stars to find them. We'll keep you functioning. You're not going to meet the gods yet."

CHAPTER 31

Jasen pulled his coat close and peered around the silo with Karmeena. Out on the snow-sprinkled square of Meena, people were bustling through afternoon errands, eager to get home before the evening flurries.

"I really don't sense anything," said Karmeena. She'd be thirteen soon, old enough on most worlds to have extensive mind-reading skill. But it was understandable that she'd be behind. Jasen had only begun to train her about four years ago.

"It's all right," said Jasen. "Remember that they're naturally blocked and you're not supposed to sense much, just a vague presence, an impression of emotion." He caught sight of a familiar figure heading across the square: Vecle, a woman he'd been sleeping with—he'd promised he'd see her tomorrow.

"You're lovers, no?" said Karmeena.

"You sensed that?"

"From you, not her. I can't sense them, Jasen."

Jasen got his own blocks back up, felt the hum of the minds on the square recede from his consciousness. She was doing sufficiently well. His plan was simple. Karmeena was still young enough to be tested for potential as a Jetho. If he trained her to mind-read and she got tested, there was a chance the Jethor would believe she was a natural prodigy and accept her. And children accepted to Zerin were allowed to bring a companion to the island. This could be anyone: relative, friend, or acquaintance. Karmeena's companion would be Jasen.

Jasen knew Illia, even more than Leric, disliked the plan. She didn't want her daughter on an island balanced between duties to the king and the Borderals. But she couldn't deny that Karmeena might find uses for mind reading. It would give her an edge as a Borderal, help her to spy and stay safe. So Illia had allowed Jasen to train her.

"What are you two doing, lurking there?" A group of Jasen's friends came up smiling behind them. He didn't want to lie to them—they were trustworthy Borderals after all—but the fewer who knew about his plans, the safer for everyone.

"We're studying for Karmeena's history exam."

"Oh yes? That's why you don't have any books out."

"Well, she does have to have it memorized." Jasen glanced at the darkening sky. "But we should be getting home."

"Wise call. Studying in the snow will freeze your neurons."

≈•≈

That night, after a long practice with Karmeena, Jasen sat up by the fire, trying to relax his mind. But it wouldn't relax. He was strained to the teeth. It wasn't the usual sort of mental fatigue he experienced after working with Karmeena. In fact, he realized suddenly, it wasn't related to Karmeena at all. It was a warning, a presence outside the house.

He bolted to his feet.

A sense of wrong filled his consciousness, sensitized by hours of thought exchange. His first thought was a City attack. He tensed, ready to flee. But flee where? He reached out with his mind to try to gauge the position of the attackers—and he gasped in relief when he met the familiar, veiled presence of Illia, back after three months on assignment. But the wrongness clung like fog around her. He padded to the back door just as she was slipping in, a wraith against the moonlight, trailed by a stab of winter air.

"Were the gods loving, Illia?" he asked. "Were your raids a success?"

She jumped. "Jasen? Dear gods, you're like a cat on a bird." She shied away from his gaze. "Jasen, I need to talk to everyone, except Karmeena. She can sleep."

"What's wrong?"

"Will you wake your mother for me?"

When they were assembled in the center room, Illia sat down by Leric and looked at her hands in her lap. "Sherayna's been taken prisoner."

≈•≈

The next day was sunny and chilly, pleasant for working in the winter orchards. But Jasen lingered in the kitchen with his mother and Illia after breakfast. Karmeena had yet to show her face; she was a late sleeper on any day that she didn't have school. The kitchen was sunlit. Sylan's pen scratched as she organized a chronology of failed fusion experiments. A pretense of normality.

Then, Karmeena came in, and he realized who he'd stayed in for. Her first words were "Mama, you're back!" and, checking herself, "What's happened?"

Gently, Illia sat Karmeena down and explained.

"Rayna will get away, no?" said Karmeena.

"She will if we have anything to say about it."

"We don't have to worry, then?"

"Rayna's as tough as they come."

Karmeena asked no more questions, but as soon as her mother had gone to the fields, she said, "Mama doesn't think we'll get Rayna back."

Sylan looked up at her. "Well, but she was right when she said that Sherayna knows how to take care of herself. But I think your mother doesn't like not to know when she'll see her again."

"Is that what it's like thinking about your family?"

"Yes," said Sylan. "Yes, it's something like that."

"What about you, Jas?"

"Ah . . . well. I wish I knew what my father and sister were doing." He was ashamed. He'd devoted ample energy to his plan to reach his family—but how long had it been since he'd missed them?

≈•≈

A high cloud veil had moved in by midmorning. At lunch, Shoshec and Leric tried to debate what to do about the mice in the fields, but their conversation sputtered. Karmeena started to clack her spoon on her soup bowl after every mouthful. After a moment, Leric followed her example. They grew louder and louder.

Rajaneen said, "Remind me, Sho, to go down to the potter's and order shatterproof dishware."

Karmeena giggled. Illia grinned and said, "They'd only have plastic. And you know the City doesn't endorse the use of biodegradable plastics."

Rajaneen shrugged. "So? If it refuses to degrade, we can set it as an offering for the gods to remember humanity by when we've gone."

The joke was very Kiri, and Jasen laughed.

Sylan smiled politely. "How did Sherayna become your foster child?"

"Rayna isn't a genetic relation at all," said Rajaneen. "Her parents came up from Vorna just a few months before she was born. When Rayna was only two, they were killed in a demonstration in Kepot. She'd been staying with us while they were gone, and she just kept on staying."

"No surviving family?" asked Jasen, searching for a sympathy he ought to feel but did not.

"Who knows? We didn't dare try to find her father's family in Semlona, not with him on record as a Borderal. It could have made trouble for them or for Rayna, and we never knew her mother's people. But we were glad to have her." She looked across to Leric. "And to have this one, too, when his father followed his mother to the gods."

Leric squeezed her hand.

The conversation flagged, and they passed around the bread.

"Leric," said Jasen, "was—is Sherayna one of your lovers?" He blushed to ask it. It was a perfectly acceptable question on Perdita, but Jasen was still not comfortable with such open talk.

"No," said Leric, suppressing a smile. Illia smiled too.

Ferrets, thought Jasen. *I stepped in it after all.*

But Sylan just said, "What's the joke?"

"I gave up on Sherayna early on," said Leric. "She was out in the garden, asleep in the sun—very lovely. So I kissed her."

"What did she do?" asked Sylan.

"She hit him," said Illia, "and told him if he ever did it again she'd knock his teeth out."

CHAPTER 32

Sherayna floated between sleeping and waking. The words tumbled on her ears like prayers from the gods. She had said things she shouldn't have, betrayed people and places—not finally out of fear but because she could not control what she said in her sleep. Now and then, when she thought of it, her heart lost its balance. But she hadn't spoken of home: that she knew—one never spoke of home to them.

They didn't bother to take her from her cell anymore, the warchief and the lieutenant who almost always came with him.

She was lying on her side, seeing his elbow through half-closed eyes. His voice was a loaded spring. "How did you sabotage the Leddie ship? What machines did you use? How much of a hypocrite are you? Where did you get the machines?"

Machines, she thought. *Leddie machines. Hypocrite machines.*

"Didn't," she said.

"Come, Sherayna, it didn't crash on its own any more than Nevan's ship did."

Come, Sherayna. Not on your own. Who was calling? *Crashed. Who are you who've crashed here? Not the gods from beyond.*

The lieutenant's voice, firm, not unlike Illia's: "Ethan, she doesn't know what you're saying."

"She knows well enough."

Well enough. It will be well . . . enough, when spring is in the meadows again, like when we were children, when the grass itself spoke. The grass gods. And we wove walnut branches.

The lieutenant: ". . . don't know what you think you're trying to achieve, but you're losing her day by day."

Die and achieve, day by day, is how gods live, how insects and flowers live.

The warchief rose, his arm gone from her sight. "Outside, Lieutenant." Their feet retreated, and the lock clicked behind them.

≈•≈

In the hallway, as Torna expected, Ethan spun on her. "How dare you question my authority in front of a prisoner?"

"I dare because . . ." She took a breath. "I apologize. I'm rightly reprimanded. But Ethan, I am speaking as a friend, not an officer. We've worked together for years. I know you to be a man of intelligence and restraint." She wanted to take his hand but didn't dare. "But I don't know you anymore."

"You've been hounding me."

"It concerns me to leave you alone with her."

It seemed he almost laughed. "What do you think I'll do?"

"I don't know. I don't think you know, Ethan. What do you want her to tell you?"

"How her people made those ships crash."

"I don't think she knows."

"She knows, the little tech-using anti-tech. She's ashamed to be caught in her own hypocrisy."

"And you want to catch her, in a lie?"

"By Fennoc, Torna, I do," he said. "I'd like to hear her try to justify herself."

Torna's eyes widened. "You want a justification. You want to know why."

He took a step toward her, eyes burning. "The why is everything, the only thing. If we have that answer, we can answer anything they say."

"If we have that answer, we can debate again."

"We need to be right, Torna. Don't you see? It isn't enough just to be in power."

Torna wondered how many of his words were the truth. How much was he lying to himself? She put a hand on his arm. "Listen to me. Let me feed her up, get her stronger. Then let's see what we can find." *And you will have some days away from her to calm yourself.*

≈•≈

To Torna's eyes, Sherayna still looked groggy, but at least she was conscious and sitting up in her cell. Was a half month of rest and decent food enough to restore her mind as well? Ethan and Torna sat on their knees before her, only a little higher than she was as she leaned against the wall.

Ethan asked her evenly, "How did you make those ships crash?"

"We didn't do it."

"Then who did?" asked Torna. "Theoretically, Sherayna. Who else would want to? Who could? How could they?"

Sherayna's eyes darted between them. She squared her shoulders, as if making a decision. "I don't know who. But I do know how. It's the shield. But it isn't our shield, no?"

"Shield? What shield?" demanded Ethan.

"The shield around the planet. You know it."

"Shield around the planet? Talk sense."

"Sylan told our people. You've always known we had her. She told us."

Torna glanced at Ethan. He was looking past Sherayna, lost in thought.

He shook his head. "There's no shield around the planet. We'd have picked up its emissions."

Sherayna looked away, blank and sleepy. "Sylan said . . . she explained it once. Um . . . the shield doesn't stop signals coming in, only going out. But . . . how did it hurt the ships then? The wiring? I think it's different when it contacts physical wiring, or . . ." She trailed off.

"A shield to keep us from contacting other worlds? A remarkable rebel invention. You should really consider serving on one of Cudonond's research committees." His sarcasm sounded strained.

"Not ours. We don't know how long it's been there or where. We first heard of it when Sylan told us."

Ethan barked a laugh. "Oh no, you have nothing to do with it, do you? It would just happen to isolate Perdita in precisely the way you've always wanted."

Sherayna shook her head.

"Warchief," said Torna. "If I may request a private word with you?"

Ethan glanced at her for a second, then, turned back to Sherayna. "Don't imagine this is over."

≈•≈

The implications are towering. Ethan felt like he'd been marching down a well-known street only to look down and see nothing but air beneath him. *She's lying. She must be*—but if she weren't . . .

Torna closed the door behind Sherayna. "If she's right about that shield, it would explain the *Outbound.*"

It seemed to Ethan he'd already had that thought—and at the same time, it hit him like divine revelation. His heart stopped; his mind stopped. His life stopped.

Torna continued, "If the rebels didn't destroy the *Outbound* . . ."

"No, it can't be. Someone would have picked up the emissions from such a shield."

Torna shrugged. "If it was kept a secret?"

"No. I know the Cudonond scientists. Jessec knew them, was one of them. They wouldn't keep such a secret."

"I don't understand it. But, tell me, how could the rebels possibly have done it? The *Outbound*, yes, they could have somehow gotten to it on the ground. But making two alien ships crash, before our people had even spotted them, leaving no energy trace behind from their weapons? How could they have done it?"

≈•≈

Sherayna lay in her cell, feeling sick. It had been a gamble—to find out if the City had indeed known about the shield all the time. . . . But they hadn't. At least, she now believed the warchief didn't.

A gamble to prove their innocence of the *Outbound* and the Leddie ship. A wager that their exoneration would do more good than the harm of the City's finding the shield.

But what if she had just given the City the key to space?

She had betrayed Micor.

She gasped without tears, her throat thick.

And had she done it for the good of the planet? Or to protect herself by appeasing the warchief?

≈•≈

If there is a shield, Ethan thought, *if there is a shield that's been keeping us out of space all these years* . . .

Torna seemed to believe Sherayna that the shield was some old Sama thing no one knew of till the West-of-Nows crashed. But that was crazy. It couldn't just have maintained itself for two thousand years. If it existed, then someone was running it, someone who wanted desperately to keep Perdita out of space. *And if the rebels have been using this shield all along . . . erring gods, they control the planet.*

Ethan paced the floor of his room, unable to sit still. If that shield was there, the pro-techs must get control of it.

It was deep night, twentieth hour, when he went back to Sherayna's cell. He ordered the night guard to let him in and come back in an hour to let him out again.

Sherayna was asleep, heedless of the white lights that glared on her. Ethan blinked in the sudden brightness, saw her stir as the door thudded behind them. He seized her by the arm.

"Get up." He wrenched her upright. She started at his touch and shrank away. That at least was gratifying. "Up." He pulled her to her feet, her back pressed to the wall.

He stepped back a pace. "This shield, assuming it exists, where is it? Where's its generator?"

She stared dumbly.

"I know you know. Now tell me where."

She shook her head, eyes wide as a rabbit's.

He grasped her jaw hard, letting his hand push into her neck. "I do not have time to play games. Tell me where."

"Don't know. Sylan didn't know. She knows the shield crashed her ship. It's around the planet." She sucked a breath. "She didn't know where it came from."

He pressed his hand harder into her throat. "But that's a lie, Sherayna. Your people know. You've always known. How else has it been maintained all these years? Eh?"

She closed her eyes.

He pulled her out into the middle of the floor. She gasped when he released her and weaved on her feet.

"Admit it." He circled her. "You've been using it all these years. It's obvious."

"Maybe it's automatic. I don't know."

"Automatically maintained so perfectly that even the Space Program couldn't register its existence. After two thousand years? Sherayna, even you can do better than that."

She drew another hoarse breath. "Maybe someone else is doing it. Maybe people who hate the City, not *my* people." Was that a shade of pride in her voice? "I only know of it from Sylan."

"If that's the game you want to play—all right, Sylan, where is she?"

"We don't stay in one place." Her knees shook, but her voice was getting stronger. "We know it's death to stay in one place. I don't know where she is now."

"But you could find her."

Silence.

"You have to know how to contact your people, no? Stationary or not?"

Still she was silent.

He shoved her back against the wall. She coughed and let herself sink to the floor. Did she imagine she could win this? He wanted to strike her.

"You will help me, you know," he said, standing over her. "One way or another, you will."

Behind them, the door creaked.

"I said to come back in an hour," barked Ethan and turned to see Torna.

"Warchief, may I see you for a moment?"

For an instant, Ethan wanted to strike her too. How dare she be here? Here! Now. But his indignation was ridiculous. She was on his side. She was one of his officers. He let her lead him to the hall.

"What are you doing here?" he said.

"I might ask you the same thing, Ethan. It's the middle of the night, and this prisoner isn't scheduled for interrogation."

"The guard. She woke you, didn't she?" He laughed. "I'll see her demoted to janitor."

"She acted appropriately, Ethan. Your presence here is outside protocol."

Ethan stared at her. "What do you want?"

"I want you to get some sleep—and take a few days off."

"You don't command me, Lieutenant."

"No. But I could file a report on your undocumented presence here this night."

Ethan shook his head in disbelief. "Why are you standing against me, Torna? Don't you want to know the truth?"

"Yes. But you know as well as I do, interrogation under excessive duress does not produce reliable information. It only hurts the gods. We must act sensibly, cautiously, as you acted to capture Sherayna."

Ethan passed a hand over his face. "I don't know. Nothing seems right."

≈•≈

Sherayna fingered her bruised throat. Everything she'd done had been wrong. She'd walked into a trap, betrayed Micor, and now the warchief would not let her rest until she'd betrayed him completely, revealing his knowledge of the shield, his work with the Borderals, his stronghold in Oja. And then, the warchief would make her give him Sylan, give him Meena, give him everything.

Tears rolled down her nose. Her sore body contracted with sobs. If only she could find the strength to die before breaking. That at least would not be a mistake.

≈•≈

Ethan took the next six days off. At the end of them he still did not know what to believe. Could he trust anything he heard from Sherayna? What if this shield were nothing more than a ploy to distract him from the rebels' real means of destroying those ships? It was like walking through a house of distorting mirrors.

He sat in his room and yawned. It was late, at least twenty-first hour—two hours until the new day, an Early-Spring day. Last month, Ethan had turned forty-five, but he couldn't recall turning forty. He made himself open his eyes in the chill predawn of Oja, squinted at the blue-black window square of sky, switched on the lamp, and drafted a request for a transfer. He could no longer function here. But he couldn't let the shield rest.

The next day, he relayed Sherayna's account to Lashen. If Lashen was a pawn of the rebels, then he knew of it anyway. And if he was not, he needed to. Lashen merely acknowledged receipt of the report.

Ethan's transfer came through in seven days: he'd go to Cudonond, as he'd requested, with a dozen days of leave first. He didn't want the leave, but he had it, so he went home. The transfer brought relief, but not release. He was as tired as a runner far behind in a race, who is told that he can stop now; another's won.

His Mesa house was the same as ever, the yellow roof tile cracking and the azaleas unpruned. The grass, at least, was decently cut, bright with short red bow-ax flowers, and the house had been repainted as his tenant, Niric, had promised—the exact same shade of beige, it seemed, but the old weather stains were covered over. As soon as he got home, Niric told him that the roof of the work shed was leaking again, just enough to keep the room damp amid the spring fog and showers.

Niric and the man who was living with him invited Ethan to take his childhood room. But Ethan always slept in his father's work shed. And he was tired. He'd rather spend the night alone and damp than making conversation with Niric and his lover. So, as soon was the sun was gone, he bundled himself on his mattress in the creaking, musty shed and slept.

But Sherayna stalked his dreams. He could see her crouching in the corner of her cell, her blue eyes boring into his. "I've done nothing." She droned it over and over: "I've done nothing. I've done nothing," till he thought he would go mad. He screamed for her to be silent, but she droned on. He bent over her and seized her neck in his hands, crushing her soft throat till the blood vessels burst red in her eyes, while still she repeated, "I've done nothing. Ethan, it was the shield, not me."

He awoke in a cold sweat, certain for a moment that his dream had been true.

Dear gods, what did I do to her?

Slowly, reality returned. He hadn't killed her. He'd done nothing that wasn't justified. Best now to forget her.

He stayed in Mesa a few days, patching a barely leaking roof and resenting the waste of time when he might have been searching for answers. He wrote to Nevan and casually embedded the question:

Have you ever considered the possibility that Perdita might be electromagnetically shielded from outer space?

Nevan wrote back:

That's an interesting idea. The Samas used such shields at the time of the War. Beyond that, I really can't comment.

That was comment enough. Nevan was naturally loquacious and pedantic. Offered Ethan's insight into his own imprisonment on Perdita, given even a clue as to a possible escape, he would have chattered about it for pages. Unless he already knew.

Did that mean the Zerins knew too? It would fit with Laynia's rebel leanings. Or perhaps Nevan didn't want to tell anyone. Perhaps he was searching for the shield himself, hoping to reach it before its controllers could prevent him from shutting it off. Ethan longed to question Nevan in person, but he had no pass to go to Zerin and no hope of getting one.

He was locked in with his own thoughts. And if Laynia did control Zerin and the king and Lashen, if a shield did imprison the planet like an electrified cage, had they then lost the war to the rebels already, no matter how many battles they won?

CHAPTER 33

By Mid-Spring, Ethan was in Cudonond as fourth in command of security for the Space Project. Had the quest to reach space not been emblazoned on his heart, the job would have been a joke. Since his father's death, project funding had dwindled. Investors were unwilling to gamble against the ever-present threat of rebel sabotage. So the project center stood all but forgotten some twenty measures west of the metropolis of Cudonond. Only three departments still operated: an air-travel division, streamlining jumper tech; the astronomical observatory, which saw little in the summer through the Keerina haze; and the launch simulator, still pretending to send ships into space and trying to track down what had gone wrong with the *Outbound*, after twenty-eight years.

Professor Kesoran worked with the simulator. He'd been Jessec's teacher and friend, and Ethan's as well. Now past 150 years old, the tiny, portly man was losing his eyesight, despite two surgeries. He and Ethan fell into their old friendship easily and had lunch together every sixth day, in the dining tower that overlooked the bog lands.

"Have they changed, the bogs out there?" Kesoran asked one day.

"The same as ever—swampy, brown, fallow—good for nothing but laying down a spaceport."

Kesoran laughed. "Not in our century. And the more time passes, the less gets done. There was nothing wrong with Im Jessec's ship. After all these years, all we can say is that it should not have gone down."

This was the moment. Ethan told Kesoran what Sherayna had said about the shield.

Kesoran was silent a long time. "You'd think our satellites would pick up some distortion from that kind of shield."

"But if it were a piece of old Sama tech . . ."

"I suppose it might be sophisticated enough to fool our sensors . . . if people who knew what they were doing were keeping it calibrated. After all, hiding signals is what those shields were invented for. But who on Perdita could have maintained that level of skill all these years, throughout all the tech purges?"

"All I know is that such people should be our allies. Why pretend to be our enemies and hide such marvels of tech from us?"

≈•≈

The professor got permission from Senarna to place a moratorium on the program's simulator experiments and use the budget to launch a satellite instead. Some satellites had been up in low orbit for centuries. This one would be placed in a higher orbit. By summer, the satellite was ready.

It exploded—at the same altitude as the *Outbound*.

It was thousands of measures south of Cudonond when it went, and Ethan was glad there was no chance he would see it—one more blaze, like a funeral cracker in the night. This time, he saw a surge on the telemetric readout and a radar blip fading into nothing. *This is not the* Outbound. *No one is dead. There is nothing to relive here.* He closed his eyes and leaned against Kesoran's console, his knees like jelly.

"She was telling the truth," he murmured. "It's there. All these years, it's been there."

≈•≈

Ethan relayed the findings to Lashen and received the usual acknowledgment of receipt. Days crept by. He longed to report directly to the king, but the chain of command required that he report only to the warmaster, and breaking that protocol would challenge Lashen's competence. Perhaps he was wrong about Lashen's complicity, and even if he wasn't, he would gain nothing by writing the king but alerting the queen. He was more and more certain that she knew about the shield. The way she had come to him after the *Outbound* to demand an end to the Space Project: she'd been maneuvering to forestall any more evidence of the shield.

Hoping to find his doubts about Lashen unwarranted, Ethan requested several times that the warmaster inform him of Senarna's strategy. His requests were answered with: "No information at this time."

A month after the satellite's explosion, he took a brief personal leave and went to Senarna. His plan was to skulk around the warmaster's haunts until he caught him. Once, the two of them had walked these byways together, when Ethan was newly promoted to warchief and Lashen, with customary zest, had shown the provincial Veshnan the marvels of the capital. Once, Ethan had been exhilarated wandering the teeming streets in the lamplight, fountains shouting in his ears.

He stalked those streets now, watching the people parade by in bright coats, dark-cast by the lamps—like shapes underwater. Gods, it was cold. Now almost autumn, it passed freezing just after midnight. Ethan walked, waited, shivered, asked discreet questions—and trudged back each morning to his hotel to sleep with the sun in his window. Every night, he resumed his vigil, the music from emporium concerts sailing down the sidewalks to blend with the fountains, the laughter of teenagers staging dances at wine shops, altercations at gambling halls.

On his fourth night, Ethan intercepted Lashen coming out of a dining tower. Ethan had waited less than half an hour when the warmaster slipped out his accustomed side door.

"Warmaster. Forgive me for approaching you in this unofficial capacity, but I'm troubled over the situation concerning that information I relayed more than a month ago."

Lashen turned and said, "Good evening, Ethan. And exactly what troubles you?"

"I want to know why I've been cut out of the circle."

Lashen clapped him on the shoulder. "But you haven't been, Ethan."

"I assure you, sir, I've been given no information whatsoever on the subject."

"You misunderstand me, Ethan. You haven't been cut out because you were never in. Oh, don't look so icy. We're all impressed with your work, of course. But frankly, in this, you weren't considered quite the right man for the job."

"But my familiarity with the Space Project—"

"Exactly. You're too close." Lashen smiled. "Now, you trust the regime, no? You believe that we're doing all we can in the most prudent way possible?"

"Candidly, Warmaster? I think if you were doing all you could, you'd be utilizing my training and my desire to be of service."

"Shall I note that for the record?"

"As you wish, sir."

Lashen nodded. "Last I heard, you'd called in a leave. Very sensible: your last one was too short. If you take my advice, you'll go back to Mesa and track down old lovers, not spend your time scurrying through Senarna in the middle of the night, ambushing your superiors."

Ethan returned to Cudonond the next day.

≈•≈

Ethan's fatalism grew as funding for the program was gutted. News of the satellite's explosion, yet another *Outbound*-like debacle, frightened the Keerina investors—or so ran the official line. But that scarcely mattered now. There was nothing to do but analyze the explosion, and the equipment for such analysis had already been in place for two decades.

One evening in Mid-Autumn, Kesoran called Ethan to see him. "It seems she was right, the rebel woman." He sat heavily on his desk cushion and rifled through his graphs. "Look here, within half a meter of the altitude where the *Outbound* exploded, the satellite experienced a similar power surge without traceable internal cause." Ethan sat on the floor beside him and picked up the graph. "In both instances, signals were skewed, as if the circuits had been miswired. The pattern could reflect extensive, system-wide sabotage, as we'd assumed. But it could also reflect a scrambling field."

"Why wouldn't shielding like that affect our perceptions of light from space?"

"Judging from the few texts the anti-techs managed not to destroy, I'd say there's a descrambling matrix at the lower margin of the shield. It could resequence code, but it might not repair physical damage already inflicted."

"Such a shield would be a fearsome weapon for the rebels. And they would make use of it. Anti-tech or not, mark my words, they would—and they do."

≈•≈

He sent the professor's findings to Lashen. As he expected, nothing was done. Ethan went on with security duties, thorns pricking his flesh all the while, driving him toward action when no action could be taken. Watching Kesoran work no longer interested him. And worse, it dawned on him that it had always been this way. His whole life, at least since his father's death, had been marked by fleeting moments of peace, which melted into sleepless energy—which itself burned out into numb fatigue. And then he would dream about the dark lake.

Lashen was guilty. And the warmaster controlled the army, and the queen controlled both Zerin and the king: Zerin, the home of the mind readers, and the king, who had the final word on the flow of money into research and development. All of them served the rebels.

He dreamed again of Sherayna, her face black and blue as if badly beaten, her eyes burning in the swollen mask of her face. "You cannot hurt me," he heard her say. "I own this planet."

He was on watch one Late-Autumn night when the air seemed to hum with ice flakes and the damp rolled off the bogs. Passing the statue of Leva, a pretty plaster woman arcing a circle with a compass, it struck him that he'd heard much of her worship lately. A new prayer had been circulating. How did it go?

> *Dear Leva, when we make machines*
> *To bring to dawn a brighter day*
> *Let us not only make machines*
> *But make them in a better way.*

But that was a Zerin prayer, a rebel ploy. Make machines in a better way—the old excuse for making nothing. No way could ever be good enough, safe enough for them. They did own the planet. But they did not own Leva, not the goddess in his heart.

He fixed his eyes on her and prayed an old prayer of his father's: *Leva, lover of science, may you be thinking of the program.*

But the Space Program was not the problem now. Not when his life was thus disunited.

I cannot overcome myself.

He would pray for help, he decided. An admission of desperation, for to speak to the gods directly was a gamble at best. They might hear and take pity on you. More likely, you'd simply come closer to their world, make yourself a target for the acting out of their passions. He crossed the empty lot from the statue of Leva to the big Nama-Sor and stood before it. In his mind, his patron had always been Fennoc: the god of invention and duty. But he did not speak to Fennoc now.

Brother and Sister, I dream of your reunion. I hope for it with all my love. And if you are together now, hear me and help me. Light for me the way to action and to patience.

As the days passed, his prayer was not answered. He hadn't expected it to be. He was far from certain the gods existed and wondered sometimes at his own instinct to think as if they did.

He began to shun his lunches with Kesoran, because he loved the old man and was ashamed to deceive him with forced smiles. He stayed away to keep from worrying his friend, but his absence worried him. And when Kesoran asked him gently one day, "What is this spirit of Tep living through you?" Ethan knew the time had come for him to go.

And there was only one place to go. He needed evidence to implicate Lashen in the circle of rebels. And he had a rebel, a commander, who might lead him straight to the warmaster or the guilt of Zerin. She was still the key. In Mid-Winter, a year after his departure, he was granted his transfer back to Oja.

CHAPTER 34

When Sherayna had first been taken prisoner, she might as well have been flung into the fires of Soruc the Wrathful. At times, she had seen the very flames leap up, sucking her out of the human world to the hell of the gods. She had wondered if she was dying. She had ceased to be conscious of the venomous glare of the warchief long before he had actually gone away.

It was in that time that the words had begun to speak to her, beckoning, comforting, talking of the meadows of home. At first, she had not understood what she was hearing. But little by little, the truth blossomed. The City searched for the gods in the sky, as if space were a divine doorstep. But the doorstep to divinity was everywhere, and everything was managed by its own spirit. The gods were all around. Maybe not the great named gods, but the spirits of trees and grasses, wheat spirit and dew spirit, spirit of the magpie. And the spirit of her white cell walls and this stale air: imprisoned, mourning spirits. Her kindred.

The voices passed away when her captors began to feed her properly, but the feeling remained, the stronger the more they left her alone, which was often after the warchief disappeared. That was after she'd told him about the shield, hoping to bring peace at last, exoneration from the *Outbound.* Or to hurt Micor? Or because she wanted the warchief to know. . . .

No matter. It had been the greatest mistake of her life. But after a while, she couldn't care. She lived moment to moment, like the gods.

Everything we do reaches out to the gods. Every word and gesture.

She wanted to help her cell, to restore to it all that was good in the world. She wanted to give it leaves so that it could feel the forest. For a time, she drew leaves on the walls, in blood from her knuckles, which she bit open. The stout, gray woman, the lieutenant, thought that was crazy—Sherayna could see it in her eyes. She brought Sherayna paper and pens. Sherayna scarcely used the paper, but the pens let her draw better leaves on the walls: a victory for Sherayna, not so crazy after all. She drew till her walls were tapestried with vines.

156

Sometimes she remembered the outside. Had her family given her up for dead?

The fires of Soruc seemed far away then, as when the cool robes of Nama cloak his shining shoulders—or so an old song said, or something like that. She chafed, dreamed of freedom, longed for judgment, even though that judgment must bring death. She'd given the lieutenant ten times enough information to convict her of capital anti-tech treason. And even execution would be better than day after day of sitting.

I am not in the fires of Soruc. I am in the Ice of Tep. The dead do go there sometimes. Then why should I long for death if death is nothing more than this endless immobility? I remember the tale of Fennoc's being frozen in his brother-self's ice. Eons he languished there before the tears of Feeshap, his wife-self, melted the ice, and she drew him out.

But when he was there, his mind slept too, imprisoned as his body. Yet my mind wakes. I am not in the Ice of Tep, for my mind is not in his ice. And if I die, I cannot go there, for I'm nearer to the living gods. My body falters, but my spirit soars. My eyes see the ice, but my mind sees the fields of Meena and these mountains of Oja whose spirit I breathe. From these gods of Perdita, I'm never widely sundered. To them I owe my homage.

Most times, she still felt nearer the ice than the Ojas. Yet patience spread through her like the morning. To be parted from her family now was not so heart destroying. *For they are still closer than Tep.* It was then that she took up the paper the lieutenant had given. This time she did not sketch but wrote prayers. One prayer she liked best:

> *The small gods make the world live.*
> *The great gods light the heavens*
> *And twirl star fires into planets,*
> *But the small gods wash the waters clean*
> *And breathe the breathing waves.*
> *When the ocean lies back into the sun*
> *And mirrors back the sun's face*
> *A thousand times brighter than the scales of   a*
>   *fish,*
> *Which god's light is shining then?*

Soon after she'd written that small verse, she awakened to the warchief glowering over her, as if pondering where to drive the knife. He reached for the door when she opened her eyes.

"Don't get too comfortable, Commander," he said and left her alone again.

≈•≈

When Ethan saw Sherayna, he was relieved at first. She was pale and weak but sane; Torna had cared for her well. Too well. *She's smug,* he thought, *like a spoiled child*—and the fear in her face when he woke her was far too slow in coming, as if she understood that his power was an illusion.

In that instant, his relief dissolved into fury.

He strode into Torna's office straight from his first sight of Sherayna. "You've coddled her, Lieutenant. I'll wager she's told you not a thing since I left."

Torna remained respectfully seated on her cushion behind her desk. "Since you left, sir, she's given us eighteen sworn statements of her reasons for joining the rebels and confessed to a role in twelve assaults over the last ten years."

"And information we can use? How many arrests has she given us?"

"None."

"In a year, Torna? Even in the brief time I had her, I got four!" He glared at her, and she gazed back.

After a moment, she said, "She's confessed her guilt. How much longer do we question her before she's sent to execution?"

"I have only one more question for her." He told Torna all he suspected of the complicity of the warmaster and Zerin. Torna listened and, when he was finished, turned away.

At length, she said, "She won't answer that."

"She will. Given time, she'll answer anything. That's human nature."

"Just time? Ethan, I have another idea. One I've wanted to present to you for some while."

"And what is that?"

"We let her go."

Ethan laughed and fell onto a cushion before her.

"Listen to me," she persisted. "Holding her is not good for us. Imprisonment is by its nature cruel, all the more so when the jailer and jailed are in close contact for too long. Cruelty, Ethan, hurts the gods."

"We need to irradiate this rebel cancer, Torna. Some cruelty in exchange for the health of our civilization. That must help the gods more in the long run."

"If we achieve it. But there's more to it than that. She was high up. If she were freed by her comrades, it wouldn't be long before she'd end up somewhere suitable for a rebel commander: a training ground, a meeting place, a haven where she can recover. If we tracked her, we'd track many of them—follow those and track down others. We could gut a huge section of rebel hierarchy—"

"I tracked her for five years with no such luck."

"We can do it," she assured him. "I have a plan."

CHAPTER 35

Some days after the warchief's return, they stopped feeding Sherayna again. She had been used to eating so little that the hunger pangs passed quickly, leaving only lassitude. She lay on the floor in the white lamplight, oddly comfortable, thinking sometimes: *Well, this is a novel form of execution.* And sometimes: *If death is like this, then it won't be so bad.* And sometimes she thought of her childhood, like a remembrance of a decades-old dream that had lost its potency. Most often she thought about nothing.

Two footmen barged into her room, pulled her up, and made her walk out into the hallway and up ringing metal stairs. Her body felt disconnected from her feet; her legs cried out to stop, but her mind stayed fuzzy, half-asleep. They pushed her through a heavy swinging door. She blinked, blinded by sunlight blazing low over a concrete lot—and mountains: brilliant blue in the distance. The scent of spring conifers assailed her. The air raked itself over her body, burning. Her legs collapsed beneath her, and her vision went black.

When she awoke, she was tossing in the back of a transport, and she had the sensation she had been there before.

If I'm going to die, I want to see the world again. She had not been bound. She crawled around the compartment, searching for any crack in the sides that would offer a view to the outside. There was nothing. *But I will see it. When they take me out, I will see it.* She leaned into a corner and waited.

She must have been asleep again when a thunderclap struck and she found herself flung into the front wall, the air knocked out of her lungs. The transport creaked and roared but stood still. She could hear hollering and shots fired. Gasping, she sat up, listened to an almost unheard-of cry: a surrender. Who was surrendering? Quieter voices. The back of the transport opened. It was almost as dark without as within—a silhouetted figure loomed against an overcast night.

"Sherayna?" said a man's voice, a voice she knew but couldn't place.

"Yes?" she croaked.

The man came nearer, and she felt herself lifted in arms like rock. Her back burned where it had hit the transport's wall. She shivered.

"The gods are loving," he said. "We'd given up hope of finding you."

"Olloan. I think it's you."

"You think rightly." They were moving among dark figures through the forest. He laid her down on something soft—in a tent?

"How long?" she asked sleepily.

"Just over a year. It's the eighth of Early-Spring."

"Where are we?"

"Western Oja. They were taking you to Senarna for trial. Callin unfiled their plans, by the love of the gods."

"I want to see the cedars," Sherayna murmured and sank into sleep.

≈•≈

The next three days were the happiest of her life. While three of Olloan's people disposed of the City footmen, she, Olloan, and his two remaining companions traveled through the forest southwest toward the river.

Olloan told her, "We've planned a diversionary attack in the foothills. While the City's occupied, our people will meet us at the river and take you down to Meena."

That sounded fine. She trusted Olloan. All day, he carried her like a child, her featherweight nothing to his sverra strength. She looked at the trees, always slender skeletons in Oja, gray needles too sparse to cover twigs knotted like old women's fingers. The ground was gray dust, the air dry— colors soft, quiet. Iltan was quiet, but it teemed with life, hidden, watching. Life in Oja seemed rather to sleep: a rare birdcall, a shaft of sun in the midst of the bony branches.

It was cold in the foothills. The prison, if nothing else, had been warm. On the third evening, Sherayna came down with a fever. She shivered, burned, ached, and took no more joy in the forest. She was dimly aware of being handed into a riverboat in the dead of night, of rocking on the waves for a long time.

≈•≈

She woke up in a room she knew, a small walnut-wooded room filled with old furniture, a shelf overflowing with dust-caked books, toys. Her childhood room. The sun spilled in silver through the dusty windows. It seemed she had been dreaming.

How old am I really? Am I still in school?

But she distinctly remembered Olloan saying that it was Early-Spring in 2031, or 2041 Standard, Sylan would correct her. That made her forty. *How did I ever survive to be forty?* She was fully awake now and knew where she'd been. She lay still for some time, until Illia came in.

Illia's hair had grown longer. Illia was in tears. She sat on the edge of the bed and sobbed. It was intensely unpleasant, yet Sherayna believed that she might have cried too if she hadn't been so tired. As it was, she could only offer soothing words that she couldn't remember later.

But she remembered Illia saying, "I was sure . . . I was sure I'd lost you. I was sure this was the last time. And Karmeena passed the mind-reader's test for going to Zerin, she already has her pass. She's going to go off to Zerin at the end of the school year. Who knows what will happen to her, even if she does take Jasen as her companion? I kept wondering if anything was left."

Sherayna remembered something about Jasen training Karmeena for Zerin, but she couldn't concentrate on it. Instead, she held Illia's hands. "It's strange, Lia. I feel like I've never been away. I don't feel like I've been robbed of a year but more like I've gained something." All at once, the white-lit cell was close, as if it lay just behind her eyes. "I learned . . . I've met the gods, and I know why we're fighting as I never knew before."

Illia wiped her nose on her sleeve. "Why is it, then?"

"Because Perdita is our sister, and with every spirit of every stream or rock or tree that dies a part of our soul dies—but if they live, we live forever."

≈•≈

Leric was on assignment, but they spared him a few days to come home to see her. He arrived on her second day awake in Meena, looking grave—how eerie to see Leric look grave.

He sat by her bed and kissed her cheek. "Now, hit me."

Sherayna tapped him on the chin.

He smiled sadly. "I didn't think we would get you back. I never said so, but Kara knew. Since Jasen and Sylan have been teaching her to mind-read, I've started to think she knows everything."

Sherayna tried to think of something comforting to say. "I'm glad to come home, to have a home to come home to. That's why the gods are insane, Leric. Their places, their people are forever shifting, and the gods never know if they'll find those places where they left them. It would drive anyone insane, no?"

Leric took her hand. He seemed to be studying her fingers. "And our people shift and melt in tandem. We have you back, and we'll lose Kara. I pray Micor will be watching after her and Jasen while they're on that island with that secret shield. We told Kara about the shield, Rayna. We had to."

The shield! Paralysis spread through Sherayna's limbs. *Powerless. I betrayed him, and I'm powerless to take it back.*

"What is it?" Leric frowned. He laid a hand upon her forehead as if afraid her fever had worsened.

"Oh, Leric," she whispered. "I remember. Oh, Leric, I've done a terrible thing."

"What did you do?"

"I told them. I told them about the shield. I told myself I did it on account of the *Outbound,* but the City knows. I may have just opened Perdita up to space."

He was breathing hard as the seconds stretched on. "Did you tell them where? Did you tell them it was on Zerin?"

She struggled to remember—those days were a long stretch of vertigo. "No. No, I didn't say where. No, because I told him I knew about the shield from Sylan, and Sylan had no way of knowing where the generator was."

"All right," Leric said and then repeated, "all right. We'll tell Micor. Maybe . . . maybe it won't be that bad. Maybe even with the shield down, we could knock out the old Sama superlight communications, so the City couldn't contact other worlds. That would buy us time."

"I should have died there."

"No."

"Micor should kill me for a traitor."

"You were under duress."

She scarcely heard. She was gazing at the shelf by her bed: old books, old toys—childhood in dust. "I betrayed Micor because I didn't trust him. I didn't trust him for not trusting me. And he was right. I'll never doubt him again."

CHAPTER 36

Torna ought to have been pleased. The plan flew smooth as a jumper in a still sky. They drugged the last meal they gave to Sherayna, and while she was unconscious, a medic placed a transmitter under the skin of her scalp, covered by her hair so that she'd never notice the scar. Then, for three days, they didn't feed her. The weaker she was, the slower her rescuers would be able to move, the easier to follow their progress.

The transmitter had an operating life of less than four months. But while it functioned, it made Sherayna easy to track. The tactic was illegal, an infringement on the freedom of bodily integrity.

A good law, Torna reflected. *Who would want a regime that could monitor its citizens' every move? But, as with all laws, there are circumstances under which the higher good prevails. To strike the power base of the rebels: isn't that the higher good?*

The medic had been shown a falsified letter of legal dispensation. Ethan and Torna would do the tracking alone, and when the rebels were discovered, Senarna would almost certainly be too pragmatic to question the methods employed. Yet she was troubled.

≈•≈

When the signal halted in Meena, Torna suspected that Sherayna was merely resting before moving on to some rebel slum such as Vorna. But the blue pointer blinked on the monitor, motionless day after day. Torna and Ethan checked into an inn at Veshna Harbor and waited—ten days, fifteen. . . .

"Do you suppose she's died?" asked Torna one night.

"No."

"You sound very certain."

He was silent for a time. "Fennoc speaks to me."

"Fennoc does not always speak the truth."

Ethan half-laughed, staring into the hearth fire. "Nevan writes that the Samas didn't consider prophecy to derive from Fennoc. They thought him too bounded by reason to see beyond it to the future-truth."

"But how can one see truly if not with the eyes of reason?"

Ethan glanced at her with a rare smile in his eyes. "That, Nevan writes, is a Kiri notion—that truth best derives from empirical logic. Our devotion to Fennoc, he writes, is one of the legacies of our Kiri ancestors whose religion is based on physical observation rather than intuitive understanding."

"Nature worship? Worship of the visible world." Torna pondered. "Worship of its physical laws, of the order of things—that is like Fennoc. He may be right."

"I think he's wrong."

"What do you think, then?"

"I think if we trust in Fennoc more than the Samas did, it's because he's the patron of scientific discovery. And as vital as that was to the Sama Empire, it's more important to us. It defines our long struggle against these anti-techs."

Torna sighed. "So why has Sherayna stopped in Meena?"

"I think it's time we find out."

≈•≈

In those tense summer days, Ethan remembered a folk tale. A man once had two brothers. When one brother was murdered, the man asked a seer who had done the deed. The seer said, "Why do you want to know?" The man answered, "So I may avenge my brother by killing his killer." The seer said, "Your brother was killed by your other brother." So the man had to go home and kill his other brother, and then he had no brothers.

I am that man. And Ethan wasn't sure what he hated more: the idea of treason in Meena or the accounting he would have to demand for it.

He went back to Oja with Torna and ordered his agents into Meena. Five spies, all Semlonans with a background in farming—perfectly plausible additions to the profitable agricultural backwater.

For two months, the agents found nothing to suggest that Meena was anything but the comfortable, close-knit community it appeared to be, peopled by farmers more concerned with harvest yields than politics. The agents did not find Sherayna, though until its failure, her transmitter signal continued to blink just outside the city center of Meena. But, of course, as a high-profile outlaw, she'd naturally keep a low profile.

Then toward the end of Early-Summer, the regular patrols arrested a Meenan man for distributing anti-tech literature, an offense as common as breathing in Veshna. The man was to be incarcerated in Mesa, pending trial. But he never arrived in Mesa, though a record appeared in Oja City stating that he had. A back check into arrests in Meena revealed that fewer than 70 percent of the individuals arrested in the past twenty years had ever reached their specified destinations.

Then, in Mid-Summer, there was an attack on a dam under construction in Oja. Eleven rebels were killed. Ethan sent photographs of the bodies to his agents, who identified three of them as Meenans.

≈•≈

Torna watched Ethan stare out his office window at the blue Oja Mountains.

"How could we have missed it all these years?" he said. "If the Meenans fight us, which they will . . . Meena is the breadbasket of Veshna."

"Yes. Wait till after the harvest."

His face hardened. "No. The sooner we attack, the less prepared they'll be to fight. I want to minimize the bloodshed."

"Do you?"

"What do you mean by that?"

"Nothing, Ethan. I don't doubt you know what you're doing." Her voice was harsher than she'd intended. To soften the words, she reached across his desk and squeezed his hand. It was cold.

CHAPTER 37

The months had passed, and Sherayna remained in Meena because her family had grieved for her and wasn't ready to face the idea of losing her again. And because she herself was uncertain, not about the Borderal cause but about her role in that struggle—if she had any role after her betrayal of the secret of the shield.

Micor had written them that he'd already known of that breach. He was dealing with it, he said. That was all. No comfort or blame for Sherayna.

She hadn't worked regularly in the wheat since the age of fourteen. Then, it had been tiresome, an excuse her foster parents concocted to keep her away from the fighting. Now, the satisfaction that it gave her was almost complete. Weeding the fields, the green wheat whooshing against her legs, she heard the grass spirit calling her sister. The gods smiled, white lines in gray rain clouds. Only occasionally was there sadness, shame: when, to comply with consortium regulations, they poisoned the pests in the fields. For days, the powder whitened the grass stalks, grayed the earth, and deadened the singing of the cicadas.

As harvest drew near, the southeast irrigation line sprang its annual leak. They shut off the water main, and Sherayna went to repair it. It was high afternoon; the sun beat on her back, but her broad-brimmed hat cast a cool circle around her neck and chest. A breeze rattled the curved claws of the wheat florets.

There was a yell—lost downwind. Far down the field, the dark form of Karmeena raced toward her, dust billowing up from her feet. Sherayna got up and jogged down the furrow to meet her.

"Rayna!" Karmeena crashed into her, gasping, grabbing hold of her arms. "Rayna, the City's come. They have . . . there's footmen down in town . . . and they're retaining people for questioning."

Sherayna stepped past Karmeena and strode down the row in the direction of the town. *They followed me. They want me.* "Did they see you leave?"

"I don't think so." Karmeena stumbled into step behind her. "I was in the store with Papa, and they were gathering on the square, and he told me to slip out the back and take the ground car."

Shoshec and Rajaneen were out in the west field on the combine. Jasen had gone with them. Sylan had been at the library; there was every chance the City had found her.

"Where's your mother?"

"She went to the supply yard to look at piping."

"Good. That's not very near the square. She'd have time to get out."

Karmeena nodded, still breathing hard.

"You left the car by the house?" Sherayna asked. "Good. I'm going into town. I need you to go out to the west field, find your grandparents and Jasen, and tell them to get to our meeting point."

"But what are you going to do?"

"Deal with this." She squeezed Karmeena's shoulder. "It's all right. I've done harder things." Turning, Sherayna broke into a run, her hat falling off behind her. She could hear Karmeena pound away to the west.

≈•≈

Sherayna took her smallest gun from the house and hid it in her boot. She drove until she saw City guards blockading the main street ahead of her. At their signal, she pulled over and got out of the car. They scarcely bothered to search her but shoved her into the center lot, which was on the verge of riot. Ten or twelve people stood under City guns. Their neighbors were protesting that their arrests were illegal, the City officials shouting back that they were not. Some Meenans hovered in clumps surrounded by footmen. Others were charging along the streets, half-pursued, half-pursuing the footmen who were ransacking shops, searching for the gods wondered what. Blue army transports blocked almost every street: great, unwieldy boxes like the one that had carried Sherayna through Oja.

At the east side of the square stood the seer, in quiet conversation with who else but the Warchief Ethan.

At the sight of him, her heart began to hammer, and she almost turned and fled. Then anger flared. She clenched her fists as a footman pushed her into one of the knots of people.

She fell into her neighbor, Tana, and steadied herself against the old woman's shoulder.

"Warchief!" she shouted, moving into clear sight of him. His pale eyes fastened on her. "If you're looking for me, here I am. I'll surrender. I'm a fugitive. But you can hardly claim provocation for invading an entire township for the crime of happening to be my home." The shouting of the crowd was dying, faces looking between them to see what would follow.

"Don't flatter yourself, Sherayna," he called back. "You're not the only rebel here. We'll take you in—and every other traitor in this traitorous population." He addressed the square at large. "Your seer has examined my orders. I have warrants to arrest twenty-five of you on sight and to search every building, public or private, in this township." The crowd roared, and he shouted louder over them. "If you do not cooperate with our investigation, I am authorized to put your fields to the torch." Cries of indignation. The warchief's voice rose above them. "Your seer has approved the legality of my documents."

All eyes turned to the seer. "I would not use the word 'approved,' Warchief," he said, "but they do appear to be legal."

"What's legal?" someone shouted. "Planet murder is legal on Perdita!"

Everything was happening too fast. Footmen moved to restrain citizens. Citizens pushed back against footmen, broke out of the groups into which they'd been herded. On the streets, crashes and cries, windows breaking. Sherayna was caught in a jostle of bodies. People ran, fell. Inevitably, there came a gunshot and another. She ducked and leapt and rolled through the crowd, toward the outskirts of the lot, reached a few meters of open space, sped behind the wall of the post office, pulled out her gun.

If she could not exchange herself for Meena, she had no way to save the town. Many Meenans were trained fighters; they would have to save themselves. Now all she could do was keep a lookout for her family and help where she could.

She dove around the back of the post office and shot a footman bearing down on Vecle, one of the maize grower's daughters. She darted back roughly the way she'd come, into the transport junkyard. Several people rushed past as she crouched behind the remnants of a steering train. Through the cacophony came an old bird whistle from the Iltan days. She whistled back. Illia appeared from behind piled steel siding and scampered to her side.

"I thought I saw you vanish this way," she whispered. "Kara got back home?"

"I sent her to tell Mama and Papa and Jasen to get to the shelter. Where's Leric?"

"Behind the silo. We still have to look for Sylan. But when we heard you speak, I told him I was going for you first."

"Let's get to the silo."

To reach it, they had to cross two lots. As they sprinted between the consortium office and the car shop, a footman called out to Sherayna to stop. She did stop, and fired at the same time he did. Her leg fell out from under her, and she crashed onto the pavement. She must have hit the footman, for he wasn't on them yet. Illia was pulling her to her feet. Her leg was warm, wet, fire to stand on, but she could limp on, her arm around Illia's neck, behind the car shop and transport lot—one of the transports was in flames—and finally the last few meters to the silo.

The noises were muffled there. Sherayna collapsed onto the dirt as Leric dropped to the ground beside them. She looked at her leg, a deep gash in her shin. It had missed the bone but was bleeding profusely. Leric started tearing her pant leg open from the bullet hole.

"I have a blade." Illia took it from her pocket and handed it to Leric. "I'm going to go for Sylan."

Leric looked up from Sherayna's leg. "I was going to go."

"But you need to help Rayna get out of here. You're stronger than I am."

He hesitated no more than a second, nodded, finishing his cut of the pant leg above the knee. Illia knelt to examine Sherayna's leg, squeezed her shoulder. "Don't linger. They'll be back here soon. Sylan and I will meet up with you."

She pressed Leric's arm, and he touched her hand quickly. Then she sprang to her feet and darted off around the silo.

When Sherayna's leg was tied up, they moved as fast as they could into the shelter of a walnut orchard. The people of

Meena had planned for these exigencies. A network of dense orchards and junk piles ringed most of the township, a hope of escape in the event of a City attack. The City did not appear to have noticed the logic behind the formations, for here the bees buzzed louder than the ruckus in town. Sherayna and Leric had ended up on the wrong side of the center street and had to circle some twelve measures to reach their meeting place. At first, Leric carried Sherayna. When he tired, he supported her as she staggered beside him, through the walnuts, through an old transport yard, through the rosid trees, the apples, pears, walnuts again, finally out into the west field by the bristlenut orchard, and to their shelter just at sunset.

It was underground, its entrance hidden in debris near the fence that marked the division between the claw-wheat and the bristlenuts. Leaves and grass were routinely glued to the door to ensure it was never exposed. Leric let Sherayna fall to her knees and knelt beside her, knocking three times fast, four slow on the door.

Rajaneen opened it, and they tumbled down the stairway to the battery-lit room.

Karmeena flew into Leric's arms. "Where's Mama?"

"Where's my mother?" Jasen echoed at once.

His arm around Karmeena, Leric told all they knew, while Shoshec treated Sherayna's leg, still bleeding thickly, and gave her an oral antibiotic. Ordinarily, Borderals eschewed such drugs, which selected resistant strains of disease. But in times of crisis, personal safety came first—the cause would not be won if the fighters were dead.

They waited. Boxes of supplies littered the floor, making the room too close. They made themselves eat and drink from their rations, and Rajaneen laid out cushions to sleep on. Jasen withdrew for an hour to the tiny adjoining chamber that was storage room and toilet. The room was more open without him.

Night fell. Every few minutes, Shoshec glanced at his watch. Karmeena sobbed softly with the same regularity. Sherayna stretched out on the cushions and elevated her leg. Though her heart was pounding, her eyes were heavy. She felt helpless and slightly sick.

She awoke with a start to Jasen's voice.

"What's the time now?"

"Seventeenth hour," said Shoshec, "six hours till dawn."

Illia and Sylan had not come. Sherayna sat up.

"Shouldn't they be here by now?" said Karmeena.

"Not if they had to hide," said Rajaneen.

"But it's been dark for three hours," Karmeena protested. "They should be able to escape in the dark, no? So why aren't they here?"

"I'm going back," said Leric.

"No, don't go, Papa!" Karmeena sprang forward to grip his wrist. "They probably are just hiding. Mama knows how to hide from the City. She's just being careful, no? So we should stay together and wait."

"You're probably right, love, but it's also possible she might need help." Leric got to his feet, holding onto her hands.

"But you shouldn't be the one to go," said Rajaneen. "You've already been out there for hours. You had Rayna to carry. You need to rest."

"That's true too, Raja, but I have to be the one. As you say, I've been there, so I know the situation. And you and Sho haven't dodged the City for years, you're out of practice. And Jasen and Kara have never been trained. And Rayna can't go." He smiled grimly. "I'll be careful."

Turning to Karmeena, he smoothed the tangled hair back from her face and kissed her forehead. Quickly, he kissed the rest of the family, grasped Jasen's hand, and vanished into the night.

≈•≈

Ethan shuddered when he heard Sherayna shout, "Warchief, if you're looking for me, here I am!"

He spotted her at once in that Meenan crowd, the afternoon sun glancing gold off her hair, her voice as strong as that day in the snow of Oja when he'd seized her. And here she was, offering herself in exchange for her people, even as her first words then had begged aid for the two Ojan men gunned down beside her.

He didn't want to see her. He'd hoped that she'd just be arrested by one of his footmen and he'd never have to see. But why? It was what he'd come to do: arrest the rebels he had warrants for and establish a military presence to watch the rest of the township. Yet suddenly it seemed doomed to failure, his commands empty, his threats idle.

When the rioting broke out, it seemed to him he was two people: the government officer, fighting rebellion, and the man who could see the futility of it with the clarity of a seer. The shots rang out, as they had to.

Now they'll fight. Can't expect two seconds of intelligent behavior— to know when they're beaten.

He lunged to the ground, pulling the seer of Meena down with him, drew his gun, spoke to the four chief footmen crouched beside him. "Fan out around the town, block their escape routes. Demand surrender. If they drop their weapons, incarcerate them. If not, shoot as needed." As they dashed away, he placed a hand on the seer's shoulder. "Are you all right, Im Seer?"

"Alive," said the old man. "Better if you can get the shooting to stop."

Ethan nodded, leapt to his feet, and sped round the corner of the nearest building, out toward the transport yard. But, foolish!—there wasn't a Meenan there. They were rebels, after all; they'd run to the fields, not the transports, disappear into the wilderness. No, not the fields, the trees. The orchards. He scanned the scene. Behind him, to the east, there: a tree line and the shapes of people. Too late to catch them probably, but more would come. He darted round the transport yard, nearer the orchards.

That's where they'll be.

He picked up a footman, and then two more; the four of them headed off a knot of four rebels, one armed. Ethan shot him, saw the other three tied with the light flex chain they'd brought in their waist packs. Ethan had one of the footmen take them back to the transports for holding.

Minutes passed. The routine turned automatic. Head off a rebel or two or three. Call for surrender. Tie them and cart them off. Few Meenans tried to shoot. Good to know not every Meenan brought guns to town habitually. He maintained hand-radio contact with his chiefs though his radio was plagued by static.

The crowds thinned, scattered, vanished as in Iltan. Ethan ordered a fleeing man to drop his gun. The man ignored him.

Ethan aimed for his shoulder, shot, hit his back. The man fell in a spurt of blood. Out of the corner of his eye, he saw a footman tying up a teenager. For a moment, all was quiet.

Then, Ethan heard voices calling distantly behind him. Now one, now many, frantic.

Fire.

Great gods. It had to be a mistake. He reached for his hand radio: raw static. Damn shoddy design.

He spun back toward the town center to see Torna running toward him. "Fire, Warchief! I've been trying to reach you."

"Where is it?"

"East of town—someone set the fields off."

"On whose authority?"

She shook her head.

"Damned to Tep." Ethan was already running. "Is it quartered off per the king's orders?"

"I don't think so," said Torna beside him. "Looks wild to me."

He could see the smoke pouring west on the wind. "Torna, get to the local fire center, south side of the transport yard. Take twenty footmen and man the fire transports, send all the rest you see to the fire."

"The rebels?"

"Aren't as important as the fields. Go."

She dashed away.

Ethan took a deep breath and shouted out across the township: "This is an over-Fennoc command. All footmen not in command of a transport move east to fight the field fire." He was painfully aware that many footmen hadn't heard him, equally aware that he'd just told the Meenans his orders. But it wasn't a question of tactics now. Let the Meenans win—better than losing the fields that fed Veshna.

He sped toward the flames now licking fast over the grass. Stifling heat. Several footmen were on the scene—no tools except a couple of shovels—the footmen were clearing a bare zone, on the west. Procedure. Good. Maybe too close.

Ethan strode into the midst of his footmen. "You two, stay here on standby as medics. You two, go to the hospital for first aid supplies—commandeer a ground car. You," he motioned to one of the footmen, "give me your handset." He threw his dead hand radio on the ground and latched the footman's on his belt. "The rest of you, go to the stores and load shovels, picks, blankets, cloths, fire coats, anything else you find to help. Go." He crossed to the diggers. "Good work, move it back. Wind's up." The footmen nodded, already pushing the cleared zone backward, their breaths ragged, flames close to their faces.

Smoke searing his eyes, Ethan jogged along the perimeter of the fire, expecting every moment to see the end of the flames, but with each pace, the flames leapt high: far more than the little space he'd been authorized to torch. His chiefs, via radio, reported that considerably more than a measure was ablaze. He forced his mind to the task at hand. It wouldn't spread much to the east in this breeze. The west was the problem. He stumbled on a water line, too thick to cut—he shot it open, but there was no water. The irrigation mains were shut off near harvest time. The mains—they would be by the house that owned this field. Ethan summoned the town plans to his mind: *to the south*, he thought, *on the opposite end of the fire.*

The footmen were returning with the supplies. He deployed them. The fire had jumped the first clearing, burning one footman in the face. He needed to get the fire transports' hoses on the west. It took Torna's team minutes to get the hoses running, and even then they were askew, water spewing randomly.

"Lean forward, you fools," Ethan cried. "Did you sleepwalk through your fire training?" He called out into the streets, "Who has experience on fire hoses?"

Two people were at his elbow at once: a man and woman, out of uniform, Meenans. "We're with the local fire team," the man barked.

"Get these two on the hoses! You, there. You, over there."

They aimed the water at the base of the flames. Now a new clearing, farther down. He sent three to the house to find the water mains, two more to do the same for the next house southwest. Good: someone was cutting cloths to cover noses and mouths. Ethan took one and jogged south, where the flames were spreading. To the northwest, he could hope, the town's pavement would block their progress. *Need more people on the south.*

As the hours dragged by, it began to look hopeless. As soon as one corner of the flames was contained, another broke free. In the end he had to take people away from the southwest to look to the town itself—hundreds of Meenans were still confined there. Turning on the irrigation scarcely helped. It was a drip system, barely enough to dew the ground. The reinforcements Ethan radioed for took two hours to arrive from Mesa. He handed command of the fire suppression to their fire chief and rotated enough of his people off the fire to provide escorts to sort through the Meenan prisoners, transport those formally arrested to the Mesa prison and as many others as possible to the Mesa army base for temporary holding. Was it a trivial concern in the face of the fire? Perhaps, but it was what they'd come for. Besides, it would be best to get the prisoners out of town in case the whole place went up.

He went back to the fire and dug trenches with his people and a dozen or so of the Meenans who had appeared to offer help, their tottering seer among them. Blistering work. Blinding work. Half-worded thoughts flew through his head: it had been a debacle, ham-handed, his fault; Veshna would go hungry; he'd be stripped of his rank, plagued by the press. Gods wept.

Like everyone, Ethan had drenched his clothes. Still the hairs on the backs of his hands were singed. Night fell. Rotations changed. He went off past midnight, back to the town to sit with the others in the relative safety of the paved center lot. He ached inside and out—too little water was being passed around, too slowly.

The fire was beautiful, orange-red against the smoke-black sky, even the constant roaring beautiful—from a distance, like a giant hearth. Like life in the cold.

The footmen in the darkness were talking among themselves: "Crazy order." "Some bright idea." A gruff laugh. "Can you imagine what this will do to wheat prices?" "Prices? How many people will we lose out there?" "Did you see that rebel helping?" "Why shouldn't they? It's their land." "I think they started it." "What for?" "Diversion." "Can you spare a drink of water?"

CHAPTER 38

Rajaneen changed Sherayna's bandage and made her lie down again. Jasen flashed Sherayna an acid look as if to say it was all her fault. And it was, she reflected. She had plainly led them here. She forced down the tightening in her throat. Later there would be time for guilt.

Weakened from blood loss, she slept. When she opened her eyes, she saw the half-open door and two silhouettes against the first gray of dawn: Leric and Sylan—Jasen rushing to embrace her.

"Where's Mama?" cried Karmeena.

Wordlessly, Leric seized her and held her close.

"I never saw her," said Sylan.

Leric nodded at Sylan. "She got out through the back of the library and hid in the bushes. When I went to the library to look for her, she spotted me. I had her wait while I searched for Lia. I couldn't find her." His words fell like lead. "It was quiet there—the City were patrolling the streets, and all the lights were on in the buildings. I hardly saw any of our people. None of them had seen Lia. Some had heard the seer was dead, but no one knew how. They . . . they were burning the fields southwest of the silo."

Silence.

"I didn't think he'd do it," Sherayna said at last. "I was sure it was an empty threat."

"Papa," said Karmeena, "we have to go back to look for Mama."

"We will," Shoshec answered before Leric could. "But now the sun's rising. The patrols will be spreading into the orchards. Wherever Lia is, she'll have gone to ground for the day. We'll wait till night. But we will find her, Kara."

≈•≈

Throughout the day, Sherayna faded in and out of sleep, half-forgetting where she was, then remembering with a jolt: *I led the City to Meena. Oh, Lia.* The pain in her leg burned like justice.

The next night, Leric and Shoshec were gone for hours, searching for Illia. They returned without her.

"They're still patrolling the streets," said Leric. "We saw almost none of our people. The fires have taken out most of the east lands and have reached the east edge of our own fields."

"You didn't leave the water on by any chance, Rayna? To check the leak?" asked Shoshec.

"No, Papa, I hadn't finished patching it."

Leric said, "We swung past the house to see if Lia was holed up there. The City had gone, but they ransacked our things like rats. They didn't find Kara's Zerin passes." He took the slips of paper from a pocket and unpacked some other smuggled items: extra medicines, tiny trinkets, pictures, an old Sama necklace from Sherayna's mother. "But, Sylan, they took your research."

Sherayna felt dizzy.

Sylan said, "The City will know where the shield is now. They'll take it down." She sounded baffled, unable to make sense of her own words.

The City would know where the shield was. *And even if I hadn't betrayed Micor, the end result would have been the same: the City knowing about the shield.*

She looked at the faces around her; they were as numb as she was.

Jasen said, "It should exonerate the Borderals of the destruction of the *Outbound*." As if that were a consolation.

No one responded.

At last, Leric muttered, "Well, what a glorious feat of overcoming then. Especially for you two. You may even get away. I envy you, you know?"

Sylan's eyes were closed now. Thinking of her own home? Of walking in her own fields? *When our fields are worse than torched—made into spaceports, or gargantuan interplanetary croplands . . .*

"It's the end of Perdita," she said, just to see if anyone could feel it.

Silence a moment. Then Leric said, "So?"

"Sylan," said Shoshec suddenly, "was there any jae information in your shield research?"

Sylan glanced up. "What? No. No, I've already sent back all my jae work to Micor."

"That's something anyway."

≈•≈

Around noon, their shelter's air soured with smoke.

"It won't reach us here," said Rajaneen. "It would have to jump the path from our fields to the trees. And we can't run during the daylight. We have to wait it out."

"It was fierce out there, Raja," said Leric, "and there's been wind. If it's not on us yet, we should go, use it as a diversion. I'm going to see." Without waiting for a reply, he went up the stairs, felt the door for heat, and opened it a crack. The smoke oozed in like a thin, black fog. Leric coughed and closed the door. "It's still maybe a fourth of a measure away. We should go."

Without further argument, they gathered up supplies and rebandaged Sherayna's leg. She leaned on Karmeena and hobbled out behind Leric. A dark cloud reddened the noonday sun. The flames flickered in the distance, as if the horizon had been hewn into a fire pit. At their feet, the claw-wheat waved bright yellow, heavy headed, ripe for the harvest.

"Meena will cease to be Meena," breathed Jasen, a prophecy—Illia had recounted it to Sherayna years ago.

A memory flashed in her mind: going with Illia, as children, to see a friend in Mesa who raised poultry. A batch of auk chicks had been scheduled for slaughter. Their friend had taken the girls to the feeding yard, and as the birds scarfed up claw-wheat from Sherayna's hand, she thought, *This is the last thing they'll ever eat.* And she had wanted so much to keep the moment forever that she'd cried when the birds strutted away.

She cried again. Just so did the claw-wheat sway in the smoke winds, unable to know its last hour had come. She reached over quickly and plucked off a claw-grained head, burying it in her pocket. She let the tears slide down her face, soothed to see Shoshec crying too, whose family had farmed this land for seven generations.

They covered their mouths with cloths against the smoke and spread out in pairs in the bristlenut orchard to make themselves more difficult to locate. Alone with Karmeena to lean on and to lead, Sherayna grew calm. For an hour, there was nothing but moving from tree to tree. Near the edge of the orchard, they met up again at a little cave carved out as an emergency shelter. Their throats were ragged and the air ashen, but the fire seemed not to have followed. Crowded and hot, they waited out the day.

At nightfall, they set off into the wild grasslands, all together, walking by the stars and the moons. Bypassing the Port of Meena, which would be guarded, they headed down instead toward the rocky coast of the Gulf of Grass some fifty measures to the south, where the Borderals kept their boats hidden.

The moons climbed east: Olay's eye part closed and Tori's full open, covering the plain in a mild indigo. Away in the east, the burning fields threw red against the sky like a midnight sunrise. In the brightness of full night, the walkers slowed, stopping frequently to listen for the noises of pursuit. The grass whispered softly on every side.

By midnight, Sherayna could feel blood squish in her boot. Sylan suggested that Jasen, the strongest of them, should carry her. He consented and hefted Sherayna onto his back without meeting her eyes. Their pace improved without her limping to slow them. When the dawn flamed up through the smoke in the west, they had covered some thirty measures with twenty still before them to the coast.

They paused midmorning to rest in the waist-high grass. Lying in the brittle stickers, Sherayna stared at the dry stalks and thought how swiftly fire might consume that entire plain. And, noting too with a Borderal eye that most of the grasses were now claw-wheat hybrids, it occurred to her that one claw-wheat blight might devastate thousands of measures. How easy to rend a planet! Easy as stepping through a spiderweb.

After an hour or two, they got up and walked forward tentatively, stopping every minute or so to listen and look. It was impossible to be sure no one was following. There were too many noises: breezes stirred the grasses, the meadowlarks twittered, the cicadas ratcheted like laborers in a machine yard. Near noon, something in the grass shuffled under their feet. Karmeena yelped, and a lark bolted into the sky. Even Sherayna started, throwing Jasen off his balance so that he plunked her down heavily on her good leg.

"We can't keep creeping like this," said Shoshec, breathing almost as hard as Karmeena.

They sat down, the grass rising over their heads, and waited out the day, having covered no more than five measures.

≈•≈

In the small hours of the next night, the wind whipped up, salty cold, and the fog swooped owl-swift over them. By the dim haze of Tori, they struggled over clumps of grass now short and damp. The voice of the ocean burst upon them like a drumroll, just as they topped the southern cliffs. The waves roiled black below. Too far below. They had come out some measures east of their port.

They wandered, shivering, till first daylight, when the contours of the cliffs reared out of the mist. Leric and Sherayna spotted the trail simultaneously—at a suddenly familiar triangular rock they had passed in the night half a dozen times.

For an instant, Sherayna was flooded with joy. It was going to be all right. They'd soon be at the boats; they'd find Illia waiting.

But no one had news of Illia.

≈•≈

The next day, they set off for Semlona South Harbor, en route to a safe house in the city of Raratin.

In the rental car on the highway to Raratin, Sherayna watched the wheat fields of Semlona whisk by, mile upon mile, enough wheat to feed the hungry hordes of Keeri-Semlona— but what of the people of Veshna? It was nightfall when they passed into the Tall Mountains, shadowy shapes under a cloudy sky.

"So this is where they died," Sherayna heard Sylan mutter.

"They should have stayed on Vorshtamor," said Jasen.

"*Vorshtamor khalnuzh,*" murmured Sylan—beautiful Vorshtamor—Sherayna had learned enough Vunizh to understand that much. Beautiful Vorshtamor. Beautiful Meena. Beautiful. Home.

At last, they came down into the valley of Raratin, through the plains and into the giant white-lit city with its great, skyward-towering buildings, each one like another. Shoshec, who was driving, got lost and Rajaneen took over. She led them across the dizzying city and into the outskirts, where houses lined streets of manageable proportion, not too much vaster than the streets of Kepot or Mesa.

The house they'd been sent to was ancient and large, the Im Dwelling of a quiet lane. They were met at the door by an old couple, Tyoroc and Sica, friends of Olloan's, in the textile business; they were also information synthesizers for the Borderals.

That evening, Sherayna retired early to her bed. Six days since the assault on Meena. They placed her in a room she'd share with Leric and Karmeena. Dark, electrically warmed, it hardly had room to fit three mattresses. She was almost asleep when she sensed a presence, jerked full awake, reached for her gun. The gun, of course, had been given to Leric, and the presence was only Leric himself.

"Sorry," he said in response to her alarm. He sat on his mattress and let his head sink in his hands.

Sherayna sat up, watching him in the murky night.

After a time, he lifted his head. "They're not going to find her."

"You don't know that."

"Do you think we'll find her—in your heart?"

"I don't know what to think." Sherayna smiled wanly. "I'm so lost, Leric, I don't even feel lost. I'm so numb I don't remember what it's like to feel."

"You mean you ever knew?"

Not as numb as all that, for the words stung.

"I'm sorry," he said. "I didn't mean that."

It was the apology, not the insult, that crunched in her chest.

"I've done everything wrong," she said as he looked at her, emotionless. "I fell into their trap in Oja. I betrayed Micor with the secret of the shield. Then I led them to Meena. I could have torched the town myself and saved them the trouble— saved us the bloodshed. And then, then I walked into town and got myself shot, made you and Illia stop to save me. And if she is dead, it's my fault many times over."

After a moment, Leric said, "There are some faces you wear with great style, Sherayna, and some that you wear very badly—and none you wear worse than self-pity."

Sherayna cackled, but her voice grew stronger. "Perhaps, but the point's true. I've been an incompetent fool."

"Always a fool, never incompetent."

A long silence passed as they sank into their own thoughts.

"The last time I saw her," said Leric, "I didn't even look at her. I wasn't thinking of her."

"You were busy bandaging me up. What can I say to that?"

"Nothing. Say nothing. There's nothing to say." He put on his borrowed nightshirt and went to bed.

CHAPTER 39

For the longest three days of Ethan's life, they fought a high, east wind that raked flames into orchards, through houses, across firebreaks. At least Torna was there; that was some relief. He spoke to her briefly near nightfall of the second day when they spotted each other off rotation.

"Gods, what a mess," he said to her—and was surprised how good it felt to say it.

"Yes." Torna looked into the orange distance. "A mess."

By noon of the fourth day, the worst was over. But two-thirds of Meena's fields were reduced to black stubble. The fire chief from Mesa had found an army-issue lighter near what he deemed the starting point—a special-issue lighter. Ethan had ordered them for his higher footmen, knowing that a controlled burn of the fields might be an option, a card he had never intended to play.

But one of his people had played it. One of his. And that meant him. Why had he made that threat in the first place? To force cooperation? He should have known they'd never cooperate; he had known it.

He ordered a casualty report, but with the overloading of the local hospital, it would take several hours to compile. Despite glowering from his footmen, he commanded that the Meenans who had helped fight the fire be released on his authority. Then, he sent a report to Lashen, augmenting the relays he'd been radioing. He could hear his career blaze away.

Later that day, he walked the periphery of the scorched plain, seeing the last flames eradicated. He was keeping an eye out for Torna, but it was a footman who approached him.

"Warchief," she said, "we found something, searching one of the houses." She held out a sooty stack of papers. "They were just sitting on a desk. We thought they might have information on the rebels."

"Thank you, Footman," said Ethan, the papers heavy in his hands. "Have you seen Lieutenant Torna?"

"No, sir."

"If you see her, send her to me. Give out the word I'm looking for her."

"Yes, sir."

He looked at the front page he was holding, mind blank, made nothing of it. He went to his ground car and locked the papers in it. Then he went to the local inn that was serving as a rest hall and showered—at least there was still water aplenty: the South Oja River wouldn't run dry. He found himself blistered and burned, not badly. His uniform was caked black. He put it back on and ventured out again, ate, debriefed, and relieved some footmen who had come back from house searches that revealed almost nothing, only a suspicious letter here and there.

Where was Torna? When had he last seen her? Two days before. Too long. He checked the hospital.

≈•≈

"Can you believe them, Warchief?" the medic said. "She must have come back to town to help keep the fire off it, and what do they do? They shoot her, for fighting a fire, a fire I warrant they started. Shot her and left her by some smoldering shop."

Ethan listened, scarcely hearing. "How badly is she hurt?"

"The bullet missed the major arteries, but there was still massive internal bleeding before we found her. Smoke inhalation didn't help but wasn't bad, she was on the ground. The bullet hit her liver—"

Ethan waved a hand. "Thank you, Medic. I'll see her now."

She was not asleep, burned and bandaged and hooked to tubes as she was. He sat on the cushion by the head of the bed, murmured to her for a few moments as she looked around the room, groggy with painkillers.

"Ethan," she whispered, fixing on him. "My remembrances . . ."

He cocked his head in question.

"My remembrances I wrote—in my pack . . ."

"You want me to bring them to you?"

She tried to shake her head, could hardly move it. "No. Send them to Demdor. You know—?"

"Your son, yes. Of course."

"Write for me: I love him. I'll watch him when I'm with the gods."

Pain knifed him at her words, but he did not tell her she must live. She was a seer. He yearned to ask her all she'd seen. *Tell me what I've done wrong.*

She went on, "He lives in Keshot, you know. My home city. He's a drug distributor for the hospitals, like his father. Maybe . . . maybe he sent these here." Her eyes went to the tube that fed into her arm.

"Yes, it's a vital job." Ethan had heard this before; he couldn't remember when.

"I've been in Veshna too long. When I'm with the gods, I'll try to go back to Keerina. . . . Ethan, it's hard to focus."

"Rest then."

She closed her eyes, and her breathing slowed. Then, she looked up at him again. "I was going to say, being here, away—I tried to look after you. I . . ." With an effort, she held out her hand. He took it in his own. "I'm sorry about your mother." She looked at him for a moment more, then closed her eyes and went to sleep.

My mother. I never spoke to her of my mother. She was, she is, a seer.

When he came back the next night, she was dead.

≈•≈

Her personal effects would be at the army sub-base in Mesa. But before he could get them, he would have to go to Senarna to explain himself. When he got into his ground car to leave Meena at last, he saw that stack of confiscated papers on the seat beside him. He picked them up and realized why they'd meant nothing to him. They were in Vunizh. Newly written text in ancient Vunizh. Sylan.

He thumbed the pages, picking out words. By and by, he saw one repeat often. A word he had recently taught himself: *denzhen.* "Shield."

Erring gods—that shield.

CHAPTER 40

The flames were raging around Sherayna now, a seething wall on every side. She kept filling her bucket from the leak in the water line, but each time she turned to the flames, it was empty.

"Illia," she shouted, but Illia didn't come. Where could she be? She was supposed to be helping. It wasn't like her not to be there.

"Illia!"

A cackle answered. "You won't be seeing her again." Sherayna spun around to see the warchief before her, his mouth a red gash, his eyes pits of light. Around him, all was darkness, the fire's roaring vanished with the fields and the sky, under the cold white of the interrogation room.

"She's decided to stay with her family," he explained.

"But I am her family," Sherayna pleaded.

His mouth opened in an inhuman, wide grin, the words pouring forth from unmoving lips. "No, Rayna, you've never been one of them. But you're one of me now. Welcome back to your home." His mouth kept opening wider and wider until it filled her eyes.

≈•≈

She opened her eyes in the dark of her room, adrenaline ramping up her heart. Awake . . . here with her people in Oja—no, in Raratin—with the family in Raratin. All but Illia. By the time her heart slowed, she was sweating, defeated. She couldn't make the nightmares stop. Even recovering from her imprisonment, she had never lost her way so in the darkness of her mind.

I was strong enough with love then to keep the gods serene, to keep them from bleeding into my brain. Where's that love now?

The room was the gray of an ocean storm, moonlight hiding high over the thick, motionless clouds that forever hovered in the valley of this city. She stretched and sighed.

"So I'm not the only one who can't sleep," came Leric's voice from his mattress.

Sherayna sighed. It was lucky they'd cleared a spare room for Karmeena; at least they wouldn't keep her awake—unless she was having nightmares too. "There's nothing to sleep for, is there?" she said. "Nothing to be rested for tomorrow, except examining more reports and helping with the textile trade."

"A perspicacious observation." Leric paused. "Since there isn't any hurry to sleep, let's play a game."

Sherayna rubbed her eyes. "A game?"

"Find the First Cause."

"Leric, it's late."

"I'll begin: why are we here?"

Sherayna sighed again. "Because Meena burned."

"Why did it burn?"

"Because the City found it."

"Why did the City find it?"

Her eyes stung. "Because I led them to it."

"Why did you lead them to it?"

"Because . . ."

"Yes?"

Nothing came to mind. "Because I let them."

"Be led there? That's circular."

"Leric, why are you such a cruel man sometimes?"

"Are we switching sides? You forfeit your point?"

Sherayna turned over to face his dim shape. "Yes, all right! I forfeit my point. So answer."

Leric sniffed. "I am cruel sometimes because I force— no—I try to force honesty."

"Why do you try to force honesty?"

"Because I like things to be clear."

"Why do you like them to be clear?"

"Oh, I . . ." He halted. "So I know I can trust the people I trust . . . think I can trust."

"Why do you want to know you can trust them?"

"Because my life depends on them—no, that's a coward's answer. Because I love them."

"Why do you love them?"

He was silent a long moment. "Because they love me."

"Why do they love you?"

He laughed. "Gods know."

"No. Answer. Answer or concede."

"They love me because I love them."

"You'll never get back to first causes that way."

She heard him chuckle again. "I think I just did. What is a first cause if not love?"

"Yes, but personal love is not creation love—"

"I contend all love is one."

"Then you love everything the same?"

"No, but all my love and theirs and the gods' is part of one whole of creation, no?"

Sherayna lay back. "You're too philosophical to play this game."

They were silent for some moments.

"Do you know what I've been remembering?" he said at last. "I've been remembering how at night, Lia would move through the house and turn out all the lights, starting at the east corner of the center room and proceeding to the west corner of the kitchen. I would hear her feet creak across the floor. And it's hard to go to sleep without the sound of her feet. Each time I hear a footstep pad past at night, I think for an instant that I'm hearing her steps and she'll be by my side the next moment."

"Leric, I have to get out," said Sherayna. "I was a prisoner for a year of my life. I can't imprison myself in this house when there's work to be done out there. You talk about her feet. I could tell you stories too: how I hear her laugh in my ears. Such things control us, Leric, when we have too much idle time. Give me work, and I'll never complain of it."

Leric didn't answer at once. "You have work here."

"It isn't the same."

"No. It's safe."

"Maybe I need risk."

"Maybe you want to kill yourself for letting Lia die."

The blood rose fast in Sherayna's face. "You have no standing to say that to me."

"You said it yourself," he snapped. "You let the City take Meena. Let them destroy Meena—let Meena cease to be our Meena, as the seer foretold. You led them to us. You led them to her."

Sherayna fumed in silence.

"You don't even bother to deny it."

"Why should I?" demanded Sherayna.

"Because it isn't true."

"Isn't it?"

"No. Of course it's not. You're just too much of a coward to admit it."

Anger bloomed in her. "And how do you arrive at that conclusion?"

"No one could be responsible for the things you hold yourself responsible for, as if you were stronger than the rest of us. But only a coward pretends to be stronger than her peers—afraid of facing us as equals on our mutual terrain."

"Then maybe I'm weaker than you. And maybe that's why I'm driven to go. You be strong then. You stay here and fill out reports on reports. For me, I'm still going to go away, leave all this behind."

Leric sat up with a thwacking of blankets. "Damn you, Sherayna. Don't you see anything? Can't you see? We need you now. I need you now." He flopped back in his bed. "How dare you run."

"I'm not what you need. Let me go where I'm suited."

"I'm not going to stop you, am I? Why should I expect you to start listening now, after all these years between us?"

Sherayna turned away to signal an end to the conversation. It would be good to get away from all of this, to be thoughtless and useful, planning bombings again in Oja—where she should have stayed from the first.

CHAPTER 41

At his hearing at Ayer Senarna, Ethan told the facts as he saw them—curious with an intellectual detachment to see what his superiors would say.

"You place us in a difficult situation," concluded Lashen, standing high above him in the small conference hall. "This whole plan of yours has been the most poorly executed of your career. Your briefing was inadequate, your fire training ludicrous, your control over your footmen virtually nonexistent, it seems, as you allowed one of them to set afire the fields of Meena. Your overzealous and overhasty threat to torch those fields does not improve the public perception that you yourself set the fires. The communication protocols among your troops were so poorly enforced it's a marvel to me you managed to coordinate a fire-fighting effort at all. Of course, much of that coordination derived from the fire chiefs of Mesa, Vorna, and Oja City, who were forced to come to your assistance. What do you have to say for yourself, Warchief?"

"That all you say is true, Warmaster," said Ethan.

Lashen heaved a sigh. "I move on to the numbers. Approximately 60 percent of the Veshnan wheat crop was burned. The prices of grain have already become hyperinflated. As for the rest of your assignment—consider a Meenan population of some 2000 people. About 330 were out of town, 78 fatalities. About 70 citizens cleared of all wrongdoing, 4 after their deaths, 94 children removed from their families, 307 arraignments. Of those, 242 convictions, by which measure your assault on Meena is the most successful anti-rebel campaign in the history of the post-Progressive Tech Statute era, with 400 resident citizens still under investigation. The rest, some 600, unaccounted for." He fingered his mustache. "In fact, your assault has been a military triumph and a domestic and economic tragedy. How, then, can we evaluate it?"

In the end, they allowed Ethan to retain his rank as warchief but drafted a public statement announcing his retirement from active duty. Thus, by refusing to demote him, they granted their approval to hard action against rebel activity, while by retiring him, they condemned his poor judgment and assured the public that such a scenario would not be repeated. Until further notice, most likely for the rest of his life, Ethan's career would be purely administrative.

≈•≈

Ethan felt relieved. His brain was in no state to make military decisions. He didn't understand any of this, didn't understand those numbers. Tragic, triumphant . . . grotesque?

Done can't be redone.

He was given a mandatory leave. Looking back, he couldn't tell if it had gone more right or wrong. He didn't know if he would do it again. He went home that Mid-Autumn to figure it out.

Niric, who was living alone again, had Ethan's old room on standby. All the childhood possessions that he hadn't parted with were stacked in boxes inside it. The room, facing north and shaded by oaks, was dank and musty. Ethan spent as little time as possible inside it, preferring to be in the work shed, surrounded by his father's things. He avoided the people of Mesa as well, many of whom still recognized him as Jessec's son and would hook him into conversation if they saw him, especially now, when his name was decried in the pamphlets: "The scourge of Veshna," they called him. He tried not to pay attention.

He didn't want to talk. He wanted to think; he needed to. So he wended his way to the botanical gardens and walked hours daily on the roughest, hilliest paths, through brambles and brush—thinking, reliving, reasoning.

What would Torna say?

The Meenans had been both more militant and better prepared than he'd anticipated. Too many had escaped. Too many more had been killed. Too many children had been trapped in the middle. And yet the rebel hive had been crushed, rebel forces routed. Since the assault, accounts of rebel activity had declined by some 70 percent planetwide.

And then there were the shield papers. More than evidence of its existence, they explained its history and function. They were proof as well that Sylan West-of-Now had been alive and in Meena just before the assault. Ethan had turned the papers over to Lashen—but not before he'd hidden away a copy of his own, which he'd been translating in his own time. He'd considered writing Nevan but didn't. No good in telling him his wife was almost found only to admit she was lost again. And he had no wish to speak to Nevan about Meena.

The fire was meant to be a last resort. A scare tactic. He had not planned to do it. He had not done it. Lashen's investigators had identified the footman who had done it. Yet he had been the officer—the responsibility was his.

Now grain prices were rocketing up. Many of the poor would be unable to afford the wheat that was their staple food. Meal after meal, and no bread, no grain, no flour. Moreover, the consortium projected that yearly yields would be down for at least five years: a combination of property damage and the loss of several hundred experienced farm workers. So much hardship for so many Perditans. *My people, my family.*

And I have done this.

He wanted to weep.

Badly planned. Careless. But what should he have done? What would Torna tell him, if she were here? Twenty-four fatalities out of Ethan's four hundred soldiers. Not bad. Could have been better. *Why did one of them have to be Torna?*

He should have attacked by surprise. Shouldn't have hoped to reason with them. Should have . . . what would she say?

≈•≈

In the back page of Torna's diaries, he'd written to Demdor: "Your mother said to tell you she loves you." The diaries contained a fantastic amount of classified military information. Not in a century would he obtain permission to send such a document to a civilian.

He sent it anyway, by routine post, along with a headnote quoting regulation 3.44.583:

Demdor of Keshot:

The information contained herein being considered classified, it may not be referred to, in fact or by implication, in any unauthorized communication, under pain of military prosecution.

That duty done, he walked the botanical gardens, among the leafless autumn oaks and flowerless azaleas, replaying his life like a recording, every nuance unalterable.

CHAPTER 42

Nevan's Journal
Perdita: 1 Mid-Autumn, 34.06.2041 After the End

At least my family is safe. I asked Laynia again today when we could expect to receive a letter from Sylan and Jasen, and again she told me, "Not for a long time." Laynia did us a service by sending us word that they were safe in Raratin as soon as she knew—almost as soon as we had word of the fire. Knowing that, we have the strength to wait.

But it is hard for Miri especially. She's young, which makes the waiting longer—yet there's more to it than that. This disaster in Meena has confounded her plans.

Tomorrow, she becomes a full Jetho. And all her study, her practice, her pretense (and perhaps the truth too) of a loyalty to this island—all of this, she did so she could go away. To depart from Zerin as a Jetho, after years of being perceived as a weird offworld creature to be guarded as if in a zoo.

To be trusted.

To go to Meena and find our family there.

But they're not there. They're in Raratin, no one will tell us exactly where, hiding with a group of fugitive anti-techs terrified for their lives. They will not risk letting Miri come to them. And so, once more, we wait.

Nevan's Journal
Perdita: 2 Mid-Autumn, 35.06.2041 After the End

Today was a strange, warm day for autumn. The blue jay who lives outside my window was hopping happily in the sunny pine branches.

It was Miri's graduation day—or might have been if not for Meena.

She's grown up all of a sudden, left behind that adolescent cynicism that nothing matters. Now, she is gentler again, valuing small things for themselves, experiencing the here and now. She has grown up—she's eighteen. And today, she became a Jetho.

The ceremony of Miri's final vows was beautiful and overhung with the absurd. All of Wolsenond's population gathered on the great earth floor of the keep. We onlookers—the novices and the non-Jetho companions—stood in a loose circle and watched as the full Jethor danced to a slow and fluid song that made very Kiri exhortation to protect the living land, veiled over with a Sama mysticism:

> *Burn like a star out of blackness to preserve in honor*
> *and ever to forward the unity of all.*

That's a line that stayed in my head: "unity" is a Sama motif—and yet so vital to Kiris too.

Miri danced mellifluously, the best dancer there. For a moment, I couldn't help but worry that she was choosing the wrong path to be a Jetho, not a dancer, which had long ago been her first ambition.

Then she stood in the center of the giant room and spoke her vows before Olwer.

To serve the cause of Zerin and betray none of its secrets.

To protect Perdita by teaching respect for all things.

To foster progress and hone the striving of the human spirit.

To use her mind skills to gain power over another only at the express command of Zerin.

As I listened to her swearing herself to this, a terrified perplexity crept over me. She is tying herself in inextricable bonds. For if she means what she swore, she is enslaving herself to this island. And if she didn't mean it, she is a liar and forsworn. Why did I stand back and let her give herself to this? Then again, what right have I to tell her what to do with her life?

And yet, she was so young when she chose this course. Should I have dissuaded her?

The ceremony ended. There was general singing and dancing, congratulations, chatter, eating.

Miri and I spoke to Olwer.

He was smiling his usual smile and said, "You'll be a great boon to us, Miri. I know you've been longing to go abroad, and I'm sure that you shall when the time comes."

Miri smiled back in kind. "I see. When the time comes." Her mind was tightly blocked. I could imagine the anger behind the words. All this—and no closer to seeing our family.

Olwer laughed. "All things boil down to a matter of time, no?"

Miri laughed too. "If you want to play that game, Im Jetho, anything can boil down to anything."

"Freeing, isn't it?"

"Not really," I said.

CHAPTER 43

In the days that followed their arrival in Raratin, Sylan stayed away from the others. She could not share their anguish, however fond she'd been of Illia. Jasen could share it; he'd grown to adulthood on this planet, and these people were his people, almost. Sylan was sorry for them. She missed Illia. But her fury was transient. She was remote. More than that, Sylan was at rest, especially after she and Jasen received a message that Miri and Nevan knew they were safe. She felt unaccountably hopeful. Often, in the morning, when she awoke to a lemon light in the window, it seemed that her long wait was ending, and the morning spilling over the mountains reflected a new dawn in her life.

Raratin, by tradition, was an intelligence network for the Borderals. In the middle of Semlona, near the seat of City power, it was better placed to watch the City than fight it. Raratin was also a seat of Perditan manufacturing and a monument to technological dependence. Set in the deep artificial valley that the Samas had constructed in the midst of the Tall Mountains, it had virtually no natural resources of its own: little wind, no arable land, few trees. Moreover, it could only be reached by a couple of lonely mountain roads or by air. Since the Borderals seldom used airships, it was generally assumed that they could mount no significant infiltration of Raratin. So business continued profitably, while the Raratin sales executives traveled to see customers in Senarna, Cudonond, and Veshna—and to Veshna delivered the City secrets they unearthed in Cudonond and Senarna.

But even in populous Raratin, a sudden influx of new people in the wake of Meena might arouse suspicion. So Sylan and the others remained all but prisoners inside their large, quiet house. Their hosts, Tyoroc and Sica, ran a textile company. Now their profits would have to increase if their guests were to be housed and fed. To that end, the two old companions turned over analysis of intelligence documents to the Meenans and devoted their own time to increasing productivity.

≈•≈

In Late-Autumn, the official report of the casualties of Meena found its way into their hands.

"It might not be her then," said Karmeena. "The ID is tentative, right? It says so."

The house felt big and empty. Tyoroc and Sica were touring Keeri-Semlona with their wares. The rest of them sat at the polished dinner table on dusty cushions in the last light of afternoon; it was like sitting inside a monument to some ancestor, windows welded shut with years of rust, preserving the mustiness.

"Kara," said Leric, "you know there weren't many dark-skinned people in Meena. Besides our family, maybe thirty—about fifteen women. Two of them are positively identified among the dead. One is listed among the arrests. If they think it's her, then we must accept it. We can't overcome it. She's . . . gone." He tripped on the word.

Rajaneen put an arm around Karmeena's shoulder. "She's a pilgrim to the world of the gods now," she whispered. "She'll help them. She'll help them help us."

Karmeena was rigid. Shoshec's shoulders shook. Sherayna closed her eyes and pressed her hand to her brow as if her head ached. Leric continued to look at Karmeena, the corners of his mouth turning deeply down in a way unnatural for him.

"But they don't know," said Karmeena. "You can't just give up. No—" She threw out her hand as Leric opened his mouth. "You can't. It's too important not to play the long odds." She got up and marched out of the room.

≈•≈

Sylan withdrew further. Her sense of new hope faded, and again she felt imprisoned. And still she could not grieve with them—or would not.

I know what it is to lose family, home, freedom. I will not relive it with them. I don't have that kind of strength. I have the strength to survive, and so do they.

≈•≈

A household in Kepot was found to shelter Shoshec and Rajaneen. Overcrowded and overburdened as the Raratin house was, they could not refuse the offer. Sylan stood by as Karmeena consoled herself by pretending that her grandparents were returning to Veshna to look for their daughter. Was it right to let her hope when there was no real hope? Did a gradual decline into despair hinder or help a child's grief?

One day, while Sylan sat idly tapping her pen, Jasen said, "She knows, you know."

"Who? What?"

"Karmeena," he said, still typing numbers in his ledger. "She knows Illia's dead. She's simply not ready to think about it. So she's clinging onto fern fronds to keep from falling down the mountain. The fronds will break, and by the time they do, she'll be well versed in slipping and sliding with no solid ground under her feet. That's what she thinks anyway."

"She told you that?"

He looked up. "Not in so many words, but the ideas are there. I've thought them myself."

He doesn't touch my mind anymore, she thought. *And I don't touch his mind either, as if to do so would betray a trust between us.*

≈•≈

In late Late-Autumn, Sherayna left. A post had been secured for her in Micor's territory.

"Frankly, I'm glad to have her gone," said Jasen at dinner.

"Why do you have to hate her, Jas?" asked Karmeena.

Leric, Sylan saw, was watching Jasen intently.

Jasen softened his tone. "I don't hate her, Kara. It's only that she's a little maniacal, like the City—yes, I mean it. Their burning down Meena, her blowing up our ship, it's exactly the same except in scale."

"A mouse and a plague of mice are exactly the same except in scale," said Leric. "If you despise her for her Borderal acts, you despise every one of us."

Jasen shook his head. "You're not the same. You may sometimes do the same things, but she does them more blindly. There's something fundamental that she misunderstands about what it is to be human."

"You mean 'human' as the old Kiri insult?" snapped Karmeena.

"I mean 'human,' as a member of that particular social species."

Sylan tried to decipher what was in Jasen's mind. Out of the corner of her eye, she caught sight of Leric, his gaze now steady on her. When she met his eyes, he looked away, pensive.

He has lost his lover, Sylan thought. *And has he found any other to help him grieve? Sherayna?* But it didn't seem so. . . .

≈•≈

That evening, Sylan and Leric worked an hour in the sun room, she on the textile accounts, he on an evaluation of the environmental impact of three Space Project funding proposals.

"Would you Borderals accept any of those proposals?" she asked.

"No."

"Then what's to compare?"

"Some are worse than others. Some we'd risk lives to stop, some we wouldn't. I have to determine, for instance, whether paving bog land for a building site is more or less dire than draining bog land for agriculture."

"Oh, I think they should do that," said Sylan, serious, though her voice was light. "Even if it isn't high-yield land. Something has to be done to make up the grain losses from Meena."

Leric sighed and threw his papers on the floor before him.

Sylan said, "You'd worry about . . . what, habitat loss? Pesticide use?"

"I don't know. I don't care."

Before going back to her work, she watched him for a moment gazing blankly at his ankles. Unlike himself.

≈•≈

In the dull cold, she retired to bed early but had scarcely lain down when a knock sounded.

"Come?" she called out.

With only the dim light pouring in from the street lamps, Leric closed the door behind him and stood before her. He looked as if he were about to speak; then he shattered and sank to the floor. Struggling out of her blankets, Sylan hurried to him. The cold seeped through her nightshirt, but he fell warm into her arms and fit. He cried a long time, and she rocked him as she had rocked her children long ago.

"I can't stop it," he said. "I never envisioned my life without her. Oh, I told myself I had, that I'd accepted that in a Borderal's life there is no certainty, but I had no idea . . ."

Sylan shivered in the silence. "It's cold here on the floor."

He pressed his head against her tighter. "I need you, my friend. Please don't send me away."

"I know." She drew a shaking breath.

"Where are the children?"

The *children*. Sylan prodded at Jasen just a little with her mind. "Still upstairs."

"Sylan, have you gone to bed with anyone since you've been here?"

"No." She should feel proud, loyal. She felt embarrassed.

"So—damn—you're not on contraceptives then?"

"Oh." That was all he was asking. "I was sterilized after my daughter was born."

"The gods smile." But his face was drawn and sad.

Sylan was not cold anymore. Her heart hammered as she got up off the hardwood boards and lay down again in her bed. Standing before her, he took off his clothes, his face still etched in dour lines. Awkward, exposed, she shuffled out of her nightshirt, felt him slide under the covers beside her.

All at once, it was as inevitable as breathing. His body was compact, young, his hands cool against her shoulders. He felt to her arms much as she'd imagined. She'd imagined more often than she'd realized. Why had she made them wait till now, when Leric had always been willing? Nevan's pain at this betrayal could not be greater than their loneliness. What Leric was thinking she could only guess.

Later, he lay on her, his head heavy on her chest. She pulled the blankets up against the chill.

"Do you feel better?" she asked him.

"I do," he said, muffled. "I didn't think I would, not really. But I do." He yawned. "Probably just too weary to hurt."

"I'm surprised that you didn't go to Sherayna, when you both loved Illia so much."

He said nothing.

"You didn't—did you? Only, you seemed so alone tonight."

"No, only you."

"She is too much like a sister?"

After a moment, he said, "It would have been unkind."

"Unkind?"

But he shook his head and rolled onto his side, his arm around her sleepily.

"I worry all the time," he said after a while. "I worry about Karmeena. How she insists on believing Lia may be alive. Perhaps she is alive. I feel vile denying that and too terrified to cling to hope. I worry that Kara will separate herself from reality—a Borderal cannot do that. We have too much at stake."

"Jasen says she knows Illia's gone. He can see it in her mind."

"Have they gone to bed together yet, do you think?"

"God, no! Karmeena's a baby to him."

"I was sleeping with her mother when I was her age."

"No, Jasen's too old for her," Sylan repeated. "Besides, he sees her as a sister. He sees his sister in her. I've been the worst mother in the world to stay away all these years, not finding a way to reach Miri. There must be a way, without the City finding us."

She could feel him wince. He kissed her throat and said, "There are times I think we are as powerless against life as the gods fleeing the Flood of Sobai. There are times I would rather surrender to the waters."

CHAPTER 44

It was the first of Early-Spring, the first day of the new year. From the corner of the hallway, Karmeena watched Jasen and her father washing the breakfast dishes.

"She still has her Zerin passes," Jasen said. "Enough time has passed. It's silly for us just to sit here—it's silly for her in particular. She has no friends, no school, no work but filling out textile inventories."

Leric dried a plate with slow swoops. "Illia was afraid to let her go to that island. I don't want to imagine the look on her face if she saw me risking Karmeena."

"And you don't want to lose Karmeena—that's natural. But I think we ought to go."

Yes, thought Karmeena. *That's it: leaving Papa may terrify me, but we need to go.*

Leric put his plate away and leaned with his palms on the counter. "And you want to reach your family. That's natural too. But to tear what's left of my family apart to do it? Or is this vengeance because you still blame us for the deaths of your mother's family?"

"That's not fair. Are you going to say next that I'm glad Illia's dead—because it evens the score?"

Illia's dead. A hard ball formed at the back of Karmeena's throat.

"Of course I don't say that," said her father. "I'm sorry. If my words were unfair, I am sorry. But to take Kara away now . . ." He threw his dishcloth on the counter and stepped away. "No. My answer is no."

Indignation swallowed Karmeena's fear.

"It's not your choice!" She burst into the kitchen. "It's my risk to take. All my life you've kept me at home. When you were my age you were fighting the City, all of you. But you never taught me to fight. Maybe you thought that I was too soft to be capable—"

"Kara, you're capable of any feat of courage," said Leric.

"Capable of going to Zerin."

"You don't have to prove yourself."

"Yes, she does—" began Jasen.

"Not for me. For them!" said Karmeena at the same time.

Leric glanced between them. To Jasen he said, "What are you saying she has to prove?"

"Nothing," said Jasen and Karmeena together.

"She simply needs to grow up," Jasen added.

"She's barely fifteen!"

"Leric, we're fugitives here. Nothing is sure in our lives now. And what would you save her for, childhood? Here? It's too late for that. I was a child at her age, but I had not seen my mother murdered or my home destroyed."

Leric's eyes sprang to Karmeena.

"The truth is . . ." She stumbled but plowed on: "you . . . never raised me to fight like a Borderal. Now, let me tell you something. There's a good that is higher than the Borderal cause: to serve our friends. To make up for the pain we've caused. To help the gods. That's . . . higher . . ." She broke off, crying like a two-year-old.

"Micor encouraged her to go," said Jasen. "He must believe we'll be safe." He stepped close to Leric. "Look, I don't deny there will be some risk if the City picks us up before we reach the island. But that doesn't seem likely. Why would they stop us? Our passes are valid. And who would recognize us as fugitives? And once we're there, we'll be with friends. Micor's contacts will keep us safe."

There was a silence. Karmeena kept her gaze on the ground.

"You're certain?" she heard her father's voice. Looking up, she saw his eyes on her.

She nodded.

After a time, he said, "It's a dangerous thing to spend too much time from home. I've done it, and it's kept me from knowing you." He smiled at her sadly. "When you return, I'll expect you to teach me all the things that I've misunderstood."

≈•≈

When they left, she kissed her father quickly, knowing that if she threw herself into his arms, she'd never have the courage to go. She and Jasen walked down to the center of town. Wooded streets gave way to broad avenues, pulsing with movement and noises of transports and feet clacking, of voices, bells, and beeps. Karmeena clung to Jasen's hand and gazed about in wonder.

They took a public transport to Senarna, over the mountains and down through the snow-covered fields of Semlona that stretched far as the eye could see, so much vaster than the fields of Meena.

"Is all this the Semlona farmland?" asked Karmeena.

"A lot of it, I think," said Jasen. "But I read that a lot of this land's too far north to have a substantial growing year."

They reached Senarna in the middle of the night. Karmeena's head pounded from the long ride; her muscles ached. Squat towers crowded the city's narrow streets, which glowed with eerie emerald lamps and echoed with chatter. Their hotel room was tiny and smelled sticky with rosid-fruit wine, but it had a bed and forced-air heating. Karmeena fell asleep without even noticing she hadn't had her supper.

≈•≈

When they had crossed the island of Refomin and reached the Zerin ferry, Jasen grew agitated, and it frightened Karmeena. Her Zerin pass was in her true name and listed her homeland as Meena. And while it was no crime to be a resident of Meena, it was conspicuous. Her story would be that her family had relocated to the Remote Islands shortly after her test. With his accent and false pass as an Islander, Jasen would play her cousin. But would they believe it?

At the kiosk, Karmeena showed the Zerin passes and stammered through her lie.

"I'm sorry I'm talking so silly," she said, after mispronouncing the name of her home island twice. "It's just, I'm nervous. I've never been so far from home before."

"It doesn't get much farther than Zerin," the overseer said and disappeared into the inn with the passes.

After far too long, he reemerged, accompanied by an older woman, in Jetho's gray, who greeted them heartily.

"You've taken your time in deciding to join us." She inspected Karmeena's pass.

"My mother didn't want me to leave till I was older."

"Well, that's understandable," said the Jetho.

By the time they settled in the boat, the sun was sinking low and the temperature near freezing. The Jetho asked a stream of questions, and Karmeena was in a constant state of anxiety. On the far side of the straits, the Jetho ushered them into a carriage pulled by two shezmar with sloping, striped backs. The journey to the town of Vojin meant hours of clopping through the snow in the moonlight. Karmeena closed her mind completely and spoke as little as possible. She was just starting to nod off when she was thrown against the side of the carriage. They spun a full circle, the shezmar shrieking.

"It's all right!" cried the Jetho as they came to a stop with a thump. "We just hit an ice slick. Are you two all right? I'm going to see to the shezmar." She scampered out into the night, a blast of freezing air sweeping through the open door. After a few moments, the shezmar ceased to squeal and pull. The Jetho got back into the coach.

"We can't pull it out of the drift," she said. "But it's just half a measure to Vojin. It won't be a bad walk. I really am so sorry. I should have put you up at the pier. Only I didn't wager on such wretched visibility. I am really so very sorry. . . ."

The Jetho talked on. They bundled up and followed her as she led the shezmar along the icy road. Karmeena's shoes were not made for ice, and she slipped frequently. Her hands and feet were burning by the time they saw the lights of Vojin.

In the town, the Jetho ushered them into a cold chamber lit by dim oil lamps. The next moment, the room was buzzing with five or six people, building a fire, piling cushions and blankets, and checking Karmeena and Jasen for frostbite. Karmeena's toes were slightly frostbitten, and the Zerins made her soak them in a tub of lukewarm water. Her feet and her hands stung.

When she looked for Jasen, she found him standing with his back to the fire, gaping ridiculously. She frowned, following his gaze.

Before them was a very beautiful woman. Her mouth gaped liked Jasen's, but unlike him she didn't look silly. Her gown swayed about her ankles with the grace of a well-helped goddess. Dark hair framed her oval face like a hood.

She took a step toward Jasen. Then, they came together fast and held on tight, she standing on tiptoe to fit her chin across his shoulder.

"Miri," Jasen said, and something else in the Keshnul tongue.

Jasen's sister. How could Jasen have a sister like that?

Something her mother had said floated ghostly through her mind. Every day, life sends things we would never have imagined. How can we know what we'll do when faced with the unforeseeable?

CHAPTER 45

The first thing Jasen noticed was the way she leaned over to smooth blankets onto the mattress: stiff-backed like Miri—a habit she'd formed as a five-year-old in a dance class. She was the same. She was entirely different.

"It is you," she whispered in soft, strange words. He pressed his palms against her brown cheeks. "How did you get here? Wait, I'll get Dad." She turned to the others standing by and giggled. "This is my brother, Jasen." She wrapped her arm around his waist. Only when she switched to Tapanayn did he realize it was Keshnul they'd been speaking.

And now she'd announced him publicly. Had that been a mistake?

Miri had already skipped away to the door. Singing out, "I'll be right back," she vanished into the night. The others laid out food and tended Karmeena's feet. Then, with quiet goodnights, they left him alone with Karmeena.

She stared at the door, eyes wide. Was she jealous that he had found his sister when she herself had been a sister to him for so many years? But Karmeena was still his sister. He tried to tell her that with his mind, but her mind stayed closed. He sat down next to her and rubbed her clammy hands between his own.

A few minutes passed, long enough for Jasen to feel apprehensive. Would the City come for them?

The door opened. There with Miri stood his father: a middle-aged man pulled out of his bed, armed only with his nightshirt, a crooked coat, and a pair of snow-soaked boots.

"I thought I was dreaming, but I see you here," his father said in Keshnul.

"It isn't a dream," answered Jasen. *But it will be a battle*, he thought with a pang. He hadn't intended this resentment. *I got here. But you . . . couldn't you find a way to bring me here in all these years?*

Jasen came into his father's embrace. How small the man was, shrunken, fragile. His father—more like his son. It wasn't Nevan's fault that he was a weak man, that he'd sat here all these years, writing them the occasional letter. And had he taken down the shield? Jasen didn't even have to ask.

≈•≈

Nevan's Journal
Perdita: 10 Early-Spring, 22.09.2041 After the End

It's well past midnight. The words swirl before me black on purple as I scribble in the shadow of the fire and the moons. I am writing in the dark because my son is sleeping near me, and I won't disturb him by lighting a candle.

He came back tonight. There's no momentous way to say it. Back? Forward: a new-made Jasen to a new-made Miri, and even a newer Nevan.

I have paused here several minutes just to look at him. When his face seems to shift, it is only the shifting flames in the grate. But his face shifts also in my mind with the years. He still has my big eyes, still the curve of his mother's chin, but hardened and broadened into the face of a man I do not know. His hands are large—flat, strong hands. Sylan's, I suppose, in male form. They surprised me, his hands, when he embraced me.

He is so angry at me! And he faults me rightly. I was a grown man when we parted, placed in a position to gain some influence with the king and queen themselves—and instead I became a coward and prisoner. His condemnation pierces me, yet it pierces deeper to see him condemn himself. He is torn by remorse for all the things he imagines he has failed to do, and his anger at me is his anger at himself.

He can't see how much he's accomplished. He was a boy when last I saw him. Now, barely twenty-five, he's a well-traveled, confident man. He's seen more of this planet than Miri or Sylan or I—he understands it better. And still he harbors such shame.

I won't write tonight all the things he told me. I will write a thing he didn't tell me, a thing he didn't want me to know—but he was so sleepy and his mind so open that I saw it all the same.

His mother has a lover. That shouldn't leave me feeling like she's shoved me off a cliff. Eight years is a long time to live celibate. Yet I expected something else of Sylan. How unfair to her that is.

CHAPTER 46

The letter was in Jasen's scrawl. It began:

> *Mother, we addressed this letter to you because it most nearly concerns you, but we ask that you read it aloud because, as your respective children, we want you to hear together.*

She looked up at Leric, sitting across the table with eager eyes.

"Well," he prompted, "is there news?"

She cleared her throat. "'We arrived on Zerin without incident and are both well. They knew us—and they've accepted us.'"

She glanced up at Leric.

"So far so good." He nodded for her to continue.

"'We have met with my father and sister.'" She stopped, and the sentence repeated in her mind in fragments. It was exactly what they'd hoped for. Why was that so frightening? She looked to Leric for support.

He sat composed, hands folded on the table. "Go on."

She took the letter up again. "'They are both well and eager to see you. The Im Jetho has given his permission for you to come to Zerin at once. You will not require a pass. They will be waiting for you at the ferry. We will explain more when you get here. K. sends her love to her father and wishes, as I do, that he could be with us. Regrettably, the Zerins ask that you come alone. Gods' love from your son and K.'"

Sylan stared at the page. "At once," she repeated. "After all these years—at once. They must have found a way to get me past City surveillance. They must. They wouldn't let me through otherwise."

They sat for some moments in silence.

"When you see them," said Leric, "give them my love. All of them: mine and yours—why not? Why shouldn't we love them all for the gods?"

"You're talking to yourself."

"When will you go?"

"At once, as they ask. A couple of days to prepare." She looked across at him. He was watching his thumb tap gently on the table, nodding slowly in time with it. She stood up and went to the window, dull yellow light falling onto the dusty sill.

"It's like a tomb in here," she said. Then it struck her like lightning: in a very few days, she would see her daughter, an adult, almost nineteen. She tried to imagine all the little changes she'd missed and could never make up for. She put her hand to her mouth. This was joy, she thought—joy that she was weeping for. Joy first and sorrow second: the future first, the past second.

She didn't cry for very long, as if the emotions were not quite real. She looked out the window, at lavender hills under lavender clouds, and wondered how in all that lavender, the room light still filtered in yellow. An hour had passed by the wall clock when she looked around again. Leric was gone.

They typically spent their days in the house; it remained unsafe to be seen out too much. Tyoroc and Sica were sometimes there with them but often away on business. They were gone today.

All afternoon, Sylan heard Leric creaking here and there over the upstairs floorboards. She did not work. Sometimes she almost cried again but ended by feeling only vaguely sick, trapped, as she had felt toward the end in Melnar. But it struck her that in this dank house she had sometimes felt free. She didn't see Leric until dinner. They spread out cold chicken with fruit and tea.

"I'm happy for you," he said over his teacup, flatly, as if making a painful admission—or telling a courteous lie.

"Thank you."

"You've been a Borderal prisoner all these years, no use pretending you've been anything else. We're to blame for everything you've suffered here. Jasen thought so, though he blamed it all on Sherayna."

"Destroying our ship, you mean?"

"Yes."

"Yes," said Sylan. "You are the obsessive people. Not the Borderals, the Perditans. But I couldn't tell you how to do differently after so many years of digging in your lines. I can't blame you. Your ancestors did it. We all do it. Maybe the Kiris are right: the sect that says there's no hope for humanity."

They ate in silence and, when they'd finished, stared at empty plates.

"I'll tell you something," said Leric. "All Karmeena's life, when I've looked at her, I've seen Illia and me as one. Well, that's a common experience of parents. But since Illia died . . ." He sighed, resting his fingers against his forehead. "Since she died, I have had the strangest impression that she never really existed. And when I've looked at Karmeena, I've seen someone partly me and partly dream. And now, Kara's gone, and I feel that I am the dream, that the departed are the real ones."

Sylan found nothing to say. She cleared away the dishes, washed them, dried them, set them in their cupboards. Leric sat at the table all the while. She sat beside him—not across, but on the floor, by his cushion, setting her standing slightly beneath his own in a gesture she could not explain to herself.

"I have never felt unreal," she said. "But I have felt forgotten. But I do not forget."

He looked at her fiercely. "What have I done to make everyone leave me? Don't answer that! I know the question is childish. But the reality remains. My parents are gone, Illia, Raja, Shoshec, Sherayna, Karmeena, and Jasen, and you too. So go. Go back to your family."

He stood and strode out of the room. Sylan followed him into the center room. The windows were not so yellow there. The pale purple light of evening bathed the furniture like cool water.

"Do you know what I've done?" he spat suddenly. "The computers. I loved them too much. Illia said it was bad for us. Everyone thought it was bad. Everyone but you—you and me. I let you show me how to use them, how to crack City codes. How to need them, just like the City, unable to live without the machine. Illia knew—it was always stupid. I never told her what you showed me, but she knew. I don't think she ever forgave me for that."

"You're ranting," said Sylan. "You're not to blame. But I do have to go to my children. It has nothing to do with you."

He laughed. He refused to look at her. They both stared out onto the evening mountains. He laughed again, softer. "Nothing. Exactly. I am not your prison warden anymore." He spun to face her, dark against the window. "So why are you justifying yourself to me?"

Sylan held out her hands. "Leric, I misspeak. Your language is not my language. I meant, me going has nothing to do with you. No, I meant, if I didn't have to leave, I would stay. I meant, I want to go to see them, but I wish that didn't mean to leave without you. That is what I meant."

"I'm touched," he said harshly. "But I am no responsibility of yours."

Sylan felt her throat close. She tried to speak like a Perditan, as if to help the gods. "I love you."

"How can you?"

"Like this." She drew him into her arms, half-expecting him to pull away, but he fell into her embrace.

"Maybe it will be a new world," said Sylan. "Maybe if I can get the shield down and call for help, the other worlds will help you too after all."

Leric stepped back, still holding her arms. "If you think we've fought spaceflight all these years, died to prevent it, killed to prevent it, without thinking of all the eventualities—" He shook his head. "No other world can recreate Perdita. They would give us new tech and the conflict would be the same. Or they would give us new attitudes, but the old attitudes would remain, and the conflicts would be more complex. Or they would teach the City that they can go to the stars and live without Perdita, and the City would have lost their only incentive not to let the planet die. A new world can only be born out of fire."

CHAPTER 47

Miri talked with Karmeena of things Karmeena could never remember the next second. Her replies must have been almost nothing, for in time, Miri spoke to her less.

Perhaps I don't interest her anymore, thought Karmeena with a stab in her chest.

But one Early-Spring day, when Karmeena and Jasen were chatting in Karmeena's room, Miri came to see them. Under her coat, she wore a warm maroon gown. With her ruddy face and her red-brown hair, she drew Karmeena toward her like a furnace in the snow.

"I told Olwer I'd teach Karmeena about the ways of Zerin today," she said.

"Just Karmeena? Your own brother isn't allowed to learn?" said Jasen in mock incredulity.

"You," said Miri, "get to listen to your father. After all, you and Karmeena come from different backgrounds, and you'll probably have different questions. And if you're very good, Jas, maybe my friend Elri will show you some sights later on."

Jasen laughed too. "The orange-haired girl? What sights is she going to show me?"

"What indeed."

In the midst of their laughter, Karmeena felt unbearably lonely. She sat dumbly when Jasen left, wanting nothing more than to be alone with Miri and nothing more than to escape.

Miri sat opposite her. "I don't know very much about the Borderals. I hope to learn about them, and you too." As she spoke, she leaned over to meet Karmeena's downcast eyes, like a teacher trying to draw out a timid child.

The condescension infuriated Karmeena. "The Borderals believe that humans should live in the way they evolved to live: simple and close to the land. They believe that tech and urbanization only separate humans from nature and lead to ecological collapse due to a lack of understanding of the world." She glared at Miri. "They believe the Kiris are hypocrites for pretending to abandon high technology but still keeping it in their tech centers."

Miri smiled. "Well said. We're a little different from the Borderals. Zerin, like the Kiris, believes that high tech can be utilized without negative consequences. No, that's wrong. The Kiris believe that it must be utilized as a lesser evil. For example, a weapon of mass destruction might accidentally destroy one's own world, but it's better have it than to lie open to enemy attacks specifically designed to destroy one's world. But the Zerins believe that high tech can be utilized for the good, for example, that tech should be used to cure illnesses."

Karmeena said, "We believe, in the long run, it's better to let people die if they can't be easily cured." She spoke bravely, thinking of her mother.

"We think so too—the Kiris, I mean. The Zerins don't believe that."

"Then what do they want? They sound like the City."

"They want safe development of tech, development that won't fracture humanity's relationship with the rest of nature."

"What's this 'safe?'"

Miri rested her chin in her hands. "That's the question, no? The core reason that the Zerins are currently supporting a moratorium on tech advancement. They believe there must be firmer rules in place."

"Firmer rules? City rules are no rules!"

Miri sighed. "We can't go on like this."

A lump rose in Karmeena's throat. How could she have spoken that way? "I'm sorry."

"Don't be sorry." Miri stood up.

"Don't go!" cried Karmeena, bolting to her feet.

"I was hoping to go along with you, Karmeena. I have a place I'd like to show you." She handed Karmeena a pair of snow boots.

≈•≈

After a few minutes of walking, the cold didn't bite hard. The sun shone and the melting snow glistened and cracked icily underfoot. They hiked north. Soon, the tall pines blotted out the sun, enclosing them in a veil of snow and shadow, punctuated by flares of sunlight that reminded Karmeena of moments of clarity in dreams. Miri looked behind her and held out her hand.

"Jasen has been telling me about you." She pulled Karmeena alongside her. "He loves you very much, you know. But he thinks of you as a child."

"You think I want him to think of me differently?"

"I think he doesn't realize how much it must have changed you to lose your mother."

"She may still be alive," protested Karmeena, a wave of longing flooding her.

Miri looked her in the eye. "You don't believe that. I can't imagine how you must feel."

"Of course you can."

"No. I can't. I'm going to have my mother back soon. Your strength astounds me, Karmeena."

Karmeena marveled to think that she might have a knowledge of life Miri lacked. "What strength? I survive because I do that or I die. And dying doesn't feel like much of an option."

Miri let go of Karmeena's hand to struggle up an incline.

Coming up beside her, Karmeena said, "Jasen told me once that Miri's short for Mirllagíra."

Miri looked up with a smile. "That's right."

"What does it mean?"

"'The daughter of *mirlla*.' We are all sons and daughters of *mirlla*, whatever some others may think."

"Miri, I like your language. Your father's language, not Vunizh."

"Keshnul, yes. It's not strident like Vunizh."

Karmeena felt her face grow hot, but she made herself ask it: "How do you say, 'I love you' in Keshnul?"

Miri gave her half a smile. "*Llef ze melez.*"

They crossed into a grotto. Miri scrabbled down the rocks onto a narrow floor of snow. Following her, Karmeena saw that they stood before a small cave entrance.

"Wait for me." Bending to her hands and knees, Miri vanished into the darkness. The orange of a lamp flared inside, and she called for Karmeena to join her. The cave was just high enough for one to stand stooping; it was roughly five meters deep. In addition to the lamp, there was a straw mattress and a wooden chest.

"This reminds me of our Borderal hideouts." Karmeena sat by Miri. "It's so warm in here."

"Hot springs run under the rocks, down from the mountains."

"How did you find this place?"

"It was my friend Elri's. And someone else's before her. Everybody knows I use it now. We don't have many single rooms on Zerin, so lots of people find hideaways to have some privacy."

"Why did you want to see me privately?"

"Because I thought I might find things I'd want to say without other people walking in."

"Like?"

"Like there's more to you than meets the eye. You're brave and you're smart, and there's no one else like you here."

Karmeena shook her head. "Miri, I've never done anything. I'm not brave and no smarter than anyone else."

"You escaped from Meena, helped your family escape. You've been the center of the whole plan that brought you to Zerin. That's nothing?" As she spoke, she scraped her hair back from her eyes with her hand, a graceful turn of her head and wrist.

"Miri," blurted Karmeena, "you look like a goddess."

"I'm flattered, and I only hope the goddesses aren't offended."

"Miri, *llef ze melez.*"

Miri glanced at her with a gentle smile. "Karmeena, do you think you know me well enough to say that?"

"I don't think it matters what I know, it's what I feel." Her heart was pounding.

Miri placed a slender hand to Karmeena's cheek and kissed her lips.

PART FOUR

THE JAE PROJECT

CHAPTER 48

Nevan's Journal
Perdita: 19 Early-Spring, 31.09.2041 After the End

Miri, Jasen, and I were gathered by my hearth fire when Miri's friend, Elri, informed us that Sylan was in sight. We went out into the sleet-soaked afternoon just as she climbed down from the cart. She hasn't changed at all.

She walked like a blind woman until she recognized Miri through the white haze that pummeled the ground between them. She slipped and slid across the last few steps and raised her hand to Miri's cheek but did not touch it, and she cried. I hate to see my wife crying because I know how much she hates it. Miri took her in her arms, and Jasen hugged them both. I couldn't. It wasn't my time.

Back at my room, Sylan sank onto the sitting cushions by Miri's side and hid her head on Miri's shoulder. After a time, her eyes lit on me. She grinned in a way I can only describe as genuinely friendly.

Embracing me firmly, she said, "It is such a relief—such a relief to see your face again."

I cried too.

As we talked into the night, Jasen hung back from saying what was in his mind, granting Sylan and Miri time for one another.

But at length, he said, "*Mila*, I wrote you that I'd explain why they let you come here." A smile broke across his face. "They say they want you to shut off the shield."

Sylan stared at him. "They *want* me . . . ?"

"They say that the king is demanding it, which I don't doubt is true. Olwer says their records don't give them full instructions for shutting it down. That may be true. He *says* they need your expertise to make sure it's powered down correctly and not damaged. That I don't believe for a second. They wouldn't smuggle you in past the surveillance stations just to shut down the shield. It can't be that hard an operation. They need you here for something else."

"For what else?"

"I don't know."

Sylan glanced at me.

"I don't know either," I said, "But I agree with Jasen. They may have no choice but to lower the shield, for now, but they could figure out how to do it. I could figure it out."

Finally, Jasen shook his head. "I only know that if they give you the chance to get the shield down, you have to take it. Send a message out. And then it won't just be the Zerins or the City. Then we can bargain for ourselves."

≈•≈

23 Early-Spring, 35.09.2041:

Yesterday evening, I was writing by my little fire when Sylan arrived unexpectedly.

"You certainly hide a good deal in here," she said as she sat down.

"It's cold outside."

"Most people are in the common room. Some of the children are putting on a dance."

I smiled. "But you decided to hide here with me."

"I have missed you, my old friend." We reached across the little space between us and grasped hands.

"Sylan." I looked down at her hands in my own. "We aren't really married anymore, are we?"

"No."

I nodded. "You've found someone else."

She gave me a gentle look.

"I still love you," I said. "I still love you as my wife." And at that moment, I wanted nothing more than to travel back a decade to our house in Melnar—she and I and our children. Perhaps, after all, I'm not in love with her anymore. Perhaps that's why I longed for the memory.

Her voice grew flat, as it did when she had to speak of difficult things. "You love me? You wouldn't if you had to live with me."

"But your new lover, he doesn't find you difficult to live with."

"He isn't married to me."

"Meaning?"

"He isn't bound to me. You would be." She was silent a while, and there were tears on her cheeks. "I know you love me, Nevan. Maybe I should never have let you love me. But now, I have to set you free—and I need to be free of you."

This has been a long time in coming: more than eight years, since Melnar. My heart has known for years that I can't hold her.

We spent that night together: to say good-bye, she said. The next morning, I kindled a fire while Sylan set water to boil. We sat by the hearth, still wearing our thick nightclothes with woolen shawls wrapped round us as the sun peaked fraily through my western window.

I clutched my teacup, watching Sylan watch the flames.

"You're contemplative," I said. My mind was still caught in the currents of the night, and I was frightened by her silence.

"I know how the War ended."

"What?" It was the last thing I expected to hear.

"I pieced it together from my own research and Micor's documents. I never wrote anything down," she said. "It didn't seem relevant at first. And later, too relevant. Too much information on jae."

"It was jae then?"

"After a fashion." She sipped her tea. "For decades, the Samas were looking for a cure for the plague. They finally came to the conclusion that the only way to combat the jae contamination was to remove it from the environment. So they began searching for a way to shift the unstable, semishifted particles back into a stable phase. They called it the Jae Reversal. But it would only be effective if they pulsed the Reversal energy matrix directly into contaminated areas. If they kept the Reversal pattern inside a generator, it would merely shift particles confined in the generator. That wouldn't do anything to help open spaces already contaminated."

I was trembling. "They released a jae field into an open space."

"They had plans to release it along communication pulse lines." She paused, watching me take that in. A jae matrix released into the open environments of every planet in the

Sama Empire not on comm silence: no wonder almost all macroscopic life died! Will we ever understand such folly? Or do we already understand—that sometimes humans make mistakes: a small mistake, perhaps. Perhaps an order misunderstood, a mistake magnified by the absurd immensity of human might?

Sylan went on, "The field was so low energy it read almost zero. The last record I found was a piece of a report that cited the Reversal Project as complete and standing by. That was in the year 3196 of the Sama calendar."

"The year of the End."

She nodded. "They implemented the Reversal. My best hypothesis is that unforeseen effects caused a violent shift that destroyed virtually all cells that came in contact with it. Then, the field shifted back toward normal phase—hence the lower contamination levels found after the War's End. In that sense, at least, the Reversal worked." She paused. "My mother must have gotten a lead that this information was stored on Perdita. Nevan, if the City learns about the Reversal, they might assume it means jae can be used safely. They might cling all the harder to the idea of developing jae."

I kissed her. "Just when it can't get heavier, it gets heavier."

After some minutes, she said, "Once I've brought the shield down, I'll find the communication relays and get a message through to the nearest planet. When they send a ship, we'll tell them about the War, and with the force of their presence behind us, we'll make the Perditans listen too. Contact with a foreign power will unite them, it has to. They'll be Perditans alone amid the whole of Afebat. They'll have to stop fighting."

I don't believe Perdita is ready for that contact. They'd try to transplant offworld crops—that much is certain, and that alone could cause ecological mayhem. But to resist Sylan, at that moment, seemed as senseless as resisting the tides of history. Perdita cannot stay hidden.

I tried to conceptualize War's End, dozens of planets stripped of life. Suddenly it mattered very little to me.

"I wish we could still love," I said.

"We can, if you can learn to love me without holding me."

CHAPTER 49

The melting snow sent rivulets running down waterworn rocks to the creek. Micor pulled his coat around him in the cool morning of the east Oja spring and wondered again why Olloan had requested that they meet in the remote forest. But Olloan would explain soon.

For now, I am here, and that is enough. I am here, white like the snow. This place is me. He reached out to touch a wet cedar trunk, and it seemed he was holding the hand of a brother. Then he heard the familiar footsteps.

Olloan emerged into view, shrouded in a shapeless coat. There was a hiddenness in his face too—a courteous blankness that dropped a rock on Micor's heart.

"What's happened, Olloan? Is it bad as all that?"

Olloan came to a halt, scratched his nose absently, as if he didn't know how to begin. "I've just come from Senarna."

"Senarna. I thought you were going to investigate the Jae Project site by the Lo Ren."

"I did. I got within about three measures of the site itself, but Laynia told you the truth when she called it impregnable. The project center is buried deep between the mountains and the lake itself. There's one access road. I saw no way in. So I went to Senarna to spy on the administrative side instead." He walked past Micor to stare at the eddies in the creek. "I followed Laynia, which isn't easy, as you know. I had to bring in some of my own agents—people I trust from Oja. Yes, I know you didn't want any more Borderals to know yet. But they will find out soon in any case."

He looked up at Micor, awaiting some response.

"Yes. You found?"

"You were right. Her control over the project has dwindled to almost nothing. Warmaster Lashen pretends to listen to her, but the pretense is obvious."

Micor pressed a foot against the comforting solidness of a rock. "Olloan, I don't know what to do. You say our Borderals will soon find the truth. And what then? They'll be frightened, and frightening people into an aggressive assault against a jae reactor is the last thing we want."

Olloan nodded. "I agree. Either the assault would fail outright, with loss of lives—or it would succeed, the reactor would be destabilized, and it would be the War's End on Perdita."

"What do you suggest?"

Olloan replied like one delivering a speech: "This new project is based on the West-of-Nows' *Jae History*. Their report uses information from pre-End sources. What that gives the City, if they interpret it all correctly, is faulty but functional jae tech that will disperse jae contamination throughout the planet. And if they tried to use it to launch a ship with the shield up—"

"The shield will be down in a few days. That's taken care of."

Olloan sighed in relief. "That's good, Micor. Thank you."

"And then . . ."

Olloan's eyes flicked like an animal peering through a cage. "There's the Correction."

"No!"

Olloan stepped up to him. "What else can we do? We can't stop them."

"We can negotiate."

"Our best negotiator is Laynia, and she's failing."

"But if they knew the severity of the particle shift, even in the short term—"

"We can't prove that it will be 'severe.' We don't have hard numbers for it. It's even conceivable, Micor, that it won't be as bad as we fear. And if there's a chance it might go well, you know the City will take the risk."

Micor knew Olloan's solution was wrong, but he had no adequate counterproposal. He needed time to think.

Then Olloan was standing before him, embracing him, laying his chin on Micor's shoulder.

"Listen," said Olloan, gently drawing away, "if we cannot stop the City, we can at least give them the Correction. Then, they have the benefit of all the information, and we can hope that this time the kind of jae they create will shift correctly— jae without appreciable contamination, at last."

"'Hope.' The Correction has never been used. The last records show only the earliest practical trials. You know I have grave doubts. I've seen calculations in the papers that do not make sense to me."

"I know, and yet it's our best hope."

Micor shook his head. "We can't do it."

Olloan drew a deep breath. "It's done."

Micor stared uncomprehending.

"I've done it. I turned the Correction over to the warmaster."

Micor's legs gave out, and he sat down in the snow. For a long time, he neither moved nor spoke. The meltwater swirled in the creek with a voice as even as a sleeper's breathing.

Finally Micor whispered to the air, "You! Of all the people I believed I could trust. Your mother died because the City lost the Lost Lands—and you, her own son, join with them. You take away our only bargaining token, that jae is deadly. You give them a document they can wave in our faces saying, 'Look! The problem is solved!' It is not solved! I do not trust the Correction! For all we know, it may backfire as completely as the War's End itself. And you, you gave them this . . . means perhaps to eradicate life on this planet." His voice trailed away, and he felt tears hot on his cheeks.

He looked up to see Olloan sitting by him in the snow, his face contorted in misery.

After a long space, Olloan said, "Perhaps I was wrong. At any rate, my agents will learn about this soon. They've been watching the Jae Project too closely not to notice a major advance in its development. And if I don't tell them the Correction comes from me, they'll tear the planet apart till they find out. And when they do find out, they'll kill me—they'll have to. They can't trust me, and I know too much."

Micor was weeping freely now. "You could go to Zerin."

"Probably Zerin wouldn't sanction my action any more than you do. And Zerin and the Borderals will have to be able to stand together in the time to come. I won't divide them."

"Gods help you, Olloan. What do you plan to do?"

"Micor, I plan to die."

Micor slipped down into the snow and reached out a groping hand.

Olloan grasped it. "There is no better way. If I went to the City, they'd make me denounce the Borderals, and if I did not, they'd have to execute me by law as a rebel. Or they'd forego the law and hold me prisoner, try to use me. I won't have it."

"I'll hide you."

"Our Borderals will need you. You can't waste your time on me."

Tears slipped down Micor's face.

Olloan took a couple of steps and stopped. "I do love you."

"I love you too," said Micor dully. In his head he followed up with some platitude about finding a solution. They had to, didn't they? But he didn't say it. He was tired, suddenly. He needed time to reassess; solutions appeared in their own time. Didn't they?

Neither spoke. The only sound was the thawing creek. The snow stilled the world; it fell like peace. But it was false peace, a frozen peace, the peace of life absent.

A gunshot burst the air.

Micor jerked and looked up to see Olloan fall down the slight slope. His blood gushed red around him, melting the snow so that he sank before Micor's eyes. He knew he should run to his son, shake him, beg him to be alive. That was what any father would do. But Olloan wasn't alive; the bullet had gone straight through his brain. And Micor didn't do any of that. He sat still, going mindless as the rocks.

I must have lived too long to feel like a living being.

At last, he went to his son's body. The blood now flowed only sluggishly from his blasted head. Micor pulled the body out of the red cavity into which it had sunk. He carried it to the side of the creek and washed off the worst of the blood. Then he took the body up in his arms and began the long walk to the road and his transport.

CHAPTER 50

The rain pelted the window of Ethan's office in the Mesa prison. He tapped at his keyboard, filling out "Prisoner Transfer Triple Confirmation" forms. Since Meena, three separate officials had been required to identify each incoming prisoner. But identity papers were still too easy to forge. A move was afoot in Parliament to delegate Senarna record-keeping rights so rebels and their movements could be traced more effectively.

But the seer schools were fighting the proposition. Give the central government access to records on every citizen's life and the most innocent people would live in fear that their movements might be misinterpreted as rebel acts. They made a strong case. Both sides did. Ethan reserved his judgment. The only thing he wanted now was a job where he would not have to think.

His hands were sluggish with cold. With a sigh, he corrected three mistyped words and switched on his box heater. The department had told them to conserve energy. Any savings, they said, would be paid out to their employees to offset the newly inflated food prices. Still, the work would not get done if he could not physically do it. He flexed his fingers over the heater until they were hot and then returned to his typing. He was signing the form when his aide knocked.

"Sir, you have a visitor." The aide was peeking round the door with an uncharacteristic timidity.

"Yes?"

"Queen Laynia, sir." No sooner were the words out of his mouth than she brushed past him, elegant in a long green gown and dark rain cloak.

"Thank you." She waved the aide away. The aide closed the door without a glance at Ethan. "Cold downpour for the time of year," she remarked, pulling off slim black gloves.

"What do you require of me, my Queen?" Ethan peered up from his seat on the floor.

A smile fled across Laynia's face. "Admirable directness. I sit low before you." From a pocket, she produced a paper. "I have here a mandate commanding your attendance at Senarna in seven days. You may verify the king's signature."

She leaned over and set the paper on his desk.

"May I ask, my Queen, why you have been troubled with delivering it?"

"I told my husband that Lashen had need of your perspective but feared that if he asked for you, after the Meena affair, his judgment might be called into question. Since *no one* would question the king, I convinced him to make the arrangements himself by sending me. In a way, it's all true. Lashen does need your perspective, and he would never ask for you now." She crossed to the front of his desk and stood before him. "But your meeting with Lashen will be for show. You will stay at Ayer overnight and then come with me to Zerin."

"The king knows this?"

"The king knows what I want him to know. If you, or Lashen, tell him otherwise, he will still believe me."

"You are the power of the planet then, my Queen?"

She sank on her heels before his desk, lowering her standing. Her look was stark: not false, not true. "Warchief, you will come to Zerin."

CHAPTER 51

On Sylan's sixth day on Zerin, Olwer took her and Nevan to the shield control center. It was like stepping back a millennium. The room was huge, bristling with control panels and readouts with a hard gloss sharpened by a glowing white ceiling. Sylan breathed the antiseptic air.

If only Mother could have seen this. The thought sent a pang over the gladness.

Olwer walked to a console where a readout glowed: energy emissions plotted out in neat graphs. "These are the main power controls." He pointed.

Now she was in her own arena. She glanced over the readouts, Nevan coming up close behind her.

"Quite a fine maintenance job," she said. "You're only one millionth off on your secondary scattering pattern. She glanced at Olwer. "Jasen was right. Your people must know how to shut it off. You've never needed an outsider."

"Our people lost the documents that gave those protocols five hundred years ago. We can make guesses. But if you'd care to take a look, you'll see the main switch seems to be missing."

Sylan looked down. "So it is." Recalling the schematics she'd memorized, she went to the access panel for the main shutoff switch and peered at the circuits. "Three redundant sets of relays." She set to work tracing the circuits to their master switch. "The Sama Empire did not want to see this shield come down."

"They needed to guard the planet," said Nevan.

"Here." Three access panels down, Sylan found the master switch. She returned to the main power console and set to work closing down the preliminary systems.

Nevan rattled on, "Perdita was a prison planet because it was obscure—a place to keep war prisoners without fear of Kiri assaults. But that positioning also made it ideal to store sensitive information. And so it became a library bank for the Jae Reversal papers. But with such an investment in Perdita, the Samas needed to keep it safe, to ensure it could disappear if need be."

A blue light blinked on the console, indicating readiness for final shutdown. Sylan crossed back to the access panel and threw the master switch. The readouts immediately registered a decline in energy output. She smiled. "Now that's the prettiest thing I've ever laid eyes on."

It was almost over. *One more task, and I'll bring a renaissance to this planet stumbling in the dark. And Leric will see that I was right.*

"How long will it take for the shield to dissipate?" asked Olwer.

"I'd estimate five to ten hours." Sylan scanned the room for signs of a comm station.

"Fine." Olwer herded them toward the door. "We'll be sure to call you back if we have any problems."

"I ought to wait here," said Sylan. "I'm your expert, after all."

Olwer sighed. "I can't let you send any messages."

Sylan bit back a savage retort, considered her words carefully. "It's a violation of all our codes to seize thoughts from another's mind."

"I didn't read it in your mind, Sylan. It's obvious." He looked from Sylan to Nevan, bland and thoughtful. "Yes, Jasen was right, Sylan. We didn't bring you here just to shut off the shield. We need your knowledge of jae."

CHAPTER 52

It was always the same at Ayer Senarna, thought Ethan. Finely dressed people rustling amid the same swirl of tapestries. A termite's nest. The evening he arrived, he was scheduled to meet with Lashen. He scarcely had time to bathe and throw on his dress uniform before rushing to find the warmaster.

Yes, it was all for show, as Laynia had said—the warmaster in his palace office, like a prince, not a soldier. The desk and the cushions were covered in satin: no cabinets for files, no computer, only an intercom. Lashen was his old self, smiling behind his make-believe desk.

"Please." He gestured for Ethan to take the cushion across from him. "The king seems to think that I could benefit from your counsel, and far be it from me to contradict him. I'm glad you're here."

"Thank you."

"I must confess, however, I'm not aware of any operation that isn't running smoothly."

"You have no need of my counsel then, sir."

"Well, we'll see. Let me explain our most relevant project to you."

Ethan's eyes widened. Lashen surely wasn't planning to share real information.

"First, you should know that the planetary shield you alerted us to has been deactivated."

Ethan's heart leapt. Was it the truth? If it were a trick, it would have to be played fast. Given time, Ethan could check the truth of it with Kesoran. Lashen was grinning like an uncle giving out toys.

"You're sure?" said Ethan.

"Ever since you brought us your information, we've been pursuing the thing. It's down, all right."

Then, space was open to them, their ancient sister worlds. The stars, the galaxies—alien worlds: a thousand wonders. The wandering realm of the gods. "It's fantastic, Lashen. I can't tell you. You are to be congratulated."

But what if it were just another lie?

Lashen chuckled. "And you. And you. And I don't have to tell you that with the shield down, the Space Program can proceed. And it has. Faster than you could imagine. That *Jae History*, another discovery of yours, has formed the foundation for a space project that should be ready to take us across galaxies—galaxies, Ethan—less than a dozen years from now."

Ethan was not prepared for his own reaction. A jae program so far advanced? In his lifetime, how many hundreds of new worlds might he see? And yet no one could deny that jae was hazardous. It seemed better to resurrect the old program, his father's program. With the shield down, they could contact other worlds for help developing rippling engines, slower but safer. They could still walk through space.

And we wouldn't be exploiting documents I stole—the thought flickered through his mind.

"It's too much for me to take in, sir," he said. "We do know, however, that jae tech may lead to environmental contamination."

"That's so, of course. We've done all in our power to minimize the risks. We've never planned to use jae except as a starting point for reaching out to other worlds so we can meet them as equal space-farers, not backward beggars."

Ethan nodded. "That sounds viable."

"Oh, better than 'viable,' Ethan. An unlooked-for blessing rained down a couple of months ago in the form of a rebel traitor. He sent us a hearty dose of information. I can only wonder for how many centuries the rebels have been hoarding it." He broke into a wide grin. "It is no less than an ancient dissertation correcting the jae miscalculations that led to the plague."

A solution for the plague? *That's too good to be true.* "A rebel trick, sir?"

"Not possible. We've had engineers, historians, linguists tear it apart. If it were a fake, it would be the cleverest in history—infinitely beyond the power of the rebels to perpetrate in the mere eight years since the offworlders crashed and made jae an issue. Moreover, the man's motive makes sense. He realized he couldn't fight our project, so he chose to help us make it safer. He could be the first sensible anti-tech in the history of Perdita."

"But that means—"

"That the rebels somehow caught wind of the project, yes. Well—counselor, if you have any suggestions for tightening security, don't hesitate. On the other hand, I'm optimistic that they don't know exactly where we're stationed."

"How can I aid you, Lashen?"

Lashen gave him a steady gaze. "The queen."

He froze. *A trick of hers after all?*

"She has an errand tomorrow and wants you to accompany her."

"Yes. You know what she wants?"

"Not precisely. But you can believe it will bear on jae." He leaned in close again. "And her ideas are not conventional."

"I know."

"Hold that in your mind when she speaks to you. And remember I know it too. I know a great deal about her attitudes."

"Valuable information, I'd think, sir."

"Yes, indeed. Indeed it is. I haven't sent that information to market just yet, because to do so might have hindered our progress with the shield. But it will fetch its value. Soon. Ethan, press your uniform."

≈•≈

He didn't press it. The queen left a message for him to meet her next morning, dressed for travel. He wondered if he should refuse, make her account to the king for where she was taking him. But best to leave Lashen to contrive her fall, he concluded. And Ethan would discover what she'd been hiding, as he'd discovered the shield.

A gray rain tumbled out of the north. Laynia drove with a steel determination, making no attempt at conversation.

Ethan found his thoughts dwelling on Lashen. Yesterday, his world had been melting into a shape, like mercury drops merging and splintering. He had gone to bed happy on the whole, with the shield down, a space program in place, and his old friend his friend again.

Yet in the light of a muted day, his mind had grown more sober. Lashen was not working with Laynia, probably. That was good. But it did not alter the fact that Lashen had lied to him for years.

And if he lied in a good cause—as I think that he did—does that wipe away the lies? He could have trusted me. It seems I made an error somewhere: I believed that worthiness will, of necessity, derive from worthy motives. Lashen believes in what seems right to me. But if he hurts and deceives to achieve what he believes, is he any different from the queen, who probably believes, as much as he does, that her deceptions will bring about what is right? And I . . . am I any different, I who have destroyed so much? Torna knew I was wrong. Now that she is gone, who can I trust?

He felt fevered. He could not solve these riddles.

I can't trust myself, and that's a hard fate. Because, at the end, one's own reason is all there is. That's what Father said. Use reason, as the gods cannot. See each thing as if for the first time.

As if such a thing weren't impossible.

≈•≈

At the north end of Refomin, they caught the ferry to Zerin, disembarking at the village of Nac. That Nac was labeled as a village on maps was merely a courtesy. It was only the Zerin ferry station: a few shapeless hovels by a mud-sunk road. Laynia steered him into one of those hovels.

She was there, Sherayna, in blue with her hair tied back. She turned as the door opened. "You!"

He stood rapt. Afraid as she rushed at him.

She hit him across the jowl and sent him reeling. She kicked him in the ribs, dropping him to his knees. Someone shouted her name, held her back.

Where was Laynia? Had she brought him here to kill him?

His breath came like fire. He held one hand to his chest, stayed on his knees, looking down.

"He is the one!" Sherayna screamed. "Murderer!" Noises of scuffling. "Look at me, pig!"

He looked at her.

She was scrambling for purchase against the white-skinned man who restrained her.

"You. You raped our land, killed our people, starved the planet. You murdered my sister!" She pulled against the man. "Micor, let me have him!"

"Not now, Sherayna." He dragged her out the door. Micor. White. A sverra, he thought dully.

Laynia shut the door behind them. She raised a quizzical eyebrow at someone beyond Ethan. He followed her gaze to a stout gray-haired man. And behind the man stood Nevan, glancing nervously between Ethan and a woman with a thin face. Sylan? Brought to this place by her rebel holders? Nevan knelt at Ethan's side.

"Are you all right?"

Ethan laughed.

CHAPTER 53

Ethan spent the afternoon on a mattress, thinking of Sherayna and her sister. Her record in Meena had listed no relations, but it was under a false name. If her sister had died in Meena, naturally she'd hate him. And before that, he had held her prisoner for a year. Yet she hadn't even mentioned that. Why? The rain drummed the roof, passing over and over with the winds like a percussion performance. *Why?* Long after the word lost its meaning, it beat in his head in the voice of the rain.

A doctor from Vojin arrived in the afternoon and told Ethan he'd broken two ribs. The man bound his chest and gave him a painkiller. Nevan brought him water and a bowl of soup.

Ethan pushed himself up and addressed his supper.

"I'm not sure all that bandaging is going to help your ribs," said Nevan.

Ethan decided not to share his view of Kiri medicine.

Nevan said, "I've been grateful for your letters."

Ethan looked up at him, a little surprised. "Then I should have written more often."

≈•≈

In the front room, Ethan was the last to take his place at the conference table. Though a fire crackled in the hearth, the room was damp, the roof leaking, the daylight long since retreated. There were six at the table besides himself: Laynia, the sverra, Nevan, Sylan, the aged man. And there was Sherayna, dark before the blaze of the fire.

Two offworld jae experts, this sverra—one of the ones who came long ago?—the queen, a rebel commander. What scheme are they dreaming of drawing me into?

When Ethan was seated, the sverra spoke: "We may soon have a jae plague on our hands. We're assembled here to prevent it."

Ethan kept his face blank, but inside he smiled a little. Some things remained predictable.

"Then why is a City man here?" cried Sherayna.

"To help us," replied the sverra.

Ethan let the smile reach his lips. "Help you?" he asked before Sherayna could. "Why should I help you? I think your philosophy is folly."

Laynia said coolly, "If you still know how to listen, Ethan, listen before dismissing us."

"I've heard you already."

"Odd!" Sherayna spat. "Since our words have been banned from public debate."

"Enough," said the sverra wearily, "I must speak. You may listen or not. We don't all know each other, so I'll make the introductions. I am Micor, an anti-tech of old standing. Next to me is Sherayna from Meena, my trusted lieutenant." Sherayna never took her gaze off Ethan. "Next to her is Olwer, the Im Jetho of Zerin." The aged man smiled.

All rebels, thought Ethan. *Every one.*

"This is Laynia from Zerin," said Micor, "who for decades has balanced every warring faction on this planet. Next to her is Sylan West-of-Now, an expert in jae. And next is Nevan West-of-Now, an expert in jae history. Next is Ethan from Mesa." Ethan could feel the sverra's eyes on him, but he found himself staring at Sherayna again. "He is here because Laynia thinks him an honest man."

An honest man, thinks Laynia!

Sherayna smiled viciously. "To hate honestly is honest, yet still hateful."

"Excuse me," Ethan cut her off, "but I fancy I represent a little more than 'honesty.' Unless I'm much mistaken, I'm the sole representative of the official regime."

"Shut up!" Sherayna half-rose.

But Micor waved a hand to silence her, and to Ethan's surprise, she sat down again, silent.

Ethan avoided her gaze. "We all know the queen is a Borderal agent. And since the queen is a creature of Zerin, I must assume the Im Jetho is a Borderal too. Our host here, Micor, is also a Borderal, and Sylan has lived among them for years. Nevan is a Kiri and would side with the Borderals. I am the voice of the rest of Perdita here, no?"

"Voice of Perdita!" Sherayna started in her chair.

"Ethan," said Olwer, "speaking for Zerin, let me assure you we are not Borderals. We do not sanction illegal activity, except in dire need as now."

"Shut him up," Sherayna repeated. "Let his precious regime see what it's like to have its tongue torn out!"

Micor looked at her and sighed. "Ethan, you are welcome to speak your mind. Does that satisfy you?"

"For now. If you mean it."

"Good, then we can proceed. If you will bear with me, I must begin far in my past. Six hundred years ago, my family set out from our home on Shi Durn in hope of making contact with the worlds that had drifted into silence after the War. Like the West-of-Nows, we crashed into Perdita's planetary shield. Everyone was killed but my mother, my cousin, and myself. As sverra, we were exotic beings, and in time, my mother became a revered counselor to Zerin. She used her renown to gain access to the library stores of the planet, hoping to find the reason for the End. She did, but she found more.

"In addition to being a penal planet, Perdita had been a storehouse for classified Sama tech information. Ancient, archived reports told of a project called the Jae Reversal. It had been designed to broadcast an energy matrix that would return semishifted particles to normal phase. It was intended to end the plague. Apparently, it was implemented. Apparently, it failed."

It sounded to Ethan like another rebel ploy: to blame the War's End on jae. "This is documented? I want to see the documentation."

"I brought some of the old documents," said Micor. "You may see them when we've finished."

"This story is too easy. It can't be the whole truth."

"Have you ever heard a whole truth?" said Micor sharply. "At the time of the End, the Samas were researching another project, this one called the Reversal Correction. It was of lesser status, since it promised no way to eliminate the plague. But it suggest a formula for shifting particles into a full-phase variation, so almost no new semishift contamination would be generated by corrected jae fields."

Sylan spoke up. "So the old contamination would remain, but effectively no new contamination would be added, and jae tech could be used safely."

"That was the plan," said Micor. "It was never implemented. Indeed, numerous questions about its applicability remained at the time of the End."

Ethan said, "That sounds like Borderal paranoia."

"When we've finished here, Ethan, I'll explain to you the problems with the spillage inhibitors and the imprecision of the uncertainty corrections, though I can't promise they'll make much sense to you without years of prior training."

Which I should have had, would have had, if not for the rebels. Yet a corner of his brain jumped at the thought of being shown the details of this Reversal Correction.

"These findings terrified my mother," said Micor.

"And rightly!" Sherayna burst out. "How is it these documents escaped the purge?"

"We can't be sure. Probably, they were saved because they were marked 'Reversal' and 'Correction,' and seemed to constitute possible aids in fighting particle-shift effects."

"Seemed?" said Ethan.

"Were," said Micor. "But my mother feared that if the importance of these documents was understood, it might spark a resurgence in jae research. And since the Reversal had failed and the Correction was untried, the risks were too great to permit that to happen. So she excised the files from the library system and took them into her own safekeeping."

"She stole them," put in Sylan.

"Why didn't she destroy them?" demanded Sherayna.

"Because knowledge cannot be destroyed." Micor rattled it off as an axiom.

Ethan almost laughed. "She acknowledged their value. She wanted them kept safe in case they were needed."

Micor fixed him with a look of undisguised pain so unexpected it silenced him. "When my mother died, my cousin and I became the guardians of these documents. And when our son was old enough, we took him into our confidence. Finally, we withdrew from public life, the better to protect what we knew."

The wind hissed through the pines outside, rattling the door of the hostel. Hail battered the window.

Micor continued, "After the West-of-Nows crashed with their own more basic *Jae History*, the government did what my mother always feared. They undertook a jae research project. In the past, the Borderals had stopped pro-tech projects through sabotage—"

"With disastrous results," said Ethan.

"Yes," said Micor, looking hard into his eyes, "but if results were disastrous before, they could be world-shattering now. Any destabilization of a jae reactor can lead to massive contamination, and it needn't be massive to scourge Perdita. We have seen the planet suffer from a simple grain shortage out of Meena."

No, I refuse to look at her.

"A violent assault against a jae reactor is not an option," said Micor.

Ethan's eyes widened in approving surprise. *Then what is he planning?*

"My son saw this," Micor was saying, "and he chose to act by giving the government the Reversal Correction."

His son—the traitor Lashen spoke of.

Micor took a trembling breath. "I dispute the wisdom of his choice. As I've said, the Correction is a preliminary piece of research, never practically implemented."

Sylan spoke softly. "Well, at least with the shield down, there's no possibility of a jae-powered ship exploding in an energy matrix that would spew contamination all over the planet."

"Yes," agreed Micor. "That's why the shield had to come down."

"It should have been shut off centuries ago," said Ethan. Sherayna started to protest, but he plunged on. "If the shield hadn't been there, we'd have had space travel long ago. We wouldn't need jae. We'd be one with our sister worlds. This jae situation you're lamenting is entirely of your own making."

"There may be much in what you say," said Micor, "but consider how powerful jae can be. Instantaneous travel. In its day, it revolutionized the entire Sama economy. The other Nations have shunned it because they recognize its danger. But give them a Reversal Correction, a hope for a safe way to use jae, and will they reject it? Or will jae and jae's plague spread again across the galaxies? We won't take that chance. That's why we kept the shield—until doing so came to threaten Perdita's very existence. And then, selfishly perhaps, we—I—chose the short-term safety of our planet over the protection of our sister planets."

"But surely it's true," said Ethan, "that the situation is much improved by the Reversal Correction."

"It is untried. And yet such a seeming panacea will almost certainly lead the project directors to demand faster progress with fewer precautions."

"Good God!" exclaimed Sylan. "Can we move the table?"

The rain was dripping from the ceiling onto the tabletop and her cushion. Micor rose and the others after him, lifting the table among them. Ethan stooped to help them, his chest in shooting pain, but Nevan laid a hand on his arm.

When they'd resumed their seats nearer the hearth, Olwer said, "So. If we do nothing, we're wagering that the government will conduct this project with such caution and skill that no significant problem will occur. Such caution would be unprecedented."

Sherayna barked a laugh.

"And it's obvious why," snapped Ethan. "The longer we take to study any question, the more opportunity the Borderals have to destroy any progress we make."

"And if we move against the project with force," Olwer continued, "the results may be grievous. On the other hand, Laynia's attempts to use reason have failed."

"Attempts at reason?" Ethan asked.

But his sarcasm seemed lost on them, for Laynia only answered, "Rarion; the warmaster—name me a person with influence and I'll name you one earless as Wolsena."

All eyes turned to Micor. He clearly had some sort of plan. But he only stared, dully. "What's the time?"

Laynia pondered her watch in the lamp's muddy glow. "Fifteenth hour and twelve."

After a moment, Micor said, "I don't want to say any more tonight. Tomorrow, let's speak of the future with the morning."

CHAPTER 54

Unwilling to share a room with the warchief, Sherayna retreated from the fire to a small back room. In the rainy, drumming dark, she heard Micor's voice by her mattress. "I'm glad you chose to sleep here. I need to speak with you alone."

She sat up. "Yes?"

He sat beside her. "I confess when I asked you to come here I didn't know how much you hate the warchief."

"You know what he did at Meena."

She could smell the flames in memory. She tried to put it from her mind, but it wouldn't go away.

"Yes," he said. "Yes, I know. I was foolish. I think my mind has been wayward lately."

Sherayna wanted to tell him that she grieved for Olloan. But she'd said it when Micor first came to her and told her of his death. Saying it a thousand times wouldn't bring him back. He was gone, along with Illia. There was no comfort. She watched Micor's dim shape slump in the gloom. "Why does it matter what I think of the warchief?" she said.

"You're going to have to work beside him."

"No." The word was soft but forceful. She would have killed the warchief if Micor hadn't stopped her.

I would have killed him in hate. His blood would have run under my nails. With everything else I am, I'd have been a murderer. But I'm not. Micor had saved her from that.

"No," she repeated. "I can't work with him."

"You can," said Micor sharply. It startled her. In all the years she'd known him, he had never raised his voice. "My son is dead, and I am dead, yet I am still here, doing what must be done because that is what we have to do. I do not expect less than that from you. You are here, Sherayna, you are all I have. Stop playing these games."

She wanted to run, like an angry child. Instead, she lay down and, like an angry child, kept silent.

≈•≈

She awoke to a peal of thunder. Her feet were wet. She could hear rain outside and splashes within. Micor got up from her side in the grayness.

"This is no good." He hugged his coat tight around him. "We'd better press on." He crossed into the main room, floorboards creaking.

Sherayna followed. The thunder had wakened them all. While Micor blew on the embers in the hearth, the warchief, nearest the fireplace, sat up and helped to coax a flame out of some damp kindling lying nearby. A disgusting display, how he dragged his hurt body! As if pain was something new and strange. And if it was, then she'd done him a favor—introduced him to life. She wanted to scream at him until he begged to be forgiven.

"It's five hours till dawn," said Laynia.

Lightning flashed, turning the room white. The thunder bellowed after.

"Might as well start the day," said Olwer, lacing his shoes.

After several tries, the warchief managed to catch a soggy match in the fire. With practiced speed, he ignited an oil lamp.

In ten minutes' time, they'd pushed the table near the flames, piled the mattresses around it to catch the heat. Olwer fried vegetables and eggs over the fire and swung a rusted kettle into place to steep tea. It began to feel like morning, though the night storm raged.

"So, to the Jae Project," said Olwer over his tea. "What's to be done, Micor?"

"First of all," said Micor, "can we agree that the project, as it stands, must be halted?"

All eyes looked to the warchief, and, to Sherayna's surprise, he hesitated. "From my perspective, it would serve better to maintain the project if we can be assured of reasonable safety standards. And always assuming that the present dangers have not been grossly exaggerated, which I have yet to be shown any evidence of."

"Yes, and you must be convinced of it," said Micor. "Let me try to explain." He dove into a river of jargon lost on Sherayna. The warchief, however, listened, interrupting to ask for clarifications, more basic explanations. Sherayna finished her breakfast; she was beginning to feel sleepy in the heat. At some point, Micor rose and recovered from his baggage a set of schematics. Sylan, Nevan, and the warchief huddled around him, looking over the papers, discussing shifts and contamination.

The warchief flipped through pages back and forth, back and forth. After staring at one graphic for several minutes, he set down the papers and sighed. "The levels may be a little high. If you are telling me the truth, which I don't really have enough background to judge."

"I believe this is the truth," said Sylan, "and I have no investment in seeing Perdita's space program stopped. I would like to see Perdita contact other worlds. But Micor's science seems sound. Sound enough that, *for the moment,* I'll even agree that we should not send for offworld advice, not till there's a workable policy on how best to address this Reversal Correction. We would not want it marketed outside Perdita."

The warchief eyed Sylan—then Nevan—like a gambler ready to call a bluff.

"Sylan," he said, "how does the scale of our program compare to the Samas'?"

"Let's see, for about two hundred years, virtually all Sama real goods were transported using jae ships. A Sama heavy freighter required a pull of factor ten. The light ships operated at factor five. I'd guess that Perdita, with a first-time aim of just getting a light ship up and off wouldn't have reason to operate above factor three."

"For one ship," said the warchief, "just to make contact, not for everyday travel as the Samas traveled."

Sherayna boiled. "You don't know that. You can't assume that. They'll more than likely use jae as much as they can—"

"That's an alarmist—"

"If she's alarmist, you're too trusting," said the queen. "We can't assume that the government's use of jae will stop with one ship. And we can't assume that they will even reach the stage of launching a ship without a major catastrophe. We've been talking in terms of abstractions, how safe could jae be at its safest. But it's not at its safest. There is, as Olwer said, always too much push to do too much too fast."

Now the warchief will tell us again that Borderals are to blame.

But he didn't. He turned to Micor and said, "I've heard murmurings about some plan you've hatched. Yet you seem reluctant to share it with us."

Micor drew a deep breath. "I have misgivings that our personal rivalries will render it impossible." He glanced at Sherayna. Now, that was galling. "Essentially, the plan is to win time—time to openly discuss the very issues we're discussing."

"You speak of open communication," said Nevan. "It sounds to me as if you agree with your son's action."

Sherayna thought she saw tears in Micor's eyes. She herself was still reeling from the news of Olloan's death. "I had hoped that by withholding the Correction," Micor said, "we would keep the project to a slow enough pace that we might still have time to negotiate . . . something."

"I tried it," said the queen.

"I know you did. I know."

"What is your plan?" the warchief repeated.

"I've been studying the Correction for years."

"And you've told me you may know how to correct it to maximum efficiency," said Sylan, "to make it safer than it is in its present form."

"Yes, I think so."

"So you'll ask them to hire you on?" said the warchief.

"No," said Micor. "I won't work on their terms, the threat of prison hanging over me. If I am to negotiate to help them, I demand standing."

"You wish me to request amnesty for you?" asked the warchief. "That I'd consider."

"I wouldn't trust," said Nevan. "I'd trust you, Ethan, but not the king."

Sherayna looked at him with admiration.

"I have a better bargaining tool," said Micor. "About two hundred years ago, I began a project of my own. I developed a fail-safe mechanism, an 'off box' that will damp out the main drive of a resting jae reactor."

"What does that mean?" said Sherayna.

"It means the reactor will be turned off," said Sylan. "Every reactor already has one."

"But mine is different," said Micor. "It's programmed to cause a minute energy surge that will scramble the main drive."

"But we don't want to scramble it!" exclaimed Sherayna. "If those particles were shifted incorrectly—"

"A *resting* reactor," Micor said. "That means a drive in a vacuum, before it ever makes contact with its particle feed. You see, there will be nothing to speak of to be shifted."

"So the drive will not only damp out but have to be recalibrated," said Sylan.

"It will have to be rebuilt from floor to ceiling." He gave the warchief a long look. "My latest model is a self-contained box, just over half a meter on the longest edge."

"And now you have to get it to the generator," said the warchief.

"Exactly."

"Do we know where the generator is?" Sherayna asked.

Micor nodded. "My son traced it. It's underground, off a mountain pass by the Lo Ren river."

"And you think Ethan can get you in," said Nevan.

That's it. He wants me to travel to the Lo Ren with that man.

"Wait," said the warchief. "Why should I want to be part of your plan? You want standing, you say? You'll gain it through sabotage?"

"They'll need me to rebuild the system. I can make their project stabler, more reliable. It will give me an opportunity to negotiate terms. What I'll demand foremost is an open forum. I'll demand that the Progressive Tech Statue be overturned, that the Borderals be given back their voice. And then we'll talk."

"Yes, and then you'll refuse to help," said the warchief.

"No," said Micor, "because if I do, they will simply start the project again without me—and we'll be back where we are now, but with all the Borderals alerted to the project and the City more desperate to work faster than ever, before they can be sabotaged. You see, I'll help you because I don't want to see jae kill Perdita."

Sherayna could not contain herself. "You can't mean it, Micor! You know Perdita isn't ready for space."

"Why not?" demanded the warchief.

"How many reasons do you want? Microbial contamination, ecosystem imbalance from importing crops—"

Sylan sat forward. "Sherayna, the issues you mention are pertinent. My Nation is expert in negotiating safe interplanetary contact standards. They will help you."

"It's all we can do now," said Micor.

Thoughts flashed through Sherayna like bullets. Why was she the only one to speak for the Borderals? What had happened to Micor? He said he'd died with Olloan. Had he turned traitor with him too? Why was a Kiri like Nevan silent? But shutting down the reactor—that had to be done.

Nevan was saying, "It's clever in many ways. But they won't let Ethan in. His standing's not high right now."

"He's right," said the warchief. "Lashen has probably already given a specific order to cut me out."

"You underestimate the endurance of your influence with the army," the queen told him. "Except for Meena, your record is clean. Your loyalty is unquestioned. And your father's name still carries weight."

"You've just laid out three good reasons for me to stay uninvolved."

"Who is your father?" Sherayna asked.

"Jessec."

Jessec? She thought back to news reports from that time. She could remember Jessec with his son in the photos, but she'd never imagined the warchief was that son.

"If this works," said Micor, "we will have a new order. You will still have your standing, Ethan. Higher maybe."

"They won't let me in," said the warchief.

"They will," said the queen. "I have a clearance for you from my husband."

The warchief laughed. "Truly, you dangle him like an earring."

The queen smiled tightly.

The warchief—Jessec's son?—shook his head, looked at Micor. "I want to see your plans for correcting the Reversal Correction. I want to know that you have something substantial to offer us."

"You wouldn't understand my plans."

"If I truly cannot understand them, I'm not willing to betray my own government for them."

Micor sighed. "I brought some documents. But I can't put knowledge in your head that you don't have time to learn. If I answer your questions to the best of my ability, and your ability, and the answers satisfy you that I can help you, will you go?"

"Perhaps."

Micor nodded. "One more thing," he said, addressing all of them. "The warchief doesn't trust me. By the same token, I do not entirely trust him. I am not prepared to hand over my off box to him when he might simply turn it over to his warmaster."

The warchief sat forward. "What can I do to ease your mind?"

"Nothing. I'll explain the functioning of the box to you. But my own agent will carry it. Laynia has provided clearance for you to take an assistant with you."

And now it comes.

For a moment, he stared blankly. Then, his eyes turned to Sherayna. "Not her?"

"Why don't you go yourself, Micor?" asked Sherayna.

"Because I am too conspicuous as a sverra, even in disguise."

"She'll kill me, you know," said the warchief. "The first time she catches me off guard."

Sherayna heard herself say, "No. I won't."

He laughed at her.

"I didn't know what was at stake till now. But I now understand. Micor can't go to the Lo Ren. You will have to install the off box. I couldn't learn that much new tech so fast. If I killed you, I'd kill that purpose. How dare you assume that I would place my own vendetta above the safety of my world? You, who held me in prison a year and never heard the name of Meena from my lips. How dare *you* suggest such a thing of *me*, when you are the butcher of Meena! How am I supposed to know you won't kill me?" She stood and banged out the door.

≈•≈

The storm had passed, but the rain still drizzled down in the first light of morning. Sherayna longed for the warmth of Meena. A dirty mist hung on the towering pines, the ground a river of mud. Yet it was a relief to stand there, drenched, the rustlings of the water the only sound, away from those people.

She squelched down the road toward the trees. When she had gone a little way, she heard a step behind her and whirled. It was the queen, as wet and muddy as she.

"I know, my Queen," said Sherayna. "You trust him. Micor told me."

The queen came to her side. "Let's walk under the trees. They'll be a bit of shelter."

Sherayna went with her beneath the black canopy. The air was a little less frigid there, the drops fewer and larger, plopping leisurely off the limbs. Nature's spirits with no human care.

"He won't kill you," said the queen. "He won't even try to thwart you, and here is why: because he'll reason that Micor's plan is for the best."

"How do you know?"

"I know him. I've known him since he was a child. He has a tendency to overreact—"

Sherayna laughed bitterly.

"But at bottom, he prides himself on his logic."

"Logic?"

The queen stopped walking and faced her. "He gets unstrung by his passions. We both know that's true—but it only happens under the stress of what he considers a great personal catastrophe."

"How was Meena a personal catastrophe for him?"

"It was the ship, Sherayna, losing the Kiri ship."

"That was seven years before!"

"It was all one path. But I think Meena frightened him. His conduct has been far more tentative since then."

"Because he was reprimanded."

"Because he returned to his logic. He'll conclude that reason dictates Micor's path is best. He can't deny that jae is deadly and that a project rushed too much leaves things overlooked. And he'll want to secure Micor's willing help for Senarna."

Willing help! Sherayna thought. *Tell me, please, that Micor has other plans.*

Sherayna looked up through pinched branches to the storm clouds. "I can't believe it."

"You're wise to be wary on principle, of course. But there's no time to find anyone to replace you."

"Sylan! Sylan instead of the warchief." *Yes*, she thought, *I might just go with Sylan.*

"The king will demand her presence in Senarna soon. He only allowed her a little while on Zerin to meet with her family, to earn her goodwill."

Sherayna blanched. "He'll torture her for information on jae."

"He'll demand it, yes. And I'll advise her to give it without resisting. By the time his people can use it, the generator will be shut down—with your help."

Sherayna was soaked to the bone and the queen no better. A regal woman, draggled as a wet cat. The image described their whole gathering: all causes, all duties, all noble ends, all flooded with too much living.

CHAPTER 55

Ethan sat two minutes with Micor—and missed every word the sverra said. To begin to understand this Reversal Correction would take every ounce of his concentration: its theory began with the most advanced precepts he had ever learned in quantum physics. And he couldn't concentrate.

He asked for a little time to his thoughts and shut himself in the sleeping room. Sitting on the mattress where Sherayna and Micor had lain last night, he let his head fall into his hands. Perversely, now he was alone, no thoughts would come. His eyelids were heavy.

Can it be I agreed to join forces with these rebels? And I told myself I'd be Lashen's agent here only to deceive him, more than he ever deceived me? Am I as bad as Laynia?

What had turned him from his own path so fast? What could turn Jessec's son traitor?

True, the Jae Project was being pushed fast—that was a foregone conclusion: with the threat of sabotage, there was no real alternative. A potentially deadly tech, a necessarily inexperienced research crew, a need for rapid development. It made a bad combination.

Slowing the project would be for the best. But Senarna could not agree to that as long as it's working against time to get a jae ship up before the rebels can find the installation and—

He started.

And, erring gods, the rebels have already found it! Micor knows, Sherayna knows. It's only a matter of time before they strike us. I have to tell Lashen, tell him to shut down his reactor now. But will he? Can he? What if he won't and he calls me back to Senarna where I cannot act? We'd be back to waiting for the rebels to attack our jae generator.

Could he tell Lashen just enough: be on the lookout for the sverra, the sverra was vital, he'd just been on Zerin? Yes, that seemed prudent.

And Ethan would go to the Lo Ren. With her. His thoughts stopped at that.

She'd attacked him and then yelled at him for suggesting she was capable of such an act. She was mad.

But, no, she had never pretended to be incapable of his murder. She said she'd hold back from her vengeance *on this mission*—that was it. In her eyes, he'd impugned her reason.

If she were reasonable . . . if she were loyal (unlike him), she'd follow this course.

She wouldn't hurt me, not until the task is complete. And then, for good or ill, I'd be surrounded by guards who'd keep her from killing me.

And would he really care all that much if they failed?

He rose and saw the rain falling softly past the window, the clouds a blanket obscuring the sky.

But what if it's all lies? And what if I can't bear more lies?

He lay down, stood again, paced the room, curiously glad of the flashes of pain through his side. At last, when the morning was white in the window, he hit upon the formula:

If I do this thing, the best that will happen is that we will win Micor's aid in achieving jae travel, and he will help us advance it, and maybe even bring a fair number of his rebels onto our side in the end. And if I do this, the worst that will happen is that the rebels will end our Jae Project, and we'll be back to fighting.

But if I do not do this thing, the best that will happen is that our Jae Project will work and we will venture into space. And if I do not do it, the worst that will happen is a jae disaster that could devastate life on this planet.

On the one hand, enhanced jae or the old impasse. On the other, functional jae or devastation. The probabilities speak clearly; it's my duty to do it.

CHAPTER 56

That is how it will have to be if I'm to travel with this man, thought Sherayna. *I have to do what I have to do; that is all. I am nothing but purpose.*

The warchief wrote a note to the warmaster, which Laynia read aloud: "'I've been detained on Zerin. Should be back to Senarna within six days.' Good. Hopefully, he'll believe you've been taken prisoner and see you as a piece out of play. I just hope we can disguise you well enough that his spies don't spot you leaving."

"We've planned some diversionary mischief," said Micor. "We've also sent out word that he should be looking for me— if he's wise, *that* will occupy him."

Sherayna and the warchief would take a jumper to Mesa. Air traffic being conspicuous, they would, then, drive to the project site in the Lo Renna region, where the warchief and his assistant would arrive for an unannounced royal inspection. Once in the installation, they would doubtless have to overcome some of the personnel by force. To minimize casualties, Micor provided them with a fast-acting tranquilizer and a series of ten syringes. Once injected, a person would collapse almost at once. At the first opportunity, the warchief would install the off box. It sounded simple, and insane.

≈•≈

Beside a gray road on the gulf shore, Sherayna shivered under the eaves of a clam shop, waiting for the warchief come out of the car agency. After a long time, his step clipped on the rain-pelted sidewalk. She even felt a hint of relief to see him, not a harbor guard, coming toward her.

"You took your time," she said.

"The clerk was having dinner. It took him ten minutes to get down to his office."

"It's getting late."

"The car's in the lot around the back." He started to walk away.

"It will take five hours to reach Keshot. All the inns will be closed."

He turned to her and said sharply, "We can sleep in the jump yard."

Sherayna hadn't thought of that. She had only traveled by jumper twice in her life. "Well, that will do then."

The warchief mumbled something under his breath and led her to the car. When he took out the code card, she snatched it from his fingers and memorized the numbers. He gave her a moment, then snatched it back and keyed the code to start the engine.

The measures fell away. Silver-white drops of rain whizzed past like stars, the yellow headlights illuminating only a couple of meters of roadway before them.

This is what space is like, like nothing and nowhere. Imagine light-years of this. Traveling like standing still. This is the space he loves so much. This is where he thinks the gods will meet him.

She could almost have fallen asleep in the warm car.

This is what space is like, like the peace-sleep of death before reliving.

It was past the fourteenth hour when they came to the limits of Keshot, a large manufacturing city, heavily guarded. The sleepy border guard looked over the warchief's papers and the false ones Sherayna had carried since her job in Kepot. Sherayna was only a little worried; she wasn't known here. The guard waved them through.

Sherayna had no fondness for cities. She was glad she could see no more by the streetlights than vague brown box shapes. Even in the darkness, the jump yard was appalling: a sprawling featureless lot filled with ground cars, and beyond, sickly lights fluorescing over the landing strip. A wave of nausea passed through her.

Suddenly, it struck her why the place was so hideous: it was like the City base in Oja, like the prison. When she looked at the warchief, she couldn't feel anger or fear, just sickness.

The lobby itself was not so bad. Yellow lights glared over an array of cushions and tables, a small fee window, and a food counter closed for the night. Some dozen people lay around the room, most asleep on piled cushions, a man reading a news pamphlet, a woman nursing a baby. The warchief went to the fee window to book their passage while Sherayna piled their baggage in a corner and pulled up some cushions.

"Long trip?" said the woman with the baby, a few feet away.

"From Senarna," Sherayna answered.

"Where are you headed?"

"Mesa. And you?"

"Kepot. My sisters work at the power plant."

The one whose offices Sherayna just blew up on assignment after leaving Raratin.

"I'm sure it'll be nice to visit them," said Sherayna.

"I'm going to talk to them about moving back to Semlona. There was a rebel raid. The plant lost a lot of money. It may have to hand low-skill employees their walking shoes."

"Sorry to hear that."

"Yes, pity that," the warchief echoed as he handed Sherayna her departure pass.

Sherayna led him away a few steps to get clear of the woman's hearing range. "Fifth hour?" she whispered. "That's half the day gone."

"It's the earliest to Mesa. Kepot's two hours earlier, but that would add at least four onto our driving time."

"Thank you for the geography lesson." Sherayna stuffed her pass into a pocket. "I do come from Veshna, you know."

"So do I."

Jessec's son.

"I need you to help me rebind my ribs," he said.

She looked up, startled. "No."

"Our work is important, no? And to do it I need to be able to function. And to function I need to be able to walk efficiently on this injury. And for that, I need it bound properly. I can do that with only limited success by myself."

"Ask that man who's reading."

"Yes, by all means, let's draw as much attention to ourselves as we can."

The woman with the baby was staring at them.

"I'll help you," said Sherayna, "if you let me hold half the money the queen gave you."

He looked offended. "I thought I was going to take care of our transactions so you wouldn't have to risk being recognized."

"But if anything happens and we get separated, I'll want more money to plan my course with than the pittance I brought to Zerin."

"A fourth," he said. "I'm paying for all our rentals."

Sherayna nodded and silently counted out the thin plastic slivers he handed her, then followed him to the washroom.

The bruise was a swollen purple-black, covering much of the left of his ribcage.

He deserves worse than this.

Brusquely, she refitted the brace, overcoming the urge to bind it too tight, then left him alone to struggle back into his shirt.

But I mustn't hate him. To hurt the gods by hating him—it isn't worth it, he isn't worth it.

The woman in the lobby was rocking her baby. "Is your brother all right?"

Sherayna couldn't help but laugh. "He's not my brother, and he's fine—just a little too courageous playing tackle ball."

The woman smiled. "Sorry, I didn't mean to assume. It's just the way you were talking . . ."

"Oh, people are always confusing us for siblings. But what about you? Shouldn't you get some sleep? I hear the Kepot flight's early."

The woman laughed and nodded to the baby. "I keep Foa's hours nowadays. But I think I'll try for a wink."

"I wish you would," mumbled a sleeper from the floor.

Sherayna and the woman smiled at each other and lay down in their respective places. After a time, the warchief came back and settled on his cushions, close enough to seem cordial. It was a blur to Sherayna, already half-asleep.

CHAPTER 57

Karmeena awoke when Miri came in. Miri threw some sticks on the fire and stood before the blaze, rubbing her hands.

"What did Olwer want to see you about?" Karmeena asked.

"He wanted to talk some more about the Nac conference—without my parents."

Karmeena shuddered. "He's a liar, Miri. I feel it."

Miri half-smiled and started undressing. "Of course, he's a liar. One just has to learn how to read his lies." She slipped under the blankets, snuggling close to Karmeena. "You're not asking about what's important."

"What's more important than the two of us here?"

"What he said about Nac. He fears that Micor's plan will go wrong. And if it fails, we need some other plan to fall back on."

"Like what?"

"He wants to send a Jetho to the project who will make a plea to hold off for now, in the name of Leva."

"The Zerins have pushed the worship of Leva for years. I don't see that it's changed much."

"True. Still, if you're making a net, best to tie every knot." Miri rolled onto her back. "Laynia can obtain passage. The visit will be announced in advance. It will seem more legitimate that way." She paused. "I leave tomorrow."

Karmeena stared at her. "Why you?"

"This plan will serve another function, too. The warmaster knows we had a meeting on Zerin. He'll be expecting some move against his Jae Project. And if he thinks this visit is it, he won't be prepared for Sherayna and Ethan. I'll be a decoy."

"But—"

"But I'll also be a diplomat of Zerin. I'm a Jetho, a Perditan, and an offworlder too. I don't fear space. I have every reason to want to see my old home again. If I speak for jae postponement, I might be listened to. I am the one. Don't be afraid." She held Karmeena close.

But Karmeena had always been afraid.

CHAPTER 58

Sherayna woke first at the sound of the baby crying. The mother, bobbing her up and down, was chattering with an old man.

She is one of those people who's friendly with everyone, like Illia.

Sherayna quashed the pang of grief, the flash of fire at the warchief. Besides, the woman was more forward than Illia— more like Leric. She didn't like that thought either.

In the washroom, she showered and rebraided her hair. Back in the lobby, she doled out too much money for a rice cake and an apple. She didn't want to return to her place by the warchief or be trapped again in conversation with the young mother. Instead, she left a note on her cushion, "Gone walking," and forced herself out onto the concrete plateau. The rain was almost gone, a white drizzle that curled her hair. Biting her apple, she wandered along the periphery of the car lot, west, toward the city, drawn on by a masochistic desire to encircle herself with its greenless din.

As she followed the sidewalk toward the hum of cars, Leric kept running through her mind. He had once studied code with his parents. More than anyone she trusted, he would understand this Jae Project. She wished that she could talk to him. She wanted to trust Micor, but after all the secrets and Olloan's betrayal and suicide, it was hard to know who to confide in.

She came to a fork where the jump-yard road met a broad street, signposted the East Center Way. She turned to the north, into a quarter teeming with workers on their way to jobs in tight-packed multicolored buildings, faded and grimed, painted with gods and people and scenes—wall poetry too. She paused and read:

> *When voices still, fear speaks.*
> *But silence is the final speaker.*

Sherayna could hear Illia and Olloan.

Everything was moving too fast. Could she even be sure Micor's off box worked? Sylan wouldn't lie about it. Would she? What if this was all a ruse? The Borderals would need to know. Someone needed to know, in case Sherayna met the gods before it ended.

She asked directions to the nearest post office and jotted a letter to Leric, coding the words as best she could: the situation in brief, the project's position, the off box. She concluded with:

> *Watch for our arrival at the Lo Ren if you can. If anything goes wrong, it will be in your hands. Do not attack! Remember the contamination. But if the off box works, and the generator is momentarily dead, it should be safe: it would be vulnerable.*

For an instant, she hesitated; then she pitched the letter off to their Raratin communicant, who would see it to wherever Leric was.

She came back to the jump yard just past third hour. Inside, the warchief was eating breakfast at one of the tables, deep in conversation with the reading man from the night before. She meandered close enough to hear what they were saying.

"I think his father might work there too," the warchief said.

"Do you know the father's name?"

"Sengan? Or Sentan?"

"No Sengans I know of. Three Sentans."

The warchief waved his hand. "It doesn't matter. How's the grain shortage hitting you? Are jobs secure?"

"Jobs are pretty nearly as secure as ever. Wages are depressed, though, because we've needed extra money to purchase grain ourselves—the company, I mean. You'd be surprised how many wheat-based medicines we peddle."

"Surely you've raised the price on those products?"

"Well, yes, of course. But private demand goes down when the price goes up. And we have to give the hospitals access at cost. That's the law."

The warchief brooded.

The reader rubbed his nose. "You a relative?"

The warchief glanced up. "Just a friend of a friend. Thanks for your time."

Teacup in hand, he crossed to Sherayna and motioned her over to the far wall, away from the morning crowd. "You were gone long enough."

"You'd prefer I sit and watch you sleep?"

He sipped his tea.

"What company does he work for?" She nodded to the reader.

"North Semlona Medicinal Suppliers."

Sherayna shook her head with a charitable air. "Poor pharmaceuticals industry! To think that even it is suffering over Meena."

The warchief did not look up for some seconds. When he met her eyes, he said, "My lady, I am chastened."

"Warchief, if only you were."

"No," he said, "call me by my name. We're traveling companions, remember." He flicked his eyes over the crowd.

She smiled briefly. "So you, Ethan, have a friend of a friend in that man's company. Which means you have a friend. I'm impressed."

He glared at her with more detestation than the quip deserved. "Yes, I've had friends." He walked to their sleeping corner to rifle through his pack. He pulled out a notebook, and, sitting, began to write fast.

≈•≈

16 Mid-Spring: Ethan's Journal:

There is a chamber in my mind which suspects that Laynia allied me with this woman merely to punish me for spurning her body. Sherayna is a fiend—a god, not a human creature. But, no, she's human. And I've done her wrong. For this, she meets me at every turn with knives to carve my guilt on me. Enough of this.

I had a dream last night. I was by the night lake, the one into which my mother dove. Yet now, it lacked its sluggish tar-thickness. Like the old-time dreams, it was water again, glistening. And as I looked out over the water, it expanded forever. I have never seen the lake's other side but have always imagined it small, a pond almost, oppressive as if in a cave. Now it stretched to the horizon, and I saw it was no lake but the ocean itself. Ocean under the stars. The instant I made this realization, I could hear the distant tides. And looking down, I saw I was now some paces back, gazing over a featureless beach to the white crashing waves of this black sea.

And so I woke to find Sherayna gone: for a walk, her note said, but I wonder and I doubt.

When I think of my own betrayals, part of me is glad that I couldn't find a way to send a message telling Lashen to search for Micor. Micor said he did so himself. I wonder if that was the truth.

≈•≈

16 Mid-Spring, later:

I write to you now from our jumper. I ought to have written more in my life. It quiets the spirit. Is that why you write, Nevan?

I have always found the contours of a jumper beautiful, like a horizontal tower melting outward to its wingtips, spaceship-like: a needle piercing into the plane of the gods. As we took off, I watched the land give way to a sea that skimmed soft under us.

I heard Sherayna's voice: "Ethan?" Her face was a child's, despite lines of age. "Who was he? The man you were looking for at the pharmaceutical company?"

"Are we back to that?"

"I truly wish to know. Do you think he's one of us? Are you investigating him?"

I laughed to myself. "If I were, I trust I'd be more discreet. I was a friend of his mother's, that's all."

"You *were* a friend?"

"She's dead." I turned back to the window, but I didn't see the water. She takes me back to Meena even when she's not being unkind.

On impulse, I said, "Will you tell me about your sister?"

She looked as if she would strike me again. "So you can fatten your reports on us rebel offenders? Isn't it enough the dead are dead?"

I looked away. "It was stupid of me to ask."

Traveling companions! I wanted to say, "I can be more than the agent of the government that breeds hate in you." I have not said it, of course.

≈•≈

Sherayna never knew what to make of Mesa. It was crisp now under a high roof of fog, the snow geraniums already in bloom—white, red, and variegated. From the moment she climbed down to Veshna land, she had the curious dual sensation of coming home and coming to the enemy's home. She huddled by the hedges in the jump yard while the warchief checked on a rental car.

By and by, he reappeared, gloomy as a one-moon night. "No cars available till tomorrow."

"There's that much guest traffic in Mid-Spring in Mesa?"

"No, just a very small renter. I thought you knew all about Mesa."

"I know my friends languish in prison here. I know it has the largest prison except for Oja in all Veshna. I know I'm not safe here. When I'm in my right mind, I know enough to avoid it."

"Well, there we can agree," he said, looking over her shoulder.

Turning, she saw a middle-aged man trotting toward them. Come to arrest her? She made her breathing slow and even.

"Ethan!" the man exclaimed and smiled at Sherayna. "I didn't know you were back in town. And with such a lovely companion." Another smile for Sherayna, which she returned halfheartedly.

"It's nice to see you, Decoshec," said the warchief, his face glacier hard.

"And you. Have you talked to Niric since you got in?"

"No, why?"

"The roof's leaking again. He tried to leave a message for you at Senarna, but do you have any idea how hard it is for an ordinary citizen to get a letter through to the palace?"

"I'm sure it's very difficult. I'll talk to him. Thank you."

Ethan and Sherayna exchanged good-byes with the man, who scurried away as hastily as he'd come.

"Officious chipmunk," the warchief muttered.

"Who is he?"

"My neighbor. Well, we'll be here till tomorrow anyway. I suppose I might as well have a look at my roof."

They walked three cross streets from the transport stop to a quiet, tree-lined road of modest houses. He stopped at a dusty beige place with the typical yellow roof. A profusion of shrubs grew around the front walk, azaleas starting to flower.

"This is where I live." He led her up the walk. "Mark it well—when this is over, you'll want to be sure that you torch the right one."

"Are you sure you haven't led me to that neighbor's house instead?"

Ignoring her, he rapped on the door, taking a set of keys from his pocket at the same time. Waiting less than ten seconds, he strode away round the side of the house, through a gate, and into a grassy backyard enclosed by squat ornamental trees. Just behind the house was a freestanding shed, which he tried three or four times to unlock. When the latch finally gave a clink, he shoved the warped door open on a room that was only less damp than the hostel on Zerin because it wasn't raining at the moment. Boxes covered with plastic sheets were piled on the floor.

"Charming," swore the warchief under his breath. "Move in my bed and leave all Father's books here in the wet, why don't you?"

He dove under one of the plastic sheets and pulled out an ancient volume, pages puffed with moisture.

"This is where you sleep?" Sherayna said. "Not the house?"

He didn't answer, plowing through the boxes.

"Is Niric a relative of yours?"

He pulled a long plastic case out of one of the boxes, slid out the top face and examined it, then glanced up. "Hm?"

"Niric, is he a relative?"

"Tenant." He replaced the top face and set the case down. While he inventoried, Sherayna opened the case: a scale model of the *Outbound*: long, slim, red and yellow—the Sama colors of the other world. She stared at the dustless curving hull a long time.

He's Jessec's son. He must have thought, like the rest of the City, that the Borderals killed his father. But he's known better for a long time now. He can't use his father's death as an excuse for what he's done to us.

She ran a finger along the model's aft thrusters.

How must he have felt when we blew up the Kiri ship? Nothing to what I felt in Meena.

She caught him eyeing her suspiciously. After a moment, he resumed rifling through the boxes. Sherayna closed the case and peered under one of the crinkling box covers. Household items: a cooking plate, cups, a photograph of Jessec—stout, gingery, and grinning, as she remembered him from the publicity pictures of her youth, arm in arm with a taller woman: slim and white-blond.

"Your mother?" She held up the picture.

He took it from her. "I need to move these boxes into the house."

She watched as he stooped to lift one; his face turned red as a bristlenut, but he got it off the ground.

"Oh in Nama's name, let me, before you kill yourself." She took the box, heavy with books, from his arms. "Go open the door."

"I'm touched by your concern," he said, breathing hard.

"We need you to function, as you pointed out. Unlock your house."

≈•≈

They removed the boxes into the cluttered storeroom where his tenant had stowed his mattress: his childhood room, he told her. For a moment, she hated him purely because his childhood hadn't burned with hers. Sherayna set down the last box just as a drizzle descended over the yard. Inside the house, she helped him once again to bind his ribs; the bruise was larger and yellowed, healing. Soon afterward, the tenant, a tall brown man with a deep-lined smile, came home. Apparently astounded to see his landholder with a guest, Niric insisted on their taking his room for the night, the large one, Ethan's parents' room. Ethan spent the afternoon discussing the leaking roof with him and catching up with some written work.

As if it were any ordinary day. It must be strange to find oneself at home in the middle of an epic.

Sherayna spent a good deal of time talking with Niric. He was a rosid grower for the Mesa Orchard Over-Owner. Styling herself as a Semlona farmer, Sherayna spent hours discussing the harvests and Meena—and had Meena on her mind when she retired with the warchief.

Lying on the floor by the side of his mattress, she felt her memories knead themselves, folding in and in till they imploded.

"How could you kill the seer?" she demanded.

He turned to her sharply, stark awake in the gloom. "What?"

"Our poor old seer. No harm to anyone."

After some seconds, he said, "Meena's seer? He isn't dead, not in Meena anyway. The last I heard, he'd returned to his old school in Cudonond."

Sherayna brooded. "I heard he was dead. I heard that someone heard he was dead. If he had lived, we'd have found out."

"If you were already convinced he was dead?"

"I don't believe you."

"He was one of the Meenans—one of the very few, I might add—who chose to help us fight the fire rather than running. They were all pardoned."

Sherayna's thoughts were flying. It would have been like the seer to stay and help. "I'll look for him at his school when this is over. If I find that he's there, I'll be happy for him."

"And I."

"I very much doubt that you care."

"I don't care whether you doubt it or not."

Sherayna turned her back to him and wondered that she was not more pleased that the seer might be alive.

I want to believe they killed him. So I can hate all the more—but I must not hate.

CHAPTER 59

17 Mid-Spring: Ethan's Journal:

This has been a long day, Nevan. If you read this, you have already found, out of sequence, my thoughts about discovering the shield and about the burning of Meena. Little enough these pages may tell you. Little enough they tell me. But I wrote them, such as they are, yesterday in my house in Mesa. I am sorry I have been so silent with you. I have been silent with myself.

Today began in silence: a cold morning, the night's rain passed, leaving the roads dark and gleaming. We picked up our rental car and started down the North River Road, which parallels the sinuous Oja. While she drove, I tried to lose myself to the landscape: barren, wintry orchards on rolling hills, farther south, empty hills, trees growing sparser as we neared the fork in the river.

After two hours, Sherayna said, "I have to ask this, because I have to understand. Why did you burn Meena?"

Anything I might answer would be craven, for my mind thinks cravenly on the act. I spoke to the course of the events: "I was given permission by Rarion to burn a maximum of one square measure, in controlled increments, to impel your people's cooperation. But someone, it doesn't matter who, took that threat as permission to set the fields alight, and then it was too late. It was all we could do to try to fight the blaze."

In the middle of the empty road, she stopped the car. Its engine still humming, she turned to me and said what I knew she would say: "You expect me to believe that you are not to blame?"

"I expect you to believe nothing I say." That answer I had long ago prepared. "And I am to blame. I was the commander, the acts of my people were my acts. I should not have made that threat. Not so early, anyway. Perhaps not at all. Perhaps I should have waited till after the harvest as my wise friend counseled me."

She started up the car again. "Your wise friend?"

I had been longing to talk of Torna. When Sherayna mentioned her seer last night, I thought for an instant she was speaking of Torna, a curious mind trick that kept my old friend in my thoughts.

"She died in Meena," I said. "Yes, some of us died too. You met her, Torna, when we captured you in Oja. She watched you that night, and later, after I was reassigned."

"The lieutenant," said Sherayna. "She seemed decent—as City soldiers go. More decent than you."

"Unquestionably." I was not thinking of my failings. I was thinking of her absence as a black hole in my life. "She was the mother of that man from Keshot. I told her I'd send him her journals, and I did. She was my closest friend."

This I had never said, not even to myself, and not to her to whom I should have said it.

Sherayna did not reply. We moved east along the river, its fish-scale glint flashing now and then beyond the meadows to our right.

At length, inevitably, she said, "My sister was my closest friend, and I will not cheapen her memory with talk. She was a friend to this world."

I could say as much of Torna, but I did not. My father said there is a time for each to be heard and a time for each to listen.

When we stopped to eat our midday rations, we left the car by the side of the road and walked to the riverside. The sky had cleared, and though the prairie winds blew loudly, we were warm enough sitting on the rocks in our coats, watching the river ripple.

Sherayna said, "You know why the waters of the Oja are so clear?"

"I do. The runoff from the chemical plant in Oja City has killed most of the algae." I was pleased to see her eyes widen.

"In Meena," she said, "skin irritations from the water are commonplace."

"In Mesa too."

"And what do you think of that?" she asked casually, squinting out over the soft, slow waves.

"I wouldn't object to a new way, provided that requisite changes in agricultural practice could be effected without causing grievous economic hardship."

"Meena caused hardship." I think she could not repress that.

"Yes, I mean hardship like Meena. Or worse."

"But think how many times over the problem could have been solved if only it hadn't been more profitable for the consortium to poison the land, if only they'd agreed to lower yields. It would all have been stabilized centuries ago."

I had no interest in defending the Grains Consortium. "Think how many times over it could have been solved if new technologies had been allowed to flourish, if we'd been able to ask companion planets for help. Think, with greater yields and greater profit, and all without the pollution."

"The complicated answer," she said.

"Whereas centuries of fighting is so simple."

"It's all that's kept you from destroying us."

I thought of you. "Nevan writes that our centuries of fighting are the very thing that has most endangered this planet."

"If he's anything like his wife, I wouldn't trust him."

I asked her why she disliked Sylan. She said she didn't dislike her (which, having watched the two of them, I do not believe). But she said she distrusted Sylan's *very City-like* way of presenting herself as an expert in tech philosophy. I would like to know Sylan better. You have seldom spoken to me of her. Probably you were trying to protect her from us, to hide her knowledge. I think you have spent much of your time on our world afraid, which is wise, but I wish it were not so.

We drove into the afternoon sun in prudent silence. I am impressed by Sherayna's self-possession. This woman who, I do not doubt, fully intended to kill me in Nac now speaks to me like one who truly cares to hear me answer. I begin to think she may not be unreachable. I do not cherish the vanity that I could convert her to my philosophy. But someone else, if there were less bloodshed between them, she might listen to that person. A foolish fancy, probably. I am letting myself be buoyed by the visions of Micor's new order.

As I pondered her words, I reflected that in all of the times she had berated me for Meena, she had only once reproached me for imprisoning her in Oja. This puzzled me. True, the burning of Meena loomed larger and more immediate. Yet when I held her prisoner—I myself recoil from those memories.

I asked her finally why she never cursed me for those months in Oja. I was driving then, and I could see her lean her head on her hand and stare out the window.

She said, "When you look out there, what do you see?"

"The sun." It was sinking blinding in front of my eyes.

"I see life. I see the universe. I see the gods, I see my kin, myself, my sister. I see eternity. It was hard to see it in the walls of an Oja prison cell. I had to learn to see it subtly. Now I can see it all the time—if I look. And that is worth death, Ethan. It's certainly worth that year."

I could not speak.

After a moment, she said, "The ocean lies back into the sun and mirrors back the sun's face. I wrote that there. Your lieutenant friend, she gave me paper. At this instant, the ocean is rising before us to meet the sun. That's part of infinity. Tomorrow in Lo Renna, we'll see it."

She is nearer the gods than I.

We arrived in Oja City after nightfall, the freezing sky flecked with stars. In spite of her soaring words, I think she was frightened to be so close to the base where we'd imprisoned her. She stayed close to me till we'd paid for our rooms. With the gods' love, we did find separate rooms. Locking my door, I curtained the windows and turned up the heat, and felt, for the first time since Laynia came to Mesa, as if I were safe and could breathe.

≈•≈

18 Mid-Spring: Ethan's Journal:

We set out from Oja City early, when morning lay like a cobweb on the air. I had liked living in that city, and I think she had too, before her imprisonment. Oja, like a barren compromise between our two philosophies, is too urban to be wilderness, too rural to be civilized. These thoughts fell through me as we drove into the mountains with the Gulf of

Oja glinting through the trees to our east. When the sun burst at last over the western peaks, it blazed behind the cedar needles in flashes of green so bright they seemed golden.

We hardly spoke. Our destination began to feel close, and my thoughts turned to the deceit we must accomplish. It sickens me to think of the knife I am about to thrust in the back of the army that has fostered me—of Lashen, who has shown himself so steadfast. It dizzies me, this moral duality of acting against conscience in the name of what reason calls good.

We did speak finally, to clarify our plans. I tried to explain to her, to the best of my knowledge, the principles of Micor's invention, but I think she could grasp very little, having trained herself to recoil from all machines she hasn't been forced to use. She calls it "forcing": the combines they run in Meena, the irrigation lines—the pesticides. All this, she says, they have used under duress.

Out here, the thawing waterfalls pummel their channels, sometimes flowing over the road. Once, when the flooding was deep, we had to push the car through the water.

As we waited by the falls for the electrics to dry, she said, "These waters speak with the voices of gods. If you listen, you can enter the gods' world and they yours." She is a world worshipper, perhaps the most devoted I have known. Perhaps because I have known very few.

We came into Lo Renna an hour before sunset. Have you heard the old expression, Nevan: "Lo Renna is like bad sex: a lot of climbing to get nowhere"? It hardly deserves to be called a city, this hamlet clinging to seaside cliffs, all hewn from the mountain stone as if it were a symbol of the human handiwork in the engineering of this planet.

"I have always loved Lo Renna," said Sherayna. "Time passes it by."

Time does nothing of the sort. Underneath its architecture, Lo Renna is a current city, as beleaguered by strife as the rest of the planet. But what Sherayna saw was the Borderal ideal, approximated if not realized, and I did not have enough bitterness to pierce her illusion.

After we checked ourselves in at the hotel, I walked to the headlands to watch the sunset. She followed me openly down the trails at some distance, to ensure, I presumed, that I made no move to contact the army. I emerged from the trees on the rocks looking out on the sheer drop to the sea. The wind was rising. A yellow haze blurred the horizon. She came to stand beside me.

"I have no hidden radio," I couldn't refrain from saying.

She gazed past me to the bloated sun. "I wanted to see the sunset blend in the sea, at the end of the world here."

"Have you seen it before, from here?"

"You know I won't tell you where I go or what I do."

The sun was reddening and widening at the threshold of the waves as if it were old and dying.

She said, "I'm not ready to die, Ethan. There are still things for me to see and do. And though my sister's gone, there are people I wouldn't choose to leave."

"You think you'll die in this?"

"Of walking into an army installation to destroy their supreme tech achievement? A convicted Borderal?"

"They won't accost you while you're working with me."

"Unless they realize you've betrayed them."

That was true. I looked away to the half-orb sun.

"Ethan, it's imperative that we understand each other." She said it with a swift determination, culminating some internal debate.

"It can't be done," I said. "I cannot want the world you want, and you cannot want mine—and as long as we can't understand the wanting, we can't understand the idea, not really."

She waved away my words, as if they'd already been discussed and dismissed. "Yet we're here together because we understand a common good, a need to preserve Perdita. And Micor is right, we will not survive jae, unless we, as a world, learn to overcome our worser selves, to understand the heart, if we can't understand the mind. To be able to believe we each want what's best."

"Small comfort such faith may be," I said, "in the face of the issues that construct policy."

"But small comfort is still some."

A soft purple hue was melting over the ocean. The trees behind us nodded with a noise like the dragging surf. Sherayna must have been speaking loudly, but above that rhythmic roaring, her voice sounded soft, ebbing and flowing like part of the same planet forces.

She said, "There is only one thing that finally destroys, and that's hatred. If this planet is killed, it will be killed by hate—be it the hate of those who hurt the planet or of those who hate those who hurt it."

She'd oversimplified it—but it didn't matter.

"Yes." I remembered the hate I had felt for her once, and I blushed for shame.

"I must not hate you." She looked at me, but the words were an admonition to herself. "And to understand is to not hate."

"Or to hate completely."

"No," she said sadly, "simply to pity." We stood in silence. Then, she started back down the trail. I wondered at her words—and wondered if this was a woman reborn, or merely a woman I had never met till now.

≈•≈

18th, later:

My broken ribs having constrained my range of movement, Sherayna assists me in readjusting my brace. Tonight, she stared a long time at my bruises, somewhat worsened by fording our car across the flooded road today. Her gaze bothered me. I wish I could say my own feelings were clinical, but I confess there was more.

"Why should this worry you?" perhaps you ask. "She is a beautiful woman. The flaw in you would be if you felt nothing." Yes, she is beautiful. Though I did not admit it then, it dragged me the first time I saw her.

I put a hand to her shoulders, and she did not pull back but gazed into my face with an absent expression. Then, we stepped apart as if a dream were broken. I told her I could bandage myself, and she left me without a word. I am glad it will be over tomorrow.

CHAPTER 60

Memories hung like willow branches, fragmenting the world beyond their whispering leaves. Sherayna detested Ethan, for Meena, for her imprisonment in Oja—and in Iltan—for his lies, his rage, for Illia's death. She pitied him, for his father, his beliefs. And she felt by turns regret and respect, cowing dependence, companionship, trust—that last most terrible. She had no reason to trust him except she felt she could.

In his room in Le Renna, he touched her shoulder in a gesture too personal, almost intimate, and yet for that moment, it seemed fitting.

Back in her own room, she thought of Illia, and it seemed a betrayal not to hate Ethan for her death. *Illia, you gave me a garland of walnut leaves once. I can't even remember what I did with it. And have I remembered you better?*

≈•≈

The next morning, she put on a City uniform for meeting the project engineers.

I am City. I have made the gods turn me into what I let myself be last night. And what was that? His ally? Something deeper?

Taciturn, she drove them west into the mountains. The waxing day promised the rain-washed skies of spring. The long-limbed cedars grew sparser as they climbed. Weirdly fractured granites hid grasses in their shadow.

"It looks almost like a dead moon up here," said Sherayna. "You ought to feel at home."

"Nothing in the universe is truly dead, but this is your planet raw, as it was before we humans came. You should love the naked rock."

"Did I say I don't?"

A boulder shaped like a flat-beaked bird marked the gravel road on Micor's map. There was scarcely room for a single car. A measure down the way, a sign read: "Blind Road: Lake Access South"—a bright-red, newly painted sign. They drove by it and went on.

Some measures later, the road narrowed. Ethan said, "They must time their traffic so that no two cars will meet."

"Not expecting any unannounced inspection," said Sherayna.

"But they must. It's standard, especially for a project as momentous as this."

"It won't be unannounced long anyway if we meet any cars that have radios."

Ethan made no answer.

Past midday, they rounded the mountain straight into the blinding sun. Sherayna nudged the car forward in the face of the glare, over marble-slick gravel. A tight switchback to the southeast rose before them, looking down on a sheer drop of several hundred meters. Sherayna sat up, rigid, straining to see clearly as she crawled around the curve.

With a jolt, the car lunged forward, its nose tipping down to the left while the rear wheels slid out toward the cliff edge. For an instant, she went blind with shock, but years of training made her press the brake gently and steer the car straight. It stuck.

Neither she nor Ethan moved. Then they exchanged a glance, and, precariously near the edge of the cliff, she took a careful look out the window. She could see flat ground outside, extending at least two feet from the car. She raised a finger as a gesture for Ethan to wait and eased her door slowly open. Half of the road had broken away. The car's left front wheel had fallen into the gash, slipping its rear wheels round on the gravel till the left side lay fewer than ten centimeters from the edge.

She heard Ethan's door open. "You get out first," he said, "so the weight's shifted toward the mountain."

Hardly daring to touch the car, she eased herself out onto the sheer cliff face and jumped the meter-wide gap in the road to the firm ground in front of the car. Ethan, who had a shoulder to his right, got out and stood beside her.

Sherayna shuddered. "We took the wrong road."

"We can't have. It's exactly as Micor drew it on the map."

"Then explain to me, please, how they use this as their access road."

He sighed. "Maybe they have another as well." He stooped to examine the ruptured pavement. "Or maybe this is part of their defense system."

She stooped next to him and followed his eyes. Near the break, the road was clear of rubble and scuffed with regular parallel lines. "They have some sort of makeshift bridge they lay over it to cross it."

"So it seems."

"They've been learning techniques from us."

"If we were wise, we'd have learned them centuries ago." He circled to the back of the car. "We'll have to get it across."

"Give me a lever big enough, and I'll flip it like a coin."

Ethan examined the wheels. After a time, his eyes drifted away in thought. The minutes crept by.

"We could jack it up," Sherayna said, "but then we couldn't push it forward. And we don't have the strength to pull it up without a jack."

He said nothing.

"Well?"

He sighed. "I think . . . you're right." Was that surprise in his voice? "We'll have to leave it. So much for arriving unannounced."

Ethan walked a few paces down the road, gazing out over the sheer cliff face. At length, he turned back and came to stand beside her. "We can't leave the car here for anyone to see. We'll have to push it off the cliff."

Sherayna laughed. "For anyone to hear."

"It seems to me a few moments of sound will be less conspicuous than days with a ground car sitting here."

Days. It would take days to reach the Lo Ren by foot.

"All right," said Sherayna. "Let's not waste more time."

They unloaded their baggage and positioned themselves by the rear of the car, Sherayna pushing from the side, Ethan from the back. The gravel shifted under wheels and feet; the rear wheels ground, protesting, toward the drop-off. One final heave and the wheels swung off the cliff, tumbling the whole machine backward into the ravine. Sherayna skidded on the gravel, bumped into Ethan, who slipped a little but managed to steady her.

The car scraped and clattered, and boulders crashed down in its wake. The mountains bellowed. Sherayna tensed, poised to flee. But there was no place to flee. For a long time, they stared at the tiny, gleaming wreck far below.

Ethan whispered, "Damn, damn, damn." He was breathing hard.

"Are you in much pain?" Sherayna asked.

He seized his pack from the roadside and pulled out the map. "In about another six measures, we should come around to the Lo Ren side. There ought to be more trees, maybe shelter for the night."

"A place to hide at any rate."

"We don't need to hide," he said. "We have official passage. If anything, we flag down any passing car for a lift."

"What? Correct me if I'm wrong, but didn't we just plunge that car down that cliff to avoid being seen?"

"To avoid the *car's* being seen, Sherayna. We wouldn't want someone to spot it and report it before we have time to explain ourselves. We'd put the whole base on alert, give them time to radio Senarna for instructions."

"And if any car we flag down has a radio, the base will still be on alert, talking to Senarna before we can get there."

"No, because I can order them to keep radio silence. It's unlikely we'd meet anyone who'd outrank me."

"But they would probably radio out as soon as they saw us, before we had a chance to explain."

Ethan gazed out at the easterning sun. "How would we explain avoiding cars that pass us by?"

"As I did just now. It was imperative we keep our element of surprise—in order to be true to the king's mission: that we inspect them unannounced."

He looked down at the map again. "Walking, it will be a good eighty measures. Can we spare the time?"

"We have to."

He smiled. "So much for timely progress. Very Borderal."

"Let's walk," said Sherayna and started off.

≈•≈

There were indeed more trees on the lakeward side, firs like a mantle cloaking the limbs of the mountain. The lake glinted yellow-blue below, 150 measures northeast to southwest—the *Lo Ren*: "beautiful lake land." They paused several minutes gazing over the lake, drank some of the water they'd carried from Lo Renna.

Water, thought Sherayna. *Water coursing through my body, water shining before my eyes like a mirror to the gods. But more than a mirror . . . an aspect of the gods. A spirit. One spirit in everything.*

Water in the air, in the lake, in the ground, in the trees, in herself . . . in him. It was like electricity. She stood up on her toes, almost vibrating with it—a thousand thousand crossing lines connecting all to all. She laughed, only in her mind, but the laugh rang through her. And she was the Lo Ren and the road beneath her feet and Ethan beside her. All one.

The moment passed. But a contentedness remained, bathing everything in a gentle light.

They would have to camp near the stream tonight, no difficulty in the South Mountains in spring. At length, hefting her pack, Sherayna turned, about to walk past Ethan. But then, she glanced at him and stopped. He was frowning at the water.

"Are you ready?"

He nodded.

It was by the light of Olay that they finally found a small flat glade, thirty meters down from the roadside and six from a steep, rushing brook. The weather was mild lakeside, but the year was still young and the sky cold-clear.

"We ought to have a fire," said Sherayna. "No one will see it from here, as long as we put the smoke out by morning."

Ethan made no objection but watched, sullen and silent, as she coaxed a flame from moist twigs and fir needles. He allowed her to examine his ribs. Even in the dim glow of moon-fire-flashlight, she could see more bruising.

"A mess," she said.

When they'd eaten their ration bars and changed back to their traveling clothes, Ethan took out his notebook and wrote by flashlight.

"What is that?" asked Sherayna.

"My letters for Nevan."

"Saying what?"

"What I see, what I think. He wants to chronicle what happens here, and I want my voice to be heard."

"And if the City seizes your book?"

"I'm being vague about the mission."

As he wrote, Tori rose on the western mountains, a shimmering sliver. By and by, his pen ceased to scratch. When she glanced at him, he was staring at her, but he dropped his eyes at once and fell to writing again.

"What is it?" she said. "What are you writing about me?"

He paused, looking up. "Not as much as I could."

"Is that meant to be an insult?"

"No. You cut your hair."

"After Meena. To make it harder to recognize me."

"Why not after Oja?"

"Because home in Meena, I felt safe."

He looked away. After a long time, he said, "I want to love the gods through you. I know that now."

"You should have thought of that before you killed my people and burned my fields."

He opened his mouth as if to speak but only sighed. Finally, he said, "You exhorted us to peace yesterday."

"This is not the time."

"No, and no time is the time," he said sharply.

They watched the flames. Sherayna wanted to climb into their warmth and not be burned.

"We help the gods through love," came Ethan's voice. When she looked up, he was looking at her earnestly.

He was right. He was indisputable. And Illia—it would help Illia more if Sherayna could forgive him.

After a moment, she moved to his side and held out her hand. He took it at once in a hand firm and warm and just a little larger than her own. They met each other's eyes in the firelight, then looked away and sat silent. At length, he reached his other hand to her hair, and oddly, she didn't mind, as she hadn't minded his hand on her shoulder. As he brushed her neck, his fingers found the necklace she wore beneath her shirt. Maybe that was what she'd wanted. He balanced her necklace on his fingers, staring.

"A head of grain from Meena," she said. "I rescued it before it burned and had it dipped in gold alloy."

He let the necklace drop and sat back. "We've hurt each other. I am sorry."

He was sorry, she realized, and the feeling ran in parallel to his convictions that fighting for the City was necessary. Sherayna understood that: she had killed for the Borderals and she, too, was sorry for the families and the friends those acts of hers had torn apart. In some ways, they were much alike, she and Ethan.

"You know," she said, "in a different reality, I think I would like you. I wish I'd known you differently."

CHAPTER 61

19 Mid-Spring: Ethan's Journal:

On watch here while Sherayna sleeps and watching only halfheartedly, I admit. I am letting myself lag to be fresh for tomorrow. A page or so ago, troubled by her blue-cast face as she watched Tori rising, I wrote a fiery and ridiculous thing. I wrote that I thought we were of one soul.

And I believe it. We will not be united in this life. But perhaps in this life, we can move toward our eventual meeting. Perhaps there may be an illusion of union—no, not illusion, but a first step.

She has a necklace with a head of wheat from Meena, dipped in gold, clasped in the middle of runic letters. The preservation of Meena: a passing fragment of a wheat stalk transformed into an eternal work of art. I know that she—and you—would disagree, would call the wheat the remarkable feat of creation and the gold merely simple, elemental. But gold, for the Samas, was the purest of all colors, the color of moving between the worlds, the sun -color of knowledge, the Golden Way, the Shonac—she carries it even in her very name, in the old Old Dabunè: Sherayna: , "the giver of the golden light."

I wonder how long the odds are that I will succeed in this mission before being arrested, before losing my career, before this world disowns me as my father's son. When that happens, Nevan, when I am decried as a traitor and am executed and gone, take this to be my testament:

The highest good we Perditans can attain is to journey into space, to reunite with our lost sibling worlds, to rediscover our forbears both Sama and Kiri—to voyage into the light-speed space, be it by jae or be it by rippling, to walk through the rent between dimensions, as if to reach out and embrace the gods with love. Yet none of these objects can be achieved if jae devastates our people before we can achieve them. I do not regret these steps I have taken in defiance of the Perditan government. If I could erase one thing from my life, I would erase the destruction of the *Outbound.* And if I could erase another, I'd erase the massacre at Meena.

≈•≈

20 Mid-Spring:

She put out the fire thoroughly this morning: a rebel skill—no smoke by the time the sky glowed between the mountainsides. We were wet with dew, stiff from the ground, sore from our exertions yesterday. As we descended into the valley of the Lo Ren, Sherayna grew agitated at the thought of being spotted by a vehicle. But I, for one, was not prepared to add hours to our travel time by hiking along the slippery, spring-wet hill below the road. In deference to my injury, I think, she did not press the point.

But when she heard a ground car humming down the mountain, she seized me by the arm and all but hurled me down the hill in front of her. The car passed above us without slowing.

It was near noon, and, having been forced to halt, we decided to rest and eat. We moved down a few paces to a sunlit knoll. I consulted our map as she got out our rations.

"I'd estimate we have about thirty-five measures left to go," I said.

Sherayna chewed on some dried fruit thoughtfully. "We could get there tonight."

"We could, but I don't much relish the idea of having to bluff my way into a high-security establishment, figure out its layout, then waylay my escort and perform delicate technical operations at peak speed, after a full day walking down a mountain."

"Then again, there will probably be fewer people on duty at night than tomorrow morning."

"True, but I'd rather be rested."

She nodded. "It's for you to say, you're the technician." And after a moment: "Do you think there's any chance that a new order may indeed be established by all this?"

"I can't begin to speculate. You doubt Micor's word?"

She handed me a ration packet and said nothing.

"I had the impression you had great faith in him," I pressed.

"I grew up revering him as much as any seer. I still revere him. Yet he's pretended all these years to guide us, and all the time he was guarding tech more dangerous than any of the rest."

"In order to understand it and render it safer, surely."

"Yes." But her tone was uncertain. "I miss Olloan." The rebel traitor. "I think I trusted him more than Micor, I don't know why. He was gentler maybe. Even though he betrayed us, somehow I still trust him more."

"You're doing the right thing," I said, "and a loyal thing. You're fortunate. I am doing the right thing, and a disloyal thing."

"You've earned the queen's trust. Now you're proving you deserve it. That's loyalty, no?"

A harsh laugh escaped me. "I repeat it: disloyalty. Disloyalty to Senarna, to the king, to the warmaster, who is my friend. She has always been one of you."

Her eyes narrowed. "We, whom you detest so, Ethan?"

"No," I said. "No, not you. What you are, you are honestly. But she relishes deceit and power and typing on the keys of our poor, simple king."

"You can't blame her because her husband has too much power and too little brain."

I eyed her. "You are quick to her defense."

"I spoke to her in Nac. She's devoted her life to protecting Perdita, and not for power. By undermining this project, she may well be branded a traitor like the rest of us. She's given up more, I think, than any of us."

"And all this you know because you spent a few days with her? Even if her acts seem noble, her heart is dark. I know it."

"No one knows another's heart," she said rightly.

"Very well. Let us say, I have strong reason to suspect it."

"What reason?" she asked.

I looked at the sunlight dappling the firs. I looked at the leaf litter and scraggly forest grass, and I envied these mindless things. Yet I wanted her to know, as I want you to know—I wanted to learn things and to teach things I have overlooked too long.

"I met her," I said, "during my third year in the Space Program. I was nineteen, about the age of her younger son. When she came to see me, I was honored almost to panic: the queen, to see me in my father's name! I knew it had to be on account of my father—there's no other reason she'd have heard of me. She came to my room and spoke some pretty words about what a great tragedy my father's death had been and how she hoped I would carry on in his footsteps.

"And then she began to talk of how Perdita needed a guiding conscience, of how that could be me. I said I could never be equal to that. I might acquire Jessec's technical knowledge. I hoped I shared his sensibilities, but I could never have his skill with people. She said I shouldn't worry, he had guided me far and she would guide me further. She said between the two of us, we could change the way Perdita functioned, and she put her arms around my neck and kissed me.

"I thought she was talking of preventing disasters like the *Outbound* from recurring. It sounded beautiful to me. In her arms, I was ready to believe any dream she planted in me. But at some point, I began to hear: she was talking of stopping the program, of setting tech development on hiatus, of legislating rebel—Borderal—dogma. I felt the trap closing. I called her a traitor, a Wolsena's promise. I think I accused her of murdering my father, and I manhandled her out the door."

Sherayna gaped. "She didn't have you arrested?"

"She couldn't. She had no excuse for seeing me. I wasn't really important enough for her personal condolences, not two years after my father's death. If she'd spoken of it, I'd have exposed her as a rebel—damaged her credibility anyway."

Sherayna stared at me. "If she can get us into this Jae Project, Ethan, I think she could have found an excuse for seeing you."

I do not like the idea that Laynia spared me. Yet Sherayna was right. The incontestability of her words staggered me. "Maybe."

"And you're wrong to despise her for her politics. That, to me, seems unlike Im Jessec's example."

Those words infuriated me, and I had to restrain myself from shouting in the stillness of the forest. "That's exactly the manipulation she practiced on me! Twisting my father's magnanimity into rebel sympathizing."

"That's not what I said—"

"I know," I cut her off. I knew. My fury died like a faucet turned off. "You meant that my father advocated respect for divergent views. And for the sake of the gods, I could forgive her her politics, but her nature is twisted, and she mesmerizes minds." Sherayna was twirling a blade of grass in her fingers. "Not like you."

She met my eyes. "Are you sure?"

"Yes."

"I could be playing you for a fool."

"You are not."

She looked away and groped for her pack. "We had better get back on the road."

We camped early, some ten measures from the project site in a glade of stumpy grass about twenty meters up from a creek. Taking advantage of the daylight, we washed our uniforms in the stream and rinsed the sweat off our hands and faces. Since the evening was starting to chill, we lit our fire at once, reckless, propping our uniforms on our packs nearby to dry. Sherayna scavenged for herbs and roots to add to our rations.

As we watched the sun sink, Sherayna said, "I've wanted to ask you something." She waited for me to look up. "I knew that your father had a son—you were in the news now and then when he was so popular. But I don't remember hearing anything about your mother. Did she die when you were young?"

"She left with a lover, a man my father suspected of having Borderal leanings. Maybe she was afraid my father might harass him for his politics—which he would never have done. At any rate, she left. I haven't seen her since I was seven." I do not know when I had last spoken of my mother to another living being.

Sherayna's eyes were too big with pity. "She never wrote?"

"No. And I have a question for you. Were you and Olloan lovers?"

She frowned at me. "No. Why do you ask?"

"You spoke of him with great tenderness."

Still she frowned. "What do you think you see in me?"

Another question for which I had no answer. "A woman I can esteem."

"Unlike the queen?"

"As sky to earth."

She looked away. "Perhaps too true. The sky won't catch a falling man, and the earth crushes him."

"Meaning you crush men?"

"I let them fall. Let me tell you a story. There was a man I was in love with once. And he was in love with me. He wanted me very much—only he loved another first, and she, who would have been pleased to see us lovers, she would always be first. And I was too proud to be second, and so I turned him away. That is the woman you think you want. Too selfish to give herself to her cause as the queen has, or even to her own life."

I grasped about for something to say. "I think you're too harsh."

"The truth is harsh."

I felt I ought to make some confession worthy of her own. "I have never been in love. I have wanted people, but I have never been driven to a union soul to soul, till now. Because that is what this is—for me, not you. I know that."

She barely glanced at me. "Let's take a look at your ribs."

The evening had turned milder than we'd anticipated. Standing by the fire, I was more than warm without my shirt and brace, my breathing painful and fast. But I held back from her because I have caused her so much pain I have no right to ask anything of her.

We rebound my ribs, and I put my shirt back on. And after that, she came close to me—I truly couldn't understand why at first. Then, she kissed me briefly, a brush of lips on lips. And she went back to her place by the fire.

"I need to clear my head," I said and walked out into the blue night where the breeze tickled my arms like feathers. Shivering a little and quieter inside, I returned just as Tori was rising. Sherayna was sitting by the fire, her arms around her knees, staring at the climbing moon as she had stared last night.

"Ethan," she said, "if we strive long enough, will we see each other with both eyes wide open?"

CHAPTER 62

Sherayna had the watch before dawn. In the sleeping cold of the twentieth hour, she rose from her place to drench the coals and heap the earth on top to still their hissing. At the stream, she washed, shivering, and donned her still damp City uniform. Then, she filled their ten syringes with Micor's tranquilizer and stored five in the inner pockets of her tunic.

The moons had set; the dawn was a cloak of iron behind the western mountains. In Meena, the sun would already be blazing over green claw-wheat that must by now be hiding the fire scars. Meena would recover, but would she see it?

Ethan slept on as she packed, his face lax, turned to the fire pit, one hand peeking out from his coat and blanket, palm up. If they both survived this, would they be enemies again? She had a sudden yearning for time—to speak with him, to learn, to listen, to blot out the rest of the world and keep walking through the mountains, just the two of them.

He sat bolt upright. "Sherayna!"

"What is it?" His voice must have carried for a measure.

He groped out of his blanket and took her face in his hands. "I saw it. I understand what it is now."

"What?"

"The dream. I was standing before the black ocean. The stars were wheeling above it. And then something was happening to the ocean. The waves were turning to gold: straw gold. And the horizon paled to just such a shade of gold. And then the sun came roaring up and set the sea alight. But the stars were still shining in the black above! Don't you see?" He gestured at the sky. "It was in space, it was all in space, the whole ocean! The whole time."

His exuberance unnerved her. "Ethan, every ocean is in space. Why can't you City understand that? All of us, everything, is always in space. The whole world is in space. Don't tell me it takes a dream revelation to tell you that."

"Don't you see? I was there, up there." He cocked his head skyward.

"You are always there! That is the folly of the Space Program, of the Jae Project, of all of it. You think you'll reach the gods up there? They is here! They're everywhere."

He smiled. "They are not everywhere—or where they are, we do not always see them."

"My point exactly."

"Sherayna, I'm not talking about the space that Perdita floats in. I'm talking about the space in my mind, the point where my thoughts and the gods' intersect. The dark became light without changing what it is."

He was not behaving like himself. She felt her palms grow sweaty. "Ethan, we have to face the project today."

"I know you." He lifted one hand to her face. "I know."

Her heart pounded. "Who am I?"

"You're my mother's daughter."

Sherayna laughed, or perhaps she merely shuddered. "I'm your what?"

He sat back a little. "This." He pulled her necklace gently out from under her collar. "I had only noticed the grain head before, but the old symbols—look."

"I don't read the old Sama symbols."

"It says, *Destusee*: 'we overcome.'"

"It's the old motto. Well?"

"It was my mother's. Wasn't it yours?"

Sherayna shook her head. "My father's."

"Sherayna, if your file's not lying, then you're forty-one."

"You have an advantage over me, Ethan. Yes, I'm forty-one. And you?"

"Forty-eight." He stared at her expectantly. "Don't you see? That's why she left. She was pregnant with you. And your father was a Borderal, so she couldn't risk bringing her new family into contact with my father."

Sherayna opened her mouth, closed it, finally said, "Ethan, what brought on this revelation?"

"It was the dream. Not this dream, the first dream."

"What first dream?"

"The first time I saw the water. I saw my mother dive into it. I had that dream—do you realize—the first night I ever spoke to *you*."

"And?"

"And then the sun rose out of the ocean. It was her—but it was you."

Sherayna could think of no good thing to say, but she owed him the truth. "I think you're grasping for reasons to explain why she deserted you."

He started to shake his head, then hesitated. "I suppose if she were your mother, you would have recognized her photograph in Mesa."

"My parents died when I was two and I had no picture of her—but, yes, I do think I would have felt something. And I didn't. Look, my mother's name was Dawa."

"My mother's name was Serbna—but, of course, she would have changed her name."

She looked at him and thought how much he looked like the woman standing by Jessec's side. Not like Sherayna.

Ethan rested his hand over his mouth. Then, his brow cleared, and he gazed at her with quiet conviction. "I know what Fennoc tells me."

"You're a seer then?"

He smiled briefly. "Only to see you. And your sister—my sister. My dead sister."

"No, listen," said Sherayna. "My foster sister. My sister. Not your sister. *I* can't be your sister. The odds against the two of us ending up relations, they have to be astronomical."

He was silent a long while. "My mind knows you're right. But it doesn't matter, the genetics don't matter. My soul has told me we're . . ." He broke off. "My soul has told me."

Sherayna groped for emotions. "I can't think about this now. We have to be on the road."

≈•≈

They walked down the mountain into the morning. The lake flickered now and then through the veil of trees, sky embedded in the land. The day was vibrant with spring, and even the granite road seemed more alive than mere rock beneath Sherayna's feet.

She asked Ethan, "If you've learned to meet the gods inside yourself, does that mean you recognize that there's no need for a Space Program?"

"No. I believe that physical place is important. It changes the way our minds perceive and the way the gods' minds perceive too."

Sherayna considered this. *Dare we blame our surroundings for our inner strife?* "I don't think it's the place that does that."

"Then it doesn't matter if we desert Perdita, no?"

"Our planet is the system in which we live. It's our health, not just our place."

"If we got to the other inhabited planets, we'd survive there very well."

Sherayna watched the ground flashing under her feet. That couldn't be right—which meant he must have been right about the need for a particular place. But that didn't seem right either. "Perhaps. But we have what we need right here. Why go anywhere else? It would be very hard."

"We?" he said.

They walked on in silence.

By midmorning, the road had leveled off, running parallel to a low-banked hillside that overlooked Lo Ren. Oaks and elms crept in among the firs, mottling the countryside in dozens of greens. Birds flittered through the treetops. A gentle breeze blew off the water, rustling the trees . . .

Rustling to their left, more than was natural. Sherayna saw Ethan steal a glance at the woods. Briefly, they met each other's eyes, walked on. They could excuse their presence but could not excuse taking any hostile act against the City personnel who were watching. Then, to Sherayna's amazement, came another sound: a high-pitched twittering, repeated in a pattern that was not a bird's.

"Warblers," she said. "It's early in the season for them."

"Yes, it is early," Ethan answered.

She could not respond to the signal, of course. She had not expected her people to be here. Could Leric have gotten her message so fast? Guilt crunched in her chest, to be plotting even now, deceiving Ethan.

He is still City. I have my first duties.

They walked another two measures, leaving the noise of her compatriots behind them. Around a sharp bend, the road dead-ended in a dusty turnabout. Behind it climbed a slope of boulders. To the left, the woods ascended gently; to the right, the hillside led down to the water. Ethan inspected the perimeter of the circle with an air of authority. Sherayna, meanwhile, studied the slope. It seemed just the place for the entrance to the project. But if the piled boulders hid an entrance, they hid it well. Ethan glanced her way. She shrugged.

He stepped back and called out, "I am Warchief Ethan from Mesa, come in the name of the king. You are required to offer entry to my footman and myself." He waited. Nothing stirred. "You will grant me entry or stand in defiance of Ayer."

Still nothing. After a moment, Sherayna climbed a few steps up the rock face to look closer for a passage. She heard a man's voice to her right:

"I am Lieutenant Zelmec, duty officer in charge. Warchief, why haven't you approached us using the proper codes?"

Sherayna turned to see Ethan walking toward a lanky man flanked by two armed footmen.

Ethan said, "The king wished to send an agent who was not a member of the project. Since the king himself, for his own safety, is not privy to all the code procedures surrounding the project, he was unable to brief me in those procedures. I must, on the king's instructions, require you to make no outside communication regarding our presence until my business is concluded." As he spoke, he withdrew his pass from his pocket and handed it to the lieutenant. Coming to his side, Sherayna did the same.

The lieutenant inspected their passes. "I know you, Warchief. But I hope you'll understand that I must verify your identities against our records."

"Naturally," said Ethan.

"Please come with me." With a wave of his hand, the lieutenant led them down the slope toward the river. There, on ground they'd already looked over, a horizontal door had opened, leading to a metal stairway.

Down several flights of stairs, the footmen's guns at their backs, they came to a white-lit steel passage, and then an anteroom, where the lieutenant left them under guard for several minutes.

He returned with a stern face. "Your identity has been verified, Warchief. However, our archives contain no record of your footman, Tela."

"Yes, I suspected that," said Ethan. For an instant, Sherayna's heart froze. "Footman Tela is an engineer from the Space Program at Cudonond. She was only inducted last week in order to accompany me on this mission—which, I must add, Lieutenant, is priority. I trust you will let me proceed without further delay."

"Of course, sir. As soon as I know what your priority mission is and why my footmen spotted you walking like tourists down the street."

Ethan explained what had happened to their car and spun out their story of an inspection of safety protocols. "Are you satisfied, Lieutenant? Do you require me to remind you of our respective ranks?"

"No, Warchief. Your rank is owed respect here. I trust you understand our caution in the name of guarding this project, particularly since our watches have found traces of a rebel presence."

"What traces?" asked Ethan, frowning.

"Sounds, footsteps."

"That's all, Lieutenant? I suggest you intensify your surveillance."

"We hide here by minimizing our presence, sir," said the lieutenant stiffly. "I'm sure you, Warchief, appreciate the importance of delicacy in military operations."

That was a dig about the burning of Meena, Sherayna realized.

Ethan's face was stone. "Then pray you are still hidden. And allow me to conduct my inspection."

"Of course, sir." He started to turn, then hesitated. "May I ask, is your visit at all concerned with that of the Zerin envoy?"

Ethan raised an eyebrow. "Zerin envoy?"

"This young Jetho who arrived a few days ago to lecture about worshipping Leva as a tech goddess."

"I hadn't heard," said Ethan.

The lieutenant nodded. "The king isn't having second thoughts about the project, is he? Sending her and then sending you?"

"I am not privy to the king's thoughts. But I can think of no reason he should question this project. Can you?"

"Of course not." The lieutenant hurried to assign a team to show them around the complex.

What young Jetho? Sherayna wondered. *What is Zerin doing?*

The lieutenant insisted that they have at least four guides, all specialists in particular subfields—armed escorts, really. At least, reflected Sherayna, she and Ethan had not been asked to relinquish their weapons. To do so would have been an affront to his rank.

A map of the facility showed it oriented around a core generator in which the particle bombardment would take place. From this force-shielded core ran four force-shielded power lines that would transmit the shifted particles into "travel cells," containers the size of a large book box, suitable for installment in superlight engines. The outer ring of the complex, in which they now stood, consisted of control rooms and barracks for the project personnel. Surrounding the power lines and the core was a network of automatic cutoffs that would register conditions outside normal parameters and alert the main and secondary fail-safes to switch off the generator. It was laid out just as her briefings had said.

Sherayna could not help but notice the glow in Ethan's eye as he remarked to one of their guides, "Most elegant engineering."

"The system is almost set to test," said the young man, "but we haven't yet achieved an adequate vacuum in the particle chamber." He led them into a room of glowing readout screens.

"Have you encountered any technical difficulties so far?" asked Sherayna.

"Aside from the vacuum? No, none at all."

"We did have trouble calibrating the tachyon-detector cutoff switches," said another of their guides, an older woman. "The idea of registering faster-than-light emissions is so new to us! It took us a while to get our minds around it."

"They're calibrated now?" asked Ethan.

"Yes."

"How do you know if you haven't switched on the tachyon field to test them?"

"Well, by the simulations."

Ethan nodded and proceeded to ask a series of technical questions on how the readouts were connected to detectors and detectors to the generator. Sherayna followed little of the engineers' descriptions, but she did memorize which panel they identified as the access to the relay circuits. A perfect place to set up the off box. Now, they could move.

But just as she was poised to overpower their guides, Ethan let them lead him out of the control room and down to another that looked almost identical. He seemed to be enjoying this tour of theirs.

"Now in terms of security protocols," he began.

"Oh, every computer and access panel is coded," said the young man. "And there are surveillance devices in all rooms and corridors, except the quark chamber, of course, which needs to be kept absolutely pristine."

"The surveillance devices are hidden, I trust."

"Of course."

"How many per room."

"Three."

"Constantly monitored?"

"Yes, Warchief."

"I'd like to inspect the monitoring facilities."

In the monitoring room, there were five footmen on duty, each inspecting some dozen screens. Ethan made their guides explain which screens correlated with which rooms. No control room was more than a few seconds distant from a security contingent. Sherayna began to feel like a pig corralled for slaughter.

Ethan said, "I see no rooms adjoining the travel-cell-collection chambers."

"The cameras aren't hooked up yet," said one of the surveillants. "There's nothing there, sir, just empty rooms and empty cells."

"And the links to the power lines." Ethan glared at the man who had sworn they had cameras in every room. The man blanched.

"Yes, sir," said the surveillant, "but someone would have to disconnect the cells in order to reach the lines. And those lines are inactive now, sir."

"Still, the rooms should be monitored. Make a note of it, Footman Tela." And to Sherayna's surprise, Ethan extracted the off box from his pack and handed it to her as if it were a typing pad. Mustering a professional air, she pretended to enter a code on the box's keypad.

"I'd like to inspect those cell-collection rooms," said Ethan.

≈•≈

The room was a plain steel-walled closet, kept locked from the outside. At its far end was a panel, which, when removed, displayed the travel cells connected to the jae power lines. Sherayna could see two cells: dim, opaque boxes. Their guides, trusting Ethan, consented to explain how the cells were connected to the lines.

This is the moment, Sherayna realized. Ethan saw it too and purposefully drew their guides' attention to the wall readout screen so that two of the guides stood in front of him and two behind him but still in front of Sherayna—all were looking away from her toward the screen. Sherayna pulled two syringes from her pocket. Tucking the off box under her arm, she uncapped one of the syringes, switching the other to an outer pocket. Casually, she stepped up behind the nearest footman and plunged the syringe into his shoulder. As he fell, she let the off box clatter to the floor, shoving the syringe into her pocket as she caught him. "The footman is ill!"

As the other footmen moved to help him, she uncapped her other syringe and plunged it into the shoulder of the older woman, reaching for her gun as she did so—no time to seize another syringe. But the other two had seen her; the talkative young man had his gun trained on her chest. Ethan jabbed him from behind. The remaining footman spun around, gun on Ethan.

"Warchief!" he exclaimed incredulously.

Sherayna shot him through the shoulder. Crying out, he dropped the gun, just as Ethan moved in and syringed him. As he slumped to the ground, someone else rushed in. Sherayna lifted her gun but stopped to see a woman dressed in a Jetho's gray.

"Quick," said the Jetho, heaving the door shut, "you don't have much time. Can you jam the door? They're coming down the corridor."

Ethan strode to the door panel and fired at it point blank, freezing the lock in place and sealing them in.

He turned to the Jetho, frowning. "Miri?"

Sylan's daughter—yes, there was a resemblance.

The young woman waved her hand frantically. "I think one of these people pressed some sort of alarm. Listen, you have to work fast. The Borderals are going to attack."

The glance that Ethan threw at Sherayna cut her to the heart.

"How do you know?" He picked up the off box.

"I read it in their minds, the soldiers' minds—maybe they're wrong, but they've been deploying their forces. That's why they left me in the barracks without an escort."

Ethan was disconnecting one of the travel cells. The door echoed with a deafening thud. Miri started and clung close to Sherayna, who moved to the side of the door, her gun poised.

"Ethan, give Miri your gun," she said.

He drew it and tossed it on the floor.

Miri picked it up, her hands shaking. She seemed unable to stop talking. "I read their minds to find out where you were and deflected their minds from seeing me go by. It's hard, I have an awful headache. I don't think I did it very well."

"It's all right," said Sherayna.

Noises of machinery from behind the door.

"Stand on the other side of the door where you'll have a clear shot," Sherayna ordered.

Trembling, Miri complied.

The door screeched—and there was silence.

Miri whispered, "I planted a suggestion that the rebels are already invading the base . . . I hope."

"They've gone?" Sherayna whispered back.

"I hope so."

"You can do that with your mind?"

"I hope so. It's more than I've ever tried. But they're scared, they're primed to believe it."

Sherayna glanced at Ethan. He had set one travel cell onto the floor and was hooking the off box into the power lines.

"We didn't know you'd be here," said Sherayna to Miri.

"It was arranged at the last minute. I came by jumper, a royal envoy, to try to slow—"

The floor beneath them rumbled. Sherayna put a hand against the wall to steady herself.

"What was that?" she asked Miri, who only shook her head. "Ethan?"

"Nearly," he replied, punching a code into the off-box keypad.

The floor lurched. Sherayna fell on one of the footmen, felt more than saw Ethan thrown down close to her. Another tremor. There was Miri staggering across the room, Ethan crawling back to the off box. A sudden flash: the cell that was still hooked up went blue, dazzling the steel walls. *Power surge?* The blue was gone.

A second of terrifying black.

Had that jolt activated the reactor? That blue, had it been jae? Had Ethan failed with the off box?

The yellow ceiling lamps flickered on.

Light spots dancing before her eyes, Sherayna saw Ethan doubled over by the power line. His breaths hissed in the room like wind through an air duct. A different kind of terror seized her. But something else . . .

"Where's Miri?" she cried.

Ethan slipped onto his side, propping himself on his elbow. "Gone," he whispered. "Fell against the line. No flash, no sound . . . she was just gone."

Sherayna clambered over the footmen to his side. "The off box?"

He nodded and, heaving himself onto his knees, leaned over to examine the box. He looked back at Sherayna and nodded again, his whole body weaving with the force of his breaths. His eyes went wide, and he reached out shaking hands to her.

Grasping his hands, she saw the flesh was burned raw, blood dripping black onto his wine-colored cuffs. His face was the lifeless white of clay, except for bruised marks under his eyes, and the shadows hollowing his cheeks. With a sigh, he slumped onto the body of one of the footmen, his fingers convulsing round her hands.

A stream of words poured out of her: "I'm sorry I didn't warn you about them, I didn't know what else to do. I lied, and you were honest. I shouldn't have led them here, I shouldn't have warned them. I thought . . ."

He was shaking his head. "No matter." His eyes on her face were the blue of the summer sky through the mouth of a black cave. "I still see the sun."

But his gaze drifted away. She kissed him. His lips hardly moved, but the touch pricked with electricity. His breathing was shallow, his skin taking on the sheen of a scar. She gripped his hands, though they burned her.

She did not suspect for a moment she could save him. Jae was inexorable. Still holding one hand, she laid the other on his chest and felt the pulse in his neck till it died. And for what might have been hours, she sat by his side, her hands bloody and stinging as if covered with nettles. It seemed that she had done all there was for her to do. It seemed reasonable that death should close all life.

At length, the soldiers burned through the door. The lieutenant hurled abuses that Sherayna didn't catch, shouted questions for which she had no words, then threw her in a holding cell.

CHAPTER 63

In the afternoon, the breeze came up, but Karmeena was warm in her woolen coat as she lugged a crate of pears into the eating hall. She liked the physical work more than her studies. The longer she spent as a novice Jetho, the more she became convinced that she would have liked to spend all her life on the farm.

She hefted her crate onto the counter, started back for the next one. In the hall, she squeezed past the Jetho Lulad, smiling as he tipped his crate to let her by. At the cart, she took down a case marked bristlenuts; they rolled inside like rattles, like the ones she and her mother used at dances back in Meena. The memory was like a shadow passing over the sun. She started back toward the kitchen. Then her world reeled.

She dropped her box with a crash. Standing not four steps away was a figure in a Jetho's robe, yet the robe shimmered, and her face and hair too, like sun through frost on a window.

"Miri," she said, and the figure seemed to sigh.

Lulad was rushing to Karmeena's side. She could hear him asking what was wrong. He took her arm. With the other she pointed at Miri, who stood still as a portrait. Karmeena understood that this was no live person, not Miri come home from the Lo Ren. And knowing this, she felt no horror, no wonder, just certainty that if she looked away she would lose the figure. People gathered around her, jabbering. Some stepped in the way of the apparition, yet, like a projection against a wall, she fell to the front of whatever touched her.

"Karmeena," she said, though her lips did not move—she spoke softly yet louder than all the shouting Jethor. "Karmeena, bring my family—it's hard to stay."

Without taking her eyes from the figure, Karmeena shouted, "Bring Jasen and Sylan and Nevan here now!" They were by her side in an instant.

Miri was motionless again, a video stopped on one frame. After some seconds, she heard Jasen gasp, "Do you see?"

"I see," breathed Nevan. "By the wand of Volsénlla, I see."

Sylan gasped something in her own language, a question.

"I was Miri," the figure answered, then paused, puzzled, Karmeena thought, though no puzzlement showed on her empty face. "I thought that it was important to say . . . there is a world beyond jae. There is a land of jae."

This must be made known, Karmeena thought. She didn't know what it meant, but it mattered! With all her strength, she opened her mind to the Jethor, pushed into their minds the image of the being she saw before her. She had no idea how many she reached, but she heard soft gasps close by her and knew they saw what she saw.

"I . . . wanted you to know," the figure was saying, "jae is a world of mind." Her eyes bored into Karmeena. "I wanted you to know I was sorry to leave . . . and to say I am here. Do not grieve too much, I was thinking."

"Is Miri dead?" demanded Jasen.

The figure frowned, but her mouth did not move. It was like one photo replaced with another. "I went to the land of jae."

She has died but not died. She has made her way to the plane of the gods, like so many dead before her. Yet, she—she has come back to us. She is in two worlds. She is a bridge to reunite humanity with the gods.

"We'll find you," said Karmeena, and she knew the gods spoke through her. "We will find you, pilgrim in the realm of the gods. We will follow the pilgrim." The figure was fading, but the purpose blazed in Karmeena. "See her? Love unites the two worlds. The two will be as one!" The figure was gone. Karmeena faced the Jethor. "A golden roadway lights the sky between our world and the realm of the gods. This is jae—not a highway for spaceships, a highway for the soul. This is the Shonac, the Golden Way, the Way of the Pilgrim."

CHAPTER 64

She's snapped, thought Sylan as she trailed Karmeena. *Have I?* She knew that something immense had happened, some disaster. But she couldn't comprehend it. Couldn't even feel panic. Something needed to be done, but her mind was gray. And so there was nothing but to follow Karmeena. Miraculously, Karmeena knew what to do.

They crossed to Olwer's rooms, where he kept his radio for communication with Senarna. Olwer tried Laynia's frequency first, though the chance that she'd be standing by to answer was minimal.

"My Queen, this is Zerin," he opened formally.

An aide answered, an old woman's voice: "We are receiving you, Zerin. The queen is unavailable."

"We have concerns about the waterside," said Olwer, providing the Lo Ren code. "We require instructions."

For a moment, there was silence, then, "Please stand by." After nearly five minutes, the voice resumed, "The king instructs the Im Jetho and the three West-of-Nows to report to Ayer Senarna to meet with Micor from Oja."

Olwer hesitated. "We leave at once." He broke the link.

"Good," said Karmeena. "That was good you didn't announce me, didn't give them a chance to turn me away."

"You?" said Olwer.

"Of course. I have to speak to them."

Olwer gave Kara a long look, his gray eyes unfathomable. Sylan felt herself floating away with those eyes. "Yes, Karmeena," he said, "I'll take you."

Sylan felt a trickle of relief.

≈•≈

They arrived at Ayer Senarna in the last hours of the night: the three West-of-Nows, Olwer, and Karmeena. Jasen found the castle ghoulish in the green night lamps, a nightmare to match his nightmare.

My sister is dead. I know my sister is dead, he kept saying to himself, but he did not know it. What was it they had seen? What had jae done to Miri?

Some footmen escorted them to a small beige room. A thrill of fear rang from his father's mind: this room was like the one where they'd interrogated him years ago. Jasen grasped his hand. A thin, white-haired man in rich clothes bright as autumn leaves rose from behind the room's desk as they entered. Recognizing Rarion from his news photographs, Jasen speedily dropped to a cushion beside his companions. On either side of them, two other figures sat: Micor and a large mustached man Jasen had not seen before.

Rarion spoke first. "Who is this young girl?"

Before Olwer could answer, Karmeena said, "I come as a bridge between Perdita and the Pilgrim."

The king frowned at Olwer. "What new talk is this? Another ploy, like your Leva farce?"

"I hardly know, my King," said Olwer. "We on Zerin received a visitation from an image of our Jetho Miri, whom I ordered to go to the Lo Ren—"

"To help the rebels."

"To remind the engineers to be mindful of tech safety."

"Your lies stir me as breezes stir mountains. What visitation?"

"That, my King, we do not know," said Olwer, laying a forestalling hand on Karmeena's arm. "What has become of Miri West-of-Now?"

Micor answered, "We have only one account, received just an hour ago from Sherayna—"

"Miri!" Sylan blurted frantically. Jasen saw his father grasp her hand.

Micor glared at her. "Warchief Ethan installed my off box. But before he could activate it, there was an attack on the project site. An explosion caused a power surge that momentarily kicked the jae generator on."

"Then it's over?" whispered Nevan. He seemed to be speaking to himself.

"Almost immediately, the warchief was able to activate the off box. It worked." His voice was robotic. "The active jae field ran for less than half a second at minimum power. We can hope the damage will be minimal as well. Sherayna was taken prisoner, for hours she did not speak or move. Her captors feared that the jae accident, which killed Ethan, had damaged her brain. But then she spoke. She said that Miri had been with them at the time of the accident and disappeared."

Jasen was numb. His father sat rigid, the tears flowing down his cheeks. But Sylan sank her face into her hands, doubling over till her hands touched her ankles.

"When?" she groaned, not looking up.

"About noon this past day."

Then, Karmeena spoke with a calm as inhuman as Micor's: "She's been transported into the realm of jae. This is what she told us. She has met the gods."

"But *what* has happened to her?" cried Sylan. "Have any of you stopped to think of that?"

"It's a ruse," said the king.

The mustached man made a noise in agreement.

Olwer leaned toward Rarion. "Listen, there are dozens on Zerin who will swear her words are true. This young woman, Miri, was exceptional. She had one of the sharpest minds that I have ever known. She had one of the most courageous spirits, and I sent her to your project site to speak for jae safety, and jae killed her. That is on my head. Zerin will not . . . I will not recover from her loss. But it is possible that her intellect, her insight, the precision of her telepathic power allowed her to survive this shift into a different dimension, a different state of being. It's possible. Something happened. That is no ruse. Stop seeing villains in every corner and look forward."

"How dare you?" said the mustached man.

Olwer shot him a glance, his mouth a hard line. "Forgive me, Warmaster," he nodded to Lashen, "my King. I spoke out of turn."

"Indeed," said Rarion, "you are dismissed from this meeting, Im Jetho. Out of respect for your long service, I will excuse your words this one time. The next time, you will be held treasonous."

Olwer stood, and with a stiff bow, went out.

"Hundreds of closeted rebels. Show this apparition to me."

A moment of dead silence followed. "My King," said Karmeena, "we have an obligation to look for Miri. That must be the future of jae, to create a stable bridge between the jae world and our own. Miri has made her pilgrimage. We have to follow."

"Do not trust them, my King," said the warmaster—Lashen—the name registered somewhere in Jasen's numb mind. "These rebels have devastated the project. The sverra, Micor, is one of them. Are we to sit before them and believe their tales of visions?"

"My off box is not a question of faith or visions," said Micor. "When you study its operation, you'll see, my King. I know more of jae than any of your engineers, I and this woman." He nodded to Sylan. "You can have war with the Borderals until some disaster wrecks this world, or you can use us and have jae—if you are willing to use it conservatively."

"Rebels don't compromise, my King," said the warmaster. "But they are insidious. The queen corrupted even Ethan."

"The queen is not an issue," said Rarion icily. "The queen has overstaked her odds."

"Yes, my King," the warmaster continued. "And, most respectfully, I remind you that it was I who brought you the evidence of her treason and Zerin's, gathered through years of my faithful service."

"Years indeed. But too late," said Rarion. "You let them right into the project."

The warmaster bowed his head. "I might have served you with keener skill, my King, but never with a truer heart. I beg that you listen to my words."

"My King," put in Micor, "there is much that you must learn, of jae, of the off box, of the War's End." He glanced at Karmeena. "And much, it seems, that I must learn of this supposed pilgrimage."

"We are studying your off box," said the king. "Until we reach a decision, consider yourselves in the custody of Ayer, all of you."

CHAPTER 65

They wouldn't leave Sherayna alone until she'd told them all she knew about the jae disaster. She had no objection to telling them. It was only that it had been hard to form words. She was tired, so tired that to have her dead ashes sprinkled to the sky seemed too great an effort.

After telling her tale, she slept as if she could sleep forever but awoke certain she had not slept long, as tired as before. Only the room was a little grayer, as if the life were ebbing out of the walls. She didn't mind, or not much.

Time passed. They brought some tasteless food, which she ate by force of habit. Finally, they moved her out of the installation in a ground car. She slept. When she awoke, she was lying on a cot in a small room with windows: not a prison room. A stout woman was studying a book on a desk.

"Where am I?" asked Sherayna.

The woman sat down by her bed and took her pulse. "In the secure wing of the Oja City Base Hospital."

Sherayna laughed a bit inside but couldn't bring the laughter to her face. "Is it raining?"

"No." The doctor looked down at her with a soft frown. "Why do you ask?"

"It looks awfully overcast, that's all."

"Sherayna, you took a heavy dose of that jae contamination. We don't know much about the action of shifted particles on the body . . . but it seems likely you may lose your eyesight."

Perhaps the best words she could possibly have heard. They frightened her: more than death, more than life. She felt a new strength come into her body and sat up revived. "How long?"

"At this rate, a few days."

"And jae, will it kill me?" Her voice sounded strong to her now, like her old voice.

The woman hesitated. "We don't know."

"Ah, but you think it will." Sherayna felt like dancing in defiance.

"Certainly not immediately. Your condition is quite stable for the moment. Though, you ought to know, besides Warchief Ethan, two of the people in that room with you have died. The other two are more or less in the same condition you are. More than that, we don't know. This is no time to lose hope."

Then, Sherayna did laugh aloud. "When do I go to the prison? Tell me, can I have my old cell back? The little one with the bright white lights. How long will it be before their glow becomes black?"

The doctor stood up. "You'll stay here until we have word from Senarna. That's all I can say."

≈•≈

The next five days were worse than the loss of Meena, or Illia, or Ethan, worse than a year of imprisonment in a tiny white-lit cell: a gradual, growing helplessness, a loss of self from the inside out. At first, she strove to see all she could, spent hours staring out the window onto the sterile backs of square buildings stretching for measures. She studied each object in her room, turning her head this way and that in a vain attempt to clear the darkening haze. She memorized her doctor's face, saw it when she closed her eyes, complete with the growing fuzzy blackness; never had she come to know a face so well.

She mourned all the things she would never see again: the fields of Meena, a cedar tree, the moonlight. She thought about people she'd beheld for the last time. She thought about everything she'd lost, and it seemed she had lost everything. She begrudged sleep, begrudged closing her eyes. Each time she awoke, the world was darker. One morning, she demanded a favor from her doctor: a photograph of Jessec with his family from the archives.

It lay before her, black as a charred vestige of memory. But there he was, the smiling man with his ten-year-old son, also smiling, standing beside a scale model of a prototype of the *Outbound*. She stared a long time at Ethan and could see nothing of his face but that he smiled.

"I've seen what I need to see," she told her doctor. "Let me blindfold my eyes."

Her doctor protested. How could she relinquish her final sighted days? But Sherayna was adamant. Her doctor relented, and darkness fell over her.

The first day, she suspected that her doctor might have been right. Stumbling around her room, knowing that if she tore off this scrap of cloth she would still be able to steer herself for a day or two, she almost chose that slow death. But she did not.

The days passed, and at last the blindfold was removed and the blackness remained. She learned to find her way in her room, to know by their steps her doctor and attendants, to read raised letters. The sun warmed the room for a longer space each day, and sometimes she walked with an attendant in a courtyard. Warm afternoons. Late-Spring. She heard rumors of a great debate about jae, of Micor and the West-of-Nows conferring with the king. The Jethor of Zerin had all been declared outlaws briefly, but apparently the charges against them had been dropped in exchange for their temporary self-confinement on the island.

As temporary as Nevan and Miri West-of-Now's years of confinement? she wondered.

Occasionally, she heard mention of a pilgrim. "Another new goddess," Sherayna's doctor said disdainfully. They would tell her nothing of the Borderals, except that rebel activity had declined. That subject was a sore one between Sherayna and her City guardians.

They continued to run tests on her, to poke and prod her, and study jae in her. Her doctor guessed she had two years to live. Sadder was the news that most of the others at the Lo Ren site fared little better; few were expected to survive more than five years. As for herself, Sherayna greeted her illness with equal measures of regret and relief. Her life should already be over, along with Ethan's and Illia's and the parents' she had never known.

≈•≈

One day in Early-Summer, when she was practicing her reading, an attendant announced a visitor. The steps that followed seemed familiar, yet she could not place them.

Someone stood before her. "Don't worry," he said, "I'm not here as a prisoner."

"Leric," she exclaimed, flooded with relief. "Then, how did you get here? What's happened out there? No one tells me anything."

She could feel a faint breeze as he sat down on a cushion next to her.

"You look well," he said in that quiet tone he slipped into when his soul was weary.

"Enough of that. Tell me why you're here."

"I'm here to take you home," he said. "Home to Meena."

"To Meena? How?"

"Half a month ago, the king announced an amnesty between the Borderals and the City. The conditions are simple: if we're caught breaking the law, we will still be tried on the basis of our full criminal records, but as long as we stay out of trouble, we can go home as private citizens."

"Surely you don't believe their promises, Leric. Even if they let us go home, we'll be suspects in every new Borderal action, however innocent we may be."

"I'm not unaware of that. Then again, it's a hope to have some rest."

"And the City? Have they won? Do we stop fighting just like that?"

A rustle of cloth; he'd shifted closer. "Listen, they've put a moratorium on jae use. And with most of the planet's capital being siphoned into jae research and much of the rest subsidizing the food inflation, that means little if any non-jae tech development. Most of us feel we can bide our time."

"To what end, the moratorium?"

Leric did not answer. It was like standing on an iceberg in the middle of the sea to hear his disembodied breathing—a meter away like a thousand measures. She held out her hand, and he grasped it in both his own, drawing it down onto his knee.

"The moratorium is in place while the overseers decide exactly how jae ought to be implemented. Some want to continue the old project, with Micor's Correction, to go into space." Again he paused. "Some want something else entirely. They want a fraction of the energy to be used on a human body instead of a ship's engine, to try to create a bridge between our world and wherever Miri West-of-Now went."

"Where she went? Jae killed her, no?"

"I don't know. But Karmeena saw her—so did many on Zerin—an apparition moving between our world and the land of jae. Kara is convinced that this bridge will be a portal to the realm of the gods. Since the amnesty, she's been traveling the continents, convincing others. They call her 'Im Jetho of the Im Pilgrim.' That's Miri's new name, you know, one word: 'the Im Pilgrim.' *Imasrase.*"

How bitter he sounded.

She laid her free hand over his. "You think Karmeena's deceived herself."

"I don't know what to think. I've only seen her once since this. I tracked her down on her travels. She's not the daughter Lia and I raised up." He clenched Sherayna's hands. "I'm afraid for her, Rayna."

Sherayna squeezed them back, then felt her way up his arms. He folded her into his embrace, resting his face against her neck.

"I don't think I can fight this if it's her will. And I don't think Perdita will fight. They want to believe in Imasrase." He sighed. "I can only do what I can do, I can take you home."

"I'm going to die, you know."

"And I thought you were a spirit immortal."

"I mean it. They say I have two years, maybe, they're not sure."

"They told me so," he said. "Would you rather spend them in Oja?"

"I would rather spend them in Meena."

≈•≈

They released her from the hospital the next morning. The walk to their rental car left Sherayna dizzy and disoriented. Her stomach lurched at the vehicle's every motion. But by the time they reached the River Road, her stomach settled, leaving her only timorous and melancholy.

"The last time I was on this road," she said, "I was looking at the glitter of the river."

"And headed on a wild mission with an enemy into an enemy base."

"I don't know if this is worse or that."

As they drove, he told her in greater detail of the events of the past two months. After some initial resistance, the king had agreed to rigorous safety standards in exchange for Micor's help in developing jae. Till the amnesty, Micor had been under arrest in Senarna. He was free now, technically, but he had yet to be seen outside that city. Sylan too had been held in Senarna. She was currently refusing to aid the project unless it followed Karmeena's ambition of finding Imasrase.

"At least they can't hurt Sylan when she's so much in the public's eyes," said Leric.

"You grew very close to her," guessed Sherayna.

"I thought so," he said. "Zerin, the West-of-Nows, Micor, even the Space Engineering Consortium, all support a proposal to make no attempt to contact other worlds until the jae question is resolved. The king has accepted the proposal for the moment."

"I thought the West-of-Nows would want to go home."

He made a soft sound that was not quite a laugh. "I think they want their daughter more. And besides, I think they fear that Perdita might reintroduce jae to other planets."

"And the queen? What does she say?"

"Nothing. Warmaster Lashen was apparently compiling incriminating information on her for years. When the king found out she'd betrayed him, he impounded her assets and exiled her to the Remotes."

Sherayna tried to imagine the queen's intellect locked away on those little windblown islands. "I'm glad he didn't execute her. She deserves to live. But whether she's exiled or dead, our king is blinder without her."

≈•≈

They came into Meena in the thick warmth of evening. Sherayna knew every curve in the roads, could have walked them alone unerringly.

"Back to the old house?" she said when he stopped the car.

"Only half of it was burned up. The family that moved down from Semlona to take over the fields built a new place. Senarna is letting them retain ownership of half our fields, but Raja and Shoshec were given back the east half."

"They're here?" She hadn't dared to ask till now.

"At Cudonond, working with the intelligence net—nothing aggressive, not even strictly illegal. They should be back next month."

"Oh. Cudonond. Our seer's there."

"That's right," said Leric, surprise in his voice. When Sherayna did not elaborate, he sighed. "Well, the fire took our ground car, and I have to return this one to town. Will you be all right?"

Sherayna pondered for a moment all the answers she might make: of fear, bitterness, grief, loneliness, the joy of being home. "Yes. Is the claw-wheat high?"

"Unkillable as the weeds in the sidewalks of Oja City. When the breeze comes up you'll hear it."

She sat on the porch listening to the humid night rustlings: the grasses, the evening birds. The whispering of the gods, strangely comprehensible. Another year and no crickets—what cricket gods had died with their dying? Then she heard Leric's steps coming up the drive, already unmistakable to her ear.

"It must be getting late," she said.

"Only fourteenth hour." He sat beside her.

After a lengthy pause, she said, "I did this to myself."

"For the good of the planet, as always."

"Mm, I thought so. But I was wrong."

She heard him shift to face her. "To go to the Lo Ren?"

"To send you that message, to get you to attack the project. All I did was perpetuate a cycle that we'd almost overcome. It was in my hands, and I let it slip through."

"Let what slip through?"

She hesitated. "A common interest." She hugged her knees. "And now there's blood on my hands again."

"How?" He sounded baffled.

She felt a stab of anger. "I got you to attack—and it killed him, and her, and me. And all those others. How much simpler do you want it said?" She stood and took a couple careful steps. "Now, tell me not to wallow in self-pity, you do it so well."

"Sherayna, I didn't get your letter till days after the fact. We had the attack staged long before you wrote me."

She turned around. "Then who . . . ?"

"Olloan's agents who'd helped him spy out the project in Senarna—I was one of them. I helped break one of the Senarna–Lo Ren codes. We knew almost from the first that Olloan had betrayed us. When Micor disappeared onto Zerin, we decided we'd have to act on our own."

"You signaled to me when I came in, as if you were expecting me."

A silence. "Me? I wasn't there. You thought I was there?"

"You said you'd planned—"

"I helped plan the attack, yes. I wasn't on the ground. You thought I was there and saw you there and bombed that facility anyway? That's what you think of me? After losing Illia, you think I'd let you die?"

Dizzy all at once, Sherayna sat at the bottom of the steps. "I'm sorry. I wasn't thinking." She reached out for his hand. A few seconds passed—an interminable gulf—then she felt his firm grip.

"It's all right. Our heads are all burned," he said. "Our team on the ground didn't know why you were there. They hoped if they whistled you'd give them some indication of what you were doing. When you didn't respond, they decided it wasn't worth the risk to wait, and they took the coming of the warchief as an ominous sign."

"He saved us from an ecological disaster," she snapped, "when we, *our* people, were responsible for an unbridled explosion of jae—"

"Which the City didn't bother to safeguard its reactor against, as usual."

"Did I say I was on their side?"

He huffed. "You sound like it. As for me, I'd raze a thousand jae sites to answer for all that they've done to us."

"To us, or to the planet?"

He hesitated a moment, then burst out laughing.

The night was getting colder. "It doesn't matter," she said. "If you didn't get my letter, the effect was the same. I wanted that attack—when I wrote to you, I did. In the eyes of the gods, I killed Ethan anyway."

"'Ethan,' eh?" said Leric. "So we're on name terms?"

"Don't speak to me in that tone," she said. "You didn't know him."

"I knew enough, Rayna. I thought you did too. Didn't you see enough of him in Iltan, in Oja, here in Meena?"

"I'm not condoning what he did. But what he did is not who he was." A wind shimmered in the fields, wafting pungent grass smells. She breathed in the summer and made herself say, "At the end, I think I loved him."

She heard Leric stand up. He walked past her down the stairs, a few steps out toward the fields. "I find it difficult to believe I heard that rightly. I find it vaguely disgusting."

"Happily, I don't have to justify myself to you."

His shoes scuffed as he turned on her. "Have you truly forgotten Lia so quickly? What kind of heart beats inside you, Sherayna?"

I am ill. I am dying. I am too tired for this. She bent her head onto her knees and sat very still, feeling tears well sweetly.

At length, she heard Leric say, "He bewitched you, that's all. That's understandable. This jae situation made us all a little crazy."

"No. That was not his way." The tears would not stop; they were not sweet anymore. They hurt, constricting her chest and her throat, her whole body. She didn't even hear Leric sit next to her. Now his hand was on her shoulder, and she leaned into the circle of his arms.

"He should not have died," she whispered.

He held her close.

CHAPTER 66

Nevan's Journal
Perdita: 9 Mid-Summer, 20.03.2042 After the End:

I am going to write a history. It's been over a year since the Crossing, as they call it, the day my daughter died—or may as well have died insofar as any of us will ever see her as Miri again. My readers, when I come to have readers, may wonder why I chose not to include my own account of my daughter's passing. Nothing has been omitted, for I have not written a word about it till today. Her death has been beyond my expression, as far beyond as Imasrase's survival. Shall I say, "I miss her"? I miss her.

In my own tongue, I might say *eval lyne*: "let it die," the words emblazoned on the doors of every Kiri tech center as a reminder of the rightness of death, which no human device should seek too hard to overmaster. How my people would shudder to see Perdita now! Now, when the people rejoice in the streets at the thought of using jae to blast a hole into other dimensions, to seek out Imasrase, whatever that may be, to hold hands with their gods. Even most Borderals share in the rejoicing. But in my experience, gods retain their divinity only in symbol, not fact. *Eval sym lyne*, I say. Let her die.

But perhaps I will be surprised. Who can tell?

≈•≈

The Iltan Observatory. Once a post for looking to the stars, today a post for looking outward to the future, an assurance of change, of the promised new order. A battleground transformed into a meeting hall. That's the idea— and a pretty one, I suppose.

Summer on Perdita reminds me of home. The sun scatters bright splotches against pockets of shadow, the purple trees pulse with living motion. At times like these, I remind myself that whatever humanity does, life prevails somewhere: Miri once said that to me.

The meeting progresses painstakingly. The king is there, the prime minister, the governors of Veshna and Keeri-Semlona, Warmaster Lashen, Micor, Sylan, Karmeena, Olwer

316

(very quiet), engineers from the Lo Ren Project and the Space Program, leaders of major tech consortia, masters of the seers' schools, and one Borderal representative, Sherayna, very ill. I attend too, as a recorder merely.

When the meeting day is over, we file out into the twilight. I like how it vibrates with the lingering heat of the day. We eat outside in the observatory courtyard, just far enough from the great trees to be out of their lengthening shadows. In Melnar, the mosquitoes would be biting at us mercilessly. There are no mosquitoes on Perdita, and I miss them.

Tonight, I began to sound people out for their accounts, for my history. I went first to Leric, who came here as companion to Sherayna and Karmeena. I had hardly exchanged a word with him. At first, I disliked him because he was my wife's lover. But she has not gone back to him. Now, I am more inclined to dislike him over Jasen.

Jasen, like Leric and me, has come to Iltan as a guest. I watched the two of them eating together. Though Leric is only fourteen years older than Jasen, he's largely taken over my place with my son, now my only living child. Of course, he's had the best of intentions. My anger is directed at myself, not him.

I asked Jasen if I might have a word alone with Leric. Leric smiled stiffly as I sat. I told him of my plans for my history. "I would like to have your point of view," I said.

"Thank you," he said, "but I'd rather not. Ask Sherayna for hers."

"I intend to."

"Because she ought to be heard, and she doesn't have much time." He gazed across the court to where she sat with the old Space Program engineer, Kesoran. "It's not as if she's being heard here."

≈•≈

11 Mid-Summer, 22.03.2042:

I have taken a few days away from the deliberations in Iltan. They don't need me, and I have my own work. I reached the Remote Islands yesterday and spent the afternoon taking stock of them. All seven are ragged expanses of basalt and tough grasses whipped by the wind off the silvery ocean. The towns are collections of bright-painted buildings and transplanted trees, clustering close, like the islands' little sand deer that huddle together in the fields to block out the blowing sea foam.

The islands are named for gods: Fennocin, Namin, Sorcin, Etepin, Monin, Eldarin. Today, I sought out Laynia on the smallest of the islands, Sobin, named for the water god, Sobai. She sat in the lee of the wind on the terrace of the house Rarion gave her, staring out to the plains and the sea. She did not acknowledge my presence as I sat by her but folded her arms tighter in her woolen coat.

"You look well, Laynia."

Without turning her eyes from the ocean, she said, "Did you know, Nevan, that the Remotes are the only place on Perdita where the majority of the population wants a total ban on the development of jae?"

"You've brought them round fast." I attempted a smile.

She laughed shortly. "Decades of fighting off toxic dump sites have brought them around inexorably."

"Their voices won't carry much weight in Iltan."

"How astute of you."

I wished I had not come. I told her of my book and asked if she would help me.

After a silence, she said, "I was sorry to hear about Miri, Nevan. She'd have made a fine Jetho. Olwer wanted her to follow him as Im Jetho, you know. But perhaps, put that way, it's as well that she died."

When I could unclench my jaw, I said, "I thought you were his friend."

"Oh, I was. I am."

I followed her gaze to the white sea meeting white sky.

She said, "You know, I think he may have loved her."

I think so too and wish I didn't.

"I won't help you," she said. "I've done enough of helping. This is my time, and I will have it."

"Yes, you've been instrumental in saving—"

"Yes, I have been an instrument."

≈•≈

13 Mid-Summer, 24.03.2042:

In the conference, it was a bloody day for Karmeena. The Space Program, the consortia, the seers, and the government declared her too young to have any say. She demanded to be judged by her words, not her age, but the governor of Veshna called her words insane. Sylan and Micor defended her on the grounds that reaching Imasrase might be theoretically possible.

But the Im Seer said, "Speaking to the gods is not like speaking to your neighbors. Speaking to the gods can be maddening."

And all eyes fell on Karmeena. "Speaking to the gods has always been the privilege of a select few," she said. "We don't propose to open the Jae Land to everyone but only to a very few trained from childhood. I will not be among them. And if the seers wish a veto right over any such traveler, we'll give them that right, provided that enough are selected to make the journey possible."

"You've elected yourself overseer of the project, then?"

"No," said Karmeena, "I am a worshipper who wishes to see Perdita reach the gods."

≈•≈

That evening, I saw Karmeena slumped on a rock, staring out at the purple trees. Something in her drew me near, a lack of tension perhaps, a slip from the maniacal back to the living. I saw tears on her face.

She glanced up at me as I approached. "I'm not insane, Nevan. I know that she's dead—not like my mother is dead, but dead all the same." She looked at me unflinchingly but with no religious zeal. "I'm not doing this to find Miri. Oh, I started out to, but now I do believe that Imasrase is the link. It's not so far-fetched. The gods are spirits—even, some say, spirits just like our dead. And Imasrase *is* a dead spirit, except that she didn't leave our world as thoroughly as a spirit like my mother's. Therefore, she really could be a bridge between the worlds. That's worth finding, no?"

"Karmeena, it's hard for me to say. I don't believe in your gods."

She looked away. "Can I tell my story for your book?"

"I was hoping you would."

I heard a step behind me and turned to see Leric coming toward us. He smiled at me nervously.

I said, "Help the gods," and then I fled, leaving the father with his daughter.

≈•≈

15 Mid-Summer, 26.03.2042:

Today, a path was chosen. I'm inclined to call it a bad idea. But whatever one may think of the Decision on Contact Procedure, that any decision was reached at all is a tribute to our negotiators.

The project will aim for contact with Imasrase. Sylan, Micor, and the king will be the final determiners of the safety protocols. Until the project is completed or declared impossible, Perdita will not seek contact with other worlds. The Space Program will proceed in Cudonond but with only the immediate aim of placing a ship into orbit. The Jae Project will be located on Zerin, remote from the rest of the planet, in case of sabotage or accidental disasters.

The Space Programmers were given assurances that the shield would not be reactivated, leaving them free to explore beyond the sky. The seers will have veto power over every traveler selected for the jae voyage. The consortia and the king have the promise of a unique jae tech. As long as Perdita remains isolated from the remainder of space, the Perditans can develop this tech without fear of its being stolen. Once the tech is perfected, they will own the interstellar market. The plan passed with two dissenting votes, voices of an age that overnight had become antique: Lashen and Sherayna.

Lashen threw an oratorical eye around the table. "My fellows, I have made my position clear. This deal is predicated on resorting to expertise of the rebel Micor. We are placing ourselves in the hands of forces opposed to tech development, and we expect those same forces to further our tech goals. The contradiction is clear."

Sherayna came here, I think, believing her body would argue against reopening the path to jae. She said, "There is a wisdom in the Nations, in the Kiris, in Leddra, all of them. They have rejected jae and survived. The Sama Empire embraced jae, and it's dead. There are more than fifty of us now from the Lo Ren waiting to die. If every detail in this plan is not perfect, it will kill this world."

≈•≈

20 Mid-Summer, 31.03.2042:

Sherayna died this afternoon. Tonight, they will cremate her, and tomorrow they will fire her to the sky. This evening, we prayed for her, hand in hand on the courtyard of the observatory, reciting the chant for the dead:

The uttermost undrowning light
Passes the fire, passes the flight,
Slumbers in gray, gliding, gossamer night,
Youthfully opens its eyes to the sight
Of sunlight, too bright, showering its love
On us below and all above.

We ate supper quietly, flickers winging in the trees. While Jasen held a vigil with Leric and Karmeena, I found Sylan on a trail a few hundred feet into the forest, watching the sun sink in the east, pink behind black-needled limbs.

"This is where we began," I said.

"You began on Onáda and I on Vorshtamor. I have so many old friends still left there. Maybe I should have pushed for going into space after all."

"Why didn't you?"

She leaned back, face to the small, evening breeze. "You know why. I want to find out what happened to her—not to find her, you understand, but to find out what happened. I need the Jae Land program for that."

The trees were losing their definition against a rose sky.

"Can it truly be done, Sylan?"

"Reaching Jae Land? I don't know. I don't know if it exists . . . or what we saw when we saw Miri. It will take more lifetimes than ours to begin to find out." She paused. "I wonder if Rarion realizes that."

I shook my head. "Sherayna was right. It's too much of a risk."

"Any risk is too much for a Kiri. Sometimes a risk is worthwhile, Nevan, worth risking even the death of Perdita."

"Jae ought to be forgotten."

She looked at me in the deepening crimson light. "And that is why we finally have no choice but to press on. No knowledge can be forgotten."